By Kris Tualla:

Loving the Norseman
Loving the Knight
In the Norseman's House

A Nordic Knight in Henry's Court
A Nordic Knight of the Golden Fleece
A Nordic Knight and his Spanish Wife

A Discreet Gentleman of Discovery
A Discreet Gentleman of Matrimony
A Discreet Gentleman of Consequence
A Discreet Gentleman of Intrigue
A Discreet Gentleman of Mystery

Leaving Norway
Finding Sovereignty
Kirsten's Journal

A Woman of Choice
A Prince of Norway
A Matter of Principle

The Norsemen's War: Enemies and Traitors
The Norsemen's War: Battles Abroad
The Norsemen's War: Finding Norway

An Unexpected Viking
A Restored Viking
A Modern Viking

*****

A Primer for Beginning Authors
Becoming an Authorpreneur

Enemies & Traitors

THE NORSEMEN'S WAR

Book 1:
Teigen & Selby

Kris Tualla

Kris Tualla

Enemies and Traitors: The Norsemen's War is a work of fiction. Names, characters, places and incidents are products of the author's imagination or are used fictitiously and are not to be construed as real. Any resemblance to actual events, locales, organizations, or persons, living or dead, is entirely coincidental.

Published in the United States of America.

© 2016 by Kris Tualla

All rights reserved. No part of this book may be used or reproduced in any form or by any means without the prior written consent of the Publisher, except for brief quotations used in critical articles or reviews.

ISBN-13: 978-1539806301
ISBN-10: 1539806308

*This book is dedicated to the brave and resolute
men and women of Norway who
did not roll over and give up
when their country was invaded by Germany
on April 9, 1940.*

*The characters in this story represent only a small fraction
of Norway's World War II resistance,
but while they are fictional, the events are real.*

*I also dedicate this book to the tour guides and residents
who bragged to me about Norway's resistance at every chance.
Without them, I never would have known.*

*And lastly, I dedicate this to any readers who had no idea
that any of this happened.*

NORWAY

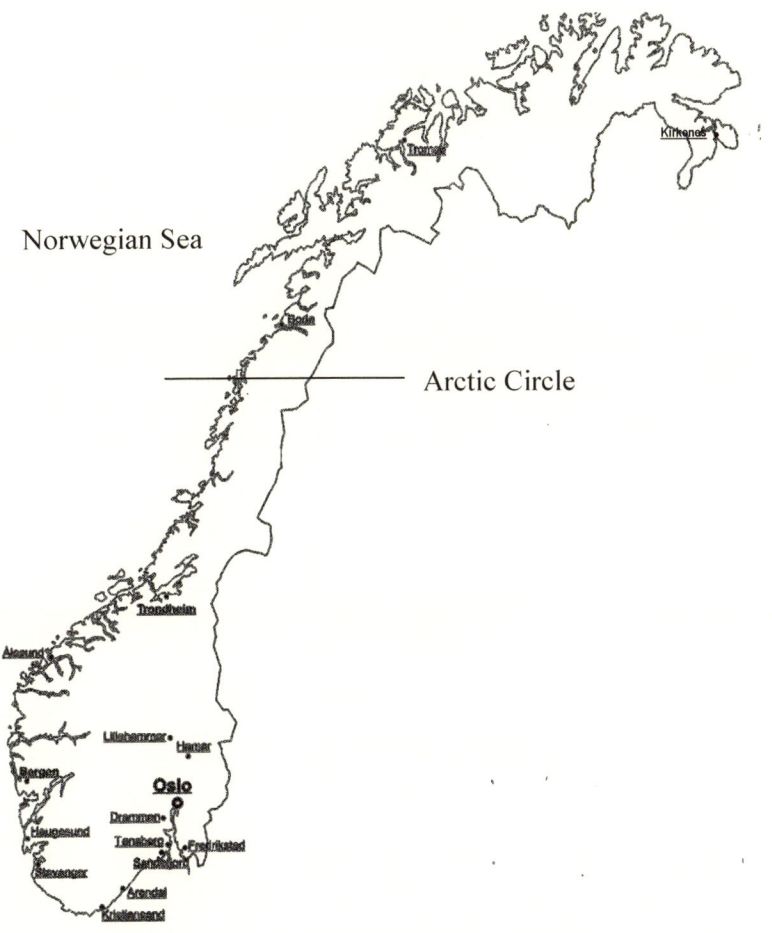

CHAPTER ONE

February 9, 1942
Oslo, Norway

Teigen Hansen slid the paper across the worn top of the Oslo Secondary School headmaster's desk. "Absolutely not. I will not agree to this."

Overlærer Oskar Jung glanced sideways at the German officer wearing an expertly fitted Nazi uniform and hovering at the edge of his desk, but Teigen refused to look up at the man. He barely restrained himself from spitting on the officer's shiny black boots.

Oskar focused his attention on Teigen and leaned forward a little. "You do understand that every teacher in Norway is required to sign this Declaration of Loyalty."

Teigen kept his voice calm and his eyes level. "I have heard the radio announcements, yes."

"And yet you are refusing?"

The light in Oskar Jung's eyes did not match his stern tone. That intrigued Teigen; perhaps he was not going to be fired on the spot for remaining loyal to occupied Norway.

Teigen nodded slowly and quoted bits of the declaration—he wanted his point to be very clearly made, no matter how the Neanderthal in brown responded. "I am. I will *not* sign any declaration of loyalty to the Nazi regime. And I will *not* agree to promote my students' understanding of Nazi ideology."

The German officer cleared his throat. Loudly.

Teigen deigned to look up at the man out of the corner of his eye. "Perhaps you need a glass of water," he said in perfect German.

The man startled, then glared at him and answered in the same language. "Perhaps you need to understand what is happening in the world."

Teigen ignored the taunt and addressed his principal. "Are we finished?"

Oskar nodded as he carefully folded the unsigned declaration. "There will be a letter in your mailbox tomorrow stating that you refused to sign this."

Teigen rose slowly to his feet. He straightened his back to make the point that at six-foot-six he towered a full half-a-foot over the glaring SS officer. "I understand."

He turned to leave the principal's office when the officer barked in German, "You have not been dismissed."

Teigen waited, looking over his shoulder at the officer. *"Was erwarten Sie von mir?"* What do you require of me?

The German clacked his heels together and extended a stiff right arm. *"Heil Hitler."*

The expected response was obvious, but Teigen was damned if he'd give it. He dipped his head, flashed a crooked grin, and answered in Norse. "Of course."

Then he spun on his heel and exited the small office, closing the door behind him.

◢ ◢ ◢

Teigen trudged through the snowy streets of Oslo toward Elsa Borg's home. The skies still held the fading green and lavender tones of dusk, though at four-thirty in the afternoon the lazy sun was already tucked in bed.

As was common, he passed pairs of bundled-up Nazi soldiers patrolling the area. Teigen kept his eyes lowered, trying not to accidentally provoke one of them; but the scarf covering the bottom half of his face hid his irrepressible sneer.

The summons to Jung's office today was expected. Each one of his fellow teachers was summoned individually, but none of them knew what the outcome would be—only that those who dared to express their opinion aloud all claimed that they would refuse to sign.

Teigen paused at Elsa's gate. The lit windows in her parents' solid stone townhome invited him in, but what occurred at the school today made him hesitate. What would he say about it?

Since that horrible dawn in April two years ago when German warships sailed simultaneously into five of Norway's major port cities, nothing had been the same. Hitler's invasion was a complete surprise, and Teigen's peaceful and neutral homeland was subdued in a matter of hours.

After the unwelcomed Nazi occupation, each of his countrymen had to choose how to respond: resist, roll over, or remain invisible. The Borgs determinedly chose the latter.

Refusing to sign the Declaration of Loyalty, however, was decidedly not the act of an invisible man.

"Then I won't mention it," Teigen resolved as he pulled his scarf down. His breath formed a cloud in front of his face as if trying to hide him from what might come.

He pushed open the wrought-iron gate and stepped up to the front door. Elsa pulled it open before he finished knocking.

"Hello, darling!" His grinning fiancée wrapped her arms around him and kissed him soundly on the mouth. Teigen tasted the bite of aquavit on her tongue. She leaned back and grabbed the arms of his coat. "Come in before you freeze."

Teigen laughed and stepped out of the way of the big wooden door which she swung closed behind him. "You keep that up and I'll stay warm forever."

Elsa's blue-gray eyes twinkled up at him. "My pleasure."

She took his coat and scarf and hung them on the rack in the entryway before looping her arm snuggly through his. "You'll never believe it—we got beef for the stew tonight!"

While the Borgs hadn't thrown their lot in with the Germans, their lack of overt objection to the occupation occasionally paid off. Every now and again their Nazi-controlled butcher would be instructed to hold back provisions which were normally reserved for the German soldiers and allow Wilhelm Borg to purchase them. The price was dear, of course, but Wilhelm would do anything for his wife and their beloved only child.

Teigen's stomach rumbled as the rich aroma of beef stew wafted toward him; his daily luncheons of lefse and herring had long grown tiresome. He leaned sideways and kissed the top of Elsa's head as she led him toward the dining room. "You spoil me, Elsa."

Her smile shifted and the glint in her eyes made his chest tighten. "I love you, Teigen."

"And I love you." Glancing toward the closed kitchen door, he paused, turned, and took her face in his hands. He slowly kissed her the way she deserved to be kissed.

It was a mistake, of course. It only reminded him of the intimacy that had been denied them since Elsa was forced to live with her parents.

Their wedding had been set to take place in early May of nineteen-forty, just four weeks after the invasion. At that point in time no one in Norway knew what the Nazi occupation meant to their lives, so their marriage was postponed. Elsa moved back into her parents' home a year ago rather than risk living alone as a single woman in a city full of enemy soldiers without much to do except frequent the many taverns.

Teigen backed away from the kiss before his reaction could not be hidden. He rested his forehead against hers and sighed.

"How much longer, Elsa?" he whispered.

"It would help if you moved to a decent apartment," she countered.

He straightened. "You know I can't afford more than the boarding house. Our wages have been cut *again*, and everything in Oslo is controlled by the brown bastards."

"Watch your words, Teigen." Elsa's brows twitched and she glanced at the kitchen door.

"If we married, we could live here with your parents," he pressed the option once more.

Elsa shuddered. "I'm not at all comfortable with that arrangement, and you know it."

Teigen shook his head, his brow lowering. "Then we remain at this stalemate."

The kitchen door swung open and Dina Borg carried in a steaming tureen. She smiled up at her future son-in-law. "Good evening, Teigen. Did Elsa mention our good fortune?"

"If she hadn't, my nose would have informed me the minute I opened the door." Teigen reached for the heavy pottery and set it in the center of the table for the older woman. "Forgive me if my stomach speaks up and says the blessing."

Dina laughed. "I do love your sense of humor."

With a grumbled clearing of his throat Wilhelm Borg entered the room from his study, newspaper in hand. "Good to see you, Teigen." He shifted his attention to his wife. "Is supper ready?"

N N N

To his credit, Wilhelm didn't mention the newspaper's recent headline until after the main meal was finished and the sweet soup was served. Made of stewed dry fruit mixed with tapioca and cinnamon, Teigen could take it or leave it. But it was Elsa's favorite.

Wilhelm pushed his empty bowl away and took a sip of the weak coffee which was substantially reinforced with aquavit. He set his cup down and his gaze pierced Teigen's.

"So what do you make of this new teachers' union and loyalty declaration, Teigen?"

So much for not mentioning it.

"I understand the Germans' point," he hedged.

Wilhelm's eyes were darker than his daughter's and they examined his much less warmly. "But you will sign it, of course."

Teigen looked at Elsa and Dina. Judging by the pleasant expressions on their faces, they obviously expected him to answer in the affirmative. But his honor was on the line as a teacher, a man, and a Norwegian.

He returned his steady regard to Wilhelm. "No, Wilhelm. I will not."

"What?" Elsa's eyes rounded in shock. "Why not?"

Teigen was struck speechless by the question. Elsa knew him well, or so he thought. How could she ask him such a thing?

"It's not as if you have to agree with them," Wilhelm pressed. "Just say the words."

That outrageous suggestion loosened Teigen's stuck tongue. "No!"

He looked around the table, stunned, and leaned forward. "My students trust me when I teach them the structure of an atom, and they would trust me if I started spouting Nazi propaganda. I won't do it. I *can't* do it."

Dina laid a calming hand over Teigen's fist which rested on the embroidered tablecloth—a fist that formed without him realizing it. "Don't be too hasty. You do have time to think about it."

Teigen's shoulders slumped and he leaned back, forcing his fists to relax. "No, I don't. I was asked to sign it today."

Elsa looked stricken. "So soon?"

"This is Oslo, not Kirkenes," he reminded her. "Once that traitor Quisling announced his edict it only took a few days to print and disperse the paperwork around the city."

"Watch your words," Wilhelm growled.

Teigen snorted. "What else would you call a self-serving Norseman who aligns himself with Hitler for his own benefit?"

"Didn't the other teachers sign?" Elsa was clearly distraught and trying to bring the conversation back to the matter at hand.

Teigen shrugged. "I don't know. Several said they wouldn't, but when a Nazi sergeant is standing over you it can be intimidating."

"A Nazi officer was in the room when you refused?" Wilhelm paled. "So they know?"

Teigen met the older man's gaze. "Yes. They know."

"You have to change your mind!" Elsa yelped. "Sign it first thing tomorrow morning when you go to work."

He stared at her, incredulous. "And why would I do that?"

"Because it's the safe thing to do, Teigen," Wilhelm stated. "And the wise thing to do."

"We all just need to get through this war any way we can," Dina chimed in. "When it's over we can go back to being who we really are."

The realization of how the two years of occupation had affected the Borgs hit Teigen in the chest like a cannon ball. Were they always like this? Or had he simply never noticed their timid lack of conviction?

"Isn't that what the German people are telling themselves?" he grumbled.

"Teigen!" Wilhelm's palm hit the tabletop making his coffee cup rattle. "That is unacceptable!"

Teigen's gaze moved around the table again, resting for a moment on each of the three Borgs with whom he had shared the last five years of his life. He shook his head slowly.

"I won't sign it. And I won't promote Nazi ideals. There is nothing you can say that will change my mind about this."

Wilhelm rose slowly to his feet. "In that case, I withdraw my permission for you to marry my daughter."

Elsa's brows flew together and her regard shot to her father. "Pappa!"

He raised one hand to shush her. "I cannot allow you to marry a man who does not have your safety and well-being as his number one concern."

Teigen felt his world unraveling even more quickly than the day the Germans invaded. Elsa had been his rock, his closest friend, the deepest love in his life. Suddenly that was all slipping away.

"Elsa," he implored. "Marry me anyway."

"I forbid it!" Wilhelm shouted.

Teigen rose to his feet and held out his hand to Elsa. He met her worried stare with as much calm determination as he could muster at the moment. "Please. Come with me."

Dina started to cry.

Elsa jumped up and ran around the table. "Have you lost your mind?" she growled.

She grabbed his arm and pulled him toward the entryway. She tossed his scarf and coat in his direction and jammed her arms into her own. Then she threw the door open and stomped outside.

What the hell just happened?

Teigen followed her into the frigid night and closed the door gently behind him. He was afraid of shaking the foundation of his world any harder than it already was.

"What has gotten into you, Teigen?" Elsa fumbled with the buttons on her thick woolen coat.

He hesitated, looping the scarf around his neck and letting his own garment hang open as he conjured a response. So many new thoughts tangled like barbed wire in his mind that the press of icy air helped sort them out.

"Regarding what?" he asked at last. "Regarding the loyalty issue? Or suggesting that you marry me in spite of your father?"

Elsa still struggled with her coat. "Both!" She looked up at him, her cheeks wet in the moonlight. "You want to remain true to your *own* loyalties, but you ask me to throw mine aside?"

It was true, she had a point. But... "My loyalty to Norway and her people has nothing to do with you—a fully grown woman of twenty-five—not obeying your father!"

Elsa threw her hands in the air, the fight with her buttons

abandoned. "What about your obvious willingness to risk *our* future by not cooperating with our captors?" She coughed a wet sob. "I thought you loved me!"

"I *do* love you Elsa." Teigen reached for her but she backed away. "I have loved you for years," he offered.

Elsa gasped and froze, her expression shifting ominously. "Is this about Tor?"

Teigen felt a familiar stab of envy. "What the hell does my brother have to do with anything?"

"When the Germans attacked, he ran off and joined the Norwegian army that same day. You—" Elsa pointed a stiff finger at him. "You had to stay behind and make sure your parents' business was taken care of."

So what.

He knew exactly so what.

"You couldn't be the war hero then, so you are choosing this battle now," she accused. "You want to be the big hero at home, don't you."

Was she right?

Doesn't matter.

"Elsa, listen to me." Teigen fought to keep his voice from shaking with either fury or fear. "I simply cannot teach impressionable students that Nazi ideas are valid or correct. Don't you understand that?"

She threw her arms wide. "Of course I do. But you can say what they want you to say without sounding *convincing*."

Teigen stared at her. "Do you still want to marry me?"

"What?" Elsa pulled her arms in and wrapped them around her body. "Why would you ask me that?"

Teigen felt his chest tighten in an entirely different way this time. "Answer me, Elsa. Do you still want to marry me?"

"I love you, Teigen."

"And I love you. Answer the question."

Elsa began to swipe her cheeks. He heard the crying spasms of her breaths.

"Elsa?"

She sniffed and ran her hand under her nose. "I can't break my father's heart. I just can't."

"The Bible says that a woman leaves her family and cleaves to her husband." Teigen drew a deep breath. "Will you be my wife, or not?"

She lifted her chin. "Will you at least pretend to teach what they want you to teach? For both our sakes?"

That question knocked the wind from Teigen. The sudden chasm between himself and his beloved Elsa gaped even wider between them and he couldn't breathe in the face of it.

"No," he croaked.

Elsa looked as if his words had punched her, and not the other way around. "Good bye, then," she rasped.

She walked past him, up the steps, and opened the door to the house. Light from behind him inked his frozen, jagged shadow on the snowy path to the gate.

His shape on the path disappeared into darkness as the door creaked closed and the latch fell with a chastising clank.

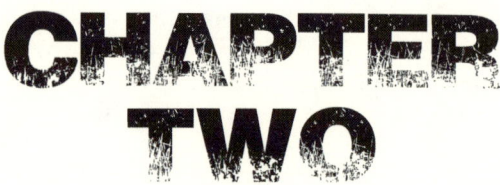

CHAPTER TWO

February 10, 1942

Teigen trudged toward the school through the frigid pre-dawn streets of Oslo, passing other men and women making their resolute ways past the ever-present German soldiers toward whatever tasks required their presence this morning. A brief nod of greeting was the most anyone offered; the faint acknowledgement of still-loyal countrymen doggedly surviving their shared Nazi hell.

After the confrontation at the Borgs' home, and the shocking ultimatum from Elsa, Teigen passed a restless and disbelieving night. When he did doze off, his dreams continued to repeat the scenes.

His head ached and his eyes were scratchy. Right about now he would pay a week's wages for a strong, hot cup of black coffee.

How did everything turn so quickly?

The question haunted him, as did the answers.

Teigen knew the Borgs' position well: keep your head down, stay out of the Nazi's notice, and appear to be amenable to their presence on the surface. What was truly felt would be tucked silently and secretly away until the Germans were—*please, God*—defeated and gone.

In deference to both his future in-laws, and for the sake of his own parents' shipping business in Arendal, Teigen had reluctantly adopted the same response. Until yesterday.

"I can't teach Nazi lies," he hissed quietly into his scarf, dampening the wool with his warm breath. His feelings were too strong to only exist in his head; they had to be spoken into the world. "I would die first."

With a start, Teigen realized that was a true statement.

I would die first.

The sentence rolled around in his thoughts searching for a viable objection, but not finding one that would stand up and knock it down.

He stopped walking, halted by the revelation.

"I would die first," he whispered.

Teigen drew a deep breath of resignation before he resumed his pace.

Tor had always been the impetuous and older brother, sometimes acting before he thought about the consequences. That was why, the morning that the Germans invaded and occupied Norway, Tor was at the Norwegian army headquarters within hours to enlist.

Teigen was always the more level-headed of the pair. He went to work that same horrible day as if nothing had happened, pretending to teach chemistry to the upper-secondary students while they stared at each other in shock and muttered unanswerable questions about what might happen now.

In truth, the occupation had been largely uneventful in regards to the war. In spite of Adolf Hitler's infusion of soldiers and the money required to keep them in place, Norway had not yet proven to be the pivotal piece in his world-domination plan which he assumed it would be. Instead, the occupation was largely a fruitless drain on Nazi resources.

Teigen formed a rueful smile behind his scarf. He was happy for his country to play that role.

Until that fascist asshole son-of-a-bitch and self-proclaimed "Minister President" Vidkun Quisling stepped into partnership with the Germans ten days ago and started stirring the pot.

Filthy traitor.

Teigen pulled down the edge of his scarf and spat on the ice.

He reached the school and entered through the tall heavy front doors. The familiar and calming aromas of chalk, floor wax, steam heat, and wet wool filled his sinuses. Up until this point the schools had remained untouched by the evil reach of Nazi control. And if Teigen's colleagues stood strong, that bastion would be held.

When he walked into the area of the office where the teachers' mailbox cubbyholes were stacked six high and ten wide Teigen faced more than a dozen teachers standing still and reading matching documents.

"What's going on?" he asked as he ducked down and reached into his box. When Teigen retrieved the envelope he expected to find, he straightened and glanced around the room.

Jorgen Lasse, the head of the sciences department met his gaze. "See for yourself."

Teigen opened the envelope. Instead of the principal's notice concerning his refusal to sign the Declaration of Loyalty, there was a short statement addressed to the newly formed Norwegian Teachers Union which outlined his refusal to accept membership, stating that to do so would compromise his conscience.

The attached explanation urged him to copy the statement, include his name and address, and mail it to their headquarters.

Confused, Teigen flipped over the blank envelope. "Where did this come from?"

"The resistance," someone whispered.

"What do we do?" someone else asked quietly.

Teigen frowned. "Is this a coordinated protest? Did every teacher in the school get one?"

Jorgen shrugged. "It would seem that only those who did *not* sign the oath received a copy."

Teigen's shoulders drooped. "So some of us did sign it, then."

Overlærer Oskar Jung strode into the office. "Only three. I've sent them home for the day." The principal faced the now silent crowd. "These papers arrived by courier at my home last night. My wife and I stuffed the envelopes before we went to bed and I dispersed them early this morning."

He paused and his regard swept the small and crowded space. "I was told that every school in Norway will have them before the end of the week."

Teigen leaned forward catching Oskar's attention. "Does this mean we have your permission to do as we're now asked?"

Oskar flashed a sly smile. "You have my *encouragement* to do so. And while I can't require you all to respond in this way, I will tell you all that my letter is already posted."

"But what will happen to us if we do this?" The music teacher cleared his throat. "I have a family to support."

"Mailing a protest letter is a much more aggressive step than simply not signing the declaration, that's true," Jorgen Lasse admitted. "But if all our teachers do it, what can the bastards do? Shut down all of our schools?"

The music teacher shook his head. "How will we *know* if they do? We might be the only ones who protest and then we'll be targets."

Bolstered by his new resolve, Teigen held the papers over his head. "I cannot allow my students to be fed Nazi filth, any more than I can tolerate our occupation in silence one minute longer." His gaze moved from colleague to colleague, meeting any eyes that were directed his way. "I will mail my letter today as well."

ᚾ ᚾ ᚾ

Teigen walked into his classroom and set the envelope on his desk with a shaking hand. His choice was clear—even clearer than the refusal to sign the Declaration of Loyalty in the first place.

Now is the time to act, not merely react.

He hung up his woolen coat and scarf. He pulled the chair away from his battered wooden desk. He sat down, opened the top drawer, and pulled out pen and a sheet of the school's letterhead paper.

With the sample text in front of him, Teigen copied out the letter of protest word for word. His hand shook again when he put his name and address to the document, but the action would be impotent without including them.

"What are you doing, Mr. Hansen?"

Teigen folded the paper as he looked up. "Good morning Brigit."

The tall sixteen-year-old girl stared at him. "The radio said all of our teachers are being required to sign a declaration of loyalty to Germany." She frowned and pointed at the folded paper. "Is that what you're doing?"

Teigen drew a deep breath as he stuck his letter into the addressed envelope. Her question made him realize that he must to decide now how much to tell his students about what had happened since their class met yesterday.

"No." He shook his head and met her gaze. "Not at all."

Teigen knew what the answer to that question needed to be. His students were on the brink of adulthood and hiding the truth from them would be a grave disservice. "When class begins, I'll explain it to everyone."

Brigit nodded solemnly and walked to her seat. As the rest of the students filed into the classroom they were unusually subdued. There was no horseplay between the boys, no giggling among the girls. Each student sat at their desk and stared, either at him or at the scuffed pine floor.

Teigen wondered which of their parents would back the teachers if the situation grew more dire. And then he wondered what any of them could possibly do even if it did.

The bell rang in the hallway announcing the beginning of the school day.

Teigen walked around his desk and sat on its edge. The ensuing conversation was going to be exactly that: not a lecture, but a conversation.

"How many of you heard about the Declaration of Loyalty which Quisling—" Teigen refused to call the man by his invented title, "—has recently required all Norwegian teachers to sign?"

Every single one of the twenty-seven students in the classroom raised their hand.

A big boy in the back row called out, "Did you sign it?"

Teigen looked straight into the young man's eyes. "No."

"Will you?" the boy pressed.

Teigen shook his head. "No."

The students looked at each other then, their gazes bouncing around the classroom like pinballs searching for others of like mind.

"In fact…" Teigen held up the newly addressed envelope and waited until he reclaimed every student's attention before he continued. "I'm mailing a letter of protest to Quisling's Norwegian Teachers Union today, stating my refusal to accept membership because of it."

Silence blanketed the room, palpable as a winter's snowfall.

Teigen dropped the envelope back on his desk. The papery smack on the wood reverberated through the otherwise silent classroom.

When he spoke, his voice was intentionally soft. "Before you ask me—no. I have no idea what will happen next."

"Then why are you doing it?" Brigit's voice trembled and her eyes were wide.

Teigen hesitated, wanting to choose his words carefully. Whatever he said to these young men and women at this crucial moment was likely to stick in their minds for the rest of their lives—and possibly shape their own decisions when facing life's undeniable challenges.

"I know right from wrong," he began. "And I know good from evil. Just as you all do."

Heads bobbed tentatively. Dozens of eyes fixed on his.

"Making the right choice often means making the hard choice." He wiped his eyes, startled that they were damp. He hadn't had time to process the enormity of what he and his fellow teachers were facing but it was clearly hitting him now. "As your teacher, I must lead the way. I must make the choice to stand up for what is right, no matter how hard the consequences might be."

One of the girls in the front row started to cry quietly into her handkerchief.

Brigit's brows pulled together. "What about the other teachers? What are they going to do?"

Teigen shrugged. "All but three of us refused to sign the declaration yesterday, and this morning the rest of us received instructions for sending our protest letters. Beyond that, you'll have to ask each of them."

He regained his feet and walked back around his desk, determined to maintain as much normalcy as possible. "In the meantime, we have a chemistry exam to review for. Please open your books to chapter twenty-three."

ᚾ ᚾ ᚾ

By the end of the day, Teigen's head was pounding. Between his lack of sleep, his distress over Elsa's stance, and the questions in every class period about Quisling's actions and what would happen next he was completely done in. All he wanted was a warm meal and his bed but wondered if he currently had the strength to get up from his desk and walk home.

"Teigen?"

Elsa's soft voice yanked his attention to the doorway of his classroom. She stood in the hallway as if afraid to come inside. Her face was pale, her eyes swollen. Though she wasn't crying at the moment it was obvious she had done a lot of it recently.

"Can I talk to you?"

Teigen stood and approached her. "Of course. Come in."

She slipped past him and he closed the door behind her. He caught a whiff of the rose oil she had used as perfume since the Nazis had claimed everything of perceived value as theirs.

Elsa walked to his desk and turned around, leaning against it for obvious support. She looked up at him, pinning her lips between her teeth, clearly unwilling to let any words out just yet.

Teigen stood in front of her and wondered if he should touch her. Would that help? Or would she pull away?

He settled on simply asking, "What do you want to talk to me about?"

Her lips slowly extricated themselves from their restraints. "I've come to *beg* you to reconsider."

The pounding in his head intensified as the hope he felt when he saw her in the hallway fled. An avalanche of anger, frustration, and soul-deep disappointment pummeled his skull.

"No, Elsa. Absolutely not."

Elsa grabbed his arm. "Why not?"

"Do you even know what the oath says?" Teigen raked his fingers through his hair. "I'd swear to be faithful and obedient to the leader of the German empire—Adolf Hitler!"

Her eyes pooled with tears. "You don't have to mean it…"

"It's a sworn oath, Elsa." He winced as his head throbbed with the beat of his pulse. "It's not a simple thing for a man to pledge his word. His honor is at stake. Don't you understand that?"

Teigen pulled her hand off his arm and grabbed the sample letter from his desk. He handed it to her. "The resistance is circulating this response. We are to copy it, sign it, and mail it."

Elsa held the paper in shaking hands and read the text aloud, her voice flat and unemotional. "I find that I cannot contribute to the upbringing of Norway's youth under the guidelines for NS Youth Service, as they conflict with my conscience. And as membership in the Norwegian Teachers Union obliges me to commit to such an upbringing, as well as other demands which are contrary to my employment contract, I cannot accept membership in the Norwegian Teachers Union."

She dropped the paper on his desk like it burned her fingers.

"You don't have to send this, Teigen. Just don't do anything."

Teigen crossed to the coat rack and grabbed his coat and scarf. He needed the actions to try and control his temper. How could Elsa ask him—repeatedly—to turn his back on his principles? Principles which were becoming more immutable by the minute.

He fisted the garments and glared at her. "It's too late, Elsa. Not only have I refused to sign that damned declaration, I've already sent my letter to their 'Norwegian Teachers Union' clearly stating that I refuse!"

Close enough.

Elsa's jaw dropped. Her shocked gasp sucked all the air from his world. "How could you?" she shouted.

"How could I *not?*" he shouted back. "And I'm not the only one. You'll see."

Teigen strode to the door and jerked it open. He whirled to face the woman who only yesterday he had planned to marry, raise children with, and grow old with and wondered how he'd misjudged her so completely.

"Is that all you have to say to me?" he asked.

Elsa grew suddenly and furiously calm. Jaw clenched, she marched to the open door and stepped out into the hallway before she turned back to face him.

"Damn you and your ridiculous convictions, Teigen Hansen," the dearest love of his life spat at him. "I hope you get every consequence you deserve."

He wanted to shout *and you as well*, but he stopped himself after drawing the breath. Hadn't he just spent the day talking to students about hard choices?

"I wish you the best, Elsa," he managed.

"Go to hell."

Resigned, Teigen watched Elsa stride out of his future until she reached the end of the hall and disappeared from sight.

CHAPTER THREE

March 2, 1942

Teigen didn't tell anyone in Oslo that Elsa had ended their engagement three weeks ago, but he did write a letter to his mother at the family's home in Arendal right away. She responded the same way that all loving mothers do to their sons when they are hurting—with food. The package of liver sausage, rice, and homemade lefse was more welcomed than Teigen wanted to admit.

"Quisling's starting to panic," Oskar Jung stated to the small group of seasoned teachers at their lunch table.

Teigen was spreading the remainder of his liver sausage on the last and admittedly stale piece of lefse from his mother. "How do you know?"

"I know a man who knows a man." Oskar winked. "He says a member of Quisling's office is feeding information to the resistance."

Teigen chuckled and looked at Jorgen Lasse. "Do you believe this man who knows a man?"

The middle-aged Norseman sporting a halo of gray grinned back at him. "Well, we can't believe the radio or newspaper, so I suppose we have to believe in something."

Teigen lifted one shoulder in agreement. "So tell us more,

Oskar."

The principal's eyes twinkled. "There have been *thousands* of letters of declination pouring into Quisling's Norwegian Teachers Union, and *Reichskommissar* Terboven knows all about it."

Teigen's eyebrows shot upward in surprise. "How many thousands?"

"Eight. Nine. Maybe more." Oskar ate a large bite of his fried potato klubb and talked while he chewed. "That's about three-quarters of all the teachers in Norway."

Jorgen blew a whistle of appreciation. "What do you think he'll do?"

"He can't arrest us all, that's for sure." Teigen licked his fingers and said another silent prayer of thanks for his mother's thoughtfulness.

Oskar's secretary Sophia entered the lunchroom in a flurry of waving arms and rapid steps. "*Overlærer* Jung! We've just received word!"

Oskar turned in his seat to face Sophia. "Word about what?"

The secretary thrust an official-looking paper in his face. "Minister-President Quisling has ordered all the schools to close. For the entire month of March."

"Close?" Teigen and Jorgen blurted in tandem.

"Why?" Oskar's eyes moved over the paper and his lips moved as he read silently.

"Is this a punishment for the teachers protesting?" Teigen looked at Jorgen and spoke the first thing that came to his mind. "So we lose a month's wages?"

"What about the children?" Sophie's hands worked around each other in an unending chase. "Where will they go when their parents are at work?"

Oskar snorted his disgust. "Clearly that pompous idiot hasn't thought this through. Those parents are going to be furious if they have to forgo their own livelihoods and stay home with their school-aged children as a result."

"My senior students are preparing to take their university exams," Jorgen grumbled. "They can't spend a leisurely month forgetting what they've learned."

Teigen leaned closer to the science department's chairman. "I'm willing to help you tutor them while we're banished, if you'd like."

Jorgen nodded. "Thank you, Teigen."

"I am, too," offered Dierks Halle, the senior physics teacher who had been listening without comment up to this point. "I'll go crazy if I have to stay at home cooped up with my wife and kids for a whole month."

Oskar folded the notification and tucked it inside his coat. "I can't believe this—especially in the winter. What a consummate ass."

⋈ ⋈ ⋈

The students were told what was officially happening, and then sent home to inform their parents that they were not welcome back into the building until April first. In the hasty staff gathering which followed, Oskar casually mentioned that teachers were free to secretly tutor students if they were asked to do so in the meantime.

Judging by the looks they gave each other, the teachers at Oslo Secondary School were bright enough to understand the veiled suggestion.

They also understood that those who would receive the illegal tutoring should be communicated with privately to keep that information from accidentally falling on German ears.

"What about our wages?" the music teacher asked.

Oskar looked like he aged ten years with the unwelcome question. "If the school is paid, you'll be paid. Unfortunately, that's all I can tell you."

"At least I can give lessons," the tall, thin man mumbled as he turned around and pushed his way out of the room.

When the meeting ended, Teigen returned to his classroom and packed up everything in his desk that he didn't want to go missing in his absence. The school was to be locked, of course, but he knew as well as anyone that the Nazi soldiers would pilfer whatever they found remotely interesting in the process.

They think they own the damn place.

Teigen carried a box of personal items to the boarding house in the waning afternoon light and then hurried back to the school to collect textbooks for the tutoring he volunteered to do.

As he selected the necessary books and thought about the coming weeks, he wondered how he would handle the isolation of his increasingly singular situation.

Teigen had met Elsa soon after finishing his university training and accepting the teaching position at Oslo Secondary. She was just twenty years old and still a student, but he was a twenty-two-year-old full-grown man with his first real job.

That was five years ago, before Hitler turned the world upside down. Three years later they were planning a wedding. Now, two years after that plan was literally blown up, he was alone.

With his few leisure hours taken up with the beautiful Elsa Borg, Teigen hadn't made many friends in Oslo. Sure, he was acquainted with the men and women he worked with, but his focus had always been on keeping ahead of his students first, and keeping Elsa happy second.

"What will you do with your time now, Teig?" he chided himself as he tucked one of each of his science textbooks into the box. "You have a whole month to fill."

He rested his hands on his hips and turned a slow circle in the classroom, evaluating what else he should grab while he could. His gaze rested on a hinged and locked case of basic chemicals used for classroom experiments.

Yes.

That.

"I don't know why, but it seems like a good idea for you to come with me," he said to the wooden box as he grabbed the leather handle. "Let's see what we can do with you."

March 23, 1942

"Make bombs?"

The question was so fervent that Teigen had to laugh. "We could, yes, but that won't be on your exams."

"Come on, Nilsson. Do what the book says to do and stop fooling around." Jorgen pointed at the instructions. "We have to be out of here in forty-five minutes."

Jorgen had been able to talk one of the Lutheran pastors into letting him and Teigen use the enclosed storage space behind the altar for tutoring during the day. But they were limited to just four hours each afternoon.

The arrangement made sense. If the Nazi soldiers patrolling the city popped into the church, they wouldn't see or hear anything.

And if the boys were stopped either going in or coming out they would claim they were catching up on their catechism classes while the schools were closed. If questioned, Father Haldstrom would earnestly confirm their story.

Teigen and Jorgen, on the other hand, entered and exited through the basement, one at a time, wearing work clothes and carrying their teaching supplies in worn metal toolboxes. Holding class while the schools were closed was strictly forbidden under Quisling's governmental policies; consequently the men needed to be cautious.

Three weeks had passed since all of the schools in Norway had been shuttered and, if Oskar Jung's friend-of-a-friend was trustworthy, the tens of thousands of protest letters from the teachers was a light sprinkle compared to the overwhelming deluge from outraged parents.

"I think they've lost count," Oskar said over a stein of weak beer in his dining room. "But my informant claims it's twenty times the number, based on the space the letters take up."

Teigen clunked his mug against Jorgen's. "*Reichskommissar* Terboven can't be pleased with his incompetent Norwegian counterpart."

Jorgen snorted a derisive laugh. "And the idiot has only been in power for seven weeks!"

"How are your students doing?" Oskar asked.

"Other than demanding to learn how to build a bomb, they are coming along. Maybe I'll dangle that knowledge as a promise if they pass their exams." Teigen flashed a grin and sipped his beer.

Jorgen shook his head. "Be careful, Teigen. Even jokes can be turned against you."

Teigen felt his cheeks flush. "That's all it was. A joke."

"I know." Jorgen scowled at him. "But those joking words in the minds and mouths of teenage boys can be much more dangerous than an actual bomb."

Oskar lifted his mug. "To parents! And their outrage!"

The jarring toast was an obvious attempt to return the conversation to its previously optimistic tone and halt the burgeoning argument between the colleagues.

Jorgen's smile was strained. "To parents."

Teigen lifted his mug. "Yes. To parents."

March 24, 1942

Someone was pounding on Teigen's door. His head ached from both the evening's earlier beer and the conversation that took a sudden turn, stealing the camaraderie from the trio.
The pounding became more insistent.
"Hold on!" Teigen bellowed. He pulled his pants over the long underwear he slept in, tucked his tee-shirt into the waistband, and grabbed last night's thick wool sweater from its resting place on the floor.
He was still sticking his arm through the sweater's second sleeve when he opened the door. What waited so impatiently on the other side nearly buckled his knees.
The stern pair of brown-uniformed SS officers was well-armed, and their appearance in the middle of the night could not be good by any stretch of the imagination. "Teigen Jakob Hansen?"
Teigen nodded and straightened his sweater.
One of the officers squinted at him. "You are Jewish?"
The question caught Teigen off guard. "What? No. Why do you ask that?"
"Jakob is Jewish name," he answered in broken Norse.
Teigen decided to take the offensive. He lifted one brow as he spoke. "I was named after an ancestor. A royal knight who served both King Christian the Second and England's King Henry the Eighth." He paused. "You *do* know of them?"
The second officer snarled. "Get your boots."
Teigen didn't move. "Where are we going?"
The answer was a fast and hard fist to his belly.
Teigen bent in half and stumbled backwards, struggling to inhale.

CHAPTER FOUR

March 24, 1942
Bergen, Norway

Selby Hovland stared at herself in the mirror, unsmiling and evaluative. In spite of the perfectly coifed platinum blonde hair, pale blue eyes lined in dramatic black, and lipstick as red as Eve's apple, the image looking back at her was hardened beyond her twenty-eight years.

The role she played was draining. If she hadn't hated men as much as she did, she would have quit a long time ago.

Or never started in the first place.

Selby closed her eyes, drew a deep breath and held it, then spritzed expensive French perfume on her bare throat. The SS officer she was meeting tonight gave her the silly luxury, hoping she would repay him by giving him freedom with her body.

Typical behavior of all of them.

Selby had lines that she absolutely would not cross, and that was the most resolute of them. Intimate but playful caresses were her limit, and the fact that the Royal Shakespearean Acting Troupe never stayed too long in any one town kept her many powerful connections from becoming too serious.

It was the hope that the *next* time they saw her, they might finally convince her to give in, that kept her carefully selected Nazi officers faithfully coming to the stage door in every town the troupe performed in.

Liberal amounts of aquavit made certain they couldn't consummate even if they grew overly insistent.

Between the ample liquor and her sultry flirtations, tongues were loosened and secrets spilled. Selby was very good in all of her roles.

She opened her eyes and set the perfume bottle on her dressing table. Another deep breath, a shake of her shoulders, and a swallow of her revulsion were followed by blazing smile and a complete transformation of her countenance.

"Are you ready, Selby 'Sunde'?" She adjusted her breasts to deepen the valley between them. "It's show time."

Selby stood, lifted her Arctic fox coat from a nearby bench, and opened her dressing room door.

ᛁ ᛁ ᛁ

"Miss Sunde! Miss Sunde! Over here!"

Camera bulbs flashed in Selby's eyes, leaving jagged blue blotches of blindness in her vision. She smiled through it all, knowing that she must appear beautiful, happy, and approachable in case the photos were ever printed in Norwegian magazines or newspapers. She was, after all, a bit of optimistic celebrity in a country buried in brown oppression.

Selby tightened her grip on Dahl's arm as the lead actor from their troupe steadied her at the top of the stairs. Together they descended the icy steps from the stage door platform into the crowd of brown-uniformed soldiers and wealthy Norwegians waiting behind the theater.

With one last squeeze of thanks, Selby kissed Dahl on the cheek, then turned an inquiring gaze over the crowd.

There he is.

Captain Rolf Schmidt grinned at her from the far side of the enthusiastic admirers. In another world, Selby might have thought of the forty-ish man as handsome. Maybe even kind. But they lived in this war-shaped world and Rolf was just one more grasping German SS officer, and thus the physical embodiment of pure evil.

Selby flashed him a mischievous smile and held out her arms.

Rolf pressed through the mixed crowd until he stood in front of her. He knocked his heels together and dipped his head. "You look captivating as always, my dear."

The warm scent of alcohol stung her nostrils, proving that young Bennett, the troupe's props manager, had done his job, generously serving the Nazi officer while he waited for the hour she required to remove her costume and stage makeup, and redress in seduction-worthy modern clothes, hair, and makeup.

"And you are your impressive self, Captain."

He gave her a chastising look. "Why must we do this every time, Selby? Call me Rolf."

Selby laid her hand on his chest. "You are your impressive self, *Rolf*."

The German kissed her forehead. "Much better."

Selby took his elbow and turned him away from the crowd. "Shall we?"

Someone spat on the ice-rimed sidewalk beside her.

Rolf stiffened and whirled back toward the crowd. "Watch yourselves," he growled.

Selby tugged on his arm. "Let's just go. Please."

"Nazi whore," someone hissed.

Rolf pulled back the edge of his uniform's coat to expose his holstered nine-millimeter Luger and unsnapped the black leather strap. "Be warned. I have no problem shooting into a rebellious crowd."

Selby dropped Rolf's arm and walked away from the theater, prompting him to abandon the gathering and hurry after her.

The distasteful reaction to her apparent treason was common and expected. To the citizens of Bergen she was nothing more than a mid-rate actress in a traveling troupe; a vapid and ornamental slip of femininity, using her sexuality to survive the occupation.

None of them could know who she really was: twenty-eight-year-old Selby Hovland of Trondheim, former seamstress, and member of the Norwegian Resistance.

She escaped Norway soon after the occupation and trained in England with the Special Operations Executive—a force preparing resistance fighters to conduct military operations in their home countries.

Selby's lips curved in a wry smile.

I could probably shoot that Luger with more accuracy than Rolf.

Hopefully she wouldn't need to prove that. And even though she embraced the subversive and secretive role she had chosen, the scorn of her countrymen still hurt.

How could it not.

"I'm sorry, Selby," Rolf offered as he draped his arm over her shoulder and pulled her close. "Not everyone understands that we are now living under a new regime."

Selby tamped down what she really wanted to say, settling for, "Norsemen are known to be stubborn."

Rolf forced a dry chuckle. "They even put us Germans to shame in that arena, I have to admit."

She glanced at the captain who was only a few inches taller than her five-foot-eight inches—in tall stiletto pumps. "So where are we going tonight, Rolf?"

ℕ ℕ ℕ

Selby unlocked the door and slid into the quiet sanctuary of her tidy hotel room. She couldn't wait to shower away the smoke of the tavern, the stench of Rolf's cologne, and the feel of his rough palms on her skin.

The captain had acted the gentleman for the first part of their evening, but the more he drank, the more his hands seemed to have a mind of their own. They slid across the exposed expanse revealed by her low-backed gown. They slipped up her thighs and under the garters holding her silk stockings in place—a gift from another one of her many German suitors.

Selby gently redirected his hands while stifling her shudder of revolt. Based on her experience men were only nice to women as long as they got what they wanted. Cross them, and you risked your life.

Selby felt safe enough to do what she did because the men she chose to spend time with were easily plied with alcohol and gladly imbibed to excess. She pretended to meet them glass for glass and flirted with exceptional skill, until they whispered classified answers to her seemingly innocuous questions.

In spite of all of their professed affections, expensive gifts, and suggestions of a life together after the war ended, she never felt guilty for leading them on like she did. They were only men, after all. Any one of them would use a woman the same way—or worse—if the situation were somehow reversed.

Selby stepped under the hot spray and let the shower's water stream over her body. She used a bar of silky French soap, yet another gift, to lather away the remnants of her evening's labors, both in the theater and in the tavern.

As Shakespeare's Jacques—played nightly by Dahl—said in act two of *As You Like It*, "All the world's a stage, and all the men and women merely players… one man in his time plays many parts."

So she was Rosalind in *As You Like It*.

And a Nazi whore in Bergen.

It was just another role.

Reluctant to stop the soothing heat, Selby was forced to turn off the water before she fell asleep standing up. She wrapped one threadbare hotel towel around her head and scrubbed her body dry with the other.

The nightgown she wore to bed was old but warm. Whenever one of her suitors presented her with a silk or satin gown in the obvious hope of seeing her wear it to his bed, she thanked them graciously, teased them about the cheekiness of their assumption, and sold the luxurious thing at a dear price to a German soldier in the next town they visited.

Then she used that money to help fund the troupe as they carried information from town to town, from resistance post to resistance post.

The irony made her chuckle.

Unfortunately, Rolf didn't have any new information tonight, though he did express his doubts about Quisling's closing all the Norwegian schools for the month.

"While I commend th' man for trying," he slurred into her ear, "I think iss not getting the results he hoped for."

"No, I don't imagine it is," Selby said sympathetically.

"You know wha' he's gonna do now?"

She shook her head. "I have no idea."

"He's gonna arrest 'em. The teachers."

Selby frowned. "All of them?"

"Nah." Rolf waved a loose hand of dismissal. "There's no place to put 'em all." He gulped the last of his aquavit. "Just a thousand of them."

"Quisling is arresting a thousand Norwegian teachers?" Selby made a mental note to look into that in the morning.

Rolf pointed a finger at her. "Jus' men. No women."

Selby smiled sweetly. "At least he's a gentleman."

Gentleman and a traitor.

"Right!" Rolf leaned back so quickly he almost fell off his chair.

Selby called the evening to an end at that point. Now she snuggled into the bed, plumped the thin pillows, and anticipated sleeping late in the morning. They were booked for five nights in Bergen, so they had time to relax between their travels.

She drew a deep breath and let it out slowly.

I wonder what sort of mischief we can cause while we're here?

CHAPTER FIVE

March 27, 1942
Bergen, Norway

"Captain Schmidt was right. The arrests started three nights ago." Dahl held up a communication that a Bergen Resistance member had managed to swipe off the desk of an SS officer. "One thousand male teachers from several cities are being imprisoned for 'defying the government's edict and holding illegal classes' while the schools are closed."

"And they're closed because the teachers refused to sign the Nazi's Declaration of Loyalty." Bennett shook his head. Is that simpleton Quisling a complete idiot on *top* of being a traitor?"

Selby turned away from the make-up mirror in the theater's dressing room, the one secure place where the members of the troupe could quietly discuss their true mission. "Is there anything we can we do?"

Bennett plopped into a chair. "We're going to make sure that the teachers' families get paid while they are incarcerated."

Selby frowned. "How will you coordinate that?"

Gunter, the second male lead in the troupe leaned forward in his chair. "We've been instructed to contact the Resistance posts in each city we visit. They will reach out to organizations in their area which are known sympathizers."

Dahl nodded. "They'll be asked to combine their financial resources and distribute them to the families of the arrested teachers."

"This situation's going to affect every single family in this country." Selby narrowed her eyes and tapped her chin with the end of a long makeup brush. "We're going to need a new idea, something to do on the ground to keep the people's morale up."

Dahl chewed absently on the paperclip he pulled from the stolen communication. "Anyone got ideas?"

Selby stared at the glint of bent silver.

Paperclip.

Paper. Clips.

Clips hold things together.

"Stick together!" she yelped.

Dahl and Bennett stared at her.

Selby pointed at the implement dangling from Dahl's lips. "Paperclips hold things together. Let's start a campaign—wearing a paperclip on your coat represents the idea of Norwegians holding together."

Dahl pulled the clip from his mouth and stared at it. "That's so simple!" His gaze lifted to hers. "And completely brilliant!"

Bennett clapped his hands together. "It's the perfect token to remind all the families that we are *in* this together, so we need to *stick* together."

Dahl gave her a warm smile. "Well done, Hovland."

"Thanks." Selby felt her cheeks heating. Dahl's attraction to her was no secret to anyone and she found the approving twinkle in his eye disconcerting.

Dahl was a man after all. And men were, well, *men.*

"Can we get a list of who was arrested?" Bennett asked. "Or do we let each town figure it out on their own?"

"Unless they print the names in the newspaper—and admittedly Quisling *is* narcissistic enough to think about doing that—figuring it out ourselves will be impossible." Selby shook her head. "We're going to have to leave that up to the individual posts."

"Fair enough." Gunter looked at Bennett. "Want to go shopping for paperclips?"

"Selby and I'll do it." Dahl stood. "Bennett, can you check that loose hinge on the tavern set?"

Bennett stretched and scratched his short beard. "Sure, boss."

Dahl turned to Gunter. "We have a new recruit coming later to talk about joining us. Will you interview him and see how we can use him?"

"You got it." Gunter stood. "Do we have packets to take to Ålesund or Kristiansund?"

"Not yet, but Karster is coming to the show tonight." Dahl turned to Selby. "Let's get lunch when we're out. There's that tavern by the SS office that had really good soup last time we were here."

Selby forced a smile. "Sounds great."

⚔ ⚔ ⚔

There was nothing obviously wrong with Dahl. Really. He was always polite and he had treated her with the utmost respect ever since they formed the Royal Shakespearean Acting Troupe last year as a cover for their select band of Resistance members.

And as a leading man in their productions he was, of course, very handsome. Standing three inches over six feet, with shoulder-length sandy hair and bright blue eyes, he was noticeable on the stage.

In person, his good looks often brought women to a gaping halt.

Watching him across their lunch table, Selby asked herself once more if she could let go of her conviction that all men were selfish and violent in their core and give Dahl the chance to prove himself to be better than that.

To what end?

Marriage wasn't a consideration at this point. With her playing the escort to multiple Nazi officers, and the entire world tangled in a war with no obvious end, the idea of engaging in either romance or love was inconceivable.

Selby realized with a start Dahl had asked her a question. "I'm sorry, would you say that again?"

His eyes flicked briefly to the side and she caught his irritation in the moment. "I said, how do you think we should disperse the paperclips?"

Good question. "I suppose we could pass them out on the street to begin with. Pretend we are inviting people to our show if we're caught."

Dahl nodded. "If we had playbills with us, we'd be believed."

"We'll have to go back to the theater and get them." Selby cast a cautious look around the tavern which was littered with brown-uniformed SS officers. "But that should work."

Dahl paid the bill for their simple lunch, grabbed the bag of boxed paperclips, and the pair made their way from the tavern. The wind outside was sharp and threw slivers of sleet at them from under a lowering gray sky.

Selby pulled her woolen scarf up over her cheeks. "The weather here is so unpredictable," she grumbled.

"Looks like our plan will have to wait." Dahl slipped his arm around her shoulders. "But I'll keep you warm in the meantime."

Selby hoped he didn't feel her stiffen under his touch.

April 11, 1942
Ålesund, Norway

Selby checked herself one last time in the dressing room mirror. Thankfully, the deep red and nearly-backless gown had held up well on its three-months-long northern journey along the coast of Norway. Trondheim was their next and final stop before she replaced it for the journey south.

At ten o'clock on this mid-April night the city would be in deep twilight—in fact the sun would dip so shallowly below the horizon that tonight's sky would never go fully dark.

While the extra hours of daylight did rob some of the perceived romance from her rendezvous, once she and her officer-of-the-day made their way into a cozy establishment the mood could be manipulated to meet Selby's goals.

Lieutenant Fritz Walder, tonight's assignation, was her youngest suitor at a mere thirty years old—and that made him her most dangerous. He and she were so close in age that his imagined future with her was by far the most appropriate of all of Selby's dalliances.

He was also brash and vain, which made him the hardest to control.

More than once, Selby considered cutting him loose. If another prospect appeared, she might actually do so. She hadn't yet needed to dismiss and replace any of her contacts and wondered if there was a way to do so cleanly.

"Selby Sunde, my beautiful rose…" Fritz waited at the front of the crowd. She noticed that those nearest to him leaned away from the SS officer. "How I have missed you."

Selby laid her hands in Fritz's outstretched palms. She stood on her toes and kissed both of his cleanly shaven cheeks. "It's so good to see you, Fritz."

As she looped her arm through his and turned to face the small crowd, she noticed how many of those waiting there—and glaring at her—had paperclips on their lapels. Selby reached out and laid her hand against the closest gentleman's chest. Her palm covered the paperclip and she pressed against it.

"Thank you all for coming to our show." Selby smiled warmly. "You'll never know how much your support of our little Shakespearean troupe means to us."

She slid her regard to the right, away from Fritz's view, and winked at the first person whose eyes met hers.

Then she dropped her hand from the man's chest, tightened her grip on Fritz's muscular arm, and allowed the officer to lead her away from the theater.

ᚾ ᚾ ᚾ

"They love you, you know." The way Fritz said it, it was almost an insult.

Selby played it off, choosing to respond as she would to a boyfriend who was unnecessarily jealous. "Oh, stop that."

She flipped an unconcerned wrist. "I mean nothing more to any of them than a night's diversion from war."

Then she laid her hand on his forearm and gave a little squeeze. "Not like it is with you."

Fritz downed a shot of aquavit and took a long pull of his beer before he fixed his dark brown eyes on hers. "How is it with me, Selby?"

Uh, oh.

She shrugged. "You know. Special."

"Special, how?" Fritz's palm groped for her thigh under the table.

Selby removed her hand from his arm and chased after his that was climbing up her thigh. Her palm landed on the back of his hand and she tilted her head to assure she had his somewhat blurry attention.

"What are you asking me, Fritz?" she murmured. "You and I are nothing more than a man and a woman, enemies according to our leaders, who are caught in a world that forbids us to be together."

"But you are here."

"And *you* are here," she countered. "Shouldn't I be asking you that same question?"

Fritz stared at his beer mug. "I'm lonely, Selby."

She drew a deep breath. "Everyone is lonely in war,"

"No. You are here. In your homeland. With your people."

A lump thickened Selby's throat. She swallowed a small, sharp sip of aquavit to tame it.

"My people hate me, Fritz," she managed.

"Because you have chosen my side," he stated and straightened in his chair. "The right side. The victorious side."

Selby couldn't look at him, afraid he would see the soul-deep revulsion she felt when she heard his pompous declaration.

She wagged her head slowly. "They don't see it that way."

"They will. They must. Or they will die. It's that simple." Fritz motioned for another shot of aquavit while his callous words fell over her like a shroud.

Selby's stomach turned. "I—I don't know what to say to that."

Fritz faced her again. "Say you'll come to Germany with me when this is over. We can build a life together there in the glorious Third Reich."

Selby could not stop herself from asking, "Are you so certain Hitler will win?"

Fritz's jaw went slack and he looked at her like she had just declared the moon actually *was* made of cheese. "Of course. It's inevitable. To suggest otherwise is treason."

And treason for me to agree.

Selby scolded herself to let that go for now. She forced herself to disguise her true feelings behind months of practiced acting skills.

"Do you love me, Fritz?"

That question obviously knocked him sideways. "Love?"

"Yes. You say you want to build a life with me." *Why was she even asking this?* "Do you love me?"

Fritz blinked. "You're a beautiful and influential woman, Selby

Sunde. I'd never be lonely again."

Selby chuckled. "That's not love, Fritz."

"Maybe not. But with you on my arm, I'd rise very high in the Reich." He downed the replenished shot of aquavit and winced at its stinging strength. "Love isn't important."

Selby was silent for so long that Fritz finished his beer before turning a stony face to hers. "What is wrong?"

Selby's brows pulled together as she considered the lieutenant. Maybe the time had come to end this particular relationship. Of course, that meant no enemy intelligence source in Ålesund for a while, but the Resistance would go on without it.

"I'm not sure, Fritz." She gave him an apologetic look. "Maybe this isn't a good idea."

He scowled. "What do you mean?"

"Planning a future together."

"Why not?"

Selby didn't move away from the soldier, afraid to provoke him further. "I always hoped for love."

Fritz stared at her, his bloodshot eyes taking a moment to focus. He pulled his hand from her thigh and shoved his chair away from the table. "Let's go."

He stood, wobbled slightly, and grabbed Selby's arm.

Selby rose to her feet, clenching her shawl in her free hand. Fritz's fingers dug into her arm but she didn't dare fight him in view of the other SS officers who frequented this nightclub. She'd have to wait until they were outside before breaking free.

Something dangerous seemed to have come over Fritz. In the pale light of the spring night outside Selby could clearly see the jut of his jaw and the anger in his eyes. Once they were away from the club, she stopped walking and yanked her arm from Fritz's grasp.

He spun around and grabbed her shoulders, his fingers clawing her painfully. "What do you think you are doing?"

"What are *you* doing?" she demanded.

"Getting what I've earned."

A shiver of realization zinged through Selby's body. Fritz was showing his true colors and proving that her theory about every man's base and violent nature still held true.

She planted her feet on the road as firmly as her high-heeled shoes allowed and refused to budge. "And what do you think you've you earned?"

Fritz swung her around, shoved her against the side of a townhouse, and pressed his body against hers to pin her there. "You've been stringing me along for months, teasing and flirting. Now you must pay your debt."

Selby put her hands against Fritz's brown-wool-uniformed chest and shoved with all of her strength. All she succeeded in doing was knocking him off balance—and inflaming his anger.

Fritz regained his stance and wrapped one meaty hand around her throat. "Go ahead and shout," he growled. "Curfew was an hour ago."

The strong alcohol stench from his breath burned her sinuses. Selby struggled to breathe past his strangling grip and think—she had combat training, she should know what to do. But her shrinking field of vision distracted her.

Until Fritz jerked the hem of her dress to her hips.

Selby reacted out of instinct—like a feral cat fighting for its life. She yowled and scratched, her fingernails raking over his face.

When she fumbled for his Luger Fritz tightened the grip on her throat and ducked away from her flailing arms.

"You bitch!" he bellowed. She heard his belt buckle jangle loosely. "I'll teach you not to treat me this way!"

Lights danced in Selby's vision. Helpless, she felt Fritz's rough hands pushing her garters aside. His insistent hardness bypassed her panties.

"*Nooooo!*" she shrieked with the last of her breath.

Suddenly Selby was free. Nothing held her up and her knees buckled. She fell hard to the pavement and sucked air through her bruised and burning throat, trying to figure out what the hell just happened.

N N N

The gentleman with the paperclip outside the stage door, whose chest she had touched just two hours earlier, walked into the spotless kitchen. "How are you feeling, Miss Sunde?"

Selby sat huddled on a wooden chair, sipping weak tea with the man's wife. "I-I am unharmed," she croaked.

The man looked at his wife, his face a question mark.

"She was not raped," the woman said. "He tried, but you stopped him in time."

He nodded and sighed his relief. "You are lucky that the lieutenant chose *our* house to attack you against."

"Where is he now?" Selby rasped.

A crooked smile lifted the older man's cheeks. "Lying by the road, half a mile away, with an empty aquavit bottle."

"They can't trace him back to you?" Selby pressed, worried that her savior would become her martyr.

"No. Don't worry." He pulled out a chair. "Now we need to get you back to where you are staying."

It was a question. "The Ålesund Guesthouse," she answered.

He nodded. "I'll telephone them now."

Selby straightened. "Be careful what you say!"

The man glanced at his wife and smiled softly. "I know someone there. They will come when I say the right word."

After he left the kitchen to make the call, Selby turned to his wife. "The resistance."

The woman carried Selby's empty tea cup to the sink without answering. Then she turned around and leaned against it, her arms folded.

She smiled softly and shrugged one shoulder. "There are many ways to fight a war."

Selby was so touched that she almost lost the cracked and fragile composure which had held her upright since the Nazi officer's attack.

"We wear a paperclip," she whispered.

"We stand together," the woman responded.

※ ※ ※

Dahl walked Selby upstairs to her room. As grateful as she was for his steadying presence, all she wanted to do right now was strip off the red dress, stuff it into the fireplace, and set it aflame with a very large match.

Damn Fritz Walder.

Damn that Nazi bastard to hell.

"Are you going to be alright, Sel?" Dahl asked gently after she unlocked the door to her room.

Selby looked up into his compassionate green eyes. "I am physically fine, Dahl. He got close, but he didn't achieve his objective."

Dahl cocked one brow. "Spoken like a true operative."

Selby *tsked*. "You know what I mean."

He leaned against the doorframe, folded his arms, and leaned his head down to her level. "I know that men have hurt you before. And I know that you hate to show weakness. Right?"

Selby felt tears welling; she rubbed them away with her fingertips. "I'm sorry, Dahl. I just want to be alone right now."

Dahl lifted her chin so she had to look at him again. "I'm here if you need me. You know that, Sel."

"Thank you." Selby managed a shaky smile.

She stepped into the sanctuary of her little room and gently closed the door. Without moving any farther she kicked off her high-heeled shoes, pulled the red backless dress over her head, and tossed it into the fireplace.

Wearing only her bra, garter belt, stockings, and panties, Selby grabbed the box off the mantle and struck a long match. She touched the flame to the dress and then dropped the useless shoes on top of it.

Selby stood in front of the strengthening fire and watched the silk fabric smoke, flame, curl, and turn to ash.

Die you seductive bitch.

And take Lieutenant Fritz Walder to hell with you.

CHAPTER SIX

April 11, 1942
Oslo, Norway

Teigen walked toward the dining hall of the recently built Grini Women's Prison outside of Oslo with his head high and his back straight. He'd be damned if he'd let these Nazi bastards defeat him.

Today marked three weeks since he was severely beaten in the middle of the night, handcuffed, tossed in a van with a dozen other bleeding men, and locked up with three of them in a cell built for two.

Concussed, battered, and bruised, his first few days in prison were hazy. He wasn't aware whether it was day or night. Food made him vomit. His head throbbed with a pulse so loud he could hear it. All he could do was curl up on the too-short-for-him bottom bunk, keep his swollen eyes closed, and remember to breathe.

One of his cellmates was apparently in worse shape than Teigen was. He disappeared to the infirmary before Teigen even learned the man's name.

While he was gone, the three remaining men put together the fact that they were all teachers, they had all refused to sign the declaration, and they had all been holding illegal classes for their students.

"How did they know?" Jans asked.

"Someone had to speak up," Teigen grumbled. "There were three teachers in my school who did sign the damned thing. I would expect the Nazi shits visited them and pressured them into turning us in."

"Does anyone know how many teachers were arrested?" The three men looked at each other. None of them had the answer.

But by the second week in prison, when Teigen was feeling able to function somewhat normally and their cellmate had returned from the infirmary with his arm in a cast, their jailors were bragging about that number.

"One thousand," they taunted during one of the two daily meals. "One thousand of Norway's brightest men, teachers of children, who were so foolish as to ignore the requirement set forth by your esteemed Minister-President Vidkun Quisling."

Several men coughed loudly at that, intentionally disrupting the mocking announcement.

"How smart are you now?" the officer shouted over the din. "You are crowded onto this women's prison because you are more foolish than women!"

Crowded was certainly the truth.

According to the newspaper article Teigen read when the facility first opened the prison was built for seven hundred women, two to a cell. Now a second bunk had been squeezed into each cell, leaving only two feet between them in the eight foot wide compartments. And from what Teigen could see, the Germans had filled the prison to its new capacity.

Though Teigen had never met his cellmates before they were locked in together, he eventually counted seventeen of his Oslo Secondary School co-workers in the total. Rumors claimed that at least a third of the one thousand teachers arrested were from Oslo and the surrounding area.

"What do you think we'll have for breakfast today?" Jans joked. "Herring? Or maybe it will be herring this time."

"I smell herring," a man behind them in line joined in. "So I think today it'll be herring instead."

"Silence!" their guard barked. "You are lucky to be fed at all!"

Teigen clenched his jaw. The pants he was wearing when he was arrested—none of the prisoners had been given anything new to wear—were loose around his waist. He knew his weight was dropping, in spite of his efforts to keep his body strong.

The men in the cells had figured out ways to exercise using the bunks as equipment. They called out to each other down the row of cells, challenging each other to contests in pull-ups or push-ups or anything else they could think of. It passed the time and released the testosterone that might otherwise cause the tightly confined men to erupt in useless fights.

For the most part, the guards left the men alone to do as they wished.

"Oh look. Herring." Jans shrugged and flashed a boyish grin. "Guess I was wrong."

Several men in line chuckled. No one made any further comment as the single file rank took their tin plates of herring and boiled potatoes to the long tables where they sat shoulder-to-shoulder to eat.

An SS officer—a major by the insignia on his shoulder—stepped up to a platform at one end of the dining hall. He had a microphone and when he switched it on the resultant piercing squeal silenced the room.

"I have an announcement to make," he said in heavily accent Norsk. "Today we will begin to transport five hundred of our unlawful teacher prisoners to a labor camp in Kirkenes. These men have continually refused to acknowledge Adolf Hitler and his glorious Third Reich as their leader and must be punished."

He clacked his heels together and held out a stiff arm. "*Heil Hitler!*" The microphone squealed its outrage as the major turned it off.

Teigen stared at his denuded tin plate, gleaming dully in the light from the high row of barred windows that illuminated the hall. He held no false sense of security; he *knew* he was going to be one of the five hundred. He was absolutely certain of it.

If that is my path, Lord, I ask that you make me strong.

The meal was officially over. The men stood up in silence and filed from the room. No one spoke as they walked back to their wing and reentered their cells. Each man was obviously wondering who would be plucked out for transport, and who would remain in the relative safety of Grini prison.

Once Teigen was alone with his cellmates, he pointed at Hal. "Your arm is in a cast. You would be useless at a labor camp."

Hal smiled nervously. "Best broken arm I ever had."

"And you," Teigen pointed to the white-haired Ole, "Are—

forgive me for saying this—too old."

Ole pressed his lips together and grimaced. "As much as I wish to disagree with your assessment, Teigen, I'm afraid you are right. I'm long past my physical prime."

Jans' face was pale under his shock of light brown hair, but the set of his jaw was firm. "That leaves the two of us."

Teigen nodded solemnly. "Yes, it does."

Jans glanced at the two other men. "I've never been so far north. Have any of you?"

They shook their heads.

"It's deep inside the Arctic Circle." Teigen plucked at his thick wool sweater. "At least I have this."

"For how many months is the sun up all night?" Jans turned to Teigen. "Do you know?"

"Sorry. I teach chemistry, not geography."

Ole cleared his throat. "The sun will be always above or below the horizon for one month before and one month after each solstice—June twenty-first and December twenty-first." He waved a hand. "Or thereabouts."

Jan shuddered. "How long do you think they'll keep us there?"

Teigen didn't want to say the words out loud because he didn't want them to be real.

"Teigen?" Jans implored. "What do you think?"

Teigen drew a deep breath. "It's possible we'll be there until the war ends."

Or until we die.

Some words needed to be locked away, even if they were true.

April 12, 1942
Oslo, Norway

Thankfully, Teigen was assigned to the next-to-last group of teachers to board the waiting cattle-cars. The Nazis chose midnight to begin their rail journey northwards, hoping to sneak the teachers out of Oslo without the residents knowing.

Even waiting the few minutes it took to load the remaining teachers into the last of the open cars grated on his nerves. The men standing tightly against him reeked of unwashed bodies and clothes.

Teigen knew he smelled as bad as anyone. He had taken the

liberty of washing out his underwear and t-shirt in his cell's sink a couple times, and let them dry as much as possible overnight before putting them back on in the morning. But his pants and sweater were in need of a good cleaning.

I don't see that happening in a labor camp.

With a loud rumble and heavy clank of metal, the door on the car behind his was closed and latched.

"Good. We should be leaving soon," someone on the other side of the packed car said.

"Not likely," Jans muttered beside him. "Now we have to wait for all the Nazi royalty to board—and they are in no rush."

"How do you know that?" another man queried.

Jans spoke louder so the others could hear him. "My pappa worked for the trains, and I helped him when I was out of school."

"How long is the journey to Kirkenes?"

Jan's lips twisted. "It's normally about twelve hours to Trondheim, assuming the tracks are clear. That's the end of the rail line."

"Twelve? On our feet the whole time?" someone shouted.

"I guess we won't get any sleep tonight."

"What if we have to take a piss?"

"They might stop and let us out once or twice." The tone was cautiously hopeful.

Teigen looked at Jans and shrugged. "One can only hope."

ᚾ ᚾ ᚾ

After the train finally lurched into motion, the wind mercifully blew away the fug of their bodies—but the sting of frost was still heavy in the air this time of year. Teigen pulled his sweater over his head, framing his face with the neck opening, to keep his ears from freezing. Then he faced backwards in the car putting his back to the wind and tucked his hands under his arms.

Most of the men copied his actions. And no one complained about being so crowded in the car. Instead, they were grateful for the shared body heat. The teachers traveled in subdued silence; some were able to doze while standing, held upright by the press around them.

"The sun's coming up." Teigen pointed to the east with his chin.

Jans looked toward the pale lavender glow on the horizon. "It must be around five or five-thirty, then."

"What time do you think we started moving?"

Jans shrugged as best he could in the tight space. "Half past twelve?"

Teigen sighed. "Nine more hours to go…"

He watched the sky gradually lighten until the train slowed to an unexpected stop. Every man in the car came to life.

"Why are we stopping?"

"I don't know. There's nothing here."

One at a time, each of the ten cattle cars was opened. Surrounded by armed Nazi soldiers, the men were allowed to quickly relieve themselves on the ground beside the track before being herded back into the cars.

"They had to wait until it was light enough to see us," Teigen observed as relief swept through him.

"It's too bad not everyone could hold their water," Jans grumbled as he zipped his fly. "Did you see how wet the floor was?"

"I smelled it." Teigen zipped his trousers as well. "Too bad for those standing nearby."

The train was on the move again when the sun peeked over the distant mountains. Teigen squinted as the piercing rays hit his eyes. He turned his back on the bright intrusion.

"The one day I would have enjoyed some clouds," he grumbled.

Jans leaned closer to Teigen and pointed ahead of them. His expression was grim. "That's Lillehammer."

Teigen frowned. "Is something wrong with Lillehammer?"

Jans shook his head. "It means we're traveling more slowly than usual. This route should only take three hours, but we've been traveling for five."

Teigen groaned and closed his eyes. Their uncomfortable journey was going to last longer than they expected. And what would happen once they reached Trondheim?

I wonder if I could sleep standing up.

He must have succeeded to some extent because he jerked awake, roused by an impossible noise. Teigen craned his neck, trying to see over the cars in front of theirs.

"What's that sound?"

The men near the outer sides of the car reported what they saw. "There are people beside the track. Cheering."

"What are they saying?"

"Stay together."

"They're singing... Hey—that's the national anthem!"

Several men stuck out their hands and pulled them back in with packets.

"What is it?"

One of them held up the opened packet. "Food!"

Dozens of arms reached out both sides of the car instantly. Nearly half of them were rewarded with anything from a slice of cheese to dried meat or a bottle of ale.

"How did they know?" Jans asked Teigen.

"The Resistance." The man speaking wagged his finger over his head. "They know everything."

Teigen frowned. "Are you saying that the Resistance knows that this train is loaded with arrested teachers who are being transported to a labor camp at the top of the world?"

The man nodded. "That is exactly what I am saying."

"But... how?" Teigen shook his head. "They would have to have been there when the announcement was made."

"Not necessarily," another one offered. "They would only need to hear it from someone who was."

Teigen accepted a piece of dried meat from one of the men and chewed it as he pondered that idea. He knew about the Norwegian Resistance, of course, ever since the day that his homeland was invaded and occupied. But always he assumed they were just a mismatched band of radicals trying to get themselves killed while playing at being heroes.

This was nothing like that.

This was the action of a highly organized and informed group of people who were reacting to a very bad situation in a very encouraging way.

In fact it was the Resistance who delivered the letters of declination to Oskar Jung the day after the Oslo Secondary School teachers were asked to sign the Declaration of Loyalty.

He took another nibble of the jerky and chewed slowly.

Huh.

CHAPTER SEVEN

April 13, 1942
Trondheim, Norway

Over the next ten hours the train passed through Ringebu, Otta, Kongsvoll, and Støren. In each town the crowds mimicked the ones that came before. The people cheered for the teachers, sang traditional songs, and handed out packages of food—until German guards drove them away.

Several of the men in Teigen's car were reduced to tears, moved deeply by the idea that their countrymen even knew they were on the train.

And more so that these men, women and children had waited for who knows how long beside the tracks for the train to pass through, just so they could ease the teachers' frightening situation with food, water, ale, and encouragement.

As it turned out the train did make two more comfort stops, both of them in deep forest and miles from any towns. Teigen welcomed the chance to stretch his legs and relieve himself on a tree, rather than add to the stench of the fouled rail car.

His lips curled in a wry grin.

Small mercies.

"That last town was Støren. We should pull into Trondheim in less than an hour," Jans said.

Teigen coughed a laugh. "Have you memorized all of the train routes in Norway?"

Jans blushed and turned his face toward the side of the car. "It was one way I could connect with my father. So yes, I did."

The men were quiet for a while until one brave soul asked the question no one else had thought to ask. "How do we get from Trondheim to Kirkenes?"

Teigen looked at Jans. "Is there another train?"

Jans shook his head. "If I was a regular person making a normal journey, I'd take a Hurtigruten ship."

Teigen dragged his fingers through his lengthening hair. "But we're not regular people on a normal journey."

"And the Germans won't want any of us to be seen at all if possible!" a voice called out.

"They're already riled by the crowds along the way."

"Starting at midnight to keep us a secret?" another scoffed and made a rude gesture. "Take that Adolf!"

Exhausted laughter scuttled among the men.

"So if not the Hurtigruten, then..." The man who spoke from the other side of the car let the sentence dangle.

Teigen looked at Jans. "I guess we wait and see."

April 15, 1942
Trondheim, Norway

The Royal Shakespearean Acting Troupe disembarked from their Hurtigruten ship to face an unexpected scene. Hundreds of shabbily dressed and bearded men shuffled along the pier, prodded and ordered forward by dozens of heavily armed German soldiers.

"Who are they?" Selby asked.

Dahl shrugged. "I'm not sure."

A man on the dock wearing a naval uniform turned around to face them. "They're the teachers. On their way to Kirkenes."

Selby gasped. "The teachers? The ones from the train?"

He nodded and turned back to look at the prisoners. "That's them."

Before they left Ålesund, Selby heard Nazi radio announcers brag about sending the arrested teachers to an Arctic labor camp in Kirkenes. But it was the resistance members who told the troupe how residents in the towns which the train rolled through had waited beside the tracks for hours to cheer for the teachers and hand food and drink to the five hundred men in the open cars.

"Those people's actions are inspirational," one of them said. "From what we've been hearing, the whole country feels that way."

"Not to mention the refusal of the teachers to give in to that traitor Quisling. That encourages everyone as well," another chimed in.

Selby and Dahl were joined on the dock by the other members of the troupe. The group stood rooted to their spots, silently watching the first teachers make their way up the plank of the small steamer.

"Certainly they aren't all getting on that ship..." Selby said to the man in uniform. "That ship's much too small to hold them all."

He huffed his disgust. "Aye, that's the *Skjerstad*. She's built to carry a hundred passengers."

He turned back to face Selby again. "She was requisitioned six days ago by *Reichskommissar* Terboven to transport the teachers." His expression darkened. "And she's the *only* ship he requisitioned."

"Five hundred men on a ship built to carry only a fifth of that?" Dahl's expression clearly displayed his horror. "Isn't that too much weight? It'll surely sink!"

"Five hundred men will die!" Selby's chest tightened and tears stung her eyelids. "This can't be happening."

"There's some what think the boat'll be put out to sea and sunk on purpose." The seaman sniffed, cleared his throat, and squinted at the vessel in question. "Then either Allied submarines or bombers'll get the blame."

Selby stepped forward and stared at the men in line. They were husbands, fathers—sons at the very least. Hundreds of families would be facing the senseless loss of a loved one.

Please God, don't let this happen.

As her gaze moved down the line, one man caught her attention. Tall, even for a Norwegian, his tousled blond hair brushed his neck and his light brown beard was the same length as most of the other men.

Of course.

None of them had been able to shave since they were arrested three weeks earlier.

It was his straight back and proud demeanor that kept Selby staring. She could see his jaw muscles working from fifty yards away and his glaring eyes were shadowed by his lowered brow.

He's angry, she thought. *Very angry.*

And why wouldn't he be?

Selby realized with a start that she was furious on his behalf.

Why this one man?

Why not all of them?

Please don't let him die.

As if he heard her silent prayer, he turned his head and looked directly at her. Bright green eyes met hers, pinning her gaze. There was no plea in his intense regard, only seething, furious determination.

Selby forgot to breathe.

He had stopped moving to look at her. That unwise lapse earned him a sharp jab from a presumably loaded rifle.

"Move!" the brown-clad soldier barked. "Get on!"

The compelling green gaze left hers and slid to the German. But as he stepped forward to close the gap, he looked at her again.

Selby returned his regard while desperately trying to think of something—anything—that she could do to encourage the man to stay strong.

Even if he's about to drown in an overloaded boat.

Tears spilled over her lashes and rolled down her cheeks, chilling her skin as they dried in the sea breeze. Without really thinking about it, she laid her right hand over her heart.

His beard twitched as the corners of his mouth lifted slightly. His brow eased. He dipped his chin in a small, quick nod.

It was his turn to climb the gangplank. He turned away from her and commenced his ascent, walking out of her sight.

N N N

Teigen relished the brief respite from his situation that his silent interaction with the beautiful woman on the dock had offered. He thought she looked a little familiar, but he couldn't place her.

Doesn't matter.

He focused his attention on finding a place to sit on the overcrowded ship.

After seventeen cold hours in the cattle cars, the train carrying the five hundred teachers had arrived in Trondheim. In the three days of waiting for the next part of their journey his imagination had run wild, taking him through increasingly horrific scenarios, all ending with his untimely death at the hands of his captors.

"The days before things happen are always more terrible than the days they actually do happen," Jans said. "Anticipating the unknown is the worst."

"You, there. And you." A Nazi soldier pointed at Teigen and Jans. "Follow those men."

Teigen looked toward where the soldier pointed and saw a line of men going below the deck. His gut clenched at the thought of dying in the bowels of an obscure little ship off the coast of Norway. He nodded and moved in that direction, trying to breathe normally and not allow panic to swamp him.

Once they went down two levels Teigen was shocked at what he found.

In the steerage section of the passenger ship, bunks made of plywood—three beds high—had been installed in the hallway. Further on through a heavy door, the ceiling of the twenty-four-bunk room was a foot higher than the hallway. A top bunk had been added to every set of two beds. It was so close to the ceiling it would be impossible for that passenger to sit up on it.

The teachers from Grini Prison were already laying not only on half of the three-tiered bunks, but on the floor below the bottom bed as well.

"They're stacking us four high?" Teigen grumbled.

Jans shot him a resigned look. "Well it's not like we have luggage to store."

Teigen wondered if he could stand to sleep either on the low-ceilinged top bunk or on the floor beneath the bottom one. His cell at Grini had been crowded, true, but he never felt like he was sleeping in a coffin.

A cold sweat spread over his skin.

Stop it.
Breathe.

"You. Here." The soldier pointed to Teigen and then to the second tier. Teigen blew a sigh if relief and hoisted himself onto the thin mattress.

The soldier turned to Jans. "You. Top."

Teigen shifted to give Jans a place to step as he climbed to the top bunk.

"Do we get mattresses?" Jan asked.

The Nazi glared at him and answered in accented Norse. "You get a place to sleep. Be grateful you do not have to stand once more."

Teigen drew a deep sigh and gave his friend a sacrificial offering. He could not do otherwise; and he hoped other men would follow his lead.

"I'll take turns with you, Jans."

Jans' head appeared over the edge of the bunk above his. "Thanks, Teig."

While they waited for the rest of the bunks to fill, Teigen allowed his thoughts to return to the woman on the dock. The pain in her eyes meant the world to him. That a stranger would care so deeply about what was happening to him and his fellow teachers filled him with even more determination than the well-wishers along the train tracks had.

Those people had been singing, cheering, and handing out food. The mood was almost festive.

This woman was clearly stricken by their dire situation. And Teigen felt the fraught emotions he saw on her face. Those emotions were real.

One corner of his mouth lifted.

Unless she's a consummate actress, that is.

An SS officer's shout halted his reverie.

"Listen to me!"

The mumbling chatter that had filled the room stilled.

"You all have been assigned to the noon to six o'clock sleep shift."

What?

"Every day when the bell rings at noon, you are to come down to this level and exchange places with a man who has been assigned the six in the morning to noon shift."

So this isn't my bunk.

Teigen groaned softly. He would have to compete for sleeping space every day. At noon. How soon would he become accustomed to that odd time? And how long was the voyage?

"When you are not sleeping, you are to spend your time on the deck. Is that understood?"

A grumble of assent wafted from the men.

"Good. We begin now."

The officer flipped a switch and the room built for forty-eight and now holding nearly a hundred men went black. The heavy door clunked closed.

Shocked silence filled the lightless space.

"What the hell?" someone blurted.

"Sleep shifts?" Teigen heard a bunk near his creak as the disembodied voice continued. "How are we expected to sleep in the middle of the day?"

The reason was clear to Teigen. "It's because the ship is overloaded," he stated. "They don't have room for five hundred beds."

"Or even half that, judging by what I saw," Jans offered from above him.

"If we are only allowed to sleep for six hours, there must four shifts," another voice posited.

"Ninety-six of us in here, another thirty in the hallway, then."

"That would do it…"

Teigen closed his eyes. He found it disorienting to have them open when there was no light to ground him. "I suppose we should try and sleep, then."

"How can I sleep when I don't know what will happen to us?" A voice at the far end of the room asked.

"Staying awake won't help," Jans said. "We don't get to lie down again until noon tomorrow."

Teigen heard the bunks groan and crack as ninety-six teachers tried to get comfortable—admittedly a much harder proposition for the half of them lying on bare wood or the floor.

Compounding their situation was the steam engine that suddenly came to life. The hiss of steam and the deep scrape of iron seemed to be happening inside the room with them.

"Well, *hell!*" a man shouted.

Teigen lay on his side, more miserable than he could remember ever being in his entire life. Hungry, with no hope of food for another six hours at least, he tried to doze off. But even though his body was exhausted, he wasn't sleepy in the middle of the day. It also wasn't helpful that the rumble and squeal of the engine banged in his ears.

It wasn't long before he felt the ship shudder and begin to rock.

We're moving. We're going out to sea.

A voice somewhere in the room began to recite the Lord's Prayer. A dozen or more of the teachers joined their voices to his and it seemed like everyone in their cramped quarters chorused the *Amen* at the end.

At least he wasn't cold—with this many bodies jammed into the enclosed space the room should stay warm, especially being close to the boiler.

Teigen thought again about the woman on the dock.

Thank you for your kindness.
Whoever you are.

CHAPTER EIGHT

April 29, 1942
Trondheim, Norway

For two weeks Selby had been listening to every single radio broadcast on the Nazi-controlled radio stations, trying to hear news declaring that the sailor on the dock's dire prediction had come true. Certainly if the teachers' ship had sunk, as he suggested, the Nazis would be quick to blame their enemies for the deaths of five hundred respected men.

But nothing was said.

"No news is good news," Dahl reminded her. "And in this case, Quisling can't risk another major uprising."

"Bastard traitor," Selby muttered.

The Royal Shakespearean Acting Troupe had finished their performances of *As You Like It* and spent the last ten days in Trondheim refitting costumes, repainting backdrops, and rehearsing *Much Ado About Nothing* for their southern journey back to Oslo. Every time Selby passed the Trondheim pier the memory of the teacher's bright green eyes sprang to her mind.

And every time it did, she said a prayer for his safety.

She was passing there now when Dahl ran to meet her. His sandy shoulder-length hair flew madly around his head in the wind and his blue eyes were pinched at the corners by his wide grin.

"Selby!" he called out. "They made it!"

Selby's heartbeat lurched. "The teachers?"

"Yes, the teachers!" Dahl slowed to a stop in front of her. "I just heard it on the resistance transmission."

Thank God. "Was there anything on the Nazi radio?"

Dahl shook his head. "I think Terboven and Quisling want us loyal Norwegians to forget all about them."

Selby made a face and resumed walking toward their hotel. "Well I—*we*—won't. Not after seeing them."

Dahl slid his puzzled gaze sideways to hers. "No. We won't..."

Selby stopped walking again. "Can we work something into the play that will remind people that they're up there?"

Dahl swung around to face her, his expression wary. "What sort of something? What are you thinking?"

"Well..." Selby paused, rummaging through her mind for ideas. "The soldiers in the story come to Leonato's house after a war. What if we added that they had been prisoners of war 'in the far north'?"

Dahl rubbed his forehead with his thumb and index finger. "Go on."

Selby formulated the plan as she spoke. "They could say that there were five hundred of them that had been imprisoned. And that they stuck together and triumphed over their enemies, and now they're returning home."

This time it was Dahl who resumed their pace. He didn't speak, but he did tug on one earlobe—a habit that Selby realized months ago signaled concentrated thought on his part.

"We could pass out paperclips."

Selby smiled; Dahl was in agreement. "Could we have the returning soldiers in the play wear red?"

Dahl laughed derisively at that. "You want to mention five hundred prisoners in the north *and* bring the Red Army to mind?"

Selby shrugged innocently. "We'll tell the Nazis—if they ask—that the red clothing is correct for the time period."

Dahl *hmphed*. "And what about the reference to five hundred prisoners?"

"That's what Shakespeare's original manuscript said." Shelby winked. "We'll tell them to look it up."

"Of course they won't."

She shook her head. "Nope."

This time Dahl's laugh was appreciative. "Okay, Selby."

"Is that a yes?"

"It's a yes." He sighed loudly and stopped walking again so he could look her in the face. "The things I do for love."

Selby's entire body flushed with adrenaline prompting the flight response. She wanted to flee. "Stop that, Dahl. Don't say things like that."

Without waiting for him to react, Selby whirled around and hurried up the steps of their hotel. She pushed her way though the leaded glass door without looking back.

May 1, 1942
Kirkenes, Norway

Teigen survived the slow, cold, and rough thirteen-day voyage to the far north through a combination of his stubborn Norse will and the mental image of the woman on the dock who noticed him. He would never have imagined how much her simple gesture could strengthen him.

In the unlikely event he ever saw her again in his lifetime, he would thank her.

And if I meet her in the afterlife, I'll thank her then.

The *Skjerstad* only docked three times during their journey, and then just to take on coal and food supplies. In spite of the replenishment, the prisoners' two meals a day were meager and not always fresh—clearly they overwhelmed the overloaded ship's galley capacity.

Because of the sleeping shifts, meals were staggered throughout the day, each man eating with his shift mates. Yet even under these harsh and unwieldy circumstances the teachers decided to give each other lectures and sing together to keep themselves from going mad.

And, to aggravate their captors.

As they slogged forward, Teigen noticed several smaller ships accompanying the *Skjerstad* on her route.

"It's for their own protection, I'd bet. Not ours," Jans said when Teigen commented on their constant presence. "The Allies will know about our ship, of course. We won't be attacked, so neither will they."

That made sense. And at least they weren't going to be bombed to the bottom of the Norwegian Sea.
One less worry.

Once they arrived in Kirkenes three days ago, and their crowded, filthy, and overall horrendous voyage finally ended, a doctor—a member of Quisling's party based on his armband—began a brisk examination of every one of the five hundred teachers. Many of the men had become seriously ill on the trip due to their poor diet, inability to sleep regularly, and exposure to the increasingly cold winds on the ship's unprotected deck.

From what Teigen observed, pneumonia, asthma, and bronchitis were most common, but some were unable to keep food down and a few were vomiting or shitting blood.

As one of the healthier prisoners, Teigen was consequently one of the last teachers to be examined. A brown-clad lieutenant stepped up to the doctor's side as Teigen waited his turn.

"Minster-President Quisling wants his report," he barked at the doctor. "He is tired of waiting."

The visibly exhausted physician straightened and glared at the man. "Tell him that the space, food, and water supplies on the ship were totally inadequate, and there were only two lavatories for five hundred men. What condition does he *expect* these men to be in?"

Teigen lowered his eyes so neither the lieutenant nor the doctor could see that he was listening. To the man's credit, the doctor was clearly horrified by what he had seen.

Even though there was nothing to be done about it now, knowing that someone in Quisling's camp had stood up for him and his fellow prisoners was a sort of comfort.

The lieutenant stormed away.

Two more teachers were examined before it was Teigen's turn. The doctor asked for his name, and made a check mark on a list before launching into his questions.

"Height?"

"Six feet and six inches."

The doctor nodded as he wrote. "Please step on the scale."

Teigen did so. Even though he knew he had lost weight in the last month and a half, he wasn't prepared for how much. Twenty-five pounds had dropped from his frame.

The doctor looked at the scale. "Two hundred and twenty." His gaze swept over Teigen. "What was your weight before your arrest?"

"Two hundred forty-five. Or fifty."

The man made an unintelligible sound and said, "Lift your sweater."

While Teigen complied, the physician donned a stethoscope and pressed it to Teigen's chest. "Take a deep breath. Again. And again. One more."

He removed the stethoscope's earpieces and made more notes. "How are your bowels?"

"Fine."

He looked intently at Teigen. "Are you keeping food down?"

Teigen nodded and lowered the hem of his sweater.

"Sleeping?"

"When I can."

The doctor made more checkmarks and scribbles. "You pass. You're fit for work."

Teigen wasn't sure if that was good news or bad.

The Nazi lieutenant stomped back into the stark room with an ugly look of triumph plastered on his face. "Here is the Minister-President's reply."

The doctor turned his back on Teigen and reached for the telegram.

Teigen could see the typed words and read them over the shorter physician's shoulder.

The measures taken against Norway's teachers are a direct consequence of their treasonable activities. They have had their chance to recant.

Teigen spat on the floor.

The doctor whirled to glare at him.

"Sorry," he said, not meaning it at all. "Am I finished?"

May 2, 1942
Kirkenes, Norway

After the physical examinations were finished, the teachers were divided into four groups, though the purpose of the groups was not explained. German-speaking teachers were selected as interpreters and sub-group leaders, so Teigen became one of them.

"At least I can speak to the bastards," he told Jans as the men walked south from the port to the labor camp outside of town. "And if they forget I can understand them, maybe I'll learn something to help us."

The group leaders, plus the men who possessed any other skills valued by the Nazis, were housed in groups of eleven or twelve in seventeen shabbily-erected octagonal huts. The huts were made of heavy untreated cardboard and had raw wooden floors—a relative luxury compared to the dirt floors of the stable.

Jans didn't claim to have any special skills so he had been housed in the stable with the remaining three hundred teachers.

"There was hardly room even to lie down," he groused to Teigen the day after arriving at the camp. "We slept forty to a row, and we only had about a foot's width each."

Teigen startled. "A foot? How is that possible?"

"We all had to all turn over at the same time."

Teigen forced himself not to laugh as the ridiculous image of forty men rolling over in tandem flooded his mind. He felt guilty about his relative comfort and tried to downplay it.

"Remember the rain last night?"

Jans looked up at him. "Yeah, of course."

"Well, the roof of our hut is tarred, but not the walls as it seems. When they got wet they came loose from the frame."

Jans' jaw dropped. "So while I slept pressed front to back with other men, you were enjoying Camp *Pappenheim*?"

Teigen snorted. "Be nice and I might invite you to visit my paper home!"

"I suppose we could choose to sleep in the fox cages like those guys…" Jans tilted his head toward the abandoned wire-and-wood enclosures which some men had claimed by stuffing a sleeping bag inside—a few thought to carry one with them when they were arrested, apparently. Teigen had been far too surprised to even think of that possibility.

He threw a dubious glance at the cages, which were open to the arctic elements. "You could watch the stars at night…"

"Feel the rain on your face…" Jans teased.

"I already have that."

Both men laughed. It felt good to grab a sliver of humor in an otherwise humorless situation.

"What's so funny?"

Another of the German-speaking group leaders approached.

Teigen had not actually met the stranger, but he knew the man's hut was next to his.

Teigen pointed at the fox cages. "We were discussing the pros and cons between sleeping in a fox cage, and living in Camp *Pappenheim*."

"Rain on your face apparently is a benefit which both options have in common," Jans added.

The other man chuckled. "Is that what you're calling our lavish accommodations?" He stuck out his hand. "Falko Jensen."

Teigen grasped his hand and shook it firmly. "Teigen Hansen. This is my friend, Jans Lund."

As Falko shook Jans hand he asked, "Are you an interpreter too?"

Jans shook his head. "No, my only skill is knowing every train route in Norway by heart, but I'm not about to offer that information to the brown bastards."

"Good man." Falko looked carefully around while he pushed his auburn hair from his deep-set gray eyes. All visible Nazi soldiers were currently shouting orders to the teachers who were not yet settled and acting confused.

"Are you members of the resistance?" he asked softly.

"Yes."

Teigen looked at Jans, surprised. "You are?"

"Have you been to England?" Falko asked.

Jans' expression dimmed. "Couldn't go. My mother was ill."

"What's in England?" Teigen whispered.

Falko looked at the ground. "Is she better?"

"She died."

"Sorry."

Jans sniffed. "Thanks."

Teigen felt bad that he never asked Jans those questions. Granted, he met the man only five and a half weeks ago, but they had been constant companions ever since. "I'm sorry, too."

Jans rubbed his eyes. "Thank you."

Teigen couldn't hold the question in. "What's in England?"

Falko squinted at the Nazi soldiers. "The Special Operations Executive. SOE for short."

"They train men—and a few women—from occupied countries." Jans' rueful tone broadcast his regret at missing out. "They teach them to be stealth fighters, and then send them back home to conduct military operations against the Germans."

Teigen frowned. "I've never heard of this."

Falko looked at him sharply. "But you know about the Norwegian Resistance?"

Teigen felt his face heating. Elsa had forbidden him to talk about the resistance movement or do anything that smacked of rebellion. He had respected her wishes because he loved her.

But standing in a chilled and muddy labor camp, after so many weeks of crowding, starvation, and filth, being forced to do Nazi bidding, and knowing that the treasonous leader of Norway thought that he and his fellow teachers deserved all of this was quickly changing that stance.

"I do. I'm just not familiar with what they do. Exactly."

Falko's eyes narrowed. "Are you angry enough to learn yet?"

At those words, Teigen felt a surge of rage pulse through his entire body. How could he have been so stupid? So blinded by love that his brain ceased to function? Of *course* he needed to join the resistance. He was already arrested for refusing to comply with Nazi demands. It only made sense that, both as a Norwegian and a man, he began to fight back.

He clenched his jaw and stared into Falko's eyes, level with his own.

"Damn right I am."

CHAPTER NINE

May 22, 1942
Bergen, Norway

Selby sat across the tiny tavern table from Captain Rolf Schmidt. Tonight was their first performance of *Much Ado About Nothing* in Bergen and the captain attended as always.

As she made light conversation, Rolf's free hand massaged her bare knee under the table; he had pushed the hem of her emerald green dress to her thigh. Selby kept her legs crossed to prevent him from going any farther.

Rolf wasn't very talkative tonight. His sour mood was reflected in both his unsmiling visage and the number of aquavit shots he chased with gulps of beer.

Selby laid her hand over the one of his that loosely cradled his beer glass. If he drank too much too fast, her time with him would be wasted.

"What's on your mind tonight, Rolf?" she murmured. "You aren't your usual self."

His brown eyes pinned hers. "I don't remember this play mentioning five hundred prisoners..."

Uh oh.

"It's the first time we've performed it, so I don't know." Selby flashed a coquettish smile. "I have to confess, I didn't pay that close attention in school. I was more interested the dances and socials."

"Well, it was startling. That's all." He downed a shot. Winced. And took a long pull of the beer.

Selby feigned confusion. "Why?"

Clearly shocked by the question, Rolf looked at her as if deciding if she could be serious. "Because of the five hundred Norwegian teachers imprisoned 'in the north'!"

Selby gave a little gasp. "Oh my goodness!" She clapped her free hand over her mouth and giggled. "I didn't think of that!"

The captain scowled. "How could you not?"

Selby waved that hand dismissively and fought to keep her tone light. "Because that's old news, Rolf. It happened months ago."

Selby misstated the timeframe on purpose to support the clueless character she presently played. It seemed to convince Rolf in his current inebriated state because he didn't challenge her.

Instead, he took another long drink of his beer and groused, "Quisling's an idiot."

Then he pulled his hand from under hers and pointed at her. "And if you ever tell anyone I said that I'll have you shot."

Selby dug deep into her acting skills to keep her expression sympathetic. She dare not reveal the jolt of fear that his unexpected threat sent streaking through her frame. She reached for his hand and covered it with hers again, pressing it back down to the small tabletop.

"You can trust me, Rolf." Selby swallowed and adopted a hurt expression. "Don't you know that by now?"

"*Ja. Ja. Ich weiss.*" He motioned for another shot of aquavit. "I know."

She tipped her head forward and lowered her voice. "Do you want to tell me *why* you would say such a thing?"

He seemed to be considering the wisdom of doing so. Selby watched his expression slowly change from concern to blatant frustration. "Do you want to know what he did today?"

Good Lord, what now?

"Only if you want to tell me…"

Rolf waited until the waiter set down his aquavit and moved far enough away from the table that he wouldn't hear what the captain said. His bleary eyes rested on Selby's.

"This morning he went to Stabekk Secondary School in Oslo to address the teachers there. He had his Minister of Education and the head of the Norwegian national police come with him." Rolf picked up the shot glass and stared at the amber liquid. "As if that was not enough, he had twenty members of his personal guard surround the school."

Selby wondered if the resistance had broadcast this yet. Her heart pounded with trepidation as she asked, "What did he do?"

"He called all of the teachers together, and then he shouted at them like a raging maniac. I was told his words could even be heard outside the building. But that isn't the worst of it."

Rolf downed the shot and ran the lightly-furred back of his hand across his mouth. "Fucking idiot."

Selby didn't react to his vulgar choice of words. Part of her job was to appear to be on the same side as her Nazi companions and not criticize them.

"What *was* the worst of it?" she whispered.

Rolf looked at her, incredulous. "He actually ended his rant by saying *you teachers have destroyed everything for me!*"

Selby felt a rush of quickly disguised relief and joy. "He did?"

"*Ja!* As if anything happening in this country is for his personal benefit." Rolf drained his beer and said it again.

"What a fucking idiot."

ﾒ ﾒ ﾒ

Selby managed to get Rolf into his waiting car with the help of his driver, and then climbed inside with the captain. After a short ride, with the silence broken only by Rolf's snores, the black vehicle adorned with rapidly fluttering Nazi flags rolled to a stop in the front of her hotel.

Luckily she returned so late from her assignations that there were seldom witnesses to her apparently traitorous return. But the lateness of the hour didn't stop her from knocking on Dahl's door tonight.

Rumple-haired and squinty-eyed, but still gorgeous, Dahl cracked the door and peered out. When he saw it was Selby who woke him, he yanked the door open. "Are you okay?"

"Yes, I'm fine. Can I come in?"

Dahl stepped back to let her pass. He was wearing a pair of flannel pants and nothing else. Selby tried not to stare at his finely built body.

"What's happened?" he asked as he yawned.

Selby sat on the only chair in the hotel room. "Has there been any communication from the resistance about Quisling's verbal explosion in Oslo?"

Dahl shook his head. "Not that I've seen." He sat on the foot of his bed facing her. "Did Schmidt tell you about it?"

"Yep." Selby recounted Rolf's tale, but leaving out the profanity.

Dahl began to laugh. "This is good."

"It seems that the higher-ranking officers were informed so they can squelch any sort of loyalist celebrations that might result."

"Makes sense." Dahl scratched his head and yawned again. "We should hear something by morning. It seems to take about twenty-four hours for the communications to reach us."

Selby stood. Dahl's sleepiness was making her drowsy. "I'll let you get back to sleep. I was just so encouraged that I wanted to tell you right away."

Dahl gave her a sultry smile. "Anytime, Selby."

Selby walked to the door, but before she opened it she looked back at Dahl. She hated to throw cold water on her own suggestion, but to be fair and safe she needed to.

"He did ask me about the five hundred prisoners we mentioned in the play…"

Dahl's brow lowered. "What did you say?"

"I played stupid." She shrugged. "I said I didn't know anything about it."

"Did he buy that?"

Selby nodded. "And I really think he only noticed because the Quisling thing was weighing on his mind."

Dahl dragged his hand through his hair. "You're probably right. But if anyone else mentions it we'll have to cut it."

Selby nodded. "I understand."

As she walked to her own room Selby thought once more about the tall teacher with the green eyes from the dock in Trondheim.

I pray to God that you're safe.

ᚾ ᚾ ᚾ

The next day the Royal Shakespearean Acting Troupe ate their cold lunches together in the dressing room of the Bergen Theater.

Dahl read the message that they received an hour earlier out loud to the group. After reading the account of Quisling's ill-advised appearance—which matched Rolf's story to Selby nearly word for word—the actors sadly learned that Quisling had ordered the arrest of all of the teachers at that school.

"Oh no," Selby groaned.

"Don't worry. They won't be sent anywhere except Grini," Bennett stated. "After this mess, Quisling doesn't dare ship any more teachers to the arctic circle."

"I agree," Gunter the troupe's second male lead stated. "Quisling needs to try and stay on the Germans' good side. He's bungled this so badly that he can't afford another public cry of outrage."

Green eyes locked on hers floated through Selby's mind. "I hope you're right."

"Shall I continue?" Dahl asked.

Selby flashed an apologetic smile. "Yes. Please."

Dahl returned to the paper. "In spite of the arrests, Quisling's statement proves our victory. It shows that by standing together the teachers have blocked Quisling's plan of organizing a new Corporate State."

For a moment, everyone was silent, contemplating those words.

"This is good," Dahl said finally. "This is very good."

June 5, 1942
Kirkenes, Norway

A month had passed since the five hundred teachers were settled into the labor camp and they were told that their four groups would each be assigned to one of two tasks.

"Each task will continue day and night in two twelve-hour shifts," the SS officer shouted at the assembled group. He waited for the translators to repeat his words in Norwegian before he continued. "And the teachers will work seven days a week for the glory of Germany and her assured victory. *Heil Hitler!*"

Not one teacher repeated the salute.

Jans leaned close to Teigen. "So that means one hundred and fifty of us will sleep in the stable at a time, not three hundred. I suppose that's an improvement. Two feet of luxury means I can sleep on my back."

"I'm glad we are in the same group, Jans," Teigen said, flashing a crooked smile. "I would sorely miss your humor."

"When will the work begin, do you think?" he whispered.

"Attention!" shouted the same officer. "Groups A and C are assigned to road-building. Groups B and D will be unloading ships at the dock in Kirkenes."

"We'll be at the docks, then," Teigen murmured.

Jans nodded. "I'm glad. I think."

"Group A, please proceed to the fjord and board one of the boats tied there. You will be transported across the fjord to begin clearing the land." The officer's arm swung stiffly to the east and pointed at the fjord which their rough camp was constructed beside.

Then he pointed north. "Group B, please assemble at the gate for your walk to the docks."

Jans elbowed Teigen. "There's my answer. Let's go."

As the men shuffled toward their assigned gathering spot, the officer gave his last command. "Groups C and D, your shift will begin at six o'clock this evening. I suggest you get some sleep."

After a grueling month, and despite their general lack of experience with physical labor, the teachers had fallen into the demanding routine. It was the duty of the interpreters and sub-group leaders to keep the Germans informed of any illnesses or injuries among their assigned workers, and relay any orders from the Nazi officers and guards to the teachers.

Falko Jensen immediately organized regular meetings between the Norwegian leaders and made sure that both the day shift and the night shift leaders all knew what the other shift was experiencing. These meetings were the only thing that allowed Teigen to hold on to the elusive glimmer of hope that they would survive their imprisonment and forced labors.

That, and the sweet memory of the blonde woman who stared into his eyes and laid her hand over her heart.

Lord, please let me find her someday, he prayed. *I do want to thank her.*

Tonight's leaders' meeting was centered on a shared concern. From the beginning, the inexperienced and weakened teachers were forced to unload large oil drums and heavy crates of supplies from German ships.

As was to be expected, injuries were common. At any given

time at least a dozen men from Shift B were recuperating in the medical tent at the camp.

Today, however, the supplies included live ammunition—and that was the reason Falko called for this gathering.

"Live ammunition is dangerous, not to mention we're aiding our enemy," declared one of the group leaders. "I think we should all refuse to unload it."

Teigen's gaze moved from man to man, assessing whether they agreed. Their reaction, sadly, appeared unanimous.

Falko nodded. "I asked you all here tonight to come up with a solution. I don't think that outright refusal is viable. That would lead to repercussions."

"Why don't the men fake illness or injury, and get out of it that way?" another man suggested.

Teigen wagged his head, exhausted from his shift and frustrated by the direction of the discussion. "You're not thinking straight, Halsten. Every man here can't pretend to be unable to work."

"That's true," Falko agreed.

"What can we do, then?" demanded the first man, glaring at Teigen. "If you're so smart, you tell us."

Teigen sucked a deep breath. "We do need to comply if we want to survive. There is no way around that."

Halsten snorted. "So why are we even having this meeting?"

"We need a tactic," Falko said carefully. "One that every one of us can agree on."

"And that tactic would be what?"

"Well…" Teigen began, a plan forming as he spoke.

The nineteen men crammed into Falko's hut quieted and leaned forward so they could all see him. He briefly met every man's eye as they waited for him to speak.

"We slow down."

Silence.

Shifting gazes.

"Slow down?" a man asked, his brow furrowed. "What does that mean?"

"That means we still do the work but we do it slowly. Carefully." Teigen wagged his finger back and forth between two of the men. "We double up, so it takes two men to lift the crate or the barrel."

Halsten straightened, his expression brightening. "We can do less than half the work, but still appear busy."

"The bastards won't stand for that!" the first man objected.

"They will if we start spilling some of it." Falko laughed as he continued. "If we 'accidentally' drop a dozen barrels of oil into the sea, they won't grouse about us being more careful."

"The SS will probably come talk to us as group leaders about the slow down," Teigen warned. "And we will tell them the truth: that the men are growing weak with the meager meals, the mile-and-a-half walk to and from the camp, and the brutal twelve-hour shifts."

Halsten grinned. "When they do, I'll suggest that if they want to feed us more, and give us a day of rest every week, that the men would be more productive."

"Do you think they might do that?" a hopeful voice from the back asked.

The group leaders grew quiet.

Falko sighed. "No. I don't think so."

"But we'll ask just the same," Teigen said. "It can't hurt to remind them that we are humans, though *merely* human, after all."

"I want to bring up one more thing before we finish," Falko said. "You all know that part of our work is unloading the Germans' food and putting it in storage…"

"Already ahead of you," Teigen stated. "My group has been pilfering food for the last two weeks."

"Mine, too," declared another group leader.

"And mine," said the redhead next to Teigen.

Falko grinned and nodded. "Glad to hear it. The Germans are stealing so much for themselves that they can't be certain the missing food didn't go to one of their own."

He clapped his hands together and rubbed them to warm them. "My next question is: do we want to have some sort of supply exchange among us?"

The men murmured to each other until one raised his hand. "I say we make certain that those from our own groups who're injured or ill are seen to. But after that, to each his own."

"I agree." Teigen glanced around the room. "We don't want to do anything that might tip off the brown bastards."

Falko nodded again. "All right. Then we are finished."

As the men rose to their feet several shivered and wrapped their arms around themselves.

"Thor's *thunder* it's cold," one growled. "Isn't this June?"

"Has to be," another answered him. "The sun hasn't set for a couple weeks."

Teigen opened the door to Falko's windowless hut. "There'll be no sun tonight." Incredulous, he turned around to face the assembled group leaders. "Because it's *snowing*."

CHAPTER TEN

June 6, 1942
Kirkenes, Norway

"Hay, sir. We'd like some hay." Teigen stood in front of the SS captain's desk the next day. Heavy snowfall had prevented any of the shifts from working today, which made the captain's mood as dim and gray as the frigid day.

"For what purpose would you deprive our guard's horses?" he replied sharply. "They work harder and are more valuable than any of you."

"With all respect, *Hauptman* Mueller, my men are freezing." Teigen waved a hand toward the office's window and the thick blanket of white on the ground. "The hay would insulate us from the cold while we sleep."

The German captain looked annoyed. "It's June sixth. This can't last."

"In the meantime, sir—"

"Silence! My answer is no." *Hauptman* Mueller waved Teigen away. "Get back to your hut. *Heil* Hitler."

Furious, Teigen gave the officer a stiff, jaw-clenched, bow and left the room.

Two of the group leaders, Halsten and Roald, were waiting outside for him in the already foot-deep summer snow. "What did he say?"

Teigen turned sideways and answered in German so that the two sentries guarding the door could see and understand him. "He said no, we cannot have any hay to keep our men from freezing to death as they sleep on the cold wooden floors."

Roald caught on to the ploy. "But the men will come down with pneumonia and bronchitis."

Halsten jumped in now. "The stronger ones might only lose toes to frostbite, but the weaker ones will certainly die."

"*Hauptman* Mueller says his horses are more important than any of the teachers."

Teigen noticed that the sentries—young men who couldn't be over seventeen or eighteen years of age—exchanged frowning glances.

"I don't know what to tell our men," Teigen said sadly. "Let's hope that the frostbite does not turn gangrenous, or even more of us will die needlessly."

The three men turned as one and walked silently away from the camp's headquarters.

Please, God. Let them help us.

ⁿ ⁿ ⁿ

"You move the old straw from the top of the haystack, like this." The young sentry carefully lifted away the graying, snow-covered hay. "Then you take the fresh hay from underneath."

Teigen, Halsten and Roald each grabbed an armful of fresh hay. The sentry replaced the old hay so that the appearance of the stack, though slightly diminished, was essentially unchanged.

"Take a little from each of the stacks," the sentry instructed. "And they might not notice."

"*Danke schön, Privat Fischer. Vielen Dank.*" Teigen turned to the other Norsemen. "We better hurry so we aren't seen."

As the trio stomped through the snow back to their huts, Teigen sent up a silent prayer of thanks.

He dropped his armload of hay in his shared hut and told the men in there to spread it on the floor. "I'll show you how to get more," he promised. "After I check on Jans."

Jans was in the medical ward recovering from a fever. The explanation of what he suffered from was vague, and no helpful drugs were available to the prisoners anyway—they were simply kept warm and allowed to sleep on cots until they recovered from whatever ailed them.

"How are you faring, Jans?" Teigen knelt beside the cot. There were no chairs for visitors in the medical tent.

"I'm getting better, Teig. I think the fever's gone."

Jans did, in fact, have a much healthier tone to his skin.

"Are they feeding you?" Teigen slipped a packet of dried reindeer meat under Jans' thin blanket.

Jans' fingers wrapped around it and he smiled a little. "Yes. Three bowls of fish soup a day."

"That's good to hear." Teigen smiled softly and lowered his voice. "Be glad you are in here. We have over a foot of snow outside."

Jans gave a weak chuckle. "I heard."

Teigen gripped his friend's hand through the covers. "I need to go. We have to collect hay for our beds so we don't freeze."

"Thanks again, Teig." Jans shifted his position on the cot. "I should be back to work in a couple days.

Teigen doubted that was wise, but what could he say about it? He shook his head and gave Jans a stern look as he rose to his feet.

"As your friend, I say stay as long as they'll let you," he encouraged. "This is the best duty you could pull."

Teigen turned on his heel and headed for the door, tucking his hands under his arms to keep them warm.

June 9, 1942
Kirkenes, Norway

The German guards brazenly marched the Norwegian teachers through the village of Kirkenes on their way to work—every day, every shift—as a warning to the townspeople of what disobedience might earn them as well. The march was a long one as their camp was a mile-and-a-half south of the town and the road was merely a dirt path.

German soldiers on horseback accompanied the men to and from, and threatened them if they got out of line, even to piss.

It wasn't as if any of the teachers would run. There was nowhere else to go in this remote area of the world except into

Russia. But the part of Russia that lay less than three miles south of their camp wasn't populated. And Russia was at war.

Even before the discussion about working slower at the docks, the teachers had been walking as slowly as possible from the camp to the pier. By doing so, they shortened their working time and reduced the profits the Germans could make from their imprisoned labor force.

Two wins.

Exhausted and depressed by their situation, Teigen was moved to tears the first time the inhabitants of Kirkenes showed their respect for the teachers and their struggle by standing silently along the road through town toward the docks.

Though surprising the first time it happened, in the last weeks the lines of men women and children—many wearing red and, for some inexplicable reason, paperclips—had been consistently in place.

They waited while one group went to the docks to start their shift, and were still in place when the finishing group passed by on their return journey to the camp.

This evening, one man suddenly stepped forward and grabbed Teigen's hand. "God bless you."

The action earned the man a shouted warning from the guard who spurred his mount forward from ten yards behind him.

Teigen stuffed his hands into his pockets and didn't look back. Curiosity demanded that he look at the folded paper which was pressed into his palm, but wisdom forced him to leave it hidden safely away when he arrived at the pier.

When you are back in your hut, he scolded himself silently. *And not a minute before.*

※ ※ ※

Teigen didn't need a light to read the note. The sun never set this far north in June; instead its light seeped through the gaps left by the constantly wet-then-dry warped cardboard walls of his shared hut.

He took off his boots and stretched out on his hay-cushioned blanket before retrieving the many-times folded scrap of paper. He had to read the words three times to be certain of what it said.

I believe God will forgive me for changing His word (Philippians) this way. We want the teachers to know how their stoic example has strengthened our nation, and whose example is better than Saint Paul's:
"*I want you to know, brethren, that what has happened to you has served to advance freedom. That it has become known throughout Norway, and to all the rest of the world. That your imprisonment is for good; and Norwegians have been made confident because of your imprisonment, and are emboldened to speak against our captors without fear.*"

Teigen was stunned.

Ever since boarding the *Skjerstad* he and his fellow teachers were certain they had been forgotten. Not one of them felt particularly heroic, nor had they even talked about when the war might be over and who would win.

They were, by necessity, completely focused on their immediate situation—surviving from day to day without succumbing to illness or injury. Their conditions were miserable.

They were badly equipped for the cold.

They were just fed enough to keep them moving, but were all losing weight with the workload.

And there was no end to their imprisonment in sight.

Teigen wiped his suddenly damp eyes and reread the message yet again.

Norwegians have been made confident because of your imprisonment, and are emboldened to speak against our captors without fear...

He folded the paper carefully and tucked it back inside his pocket. This was something he needed to share at the next meeting of the group leaders.

But first, he would share it with Jans.

June 12, 1942
Kirkenes, Norway

The constant sun's restored glare on the last bits of melting snow actually caused physical pain to Teigen's eyes. He shielded them with both hands and squinted as the teachers who were leaving for their six o'clock in the morning shift at the docks were told to wait off to the side of the camp's gate.

A way down the dirt path and walking toward the camp was a motley group of soldiers guarded by brown-uniformed Germans on horseback.

"Who are they?" Teigen whispered.

"Russians," someone answered behind him. "You can spot the Red Army by the tall boots and the puffed-out pant legs."

"And the hats," another man said. "You can tell by the hats."

No one else spoke as the group of about two dozen men, many bleeding and awkwardly bandaged, was marched inside the camp's fence. They regarded the teachers with blurry, baffled expressions as they passed by them.

Jans leaned toward Teigen and whispered, "We're obviously not soldiers. No wonder they're confused. Guess they don't know we're famous."

Teigen looked down at his pale friend. He tried to convince Jans to stay with the medics until he was stronger, but once Jans read the note from the Kirkenes man he refused to remain in bed any longer. Teigen had been berating himself ever since.

Damn it.

Why did I show it to him?

"Teachers!" their guard barked. "Move on!"

The intentionally slow march began. The men filed out of the gate in twos or threes, and then retraced the soggy steps of the Russian soldiers toward town.

Teigen had seen his messenger beside the road for the last two evenings, always standing in the same spot. Teigen met the man's gaze and gave him a small nod both times. He was rewarded with a smile and a salute while the group moved by him.

At least he's smart enough to hold the salute and not single me out.

Teigen told everyone who had read the note that the saluting man was the one who wrote it. Though he wouldn't risk it himself, some of the teachers saluted him back.

The sharp crack of rifle fire exploded behind them. The surprised teachers halted their progress and looked back at the camp. Another shot was fired. And then another. Six in all.

"*Was ist los?*" Teigen asked their startled guards. "What is happening?"

The men closest to him exchanged confirming glances. Then one offered, "*Die Russen sind tot.*"

"The Russians are dead," Teigen translated, adding, "Or six of them are."

"They won't shoot us—will they?" Halsten asked.

"No." Teigen continued loudly in German so the guards would hear him, trusting the other interpreters to do their job and translate for the men around him. "We will not be shot because we are teachers, not soldiers. We are merely prisoners who do our work everyday and do not cause trouble."

Teigen caught the eye of the closest German guard.

He nodded, though he didn't smile. "Move on!"

ᚾ ᚾ ᚾ

Teigen remained with Jans for the first half of their twelve-hour shift. He lent his larger frame to their shared tasks, trying to take the brunt of the load off of Jans' weakened body.

Teigen waved pallets of crates into position as the dock cranes lowered their heavy burdens precariously into place.

He helped steady and guide the nets filled with bundles from the ships' holds to rest safely on the dock.

And he gave Jans instructions to count crates and bundles and log the numbers with the Nazis tasked with overseeing the work, rather than keep his friend in possible harm's way.

But when the accident happened, there was no way for Teigen to prevent it.

The barrels had been sloppily tied. Filled with thirty gallons of oil, each metal barrel weighed about two-hundred-and-fifty pounds, and over their rocking journey through the Norwegian Sea those ties had loosened.

At least, that was the Nazis' conclusion after the fact.

Jans was standing on the pier with a handful of other teachers, waiting for the pallet of nine barrels to reach solid ground when something shifted.

It was unclear whether the shift was caused by a sudden wave knocking against the ship, or maybe a strong gust of wind on the breezy day, or the crane might have moved too quickly.

None of that mattered now. All that mattered was that the pallet tipped and the barrels broke their bindings about six feet above the dock. With a sickening clang of metal they tumbled to the concrete pier, falling in all directions.

Teigen bolted down the dock, shoving men aside in his panic.

"Jans!" he shouted. "Jans! Are you hurt?"

The teachers were running after the barrels, stopping some of them from rolling into the water. One man was bellowing in pain as several teachers pulled him from under a barrel.

As soon as Teigen saw Jans, he knew. Still conscious, Jan looked at Teigen and lifted one wobbling arm to try and push the barrel off his chest.

Three men leapt to the task and lifted the oil barrel from Jans' body.

"Medic!" someone shouted.

Teigen fell to his knees beside his friend and grabbed the waving hand. "Help's coming, Jans. Stay with me."

"I think... my ribs... can't breathe..." he rasped.

"That's all it is, Jans," Teigen lied; his friend's hips were smashed nearly flat. "Just be calm. They're taking you to the civilian hospital, not the camp."

"Yeah?" Jans' eyelids fluttered. "Goo..."

Teigen squeezed his friend's hands. "Jans?"

The brown eyes that opened and met his were unfocused. "Kill... the... bastards..."

Jans did not breathe again.

CHAPTER ELEVEN

July 23, 1942
Oslo, Norway

"I'll say this much," Dahl handed Selby the Nazi-controlled newspaper. "The teachers in Norway are a tough bunch. Who would've thought it?"

Selby scanned the headlines, unaccountably irritated by Dahl's attitude. "They're men, aren't they? Norwegian men?"

"Yes, but—"

"And through their vocation they shape every man and woman in the country," she continued before lifting her eyes to Dahl's. "Teachers, by definition, set examples."

Dahl attempted to make a joke. "You know the saying, Selby. Those who can, do. Those who can't—"

"Teach others *how*." Her tone was sharper than she intended. But ever since they received word that a teacher had died in an accident at the labor camp Selby ached to know if it was 'her' teacher.

That was how she thought of him now. Her own brave warrior, fighting their oppressors on the ground just as she did.

Resistance was resistance, whether officially a member of their army or just a singular man remaining loyal to his country and his people.

"The teachers who were not arrested are still defying Quisling's demands," Dahl offered.

"This paper claims that Nazi officers are going to shoot ten of the remaining imprisoned teachers in retaliation." Selby's finger slid over the printed page. "But down here it says one in every ten."

Selby lifted wide eyes to Dahl. "Can we do anything about that?"

He shook his head. "We can't even determine if it's true, or an empty threat to terrorize the families. Look at page two."

Selby turned the page. "Teachers to be sent far north to destroy Russian landmines?"

Dahl shrugged. "It's the same everywhere. *I know someone who works at the Minister's office...* or *I know people at the office of the German headquarters...* All that these rumors have in common is the claim that something drastic's going to happen to the prisoners if the other teachers don't stop their protests."

"Will they stop?" Selby refolded the paper and sank into the chair opposite Dahl in the dressing room. "I mean, those eighteen men who escaped Grini actually *were* shot..."

"Escaping prisoners are fair game in war," Dahl said sadly. "But I don't think Quisling can risk shooting peaceful teachers, no matter what his justification."

"I hope you're right."

Selby sighed and looked at her reflection. Someone she was not accustomed to seeing stared back at her. "Are the payment packets ready?"

"Bennett finished them about an hour ago." Dahl pointed at a drawer in the chest behind him. "In there."

Selby stood and crossed to the chest. She opened the drawer and stuffed the six pockets inside her leather vest with the pay packets. She read each name as she did so.

"Still the same eight families, then."

"Yep." Dahl reached for her hand. "Be careful, Sel."

"Always." She flashed a brief smile and snuggled a leather cap over her hair. "See you in a couple hours, then."

И И И

Walking through the twilit streets of Oslo after curfew was both peaceful and incredibly dangerous. Dressed in dark, simple clothing, Selby walked quickly with her head down. Her soft-soled calfskin shoes didn't make any sound on the pavement.

Resistance workers had recently been stopped by German soldiers watching the arrested teachers' homes and the money packets were confiscated, which made delivering the replaced salaries more complicated. Now that the nights were darkening, delivering in the wee hours attracted less notice.

Since the Troupe arrived in Oslo six weeks ago, Selby had been delivering weekly pay packets to families whose husbands and fathers were either in Kirkenes or locked inside Grini Prison. Selby was familiar with the back streets and alleys of Oslo by now and had mapped out a surreptitious route to the homes.

The prostitutes she occasionally encountered were her best allies in the task, warning her of approaching Nazis as she prowled across the city from house to house. They knew Selby was delivering money from the Resistance to families of the incarcerated teachers, supporting them while their men were locked away, and they respected her for it.

And Selby respected them, in a way. After playing her role as sweetheart to a variety of Nazi officers up the coast of Norway she couldn't honestly point fingers at those women who made a living with their bodies.

I'm a Nazi whore, too.

She chuckled silently.

I just don't get paid for it.

Selby was approaching the last house on her route. This one was a little different from the others on her list because the woman who asked for assistance was only engaged to the arrested teacher. But Elsa Borg was pregnant with Teigen Hansen's child and living with her parents for now, so the payments were being made.

Besides, it wasn't Selby's decision who was paid, only to deliver the money. Once both the missing teacher and the pregnancy were confirmed, the requested salaries were replaced.

Elsa was required to answer the door because Selby was not allowed to give anyone else the packet. Her pale blonde hair was twisted in a braid disheveled by sleep. She yawned widely and held out one smooth-palmed hand.

Selby laid the envelope in Elsa's hand without saying a word.

"Thanks." Elsa moved behind the door and closed it. She threw the lock before Selby even turned around.

Shelby made a face at the solid door and the haughty woman behind it. She didn't care much for Elsa Borg.

Heading back to the theater Selby had to detour around a pair of Nazi soldiers who were roaring drunk and looking for trouble. She crouched behind a phalanx of trash cans when they crossed the alley that she detoured through, and waited until their slurring voices were at a decent distance before resuming her journey.

Dahl was waiting for her inside the theater's dressing room. "Everything go well?"

Selby nodded as she walked past him to the dressing screen where she changed back into her regular clothes. "Do you know anything about Elsa Borg?"

"No. Should I?" was the puzzled reply.

Shelby didn't answer at first. What would she say—that the woman was an ungrateful snot? "No. I was just curious."

"She's one of your deliveries, isn't she?"

"Yeah." Selby pulled a dress over her head. "She's just odd, is all."

"War makes people odd," Dahl replied in a voice expanded by a deep yawn. "You ready?"

"Yes." Selby stepped out from behind the screen and stretched. "Today's rehearsals killed me. I'm ready for bed."

Dahl's smile was hopeful as usual. "Don't tease me like that."

Selby backhanded his arm and didn't return the smile. "Let's go."

They walked to the hotel in silence.

August 29, 1942
Kirkenes, Norway

Although it was still August the weather was becoming colder. It seemed that whatever arctic summer existed had already come and gone. Life in the labor camp over the last months had alternated between humid, mosquito-filled droughts, and rousing deluges that turned the world into a muddy bog.

Teigen would have complained to Jans, but Jans wasn't there anymore. And talking to his friend's unmarked grave in a corner of the camp only made him feel worse.

Four-hundred and ninety-nine of them were still left. The other man injured in the accident broke a leg and both arms, and though he hadn't returned to wor, he survived.

A week after Jans died Teigen wrote a letter to Jans' family. He also wrote a letter to his own family assuring them he was well. He folded the two papers together and addressed them to his parents, asking them to pass the message on to Jans' school.

From there someone should know about his family, Teigen wrote.

While walking to the docks the next morning he took the chance and pretended to stumble, falling against his faithful saluting supporter and pressing the folded paper against the man's chest.

That man grabbed and pocketed the tightly-folded letter without the Nazi guards seeing it. On his way home that same evening the man caught Teigen's eye, smiled, and nodded.

Teigen pressed his lips together in a slight smile and rested a fist over his heart in gratitude.

This morning the men in Shift A were held back from their work on the road. A German doctor had unexpectedly appeared in the camp, probably because the ranks of the ill and injured had swelled to nearly a third of the prisoners.

"He is going to examine all of the men here," *Hauptman* Mueller explained to the interpreters. "We are willing to send some of your ranks home as they are unfit to work. Those inferior prisoners require too much of our time and resources, and shall be removed."

In spite of his demeaning words, the message came through loud and clear: a good number of them were going home.

"We'll make recommendations for which men should be sent home to their families, because we're their leaders," Falko said at their hastily-called meeting a quarter hour later. "Compile a list of your sickest men. We'll decide from that which names to put forward."

When Shift B returned from the docks twelve hours later, Teigen began his list. First, he walked through the medical tent and wrote down all of those names. There were eleven from the sub-group of twenty-four men he was responsible for. He added two more names—those of the two oldest teachers, both nearing sixty.

The next day, Shift B stayed back to be examined. Then Shifts C and D. At the end of the four days, Falko, Teigen, and two other interpreters met with *Hauptman* Mueller and the German doctor whose name Teigen never knew.

Falko handed the doctor a list of one-hundred-and-fifty names. "These are our recommendations for the teachers who should be released and taken home."

Mueller glowered and opened his mouth to bluster something unpleasant by the look of him, but the doctor put up a hand to stop him.

The doctor handed the list back to Falko. "Please read the names and I will consult my notes."

Teigen glanced at the other shift leaders. This was either going to go very well, or very badly. That same opinion was broadcast on the other men's faces.

Falko cleared his throat and gripped the edge of his paper. "Arne Arnaldsen."

The doctor looked at his list and made a mark. "Yes. Next."

Falko didn't look up. "Tomas Birkeland."

More perusing of the list. Another mark. "Yes."

"Dag Bjornsen."

Marked. "Yes."

In the end, the doctor and the group leaders had chosen one hundred and thirty two men in common. The remaining eighteen men which the Norwegians had selected were those who were fifty-five years of age or older. The doctor declined three of them because they were in such good health—relatively speaking—and added three men from his own list that Teigen didn't know.

He stood suddenly and faced Mueller. "I will send these one hundred and fifty names to headquarters immediately. Have the prisoners ready for transport one week from today."

He whirled in his heel and stomped from the room, leaving a stunned group of four ecstatic men and one seething SS officer staring at each other.

September 4, 1942
Kirkenes, Norway

Falko was waiting for Teigen when his shift returned after midnight. "We have a problem."

He grabbed Teigen's arm. "The German bastards just demanded that before the men leave tomorrow they sign a declaration stating that they're willing to resume their positions in the schools as members of the new Nazi teachers' organization."

Teigen stopped like he hit a wall. *"What?"*

Falko yanked his arm. "Come on. The other half of us talked before they left for their shifts. Now the rest of us need to come to an agreement."

The hut was crowded with angry men; seldom a good situation. The Nazi bastards were cursed thoroughly as the betrayal of their words was dissected by every man there.

"Can I see the declaration?" Teigen asked. He read it silently as Falko opened the discussion.

"I have had a meeting with the other two shifts," Falko began. "And we have crafted a compromise which we feel we can live with."

One man spread his arms and shushed the others.

"What is that?" he asked when they quieted.

Falko's voice remained level and calm. "We find ourselves at war with our own government. Do you all agree?"

Someone snorted loudly. "We're prisoners, aren't we?"

Falko nodded. "And in every war the injured and ill must leave the front lines while the healthy continue to fight."

"That's not the issue, though, is it Jensen?" a man bellowed. "It's the damned loyalty oath all over again! What good is our resistance if we encourage them to sign it?"

A lightning bolt of realization shot through Teigen's veins. This document was in German, not Norwegian.

"No! It's not!" he shouted, jumping to his feet and waving the paper over his head. "This is completely different!"

Confused looks bounced around the hut like a loose pinball as the uproar quieted once again.

"How is it different?"

Teigen grinned. "This statement is in *German*. It's an agreement with the Nazis—it's not caving into Quisling."

Falko grinned, his expression transformed. "That's right! It's not Quisling's Norwegian Teacher's Union—it's the new Nazi teachers' organization."

"That's just a technicality," the first man growled.

"No, it's not," another countered. "Those are completely different organizations."

"Not to mention, I don't read German," another said, grinning.

"How can anyone hold me to something I was forced to sign but couldn't read it?"

One older man stood up in the middle of the hut drawing all eyes to him. "You're saying that we tell those men who are being released to sign the paper—because we're here to resist Quisling, and not the German army?"

Falko nodded. "Exactly."

CHAPTER TWELVE

October 1, 1942
Trondheim, Norway

Selby's heart beat against her ribs as she stood on the pier in Trondheim for the second time in ten days, hoping to catch a glimpse of 'her' teacher among the men who were being returned from the labor camp.

The rapidly-spreading news that one hundred and fifty sick or injured men were being released from their arctic prison lit up Norway like nothing she had ever seen. These men were considered national heroes—they were being released from their imprisonment without ever giving in to Quisling's demands.

The pier was crowded with celebrating citizens who cheered for the men as they hobbled down the gangway from the ship. The teachers were sorted according to their situation and taken to where they could be treated best: the Trondheim hospital, private doctors' clinics, or simply a hotel where they could rest.

The assistance was given free of charge to the teachers by their proud countrymen as thanks for their loyalty and fortitude. The men were invited to stay in Trondheim until they well enough to be put on a train and complete their journey back to their homes.

Selby was deeply disappointed when the tall, bearded man she diligently searched the crowd for was not one of the passengers on the first ship. But when word reached them that an additional ninety-nine teachers were being released, her hopes soared again.

Maybe today.

Of course if he wasn't included in either group that meant he was still healthy enough to work. That was a good thing, she reminded herself.

Unless he was the one who died.

Selby didn't know his name, of course, but she hoped it wasn't Jans Lund.

No. I won't let it be.

For some inexplicable reason this stranger had become an anchor for her. He was a man, true, but a man who was safe. Distant. Unknown. Merely a symbol of how her country had pulled together in the dual faces of German occupation and Norwegian treason, resisting both at every turn. And too often at the cost of their lives.

Somehow Selby felt that if her teacher triumphed, so would her country.

It hadn't been an easy task to convince Dahl to let her stay behind when the Troupe began its hundred-mile voyage south to Kristiansund.

"I'll be two days behind you," she promised. "That gives me a day-and-a-half before we perform."

Dahl stared at her, his face twisted in confusion. "Selby, this is crazy."

She felt her cheeks flushing. "I know."

"You don't even know who this guy is."

She couldn't argue with that. "I can't explain it, Dahl. But I just want to know. I *need* to know."

Dahl folded his arms across his chest as if to protect his heart. "What will you do if he *is* on the ship?"

Good question.

What would she do?

Selby had played a variety of scenes through her mind, none with a definitive ending. "I don't know. Maybe nothing."

"Nothing?" Dahl shook his head in obvious disbelief. "You want to stay behind, and pay for your own hotel here and passage to Kristiansund, just to see if a man you glimpsed once gets off that ship—and even if he does, you're just going to walk away?"

Selby glared at him. Dahl made a clear case against her

seemingly pointless suggestion, and that angered her. Probably because she told herself exactly the same thing.

"What does it matter to you?" she groused. "It's my decision, and I really don't care if you understand."

When she said *I really don't care* Dahl's expression shifted. Selby knew he wanted her to care. Ached for her to care. Practically begged for her to care. Guilt bloomed in her chest.

"You're right, Sel," he conceded softly. "It doesn't matter if I understand."

Her cheeks flamed with mortification at Dahl's allowing her to take such an indefensible stand. "Thank you."

"A woman like you, who stands so strong and fights so well, should be encouraged to show her support for others who also resist." Dahl's declaration was stilted, but judging by the look on his face it was sincere.

Selby reached for his hand, feeling like she owed him something. "I'll be there when I said I would. I promise."

Dahl's skin was warm and his larger hand encased hers. "I know you will. I have no doubts."

Before she could pull away, he leaned forward and kissed her forehead, then wrapped her in a hug she didn't dare resist. "I'll see you in Kristiansund."

Selby gripped the collar of her expensive wool coat close to her throat to keep out the damp sea breeze. A few people seemed to recognize her and she smiled at those who stared. Not all of them smiled back.

The ship's gangway was lowered once the vessel was tied securely to the massive cleats on the dock. The crowd was silent, with women standing on the tips of their toes and children hoisted onto their fathers' shoulders.

Selby stepped to the side, standing on the edge of the crowd. When the first man appeared he looked shocked. He lifted a tentative hand and waved at the crowd, his smile uncertain.

The crowd erupted, cheering raucously and waving Norwegian flags. Women burst into unashamed tears.

One by one, the men—who were overall in better condition than the first group—made their way down the walkway toward the enthusiastic crowd. Once again, the teachers were sorted and taken to where either their recuperation or their continued journey would begin.

Selby's hopes dimmed slowly with each man that appeared, but they weren't extinguished until the last man disembarked.

Her teacher wasn't on the ship.

She turned away and walked to her hotel, her path blurred by stupid tears which stubbornly replenished themselves every time she wiped them away.

What now?

She wanted to visit some of the men in the hospital under the guise of 'famous actress congratulates returnees' to try and find out about the man who had haunted her thoughts these last five months or so, but realized the futility.

She didn't know his name, and 'tall, blond, with a light brown beard and green eyes' described half of the Norwegian men in both groups. Selby wiped her tears, drew a deep breath to quell her disappointment, and pressed the last scraps of it out of reach. She held her head high as she walked past the doorman who opened the hotel door for her.

The clerk behind the reception desk called out to her. "Miss Sunde?"

She cleared her throat and turned to the man. "Yes?"

He lifted a paper-wrapped parcel. "You have a package."

Selby flashed a bright, fake smile and reached for the parcel. Though she wasn't expecting anything, when she saw the name of the sender she was glad she stayed behind.

"Another one of my admirers, I suppose," she deflected, tucking the covert package under her arm. "Thank you."

October 30, 1942
Kirkenes, Norway

Teigen shivered in his bed, his bones aching with cold.

Two hundred and fifty teachers still remained at the camp—half their original number. Now there were only two groups of laborers, one working on the road along the fjord, and the other working at the docks.

Several of the townspeople passed blankets to the remaining prisoners who marched through their town twice a day, and the dock workers shared them with the road workers who were never seen in Kirkenes.

Since they were so far north of the Arctic Circle the sun shone less than eleven hours a day now so their shifts were shorter. That was the good news.

But with the receding sun the temperature was dropping far below freezing at night. Even the fjord was starting to freeze around the edges.

Thank you God for hay and blankets, Teigen prayed. *But could You please see fit to get us out of here?*

"If they decide to send us all back they better get a move on," Falko grumbled as he and Teigen trudged back from the docks. "Pretty soon it'll be too late."

Teigen didn't respond at first. He was too tired. Too hungry. Too cold.

"Do you think anyone remembers that we're here?" he asked finally. "Or have we been forgotten?"

Falko didn't respond to that, but instead returned to their normal daily discussion: the Resistance.

Ever since their shifts at the dock were combined, Falko had stepped up his efforts to teach Teigen about the subversive war efforts coordinated throughout Norway. In order to hide the subject of their conversations, Teigen and Falko took a place at the very end of the queue of teachers under the guise of preventing stragglers.

Two or three times during the forty-five minute stroll into town, one of them would call out a teacher's name and shout, "Hurry up!" in German, then follow with, "You know what I mean by that!" in Norse.

The man whose name was called would grumble or make a rude gesture before temporarily closing the gap in front of him. That was enough to keep the German guards satisfied so they never rode at the end of the line anymore, preferring to ride in tandem and have their own conversations.

Teigen was frankly surprised to learn the unexpectedly far-reaching extent of the movement. Falko, who was somehow receiving covert reports, explained more about the Special Operations Executive, or SOE, and that the resistance which was paying salaries to the families of the imprisoned teachers.

"I've never married and I don't have a family," Teigen said shakily, unprepared for the raw rush of emotions that statement brought; he wondered if Elsa was pining for him even now. "But I—I was wondering about those who do."

Falko's expression was quizzical, but thankfully he didn't ask Teigen to elaborate.

"Right before we were arrested they established a fleet of regular fishing boats and volunteers, called the Shetland Bus," Falko told him today. "They sail from the west coast to the Shetland Islands."

Teigen slid him a surprised look. "Helping people escape Norway?"

"That, sure." Falko nodded. "But mostly to carry all kinds of food, medical supplies, and radios *into* Norway."

Teigen scowled. "I've never heard of this."

"Good!" Falko chuckled. "Anyway, they sail from lots of places, mostly small towns where the German navy *isn't*."

"Would you leave Norway?" Teigen asked. "If you could?"

"I can," Falko stated. "But no. Especially not after this." He peered into Teigen's eyes. "What about you?"

Teigen's scowl deepened. "My brother did."

Falko was clearly surprised. "When?"

"The day the Germans attacked. He joined the army and sailed to England within the week."

"But you stayed behind," Falko said carefully.

"Someone needed to be sure our parents were safe." Even now the difference in his and Tor's situation rankled.

"Do you know where he is?"

"No."

Their conversation died there as they reached the first building in the town and the pair walked toward the docks in contemplative silence.

The residents of Kirkenes were no longer turning out in the same numbers as before. Teigen couldn't resent them for it; the prisoners arrived in April and now it was the end of October. The novelty had worn off. Even Teigen's faithful saluting supporter no longer stood beside the road.

Yet those who remained faithful to the twice-a-day parade of prisoners offered whatever comfort they could.

Their German guards seemed to be as miserable as the prisoners they escorted. They stopped scolding the people for handing food, mittens, or scarves to the men, and instead looked envious.

"They're just boys," Roald said as one urged his horse past them to open the gate to the camp. "I doubt this is what they signed up for."

"But they did sign up, didn't they?" Falko reminded him. "*Heil Hitler* and all that glory."

Teigen snorted and tightened the scarf around his neck. "The only glory here is in the sky."

The men looked up. Faint green streaks were swirling overhead as the Northern lights fought to dominate the last faint glow of the sun.

"Leaders! A meeting!" *Hauptman* Mueller barked.

Five men, including Falko and Teigen, broke away from the dock workers and joined the five road-building leaders already warming up in the captain's cramped office.

Hauptman Mueller stood behind his desk to address the men. He had an odd look on his face. Almost happy.

"I have received word today that our glorious leader is promoting every soldier and officer who has served him so faithfully in our successful endeavors here," he stated. "As a result, we are being reassigned to important duties elsewhere."

Teigen glanced at Falko, afraid to hope.

"This means, of course, that this camp is being vacated." Mueller paused, waiting for a response. When none came, he spat, "Don't you understand? You will be put on a ship in five days and sailed back to Trondheim."

But will we still be prisoners?

Teigen cleared his throat. "I beg your pardon, *Herr Hauptman*, but are we being released?"

Mueller sneered at him. "Yes. Unless you *wish* to continue serving the Third Reich?"

Teigen bit back what he really wanted to say to the pompous bastard. "Thank you for clarifying *Herr Hauptman*."

The men refrained from celebrating, or even daring to meet each other's eyes, as they reluctantly shuffled out of the warmth of the captain's office and into the frigid arctic air.

One of them said, "Look up."

The ten men stopped walking and looked into the clear sky. As if God was celebrating on their behalf an impossible swirl of green, white, red, and blue grew overhead until the heavens were filled with streams of shifting color.

Teigen smiled. *Thank you.*

CHAPTER THIRTEEN

November 20, 1942
Bergen, Norway

The seven actors and three crew members in the Royal Shakespearean Acting Troupe huddled around the homemade radio in their dressing room and listened to the covert broadcast from Trondheim.

"After sixteen days on a requisitioned steamer, the remaining two-hundred-and-fifty male teachers who were imprisoned at the Nazis' arctic labor camp in Kirkenes have arrived at the Trondheim docks today."

Oh, thank God.

Selby was elated that the men were safe, yet she couldn't help being deeply disappointed at the same time. There was now no possible way for her to ever see 'her' teacher again.

Will I forget him someday? she mused. *Or will I always wonder what became of him?*

"Though overly thin and dressed in ragged clothing," the electronic voice continued, "these men appear to be otherwise healthy. We were told that they were allowed to shower on the steamer, and that their meals were more substantial than those they received while being held in the work camp."

Glances bounced between the troupe members. The teachers

were already thin when Selby saw them in April. How much worse were they now?

"Crowds of well-wishers met the ship, singing, cheering and waving flags as the men disembarked in a stumbling single file."

Bennett chuckled. "They must have been surprised at their welcome—after all, they probably had no way to know how the first two ships were received."

Several heads nodded their silent agreement.

"I was able to reach one man and I asked him what was the first thing that he wanted to do on this day of freedom..."

Suggested responses erupted from the troupe: "Call his wife!"

"Drink a beer!"

"Eat a thick steak!"

Dahl shushed them so they would hear the answer.

The announcer laughed a little. "And he said shave and get a haircut!"

The men in the room guffawed, while the women rolled their eyes and shrugged.

Gunter, the second male lead, raised suddenly moist eyes to consider his mates. "We should invite them to a show."

Selby perked up at that. "Or do a show especially for them!"

Bennett, their props manager grinned. "That's a great idea!"

With a sigh, Dahl brought them all back to their unpleasant reality. "Except that we are heading south after this, not north."

Karolina, the troupe's second female lead and Selby's understudy, made a very attractive pouty face, one which she obviously had practiced in the mirror. "Couldn't we change our plans?"

Dahl gave her a patient smile. "Even if we could, by the time we reached Trondheim again, the teachers would be gone."

"What about when we get to Oslo?" Selby ventured. "Weren't most of the arrested teachers from that area?"

Dahl's gaze was intense. "Do we really want to risk angering the Nazis—and Quisling—by celebrating the men who successfully defied them all right under their noses?"

Selby felt as if a bucket of glacier water had been poured over her. She shook her head slowly. "No. Of course not. You're right."

Dahl's expression softened. "I wish I wasn't. I really do."

"Isn't there anything we can do?" Bennett asked.

Dahl's lips pressed together briefly and his brow furrowed. "As individuals, yes you can, though I don't know what. But as a troupe which caters to Nazi officers and sympathizers with Quisling's protection and encouragement, no."

Trondheim, Norway

Teigen moved like an automaton through the crowd, stunned by the raucous reaction of his countrymen. Men grabbed his hand and pumped it wildly. Women handed him packets of sweets. Children stared at him, wide-eyed with alarm.

"Pardon me, sir?" A man grabbed his arm. "What's the first thing that you want to do on this day of freedom?"

Teigen glanced at the children around him holding tightly to their parents and realized what he must look like. "Shave and a haircut," he said, much to the man's amusement.

Some of the teachers were herded into a nearby hotel and asked about their health. Those who didn't require any medical attention were given room keys.

Teigen handed it back to the clerk. "I can't. I don't have any money."

The man grinned. "There is no charge for any of you."

Teigen stared at the key, trying to understand what was going on. "Really?"

"Yes sir. Now, your next stop is that ballroom to your right. In there you'll find clean clothing. Take whatever you need."

The clerk indicated Teigen's now-shabby wool sweater and trousers. "Leave these outside your door and we'll have them laundered."

Teigen snorted. *As if I would ever in my lifetime choose to wear them again.* "I believe they're beyond repair."

The clerk gave him a sympathetic look. "In that case, we'll dispose of them for you. Just put them in your trash can and set it in the hall when you come down for supper.'

Teigen blinked. "Supper?"

"Your supper tonight is on the house, as well as breakfast in the morning." The man's grin grew impossibly wider. "And please let me know if you need anything else. Anything at all."

Teigen caught a glimpse of his overgrown reflection in a glass case behind the reception desk. "A barber?"

The clerk bounced a nod. "I'll send one up."

"Hansen!" Falko appeared at his side. "Do you have a roommate yet?"

Teigen glanced questioningly at the clerk.

"No, not yet." He lifted his fountain pen. "And your name is?"

"Falko Jensen." The clerk wrote the name down and handed Falko his own key. "Would you like the barber to service you as well?"

Falko shrugged and gave Teigen a *why not* look. "Sure!"

ᚾ ᚾ ᚾ

When Teigen saw himself in the hotel room's tall mirror he was shocked by the transformation of his body over the last eight months. Every ounce of fat was gone from his frame, leaving him leaner than he had ever been, even as a growing teenager.

The absence of subcutaneous padding, however, made his hard-worked muscles stand out in stark, ropy relief. He moved and flexed a little as the light from the wall lamps carved shifting, shadowed valleys over his bony frame.

I need to gain some weight back.

Jensen was taking his turn in the shower while Teigen slowly donned the new-to-him clothes. The townspeople who helped him had thought of everything—from a warm coat, down to underwear and socks.

"We just want you all to know that we support you in your triumph," one woman not much older than Teigen said to him. "It's the least we're able to do for you."

"We don't feel triumphant," Teigen muttered as he folded his new clothes into a wad. "We're just glad to be out of there."

"No matter what you feel," she demurred with a shy smile. "You and the others are national heroes."

National heroes?

Teigen shook his head at her assertion and concentrated on the long-missed feel of clean cotton against clean skin. His discarded and admittedly pungent clothing was already stuffed into the little trash can and waiting in the hall, as was Falko's.

"Good riddance," his friend grunted as he tossed the clothes out the bathroom door.

The polite knock at the room door proved to be the barber.

After plugging in a steamer full of wet towels and spreading his shears, combs, and razors on the dresser, he had Teigen sit on a chair in the middle of the room and draped a sheet over him.

"How short do you want it?" he asked as he worked a comb through Teigen's shoulder-length tangles.

"I don't care."

The man stepped around and looked him in the eye. "I could use clippers and take it all off."

"Um... no." Teigen worked his fingers through his wet hair. "Leave the top longer."

"Sides and back clipped?"

"Yeah."

Falko came out of the bathroom wrapped in a towel and collected his clean clothes from his bed. He paused and considered Teigen as hanks of hair fell into his lap.

"You're going to clean up pretty well, Hansen."

Teigen, whose mood was lifting higher than it had for the entire past year, looked at Falko from under his brows. "Well I've given him a lot to work with, haven't I?"

Falko laughed and went back into the bathroom to change, leaving the door open. "You just wait and see what I've been hiding under here," he called out merrily. "I'll be fighting off the ladies with both hands!"

The barber chuckled. "You both will. All you teachers are famous."

Teigen huffed. "So they say."

When the barber finished with both men and left, Teigen and Falko stood side by side and stared at each other in the tall mirror. Their shared transformation was nothing less than startling. Not only were they now sporting fresh haircuts, but their faces were clean-shaven for the first time since they met.

Teigen rubbed his jaw, amazed at how smooth the hot towel and after-shave lotion had left his skin. "I hardly recognized myself earlier," he admitted. "It was like looking at a stranger."

"And I hardly recognize you now."

Teigen understood that. If he had met Falko on the street looking as he did now, he probably would have walked right by the man he had spent the last seven months with.

"I feel human again," Teigen murmured.

"I feel like a hungry human," Falko countered. "Let's go eat."

⋈ ⋈ ⋈

The dining room was filled with at least five dozen showered and newly dressed teachers. Some had only washed, some had taken scissors to their beards, and others had obviously been visited by the barber.

Teigen moved from table to table, greeting the laughing and teasing men who didn't recognize either him or Falko. Their jubilant mood as a whole reflected a shared and soul-deep relief that they had survived the camp and were finally free.

"Free and being recognized as heroes," Teigen said, still unable to wrap his head around the concept. "At least here in Trondheim."

"I telephoned my wife in Bergen," one man said. "She says the entire country feels the same."

Falko tugged on his arm. "Come on. Let's eat."

The food was simple but delicious, and served right under the Nazis' noses.

Hot and delicious soup thick with chunks of fresh fish provided by local fishermen, and reindeer steaks provided by local hunters, baked potatoes, rough bread and—somehow—butter. Beer poured from pitchers to refill emptied glasses. Some men cried openly, overwhelmed by their vastly improved situation.

Teigen leaned back in his chair and listened to the rumble of euphoric voices around him.

I have never been this happy.

"I have to go see a man," Falko said when they had stuffed themselves with as much food as their shrunken bellies would hold.

Teigen felt the sudden urge to walk freely around the city. "Would you mind company?" he asked. "I need to be outdoors for a while."

Falko leaned closer and gave him an apologetic look. "I can't take you *with* me."

Teigen opened his mouth to argue when realization waved its hands. "I—oh! ...You have contacts here."

"I did," Falko clarified. "Before all of this."

"And you need to—okay." Teigen glanced around but no one was listening to them. "Can I at least walk out with you?"

"Of course." Falko placed his napkin beside his plate and stood. "Let's get our coats."

ᚿ ᚿ ᚿ

The cold here in Trondheim was different from Kirkenes. The tropical stream flowing north and east through the Atlantic Ocean from the Caribbean kept the air wetter and marginally warmer.

Teigen breathed deeply as the men walked through the dark, pre-curfew streets. He made note of the streets they turned on so he could find his way back to the hotel once he and Falko parted ways.

"It's because I don't know if the same men are working here," Falko explained. "If they aren't, I'll have to explain my own status and prove myself trustworthy to whoever is in charge of this group."

He looked over at Teigen. "You, of course, have no status as yet."

"But I'll have you to vouch for me," Teigen clarified. "Once you are vetted."

"Exactly."

Teigen drew another cold, clear breath of freedom, filling his lungs until he thought they might burst. God in heaven, it was a wonderful sensation.

"Hopefully your friends are still there," he said. "That would simplify things considerably."

"Agreed." Falko stopped at a corner. "I'll see you back at the hotel."

He turned around and walked back in the direction they had just come from.

Teigen noted the tactic and filed it away with the rest of Falko's training while he stared at the tavern across the street. A shot of aquavit sounded so good that his mouth watered, but he had no money.

A smile curled the edges of his mouth.

I guess it's time to check out this 'hero' stuff.

CHAPTER FOURTEEN

November 21, 1942
Trondheim, Norway

Teigen sat at breakfast with Falko, nursing an aching head. The 'hero stuff' was clearly true, as proven by the men in the tavern who bought him countless shots of aquavit.

He stopped accepting them before he reached a point where he couldn't find his way back to the hotel, though two of his new friends walked with him to make sure he reached his temporary home safely.

"It wasn't that I drank so much," Teigen explained. "It's because I haven't had any alcohol at all for so long, and I'm so much thinner than I was."

"Spoken like a chemistry teacher." Falko grinned and took a bite of Teigen's as yet uneaten eggs. "Have you thought about what you'll do now?"

Teigen drained his coffee cup and looked for the waiter. "I think it depends on what you found last night."

"So you *are* ready to join us?"

Teigen waited to answer, needing to be certain of his choice.

What was pulling him back to Oslo, anyway? By now his teaching position would have been filled. And as much as he hoped Elsa regretted her decision to break with him, he no longer wanted to start up with her again. His own harsh experiences had forced him to open his eyes and begin to fight back—a stance neither Elsa nor her parents would approve of.

It's time to start over.
With everything.

Teigen thanked the man who refilled his coffee mug before he answered Falko. "I am. I've given it a lot of thought, and I have more reason to fight the brown bastards than to return to my life in Oslo."

"Excellent." Falko's fist hit the table softly. "We'll go upstairs when we finish and I'll tell you everything."

ᚾ ᚾ ᚾ

While the Trondheim group's previous leader had moved on to another assignment, Falko still found friends working in the Resistance pod in Trondheim.

"And they're excited about you," he said while they lounged on the two beds in their room. "Especially because you know about chemicals."

Teigen chuckled. He knew where this was going—the same direction as his students. "Bombs?"

"Yep."

He shrugged. "I'm happy to do what I can."

"Good." Falko's expression turned serious. "Now I need to tell you what happened four weeks ago. It isn't good."

Teigen sat up on the bed, steeling himself for whatever came next. "Go on."

"On October twenty-fourth the Nazis ordered the arrest of all Norwegian Jewish males, age fifteen and older."

Teigen was stunned. The racism which Hitler was forcing on the rest of Europe had not been a concern in the Scandinavian countries who claimed neutrality. Until now.

"So occupied isn't neutral when it comes to the Jews," Teigen murmured. "They aren't safe here anymore."

"No." Falko scrubbed his smooth cheeks. "But the Resistance alerted the Jews as soon as they heard about it. They think several hundred families were able to escape into Sweden, and the Shetland Bus has been transporting others to Britain."

Teigen nodded, thinking. "And the rest?"

"Gone into hiding." Falko sat up and faced Teigen. "That's where I—well, *we* if they accept you—come in."

"Okay... What do we do?"

"Can't tell you yet, I'm afraid." Falko flashed an apologetic expression. "But we leave tomorrow."

Teigen nodded again, his mind still processing what he had heard. "Where are we going? Can you tell me that?"

Falko chuckled a little. "Yes. We're sailing to Bergen."

"Good." Teigen jumped to his feet.

Falko looked surprised. "What are you doing?"

Teigen stared down at his friend. "I had three Jewish men in my sub-group at camp. I'm going to find them and warn them, if they don't already know."

Falko clambered to his feet as well. "I had two. I'll go with you."

November 26, 1942
Bergen, Norway

Teigen and Falko were welcomed in the hotel in Bergen with the same celebratory hospitality which was offered them in Trondheim. They accepted because, as Teigen pointed out, they only had the small amount of cash that the Trondheim Resistance group had given Falko, and their future income was uncertain at this point.

Falko accepted, albeit reluctantly. "We aren't supposed to draw attention to ourselves," he grumbled as he dropped his backpack on the bed.

"Look at it this way," Teigen countered as he pulled his two spare shirts and one extra pair of trousers from his own backpack. "If we are cashing in on being heroes, how could we be covert Resistance members?"

Falko gave a one-shouldered shrug as he hung up his own meager wardrobe. "You have a point."

Falko set two small, flat, brown-wrapped parcels on his bed.

Teigen halted his walk to the bathroom, razor and soap in his hands. "What are those?"

"Our reason to be here."

Teigen met his friend's eyes. "What are they?"

It was obvious that Falko wanted to tell him, but he held back. "I... It's not safe for me to tell you."

"Don't you know me by now?" Teigen's temper rumbled unpleasantly. "What more do I need to do to gain your trust?"

"It's not my trust you need to earn." Falko scuttled his fingers through his short, dark hair making it stand up. "But I was told to introduce you to the Milorg major here and he'll interview you. He's the one who decides if and where you'll be assigned."

Teigen reversed his path and approached Falko. "Milorg?"

"It seems that while we were away on our northern holiday," Falko's lips quirked, "the Resistance and the Norwegian army began working together. The new name for the Resistance is Milorg—short for military organization."

"Huh." Teigen pondered that while he went to the bathroom and set his razor and soap by the sink. "So now the leaders are called by military ranks?"

"I guess."

Teigen stepped back into the room. "What's your rank?"

His friend's face reddened. "I'm only a lieutenant. I've been gone since March."

Teigen narrowed his eyes, assuming the answer. "And what would I be?"

Falko's face flushed further. "Soldier. No rank. At least not until you have a few successful operations under your belt."

"Huh," he said again. "So, when do I meet this guy—Major...?"

"Helgesen." Falko pointed at the parcels. "I'll set it up when I meet him this afternoon to deliver one of those."

Teigen nodded, struggling to squelch his curiosity. "And the other?"

"There is a traveling troupe of Resist—I mean Milorg actors performing *A Midsummer Night's Dream* at the National Theater tonight." Falko put up a hand. "Before you ask, no, we don't get to attend the play. We are supposed to meet the actors at the stage door afterwards and pass this to their captain."

Teigen's mood brightened at that. "We?"

"Yep." Falko grinned. "I have permission to take you on this hand-off."

Teigen's gaze shifted to the small packages and spoke his thought processes aloud. "Can't use the postal system, of course.

Personal delivery is the only way if the contents are... incriminating."

Falko's grin dimmed. "Right."

Teigen nodded slowly. There was a clear danger in what the Resist—*Milorg* soldiers were expected to do. Before he was arrested, Teigen read enough cautionary tales about men who resisted being shot in the Nazi-controlled newspapers, or heard it on the Nazi-controlled radio, to know that.

He was embarrassed to admit this to himself, but until he was arrested he never understood how widespread the network was, nor how much they did to support the citizens of occupied Norway.

Damn Elsa and her parents. He had been a fool.

Time to make up for the past two-and-a-half years.

"Well..." he began. "I've already been arrested and sent to a labor camp, and I survived. The brown bastards had their chance to break me and they blew it."

He stared at Falko. "Let's pay them back."

ᚾ ᚾ ᚾ

Teigen stood at the back of the eager crowd waiting behind the theater for the actors and tried not to be noticed, which was somewhat difficult considering he was the tallest man there. He kept an eye on the SS officer standing opposite him, carrying flowers, and smiling smugly toward the stage door.

Teigen leaned over and spoke over Falko's shoulder. "Do you know which one you're looking for?"

"The star of the show—Dahl Holter." Falko didn't look at him. "They said he always escorts the lead actress, Selby Sunde, to make sure she isn't swarmed."

Teigen's gaze sifted to the sharply uniformed Nazi. "Looks like she has a suitor."

Before Falko answered, the Nazi captain's head turned and the man's eyes bored into Teigen's.

Teigen dropped his gaze and swiped the back of his mouth with a nervous hand. Rule number one. Do. Not. Be. Noticeable.

And he'd just blown it.

The officer began to ease toward Teigen.

Falko shifted away from him under the guise of picking up something someone had dropped.

Teigen was in trouble.

He pretended to ignore the captain though he could see him out of the corner of his eye. He stared at the stage door, willing it to open with every ounce of his frame.

A German-accented voice said, "Excuse me—"

The captain got no further when the door did swing open. The excited crowd pushed him forward as they strained to get closer to the famous thespians on the raised platform.

Teigen took a step back.

Cries of 'Miss Sunde' resounded from the crowd and flashes from camera bulbs lit up the area like machine gun fire.

The captain pivoted away from Teigen to look at the actors who stood on the raised platform. When Miss Sunde's searching gaze landed on the Nazi she smiled.

The handsome actor, who must be Dahl Holter, helped the smiling, red-lipped, and Arctic fox-clad blonde on his arm down the uneven wooden steps to the paved alley. As she approached the officer in front of him, Teigen recognized her with a sickening clench to his gut.

She's the one. The one on the pier. In Trondheim.

The day I sailed north.

Teigen took another step back, afraid she might notice him.

"My dearest Selby," the officer cooed, and then kissed the backs of both her gloved hands. "Bear with me a moment while I question this gentleman—"

Falko stumbled into the captain, whirled around, and shouted at the man closest to him, "Watch yourself, you fool!"

Teigen recognized a diversion when he saw one. He stepped back again, intending to slip behind the corner of the theater.

"What are you talking about?" the man bellowed. "I didn't touch you!"

Falko shoved him.

Teigen turned the corner.

As soon as he did a shot rang out momentarily silencing the stunned crowd until shouts and heels on pavement signaled the panicked scattering of the formerly adoring fans.

Teigen swung back around to see what happened. Falko lay on the ground, grasping his bleeding thigh, and bellowing in pain. The Nazi was standing near him, but his attention was being pulled in the opposite direction by the actress.

"No! Leave him," she pleaded as she tugged on his arm. "Let's go now, before someone decides to be a hero. No one needs to die here tonight."

With horrified shock, Teigen saw the wrapped parcel sticking dangerously out of Falko's pocket.

The actor, Dahl Holter, was nowhere in sight.

Teigen made a split-second decision and dove through the confused crowd for his friend while the captain's attention was diverted. He grabbed the parcel and jammed it inside his shirt.

Miss Sunde continued to pull on the captain's arm and beg him to come with her, "Please don't ruin our evening, Rolf."

Teigen, his belly lurching in fear and anger, stood and glared at the actress as she grabbed the Nazi and pushed her lips against his.

Then Teigen turned and ran.

ᚾ ᚾ ᚾ

If only I knew how to reach someone.

The phrase pounded through Teigen's brain in cadence with his strides as he zigged, zagged, and wheezed his way through the back streets of Bergen until he found the hotel. He leaned against the stone building's side wall, panting, with dots of black swimming through his vision, and wondered what he should do now.

If only I knew how to reach someone.

He had not been followed, he was sure of that. The handful of brown-clad soldiers behind the theater was so concerned with getting out of the way of the small but randomly stampeding crowd that no one appeared to have noticed his exit.

Once he caught his breath enough to appear composed, he strolled inside the hotel, hiding his shaking hands in his pockets.

"Good evening, Mister Hansen," the clerk greeted. "How was your evening?"

Teigen forced a grimace that he hoped passed for a smile. "Fine. Thanks."

He climbed the three stories of stairs rather than get in the elevator with the cheerful attendant, and was out of breath once again when he reached the room he shared with Falko.

Falko. What had happened to his friend?

If only I knew how to reach someone.

And that Dahl Holter. What a useless…

Teigen tucked the packet under his pillow before he stripped the clothes from his sweating frame. Adrenaline aftermath, weakness, and the over-heated room made him feel faint. He pulled back the curtains and opened the window.

The rush of freezing air cleared his head. His breathing slowed. Then his heartbeat. His knees folded and he sank to the floor.

Tomorrow he would return to the theater, but during the day. He'd look for that Dahl character and give him a dressing down for running tonight. Only then would he hand off the package.

Teigen closed the window on the cooled room and stripped to his skin before he went into the bathroom. He turned on the shower and stepped under its soothing spray. He wondered how he would be able to sleep tonight.

If only I knew how to reach someone.

CHAPTER FIFTEEN

The soft *snick* of a key turning in the hotel room door lock zinged through Teigen like a jolt of electricity. Was Falko back?

He opened his eyes in time to see a young boy's silhouette against the dim hall lights before the door closed and the room was once more enveloped in darkness.

Someone was in the room with him, and it wasn't Falko.

Teigen waited, unmoving, breathing as if he was asleep. His eyes were accustomed to the dark, so by the light of the moon outside the window and the crack under the door he saw the figure start to move.

First the boy went to the dresser. His hands slid over the top. He silently opened the drawers, one by one, and rifled through the contents before closing them. If Teigen was being robbed, the youth was going to be sorely disappointed. How long should he wait, he wondered, before jumping the thief and bringing him to justice.

The boy turned toward the bathroom.

Now.

With a shout meant to terrify, Teigen threw back the covers and launched himself from the bed.

The boy yelped and Teigen pulled him to the ground and held him there with no effort. "What're you after, you thieving little lout?" he growled.

"Let me go!"

The boy was younger than Teigen expected; his high-pitched voice sounded almost feminine. "Tell me how you got the key!"

"Jensen's pocket, you big ass!"

"Big ass?" He laughed. "Is that the best you've got?"

The boy's answer was to swing his heel up between Teigen's legs and crash it into his groin. His flannel pajama pants offered no protection whatsoever.

Teigen shout was entirely different this time. He let go of his prisoner and curled on the carpet. Multicolored shards of bright light obscured his vision, and while he knew for certain that the thief was going to get away, he couldn't do one damn thing about it.

But instead of bolting out the door, the boy clambered to his feet and switched on the ceiling light.

"Where is it?"

Teigen squinted up at the backlit youth. The boy's dark knitted cap was pulled to his eyebrows and the rolled-up neck of his sweater obscured his mouth.

"Where is what?" he croaked.

"Jensen's packet. Where is it?"

Teigen was coming back into his mind. "Are you Res— Milorg?"

"Brilliant." He folded his arms. "Just tell me and I'll get out of here."

"How old are you?" Teigen grumbled as he rolled to his hands and knees.

The boy backed away. "Is it under the bed?"

Their eyes met for an instant before both of them dove on a bed, sliding their respective hands under the pillows.

"A-hah!" Teigen held up the packet. "Now tell me who you are!"

The youth stared at him, pale blue eyes narrowed in anger. "Do you even know what that is?"

"No." Teigen waved it over his head. "Should I open it?"

That question presented a clear conundrum. "I wouldn't recommend it."

Teigen flashed a sarcastic grin and lowered the packet. "Why? Because if I see what's in here you'll have to kill me?"

The boy pulled a gun.

It was the smallest gun Teigen had ever seen, true, but at this close range it could probably do some damage.

"Oh. So you will," he said.

There were two ways to go here, and Teigen chose the wiser path. He stood between the beds and held out the packet in his left hand.

"Take it."

The boy climbed off the opposite side of Falko's bed and walked around the footboard. He kept the gun pointed at Teigen as he reached for the parcel.

As soon as he was close enough Teigen grabbed the slim wrist with his right hand and forced the boy's arm straight upward. Then he dropped the packet on the floor and yanked the cap from the boy's head.

What he discovered stunned him. "What the hell?"

The pale blue eyes that glared up at him were familiar to him as were the red-tinged lips pressed together in fury. The only part that didn't match was the short light brown hair. Cut boyishly, it accentuated the delicacy of the woman's bone structure.

"Selby Sunde?" he asked incredulously, though he knew the answer.

She jerked her wrist from his loosened grasp and bent down to pick up the fallen packet. When she straightened, she stuck her pistol in the pocket of her jacket.

"Say anything about this to anyone, anyone at all, and I swear I will kill you," she snarled. "I'm not kidding."

She grabbed the knitted cap and pulled it over her head while she turned to go.

"Wait. Wait!" Teigen jumped forward and grabbed her arm. "I know you."

She huffed a laugh. "Everybody knows me, you idiot. I'm *famous*."

Teigen shook his head "No! Not like that. I saw you. In Trondheim."

This laugh declared that he did, indeed, possess lower intelligence than a common rock. "I'm sure you did. We perform in Trondheim four times a year."

Again she pulled from his grasp and headed toward the door.

Teigen didn't follow her. He merely said, "You put your hand over your heart."

Selby stopped. For the space of two breaths, she didn't move.

Then she turned slowly and looked up at him—really looked at him for the first time.

"It was back in April. I was getting on the ship." Teigen felt like he needed to keep talking because he needed her not to leave. Not yet. "There were too many men but they were putting us on that ship anyway. I stopped and looked at you. You looked at me, and then…"

Selby's hand drifted up to her heart. "Is it really you?"

He nodded. "And then the guard pushed me with the barrel of his gun because I stopped."

"You don't look the same."

"I got a shave and a haircut my first night back."

Selby's eyes widened and she gasped; for some reason that unremarkable statement seemed to surprise her.

He shrugged. "When you saw me I hadn't shaved—or changed clothes—for nearly a month." He pulled a steadying breath. "It got a lot worse after that, though. A lot worse."

"But you still remembered me?" she whispered.

"I did." He took a step closer. "And I recognized you tonight. At the theater."

"Oh."

Selby crossed to the only chair in the room and dropped slowly into its embrace. Teigen sat on the foot of his bed.

"So now you remember me?" he ventured.

Her unfocused gaze cleared and jumped to his. "Of course. I never forgot you. I was at the dock when the first ship brought teachers back in September hoping to see you again."

Teigen shook his head and said stupidly, "I wasn't on it. Or the next one, either."

She smiled softly. "I know. I waited in Trondheim for the second ship to see if you were."

"You did?" Teigen felt the sting of tears behind his lids and he rubbed his eyes to keep them from forming.

Her cheeks pinkened under her pale blue eyes. "I thought of you as my personal connection to what was happening. You became a symbol to me—if you survived, then I would survive. Norway would survive."

One side of Teigen's mouth lifted. "That seems to be a widely held sentiment."

Selby chuckled. "I suppose so."

Teigen stared at his hands as his fingers intertwined. "I didn't forget you, either."

"No?"

He shook his head. "You were *my* symbol. My hope that I would someday be returned to a normal life."

Teigen untwisted his fingers and slapped his thighs as he met her eyes again. "The joke is that life will never be normal again. Not for any of us."

"I don't suppose so," Selby said sadly. "But we need to fight for that anyway."

"You said you're Milorg?"

Selby cleared her throat. "Yes. The whole troupe is. We travel up and down the coast and carry information, supplies—" She held up the packet. "And things that will get us killed."

Teigen's regard moved from Selby to the brown-wrapped parcel and back again. "Falko wouldn't tell me what's in it."

"So you aren't in our ranks, then."

"I'm trying. I was supposed to meet with a Major Helgesen tomorrow, but—" Teigen bolted upright. "What happened to Falko?"

"We took him to the hospital. He's going to be okay." Her calm tone reassured him.

Teigen flopped back onto the bed. "It's all my fault. I accidentally caught that Nazi captain's attention and Falko tried to divert him. That's when he got shot."

A sudden memory jarred him. "Hold on!"

Teigen sat upright again. "You kissed him!"

Selby made a face. "It's nothing."

"What do you mean it's nothing?" he demanded. "He's the *enemy*."

"That's the point. Isn't it?" She stiffened in the cushioned chair. "Part of my job is getting information."

A glaring light illuminated Teigen's mind in a very unpleasant way. "You trade your feminine wiles for secrets."

She pointed at him, suddenly angry. "Only up to a very clear point. I never take them to my bed. Never!"

Teigen put up his hands in surrender. "Okay."

"Never," she repeated, her eyes flashing. "And if they press me too hard, I drop them. Like that!" She snapped her fingers.

The gal clearly had spunk.

In spades.

"I believe you, Selby." He fought the grin that fought him back. "Don't pull your gun again."

She folded her arms and glared at him. "That gun can be amazingly persuasive when pointed—" Her gaze dropped to his lap then returned to his eyes. "In the right direction."

Teigen fought the urge to cross his legs. "I believe you."

She sighed. "I can make sure you meet with Hans tomorrow. Major Helgesen," she added when his brow furrowed.

"Thank you."

"Come by the theater tomorrow morning at eleven and ask for Bennett. He'll bring you to the dressing room. That's where it's safe for us to talk."

"Okay."

Amusement sculpted her expression. "By the way, what's your name?"

Teigen laughed at that. "I'm Teigen Hansen." He tipped his head. "Pleased to meet you, Selby Sunde."

"Hovland, actually. Sunde is my stage name." She looked puzzled. "Why do I know your name?"

Teigen shrugged and laughed again. "Because *I'm* famous?"

"No," she answered as if he was serious. "It's not that. Where are you from?"

"Originally? Arendal," he answered. "But I've taught high school chemistry in Oslo since thirty-seven."

Her expression lit up like the lights in the northern sky. "Your fiancée!"

A dagger slid into Teigen's heart. "My what?"

"Your fiancée, Elsa Borg, right?"

Teigen recoiled. "No. Not anymore, anyway."

Selby frowned. "But she's pregnant."

Teigen felt a surge of joy which lasted for the split second that it took him to realize that there was no possible way for the child to be his.

"Oh, God," he moaned. "Does she say it's mine?"

"It's not?" Selby asked carefully.

"We broke off at the beginning of February."

Selby counted on her fingers. "That was ten months ago. Surely the baby is born by now."

Teigen's chest tightened. "But we hadn't been—intimate—

since she moved in with her parents a year before that."

Selby's expression was somber. "She filed for your salary saying you were engaged but arrested right before the wedding."

"That bitch." He closed his eyes. "That conniving, selfish bitch." He opened his eyes again. "Is she really pregnant?"

"Yes," she said. "According to her doctor. Her *German* doctor."

Teigen winced. "And how did you meet her exactly?"

Selby winced, too. "I delivered her the money."

"Damn," he breathed. "I wonder if her parents are in on the scam. Wouldn't surprise me at all."

"I'm so sorry." Selby stood. "It's late. I should go. Dahl will be worried."

"Yeah, what happened to him tonight?" Teigen stood as well. "He made himself scarce once the shot was fired."

Selby looked up, her expression uncertain. "He went to call for help. Why?"

"Because that—" He pointed at the packet in Selby's hand. "Almost fell out of Falko's pocket. If I hadn't dived for it, the Nazi's might have it now."

Selby blanched. "I saw... something. You must have been the man that I saw move in and then run."

"I ran, because I grabbed that." He pointed again. "I don't know what it is, but I knew it was important to keep it away from your dear Captain."

She scowled. "He's not my dear anything. He's just part of the job."

Teigen grunted. "All things considered, a thank you would be appreciated."

Selby made a face. "Thank you."

She turned and walked to the door. "I'll see you tomorrow at eleven. Don't be late. Be early."

She opened the door and Teigen leaned against its edge. "What's your rank?"

"Lieutenant." She lifted her chin. "Don't forget it."

Teigen saluted but he was laughing. "No, sir."

She turned around and walked down the hall, talking to him without looking back. "We'll see just how long you laugh, soldier."

CHAPTER SIXTEEN

After leaving Teigen, Selby's hands were shaking when she pressed the elevator button for the hotel basement. Nothing about this night had turned out in any way she expected it to.

Certainly not the Nazi captain's suspicions being raised and a consequent shot being fired in the middle of the crowd waiting outside the stage door. She wrinkled her nose in disgust.

Things like that happen when amateurs are involved.

And not the horrible near-loss of the incriminating packet of forged identity papers.

Selby had cut her date with Captain Schmidt short by claiming that the shooting had disturbed her so deeply that she couldn't be the companion he deserved. When she returned to the theater, Dahl told her that Jensen was panicked, and rightly so, that the packet might have fallen into the wrong hands.

Selby told Dahl at that time that she thought she saw a man take something from him after he fell. Dahl went back to the hospital to talk to the injured man while she waited for him to return.

"He said he thinks it was his friend who is sharing his hotel room that grabbed it. He's not Milorg—yet—and doesn't know what's in the packet." Dahl reported and handed her the room key. "He needs to keep it that way."

"Got it." Selby palmed the key. "I'll sneak in and grab it while he's sleeping."

Dahl touched her cheek. "Be careful, Sel."

She knew he meant that he cared about her, but his words irritated her anyway. "I always am. You know that."

The elevator door opened to the basement. Selby walked quickly to the janitor's closet and began to pick the lock. Even though no one was on duty at this hour of the night, she couldn't risk losing the expensive Arctic fox coat that was part of her actress persona, so she had locked the door.

That's careful.

Once inside the closet, Selby closed the door and locked it again. She rolled the legs of her trouser to above her knees. She took off the soft shoes and stuck them in the pockets of the coat, and stuffed the knit cap into her trouser's waistband. She skillfully repositioned the blonde wig over her cropped natural hair before stepping into the red pumps she wore when coming here.

The packet of identity papers was safely inside her shirt, held in place by the bands of cloth which flattened her bosom.

Donning the fox coat and adding a touch of red lipstick transformed her from thieving urchin back into glamorous actress.

Selby unlocked the closet and this time left it unlocked, just as it was when she arrived. She took the elevator up to the lobby and strode out with her head high, walking directly toward the clerk at the desk.

"Thank you again, Sven." Selby bestowed her best smile on the chubby man who was probably her age. "My pappa will be very grateful that I made time for this quick visit."

Sven blushed a little and smiled back. "I'm sure his friend appreciated it as well."

"He did. Poor man has been devastated since his wife passed." Selby made a moue. "But do me a favor, will you?"

"Anything, Miss Sunde," he promised, his expression earnest.

"If people think that I have time to visit their shut-ins or relatives, I'm going to be forced to decline." Now she looked contrite. "I don't want to hurt their feelings, you understand, but I just can't visit everyone."

Sven nodded. "I completely understand."

"Good." Selby smiled again. "This will be our little secret."

"Thank you, Miss Sunde," he replied nonsensically.

She patted the back of his hand. "No, Sven. Thank *you*."

With a wink, Selby turned and walked out of the hotel.

Curfew was long past, but Selby walked openly down the main streets. If she was discovered out at this hour, she didn't want to look like she was sneaking around.

She was two blocks from her own hotel when the order to *halt!* erupted behind her.

She did, and turned slowly to face the bright light blinding her. "Good evening, gentlemen."

"Miss Sunde?" the awed voice asked from behind the glare.

Selby shaded her eyes. "Yes."

The light lowered as the pair of soldiers approached. "Do you know it's past curfew?"

The man's Norse was stilted but correct. "Yes, and I'm so sorry. Usually Captain Schmidt's driver drops me at my hotel, but because of the scuffle at the theater tonight our plans were changed."

Trusting the Germans understood her she held out her arm. "Would you men please escort me to my hotel? It's only about two more blocks, but I would feel much safer."

As the soldier without the lamp stepped forward, clearly hesitant, Selby looped her arm through his and turned back to her path. "You never know who might be lurking in the shadows, you know?"

"Uh, *ja.*"

The man with the lamp hurried to her other side and shone it unnecessarily on the pavement as they walked.

"A dear friend of my father's, recently widowed, is in Bergen tonight and my father asked me to pay the poor man a visit," Selby prattled cheerily. "I'm afraid the time got away from me."

She giggled a little. "When I'm out with Rolf—I mean Captain Schmidt—I never have to worry about the time because I'm with him. You know?"

"Uh, *ja.*"

"Anyway, I'm so glad you two showed up. I heard a noise down that alley I passed just before you found me. I'm sure it was just a stray cat, or maybe a dog, but I was a little worried nonetheless."

"Uh..."

"There we are. Just across the street." Selby stepped from the sidewalk into the empty street. "It's getting so chilly, isn't it? I know people don't think I should have a fox coat, considering the war and all the shortages, but it sure keeps me warm and that's all that matters. Don't you agree?"

"Uh…"

Selby stopped in front of the hotel and swung around to face the two young soldiers. "Thank you so very much. I'll be sure to mention to Rolf—um, Captain Schmidt, how courteous you both were."

She kissed each soldier lightly on the cheek for good measure. "Good night."

Spinning quickly, she ran up the steps and into the hotel without looking back.

ᚾ ᚾ ᚾ

Dahl waited in the lobby, looking haggard. He jumped up from his seat when he saw her. "What took you so long?"

Selby nodded a greeting to the night clerk and kept walking toward the elevator. Dahl matched her steps as he walked beside her.

"You're never going to believe it." Selby and Dahl stepped into the open door.

"Four, please," Dahl said to the operator.

"Yes, sir." He slid the doors closed and swung the lever to take the car upward.

Dahl stared down at her. "Were you successful?"

"Yes."

They didn't speak any further. When the elevator slowed to a stop at the fourth floor, the operator opened the doors and the pair of actors stepped out.

"Have a nice night."

Selby smiled at the older man. "Thank you."

Dahl escorted her down the hall to the room next to his and waited while she unlocked it. "Should I come in?"

Selby nodded and opened the door. She crossed to the bed as Dahl closed the door and locked it. She didn't say anything while she dropped the soft shoes on the bed, removed the fur coat, the red pumps, and the knit hat from her waistband. Before she rolled her trouser legs down, she untucked her shirt and retrieved the packet.

She handed it to Dahl. "Who gets this?"

"There should be instructions inside."

Selby pulled off the wig. "I'll be right back."

Dahl was already unwrapping the package when Selby turned toward her bathroom.

Inside the small, tiled sanctuary she turned on the water, letting it run into the sink until it got hot. She carefully placed the blonde wig—one of the three she owned—on its stand. Then she leaned over and washed off the night's layers of makeup.

When she straightened and grabbed the towel, the woman who looked back at her in the mirror was one she finally recognized.

Selby combed her short hair with her fingers, pulled the cloth bands away from her chest to release her squashed breasts, and then padded barefoot back into the bedroom. She sat cross-legged on the bed and waited for Dahl to return his attention to her.

"Kristiansand," he murmured. "Captain Ustersen."

That made sense—Kristiansand was their next stop. "I assume Jensen already delivered a packet to Helgesen?"

"I would assume the same thing." Dahl looked up at her. "These are very good. Expertly made."

"Do we know who they're for?"

"The Jews in hiding." He refolded the packet. "The ones who didn't—or couldn't—get out."

"Speaking of Helgesen..." Selby made sure Dahl was focused on her before she continued. "Is he still coming to the theater tomorrow morning at ten?"

"Yes." The packet now rested in Dahl's lap. "Why?"

"Because a Milorg recruit will be coming for an interview at eleven..."

Surprise mingled with confused etched Dahl's handsome face. "Did you recruit someone tonight?"

Selby huffed a laugh. "No, Jensen did."

"Huh." Dahl's expression eased. "By the way, did you know he was one of the teachers sent to Kirkenes?"

"I do now," she replied. "Which makes sense, since I met the man he's traveling with."

"Oh, no—were you caught?" Dahl looked suddenly angry. "I know I shouldn't allow you to do these things, Sel. They're far too dangerous."

As if you could stop me, superior rank or not.

Time to deflect.

"Dahl—the man in the hotel room was that teacher. The one I saw on the dock. The one I was hoping would be released when I stayed behind in Trondheim."

Dahl's jaw fell slack. "You're joking."

"No, I'm not." Selby couldn't stop herself from grinning like an idiot. "It's the same guy."

Dahl blinked as he put the pieces in order. "And Jensen recruited him? For Milorg?"

"Yep." Selby was still smiling. "And so now Helgesen needs to vet him."

Dahl wagged his head. "Small world."

Selby nodded and yawned. "I don't mean to be rude, but I'm exhausted."

"Of course. Sorry." Dahl stood and tucked the packet inside his shirt. Then he walked to the bed and kissed Selby on the head. "Good work, Lieutenant. I'll see you in the morning."

Selby smiled. "Thanks, Captain."

November 27, 1942
Bergen, Norway

Since Norwegian hotels were forced to accommodate German guests, and not the occupied and down-trodden populace, their kitchens were allowed to purchase rations not available to the common people.

Because of his need to regain his weight, and because it was free to him as a returned Kirkenes teacher, Teigen ate a big traditional breakfast of smoked fish, lefse, fried eggs, and homemade potato klubb which had been sliced and deliciously fried in butter. The coffee was weak but hot, and he drank a lot of it to help him wake up.

After his stealthy visitor, Selby Sunde—or Hovland as she claimed—left his room, he laid awake for at least an hour contemplating what he learned. If there was no curfew imposed, he would have dressed and gone outside; since returning from the labor camp he found sleeping inside stone buildings a bit cloying, even with the window open.

Teigen cleared his throat and took another bite of smoked fish, redirecting his thoughts to the points at hand.

First of all, she remembered him. Furthermore, she said she stayed behind in Trondheim to see if he was one of the teachers being released first from the labor camp.

That stunned him. He now knew he wasn't the only one who held on to their shared moment on the dock and found significance in their brief connection.

Thank you, Lord, that you have let me see her again.

Second, once he saw Selby without the outward trappings of fame, he found her to be more beautiful than he would have imagined. Her eyes were an amazing shade of pale, pure blue. Her lips were pink enough that she didn't need the painted-on red. In fact, he highly preferred her without it.

He even liked the unusually short cut of her thick, light brown hair. Without the distraction of pinned curls or braids, her high cheekbones, slim nose, and delicately pointed chin painted a perfect picture of femininity. He smiled into his coffee cup.

How could anyone ever believe she was a boy?

His smile faded when he thought about the third thing he had learned. He set the cup down before he threw it across the hotel's dining room.

Elsa Borg was pregnant.

Pregnant.

He had last seen her ten months ago. Clearly, she hadn't wasted any time in finding herself another love.

Nor in spreading her legs for him.

And as if that wasn't bad enough, she was claiming the baby was his. And as a result she was collecting money from the resistance under those false pretenses. Money that surely could be better used elsewhere.

I'll put a stop to that, and quickly.

Of course, that would mean going back to Oslo.

How would he manage to go back if he joined Milorg? As a mere soldier, as Selby pointed out, he would be at the mercy of Major Helgesen and the decisions he made.

Maybe I could ask him to station me in Oslo.

The idea came to him hand-in-hand with obvious warnings.

He was known in Oslo. His initial arrest and subsequent imprisonment in Kirkenes were also known. He couldn't move around the city without being recognized, and those who joined hands with Quisling would be eager to expose him if his new role was discovered.

And honestly, it would be hard to hide it from his friends there, many of whom were resistance supporters themselves.

The biggest risk would come from Elsa. She and her parents were going to be furious when he revealed her deception. Not only because of their funds being cut off, but because her loose morals would be made public.

Once that came to light, the Borg family would do anything to destroy him. He had absolutely no doubt about it.

Teigen sighed and pushed himself away from the table. He needed to go upstairs and ready himself for his meeting with the major. He would just have to wait and see what happened after that.

CHAPTER SEVENTEEN

"A new recruit?" Major Hans Helgesen looked interested.

"Yes, sir," Selby answered. "Falko Jensen, the teacher who was shot last night, recruited him when they were both in the labor camp at Kirkenes."

Helgesen looked at Dahl. "Have you met him?"

Dahl shook his head. "Not yet."

Helgesen's expression turned pensive. "If I'd been arrested for no reason and shipped to the far ends of the earth, I'd be spitting fire right about now."

One of the Royal Shakespearean Acting Troupe stage hands leaned forward. "Can I have a word, sir?"

Helgesen turned to face the muscular young man with calloused hands. "Of course."

"Well, sir," he said softly as he held out a folded piece of paper. "I received this from my mother."

The major unfolded the telegram and read the brief message. Then he nodded, refolded the paper, and handed it back.

"My condolences, Olav."

"Thank you sir." Olav's voice thickened. "Can I please be discharged so I can go home and run the farm? My mamma can't do it herself..."

"Are you the oldest son?" Helgesen asked.

"I'm the only son, sir," Olav answered.

The major nodded. "I'll send word to headquarters."

"Thank you sir." Olav squirmed a little. "Do you know when I might be able to leave?"

Helgesen gave the younger man a kind smile. "You are officially released. You can leave immediately if you need to."

"Thank you, sir." Olav stood awkwardly and addressed the seven actors and two remaining crew members. "I guess this is goodbye, then."

The troupe swarmed the man and wished him well before he hurried out the stage door.

Bennett looked at Jonas. "It's just us now."

Jonas turned to Helgesen. "Maybe the new guy could join us?"

Selby's heartbeat stuttered. Her hopeful gaze shot to the major. "Is that possible?"

His brow flickered. "I can't say, Selby. Not before I meet him."

Her cheeks heated. "No, of course not," she backpedaled. "I only meant that, if he's acceptable, we could move forward without burdening Bennett and Jonas."

"While it would be convenient, he might not fit," Dahl said stiffly. "And anyway, it's the major's decision, not ours."

Major Helgesen's regard bounced between Selby and Dahl. She doubted Dahl's interest in her personally had escaped anyone's notice, least of all their commanding officer.

"Let's move on," he said. "We'll discuss that after we've had a chance to talk with him."

N N N

Teigen knocked on the stage door at three minutes to eleven. It was pulled open by a lanky young man in his early twenties with an unruly mop of red-streaked brown hair. He grinned and his eyes met Teigen's.

"Teigen?"

"Yes..."

"Come in!" Once the heavy door closed behind him, the man stuck out his hand. "Bennett Wilhelmsen. Props manager."

Teigen shook the proffered hand. "Teigen Hansen, arrested teacher. Nice to meet you."

Bennett laughed. "You've got a sense of humor. I like that.

Follow me."

Teigen made his way past racks of costumes and painted flats of scenery to the actor's dressing area. He stopped when faced with a circle of a dozen curious faces, only two of which he recognized.

Selby, of course. And Dahl, who left Falko alone on the ground and bleeding.

One man stood up. Judging by the gray in his hair and the crags in his face, he was well over forty. Even so, his back was straight as he met Teigen eye-to-eye.

He also offered his hand. "Major Hans Helgesen, Milorg."

Teigen shook it. "Teigen Hansen. Sir."

Helgesen smiled. "Have a seat, Hansen."

"Ooh. Come sit by me." The woman who spoke slid over and patted the chair she just vacated.

"Karolina..." Selby chastised.

"Uh, thank you." Teigen dropped onto the chair. He glanced at Selby who looked excited and nervous at the same time.

"So why don't you tell us what brings you here today," the major suggested. "I understand you met one of our officers in Kirkenes, but why don't you start at the beginning?"

Teigen's brows flew up. "Of my life?"

Helgesen laughed. "No. Let's just go back as far as your arrest."

Teigen's cheeks grew painfully hot. He nodded and launched into the story of the last ten months of his life, interrupted often by clarifying and probing questions from the major. He ended with, "I realize I was foolish to ignore the obvious. No one can hide from what's happening in the world and keep a clear conscience."

He paused and looked around the small group of somber, unremarkable people, all of whom now had his utmost respect. His gaze returned to the major. "It's time for me to make up for lost time, sir."

Major Helgesen nodded as he stroked his bearded chin. Steely blue-gray eyes pinned Teigen's. "What skills do you bring, Hansen?"

"Skills?" Teigen searched his mind for what sort of skills he thought the major might be interested in. "I'm a hard worker, and I'm strong—even though I look skinny now."

The major's eyes raked over Teigen's frame. "You lost weight in the camp." It wasn't a question.

"Yes, sir. I've lived through the harshest conditions you could imagine in the last eight months." Teigen pointed a finger at Helgesen. "But that's the point. I *lived* through them."

"You've got tenacity, that's obvious. And strength. And, since you were a teacher, you're obviously smart enough to get a university degree."

"Thank you, sir." Teigen drew a deep breath and gave his final plea. "Major, I'm going to work as long and as hard as I can resisting the brown bastards and our country's unconscionable occupation. I'll do it with Milorg—or without." He flashed half a grin. "But I'd rather do it *with* you."

Major Hans Helgesen threw back his head and guffawed. He slapped his thigh and wiped the corners of his eyes. "Good God, Hansen. That's priceless."

Teigen noticed the rest of the troupe smiling. Karolina clapped her hands and rubbed her shoulder against his. Selby grinned at him and winked. Only Dahl was reserved.

Then the realization smacked him.

Dahl likes Selby.

Did she like him back?

That wasn't important at the moment. He needed to focus on the matter at hand.

Helgesen heaved a deep sigh and regained his composure. "Well I'm completely satisfied. Welcome to Milorg, Hansen. Now we need to decide what to do with you."

Bennett spoke up again. "Sir, he says he's a hard worker and strong. Whoever replaces Olav needs to have those qualities."

Jonas chimed in with, "Moving the sets is hard, rough work, sir. We need another big, strong body to help."

"Yeah, we don't want to risk dropping a flat on the actors during a scene change, sir." Bennett looked seriously concerned.

Helgesen considered Teigen. "What do you think?"

"I'm very willing, of course. If you think that's where I'm needed." Teigen kept himself from looking at Selby. "But, if you don't mind my asking, what exactly does this troupe do, in relation to the fight that is?"

Dahl answered that question before the major could. "We travel with the Germans' ignorant blessings under the cover of a Shakespearean acting troupe that exists for their entertainment. As we do, we pass supplies and information to Milorg posts from Oslo to Trondheim, and back again."

Oslo?

Dahl leaned forward and lifted one challenging brow. "The packet Selby recovered from you last night is an excellent example."

Teigen nodded, distracted from the other man's challenge by the new information. "I thought it was something like that. Are you going to Oslo soon?"

This time Selby jumped in; she was the only one in the room who knew why he was asking. "We are heading south right now. We stop in Stavanger next. Then Kristiansand. And then Oslo."

Teigen faced Major Helgesen. "If they'll have me, I'll join the troupe to replace Olav."

A smattering of applause filled the room.

"I'm so glad," Karolina cooed.

"You do realize that you begin with the rank of soldier," Helgesen warned. "Bennett Wilhelmsen whom you met first is a sergeant, as is Gunter Salversen over there."

Gunter lifted a hand. "Second male lead, behind Dahl."

"Selby Hovland is a lieutenant, and Dahl Holter is the captain of the group."

"What the major is saying is that they all outrank you." Dahl smiled coldly. "And I outrank everyone."

Karolina giggled. "I don't outrank you. You can boss me around if you want."

Selby's eyes threw daggers at the other woman. "Karolina Ingebrigtsen is the troupe's second female lead. And, my understudy."

"She never gets sick," Karolina muttered.

Major Helgesen stood. "Will you come with me, Hansen? We have some paperwork to fill out."

"Yes, sir!" Teigen shot upright. "But before we go, what do I do after that?"

"Come back here and I'll put you to work." Bennett clapped him on the shoulder.

"You'll have to change hotels," Selby stated.

Teigen turned to look at her. "I will?"

She shrugged. "You are one of us now."

"What about Falko?" He didn't want to abandon his friend.

"We'll take care of him once he's released," Dahl promised. "In the meantime, when you get back here after your meeting with

Major Helgesen I'll go to both hotels with you and get you moved."

Teigen decided to take the strength position in whatever contest Dahl might think they were engaged in. "Thanks, Dahl. I appreciate it. And I look forward to working with you."

He turned to follow the major from the theater when Helgesen stopped and faced him. "I neglected to ask what subjects you taught."

"Secondary school chemistry."

The major's face spread wide with a surprised grin. "You can make bombs!"

ᛀ ᛀ ᛀ

Selby startled every time the stage door opened, but it wasn't until after two o'clock that Teigen and Dahl returned to the theater.

"He's all squared away," Dahl told Bennett. "He'll bunk with you for now, so you can answer his questions and tell him what he needs to know."

"I don't mind a roommate," the affable props manager replied with a shrug. "Now that Olav's gone, Jonas can have his turn for a little privacy."

"What about his salary?" Selby asked.

Teigen's bright green eyes widened. "Salary?"

"Didn't Dahl tell you?" She threw the actor an irritated look. "Were you going to at some point?"

Dahl scowled at her. "Of course I was. We just hadn't gotten to it yet."

Selby looked up at Teigen who was more than a foot taller than her. Without the scraggly beard and hair, he was actually as good-looking as Dahl—if not more so.

"We get a small salary as Milorg soldiers. That's what I was talking about. Dahl should give you an advance since I assume you don't have any money?"

Teigen huffed a laugh. "No. The Germans in Kirkenes didn't pay us to unload their ships or build their roads."

"Or feed you, by the looks of you." Bennett jokingly poked him in the ribs, then his jaw dropped. "Jeez, man. You are thin."

Teigen looked uncomfortable. "I'm working on it."

Selby's heart broke a little. None of them really knew what he had been through. And she wasn't certain she wanted to know.

"The troupe as a business pays for our hotel rooms," she continued. "And that includes one meal a day, usually breakfast. It also pays our passage from town to town."

"Okay..." Teigen was clearly doing mental budgeting.

"The money for all that comes from ticket sales. After we pay the theaters their percentage, of course. Just like any theater troupe."

Teigen looked at Dahl. "Is the troupe profitable?"

"Considering the situation we're in, we're lucky to break even," the actor admitted.

Teigen's face twisted. "Well... Have you considered doing plays that are more... modern?"

Dahl shook his head. "As long as we're doing classic works, the Germans pretty much leave us alone."

"And making a profit isn't why we exist," Selby reminded him. "We have a different goal here."

Teigen nodded slowly. "I understand."

Dahl reached into his pocket and retrieved his wallet. "There's one week left in the month..." He pulled out a few bills and handed them to Teigen. "So here's a hundred kroner. We'll all be paid for the month on the first of December."

"Thanks." Teigen stuffed the money in his pocket.

"Your salary as a soldier will be four hundred a month." Selby looked at Teigen apologetically. "I know—it's not much. Certainly a lot less than your teacher's pay. I'm sorry about that."

Teigen nodded. "It's less than a quarter. But I don't have to pay for a room. And I get fed every morning. I'll make it work."

"You'll get a raise after a while," Bennett assured him. "And I'm guessing a promotion won't be too far off, either."

"It's fine." Teigen flashed a crooked grin at the trio. "I just thank God that I'm here now, and not where I was at the beginning of the month."

When his smile softened and moved to Selby she knew she was in trouble.

What have we done?

CHAPTER EIGHTEEN

February 17, 1943
Oslo, Norway

Nearly three months after Teigen joined the Royal Shakespearean Acting Troupe, and exactly one year and one week after Elsa irrevocably broke their engagement, Teigen disembarked from their ship into Oslo. The rush of emotions he felt unexpectedly swamped him.

He knew he was here to confront Elsa with her deception. The fact the troupe was performing here was actually secondary to his plans. He just needed to do what they told him to in the meantime.

Taking orders from anyone grated on his ego, but taking them from Selby was particularly difficult. The petite spitfire wasted no time in making sure he understood that her word was his command.

Sometimes he thought she ordered him around just because she could.

Teigen, on the other hand, looked for ways to show his own strength of mind and character, taking initiative on projects both with the stage productions and with their work with Milorg.

The ingenious box he designed and built from scrap lumber was one example. Labeled *Comments* and placed in the lobby of the theaters they performed in, he told the highest-ranking officers in the cities where they appeared that anything placed in that box would be acted on.

The second night that the box was in the lobby at Kristiansand a tip about a raid on a house appeared. Teigen left the theater after intermission and warned the family, who were then able to hide the Jews they were sheltering somewhere else for the night. He also told them that he would make certain the fugitives received new identity papers.

"Teigen, you can't just go running out in the middle of the show like that," Selby scolded him afterwards. "What if something happened?"

"Something like what?" he countered. "Selby, there was a family of four living in that basement. All of them would have been sent to the German camps immediately—if they weren't shot on the spot. What would be worse than that?"

"I understand, but—"

"Not to mention what might have happened to the couple whose house they're hiding in."

"UGH!" She stomped her slippered foot on the rug in the dressing room. Her eyes flashed with pale blue fire which ignited a frustrating flame in his groin.

"Teigen! Listen to me!"

He drew a deep breath and held it, trying to calm his body which was waging war with itself. When it came to Selby, he either wanted to bed her or strangle her. There seemed to be no middle ground.

"Dahl and I are your commanding officers—"

"I know."

"So *act* like you know!"

Teigen dragged his fingers through his lengthening hair. This repeated argument never got them anywhere. She was always going to try to control him, and he was always going to buck.

"I'm sorry," he offered. "I'll try to ask you next time."

"Please do." Her stiff frame relaxed a little.

Teigen wanted to hug her to show her that they stood on the same ground, but he knew that would be a mistake. Selby was very reserved when it came to touch, even with Dahl whom she had known for years.

At least it's not only me.

"There's one other thing," he ventured.

Selby folded her arms and glared at him. "What?"

"I promised we'd get them new identity papers." He tried to look hopeful. "Do we have any left?"

Selby's lips pursed as her eyes narrowed. Clearly she was deciding how to answer him. That meant that they did have some. It also meant that she hated to admit he was right.

"What ages?" she asked.

And that was that. Teigen delivered the papers the next day. And to his credit he never gloated once.

Both Dahl and Selby knew about Elsa's ploy and Teigen's need to confront her, now that he was returning to Oslo.

"Let me talk to the major here," Dahl told him before they docked. "He'll have some suggestions, I'm sure, about how to go about this."

Teigen agreed, though his nerves were on edge and he felt like a mountain cat coiled to attack its prey.

The troupe went to the venue first, the National Theater near the Royal Palace. Bennett, Jonas, and Teigen oversaw the moving of the scenery flats and trunks of props, while character actress and costume mistress, Ingeborg Rossen, ordered the stevedores at the dock to be careful with her voluminous creations.

All of the actors helped, however, since the job was daunting and there were only ten of them in the group. Three hours after docking, their traveling show was organized enough in the backstage area of the theater that they could go to their hotel and take time settling in before meeting for supper.

When they reached the hotel, a trio of letters waited for Teigen.

"This one's from Falko," he told Bennett as he tore it open.

Falko had opted to remain in Bergen and work there, saying, "This city is a crucial point. Lots going on here. Besides, I'll see you four times a year."

Teigen scanned the news. "He's been promoted to captain."

"Good." Bennett was clearly not listening.

No matter. Teigen opened the letter from his parents next. He skimmed over the content looking for any bad news, planning to savor the rest of the news later.

Letter from your brother... caught his eye. Only then did he take a good look at the third envelope. There was nothing on the outside to indicate where it came from.

Teigen tore open the envelope. Inside was a somewhat ragged-edged missive in his older brother's handwriting. He tucked that away to read later as well.

"Do you have your key?" he asked Bennett. The two men got on so well that they chose to remain roommates.

"I do." Bennett held up proof and dangled it in front of Teigen. "Third floor. Let's go."

ᚿ ᚿ ᚿ

Selby watched Teigen and Bennett walk off. She couldn't help but wonder what he was planning to say to his deceitful fiancée. Had the woman two-timed him? Or did she simply fall into the first bed that threw back the covers? Whichever it was, Elsa had done Teigen very wrong.

If the tables were turned, Selby would be brutal.

But he's not a brutal man.

Selby walked up to the second floor with Dahl, eschewing the elevator. She didn't want to be confined in a small space with Teigen right now. Her feelings about him were so capricious that being near him set her on edge.

One minute she wanted to gouge his eyes out. The next, she wanted to stand by his side forever.

Selby's general mistrust of men was long held and deeply seated. Her father died in the Great War and the Danish man her mother married afterwards could only be described as cruel.

When she was young, Selby hid from him when he went into one of his lunatic rages. He screamed at her mother, accusing her of sleeping with Russians and threatened to kill her. Selby cried in her closet and prayed that God would strike him dead.

But as an adolescent she started stepping between him and her mother.

When she did, his rage turned into lust. He violated her body with his hands and pleasured himself while he did. He slapped her if she made a sound, claiming that she was trying to entice him to enter her.

"I know what you want, bitch," he growled in her ear as she struggled to swallow her whimpers. "But I won't *let* you give me the clap, you filthy whore."

Selby's mother tried to stop her from interfering at first, and then tried to stop the man Selby never called father from hurting her. Those attempts earned her mother multiple broken noses and teeth.

Selby reached her breaking point and ran away when she was fifteen. She read in the Bergen newspaper a month later that the man shot her mother and then himself.

She went back to their house and cried for a week.

Then she washed herself off, took anything that she could pawn, and returned to Bergen. Her last act before she left was to set the house on fire.

"Who are we meeting tomorrow?" Selby asked to shake the unpleasant memories from her mind.

"Colonel Berntsen. He'll come to the theater at ten in the morning." Dahl set their suitcases down in front of her door.

Selby unlocked it and Dahl carried her suitcase inside. "Thanks."

"Can I get you anything?" he asked.

"No, I'm fine."

"Then I'll collect you for dinner at six." Dahl walked out the door and lifted his case again. He turned back and smiled as he pulled her door shut.

Selby dropped onto the bed with a frustrated sigh. For years she hadn't thought about her past. But now that Teigen Hansen reappeared as a real flesh-and-blood man and joined her life, the thirteen-year-old memories were haunting her.

Why now?

Probably because they shined a light on how different he was from that horrid man.

But she couldn't know that for certain. Not until she saw how he treated Elsa.

Because Elsa was guilty.

She had forced Teigen to ignore the German occupation and act as if nothing had happened. She broke her promise to marry him when he sent the letter declining to sign Quisling's Declaration of Loyalty to Nazism.

And within weeks after that, she became pregnant with another man's child—falsely claiming that child was Teigen's and fraudulently filing for his salary after he was arrested.

Selby wanted to scratch the woman's eyes out and throw *her* in prison.

"Oh, good Lord," she moaned. "Why do I care so much? It's not my fight."

Because Teigen is getting to you.

"Damn it!"

Selby jumped off the bed and tossed her suitcase onto the spot where she had been laying. She flipped the latches, tossed back the top, and started unpacking as she always did. Some people didn't mind living out of a suitcase, but she always moved in to her hotel room. The troupe never stayed less than ten days in any city, so it was worth it to her.

"Thank goodness for hotel laundresses," she muttered and stuffed a few items into the cloth bag in the closet.

When she was done she removed her wig, washed her face, kicked off her shoes, and laid back down on the bed, closing her eyes.

Selby knew instinctively that this stop in Oslo was going change her relationship with Teigen. Right now, he annoyed the snot out of her. His refusal to be controlled reminded her of a stallion who submits to the bit only because he chooses to at the moment.

The thing that really rankled her was that his instincts were usually spot on.

All he needs to do is ask first.

She imagined his bright green eyes looking at her from under a cocked brow, as if to ask if that was really necessary.

She could almost hear his voice: "You would say yes. You know you would. Why waste the time?"

Damn it.

Ж Ж Ж

The Milorg officers in the troupe—Dahl, Selby, Gunter, and Bennett—sat at dinner together. Once their supper order was taken and a pitcher of beer placed in front of them, Dahl clasped his hands on the table.

"I received bad news today, and there's no way to soften it..." He looked at each of them. "Thirty-four men were shot in Trondheim yesterday as retaliation for the sabotage of a train carrying munitions."

Selby gasped. These things happened in war, and non-combatant Norway was no exception. But that didn't mitigate her horror.

"Do we know any of them?" she asked, afraid of the answer.

Dahl nodded. "Sadly, yes."

He pulled a list from his pocket. As they passed the list around the table, no one spoke. When Selby saw the names, tears rolled down her cheeks.

"Lieutenant Ole Arnesen. He's only been the ranking officer there for a few months." She heaved a ragged sigh and handed the list back to Dahl before wiping her cheeks. "Milorg will make sure his family is taken care of."

"His wife will probably move back up to Bodø. That's where she's from." Dahl refolded the paper and stuck it back in his pocket.

The waiter brought their soup; potato with fish. Selby stared at it, her appetite gone.

"I do have another matter to discuss," Dahl said as he salted his soup. "Promotions."

Selby lifted her eyes. "In the troupe?"

Dahl nodded. "I want to make Hansen a sergeant. He's worked hard and proven his worth. And, he could use the money I think."

Bennett blanched. "A sergeant? Like me?"

Dahl grinned at the props manager. "No, not like you. I'm promoting you to lieutenant."

"All right, then!" Bennett grinned back. "An extra twenty kroner a week and I still get to boss Hansen around."

Selby frowned. "Doesn't he give you guff?"

Bennett waved a dismissive hand. "Nah."

"He does it to you because you're a woman," Gunter stated between spoonfuls of soup. "He doesn't like taking orders from a girl."

Selby bristled. "Did he *say* that?"

Gunter shrugged. "Doesn't have to. He's a man, isn't he?"

"I never had a problem with taking orders from you, Selby," Bennett said. "Just for the record."

"You still out-rank him, Sel." Dahl's tone was infuriatingly condescending. "I'm sure it'll be fine."

Selby stood up and threw her napkin in her uneaten soup. The three men stopped eating and stared up at her.

"First of all, I'm not worried about Hansen taking orders from me," Selby ground through clenched teeth. "It doesn't matter if I'm a woman. I've got the training and the experience behind me that he doesn't have."

She stepped away from her chair and shoved it against the table. "And secondly, if any of you thinks I am somehow diminished in my capabilities because I'm female, I challenge you to back that up with a gun. You choose the time and place. We'll see who's the better shot."

She turned her back on three faces blank with shock and stormed out of the dining room.

CHAPTER NINETEEN

The elevator door opened and Selby ran right into Teigen Hansen's chest.

"Hold on." Teigen grabbed her arms and kept her from stumbling backwards in her pumps. "What's going on?"

He was the last man she wanted to see at the moment. "Let go of me!"

He did. "Selby, what happened?"

She lifted her chin and glowered up at him. "I don't want to discuss it with you."

"Fine." He stepped out of the elevator leaving the operator to gape at them. "Have you had supper?"

Her stomach growled. "I'm not hungry."

"Liar. Come on." He took her arm gently and headed into the lobby. "I know a place I'll bet you've never heard of."

For some reason, she let him lead her. Compared to Dahl's solicitous attitude, Teigen's no-nonsense demeanor and gentle touch made her willing to accompany him.

"Where are we going?"

Teigen took off his coat and draped it around her shoulders. "Two blocks. Best *fårikål* in Oslo."

Selby stopped walking. "I can't take your coat. You'll freeze."

Teigen laughed. "It's warmer here than the Arctic, I'll tell you that for sure. And I didn't have a nice warm coat there." He tugged on her arm. "Come on. Two blocks."

ⓅⓅⓅ

Though snow crunched under his boots and the night was black, Teigen truly didn't feel the cold. He was elated to have this version of Selby on his arm and looked forward to sharing a traditional and unassuming Norwegian supper with her.

He couldn't say why he invited her. But she was so unusually discomfited when she ran into him—literally—that he slipped into protector mode.

Meet her needs first, solve her problem second.

Teigen claimed a wooden booth by the window. The owner of the tavern hurried over as soon as he saw the teacher.

He grabbed Teigen's hand and pumped his arm. "Mister Hansen! How are you doing?"

Teigen grinned. "I have survived Quisling's best efforts to destroy me, Anton."

"Aw, you are too thin," Anton fussed.

Teigen glanced at Selby to try and judge her mood; at the moment she was calmly listening. "Believe it or not, I have gained back most of the weight I lost in Kirkenes."

"Well, tonight I'll feed you for free. No argument." Anton waved an expansive hand and seemed to just now notice Selby. "Both of you."

"Anton, this is Miss Selby Sunde, lead actress in the Royal Shakespearean Acting Troupe. They are performing at the National Theater for the next week."

The tavern owner blushed and bowed like she was royalty. Teigen rubbed his mouth to cover his chuckle.

"My pleasure, miss."

Selby looked at Teigen, her eyes wide with surprise. "Oh! Thank you, sir. You may... rise?"

Anton straightened. "I have a nice little bottle of wine. I'll bring it right away. Excuse me."

As he hurried away, Teigen couldn't hold back his amusement. "Well, *he* was impressed."

Selby smiled for the first time this evening. "You are still getting free food, I see."

He shook his head, still laughing. "Not normally. But Oslo was my home and he knows me."

"Did you bring Elsa here?"

Teigen tilted his head, his laughter quashed. "Why would you ask me that?"

Selby blinked at him. "I don't know."

Teigen stared back. The idea she might be jealous had hatched in his mind and was now crawling down through his chest.

"I was with Elsa for five years," he said carefully. "I thought she was the love of my life." He paused, and then said, "I have since come to know better."

What the hell are you saying?

Selby recoiled. "What does that mean?"

Teigen turned and smiled at Anton, who set a bottle of red wine and two glasses on the table.

"I hid this from the Germans," he whispered as he poured.

Teigen crossed his heart. "We won't tell."

When the tavern owner left them alone again, Selby leaned forward. "What do you mean you have come to know better?"

Teigen was at a distinct fork in the road. He had two clear directions to choose from. He chose the dangerous one.

"I never thought back then that I would find another woman who interested me."

Selby's cheeks flushed under dilated pupils. "And have you?"

"Maybe. I'm not sure yet." He took a sip of the wine. "This is good. You should try it."

Selby looked a little frantic. "When will you know?"

Teigen set his glass down and twirled it slowly between his finger and thumb. He didn't look at Selby, knowing that to say what he was going to say and be looking at her at the same time was far too direct.

"When she does, I suppose."

He thought for a minute that Selby might bolt. If their food had not arrived, she probably would have.

Instead, she drained her wine glass and poured more.

"Try the *fårikål*," Teigen urged, deflecting the conversation again. "Tell me what you think."

She seemed to be considering what to do. Eventually, she lifted the spoon and dipped into the peppery mutton and cabbage casserole. When she put the creamy deliciousness in her mouth, her disposition changed in a moment.

"This is amazing," she mumbled past the spoonful.

Teigen smiled at her. "I'm glad you like it."

The pair ate in silence for a while, the air between them lightening and the wine bottle emptying. Coffee appeared at their elbows and their empty bowls were cleared away.

Teigen ventured to ask, "Will you tell me why you were so upset earlier that you were willing to forgo your supper?"

Selby scoffed and stirred the single sugar cube she was given into her coffee. "Men."

Teigen nodded his understanding. "So your meeting of the officers didn't go well."

She shot him a dark glance. "Why do you all have to assume you're better than me?"

Careful, Teig.

He looked sincerely confused. "Why do you think they assume that?"

"Because you're all big important men, of course." She waved her palms in front of her while she spoke then dropped them on the table. "And I'm just a lowly woman."

Teigen refused to jump into that foray unarmed. He needed more to go on. "What started it?"

"Some of you are being promoted."

"And you should be, too?" he guessed.

She rolled her eyes. "No, I'm fine. I don't want Dahl's job."

"Then what—"

She slammed her fists on the table. "I just want to be shown the same respect that the male officers are!"

That cannon ball hit him squarely in the chest. "And I'm the guilty one."

She stared at him for a brief moment before answering. "It's not *just* you. But yes, it's you."

Teigen's shoulders fell. "Am I being promoted?"

Selby lifted her coffee cup in a mock toast. "Well, you're pretty darn good at what you do, aren't you?"

"At your expense."

She shook her head. "I didn't say that."

Teigen looked contrite. "You don't have to."

He sipped his cooling coffee in silence. If he really thought about it, he had been chafing at the bit under her authority. Was it because she was a woman?

No.

"If I do buck, it's because you're better than you think you are."

Her cup hit the tabletop. "What is *that* supposed to mean?"

Teigen spoke evenly, keeping all discernable emotion from his voice. "That means you don't trust yourself enough to let those under you do what they do best."

When she looked confused, he tried to explain it better. "If you allow your soldiers to fight, they'll bring you glory."

She looked gobsmacked. "Am I holding you back?"

"Sometimes. Yes. But I think you do it because you don't know how good *you* are." Teigen combed both hands through his hair and spoke the truth. "You're amazing, Selby. You're smart. You have all kinds of skills. You're fearless…"

He leaned forward and pinned her gaze with his. "Only when you step forward, do you leave room for those behind you to step forward as well."

Selby looked like she'd seen a ghost. Her face fell slack, blanched white, and then flushed red.

"That makes so much sense."

Oh, thank God.

"I'm serious, Teigen. That makes all the sense in the world." She clapped her hands on her head. "Why didn't anyone point that out to me before?"

He relaxed against the bench seat, deeply relieved. "Because as soldiers they never learned it, would be my guess."

She looked at him intently. "Then how did you learn it?"

Teigen smiled. "It's what teachers do every day."

ᚾ ᚾ ᚾ

Teigen walked Selby back to the hotel before curfew, again refusing to wear his coat and insisting he was fine.

"Arctic Circle, remember?" was all he said.

She realized again that the man she knew now was not the same man who was arrested last spring. After all that happened to him, how could he be?

"When you were in the labor camp, were you hoping to come back and teach again?" she asked.

He nodded. "At first, yes. I assumed that'd be how things

went."

"And then?" she prompted.

"As time went on, and my situation looked more and more hopeless, I got angry—and really bitter, to be honest." He looked down at her. "My livelihood and my life had been stolen from me. Do you understand?"

"I do."

"All we could focus on was making it through the day. Then through half the day. Then just taking one more step..."

Selby's throat thickened and she couldn't talk.

"I met Falko and he asked me if I was angry enough to join the resistance." Teigen huffed and his breath steamed in the cold winter air. "I told him in no uncertain terms that I was more than ready."

Selby swallowed the lump in her throat. "And that was when your future plans changed."

"Actually, that was when I started *making* future plans, not just letting my future plan itself."

That was an interesting way to put it. "And then you followed Falko to Trondheim and Bergen."

Teigen held her arm as they climbed the icy steps and then opened the hotel door. They passed through the little alcove to the second door and entered the cozy lobby.

As they approached the stairs, Selby stopped. She didn't offer Teigen his coat, because she wasn't quite finished with the conversation. "What were your thoughts when you met us all?"

Teigen looked a little embarrassed. "I knew that you and Dahl went to SOE training in England, and I was afraid you would make me go, too."

Selby found that amusing. "Why would that be bad?"

"To be honest," he began. "I had already wasted two years of the occupation pretending it would just go away. And after spending the majority of this year as a prisoner, I didn't want to waste any more time."

She frowned. "Do you think we wasted *our* time?"

"No. On the contrary, I think you were efficient."

"Efficient?"

"Absolutely!" Teigen's eyes twinkled. "You teach us what you learned and we can get right to it."

Selby laughed. "Because that's—"

"—what teachers do every day. Exactly!"

Selby nodded, still smiling, and took Teigen's coat off. "This has been an unexpectedly enlightening evening in so many ways."

Teigen accepted the coat and folded it over one arm. "Shall I see you up?"

"No. But thank you. We don't want tongues to start wagging over nothing." Especially since Dahl was probably lying in wait for her to ask why she stormed out of dinner.

Teigen dipped his chin. "Thank you for sharing my *fårikål*."

"Thank you for sharing your secret."

He winked. "I have more. Just let me know when you feel like another adventure."

"I will." Selby realized with a shock that she meant it. "Good night."

As she climbed the stairs, Teigen's simple answer rang in her ears.

When she does, I suppose.

Selby shook her head and finished the climb to the second floor refusing to give it any more thought.

ᚾ ᚾ ᚾ

Bennett was in the room when Teigen reached it. "Where've you been? I've got news!"

Teigen hung his coat on the wrought-iron coat tree. "I went to a tavern I know for the world's best *fårikål*."

Bennett's eyes rounded. "Really? Is it far?"

"Nope. Two blocks." Teigen dropped in a chair to take his boots off. "You want me to show you tomorrow?"

"Sure! We can celebrate." Bennett looked like cat with a canary in its mouth.

Though he figured he already knew, Teigen asked, "Celebrate what?"

"I'm being promoted to lieutenant!"

"That's great news, Bennett! Congratulations." Teigen was sincerely happy for the man. "You're up there with Selby and Gunter, now."

"Guess what else?"

Teigen intentionally looked curious. "What?"

Bennett lowered his voice. "Look surprised when they tell you, okay? But you're being promoted to sergeant!"

"Am I?" Teigen grinned and tipped his head. "That means more money, right?"

"Only twenty kroner a week." Bennett shrugged. "But it's something, right? Eighty more a month!"

Teigen's evening with Selby had already put him in a good mood, and Bennett's excitement topped it off. "Let's go down and have a drink," he suggested. "First shot of aquavit's on me."

CHAPTER TWENTY

February 18, 1943
Oslo, Norway

Teigen chose to eat breakfast alone as he re-read the three letters he received yesterday. The one from Falko was upbeat and excited, describing where he was living without naming the city, and describing his coworkers—calling each one by a silly nickname in case his letter was intercepted.

Teigen decided he would write back after he talked to Elsa, figuring that then he would have something interesting to say.

He savored his mother's letter and read each paragraph twice, visions of his boyhood home vivid in his mind when he read her welcome words.

Because the troupe was a professional and public group, he was able to send his mother their itinerary without raising any Nazi suspicions. And though he invited his parents to attend the plays, he knew they probably wouldn't travel to see him. At least he could look forward to her letters when he reached the next hotel on their itinerary.

I'll write her after I talk to Elsa as well.

That was going to be a difficult letter to write, but he wanted his mother to know his continued heartbreak. Even at his age, he still longed for her maternal comfort and care.

However, he hadn't told her how hard it was for him in prison or the labor camp, and he never would. That sort of news would be too difficult for a mother to bear.

The oddest of the three letters was the one Tor sent to their parents. His mother forwarded the letter after it suffered many unfoldings, re-reading, and refoldings judging by its ragged condition. Unfortunately his brother, who was active duty in the Norwegian Army, wasn't able to include any details as to where he was and what he was doing. All he could say was that he received a promotion, and he was healthy.

That does mean the most to our parents.

Teigen wondered for the first time if he and Tor would cross paths now that he was a Milorg sergeant.

"That would be an interesting conversation," he muttered to himself as he tucked the letters into his back pocket.

"Are you ready, Hansen?" Dahl clapped him on the shoulder. "We don't want to keep Colonel Berntsen waiting."

"Yep." Teigen stood and gulped the last of his coffee. He collected the coat and scarf he brought down to breakfast. "Let's go."

There were only five of them in the group that headed through the snowy streets to the meeting: Dahl, Selby, Gunter, Bennett, and himself. He had been told that he needed to talk to the Colonel about Elsa, but he figured this was also the meeting where he would officially receive his promotion.

Especially since Bennett kept elbowing him and grinning.

Once the group assembled in the dressing room they waited in silence for the Colonel. When he arrived at five minutes after ten, he wasn't alone.

"I wanted you all to meet a very important gentleman—and I wanted him to meet you." Berntsen said once he and his guest had removed their coats. "This is Jens Christian Hauge, the national leader of Milorg."

While he had certainly heard of the Oslo lawyer, Teigen was surprised at his youth. The man couldn't be any older than his own twenty-eight years. Tall with short, dark hair and brown eyes, he was unremarkable to look at.

The minute he spoke, however, it was clear why a nation of resisters followed his lead.

"I'm glad to finally meet you all," he said in a clear, strong baritone. "I've heard good things about what the Royal Shakespearean Acting Troupe has been able to accomplish, and I congratulate you on the work you're doing."

"Thank you, sir." Dahl was actually blushing. "We're honored to serve."

"I understand you have a fairly new member," Hauge continued. "A teacher who was imprisoned at Grini and Kirkenes?"

If he thought Dahl's cheeks were flushing, Teigen believed his own were now on fire. His gaze shot to Dahl, wondering if he should speak, or wait to be pointed out.

What's the protocol?

"Yes, sir." Dahl turned a strained smile on Teigen. "This is Teigen Hansen."

Teigen stood and bent over to offer his hand to the seated leader. "It's a pleasure, sir."

Hauge stood as well. He pumped Teigen's hand and smiled into his eyes. "When did you return?"

"November," Teigen said. "At the very end."

Hauge let go of his hand. "Go on, sit." Both men reclaimed their seats and Hauge asked, "And when did you join Milorg?"

Teigen allowed a half-grin. "In November."

The lawyer laughed. "Well done. What's your rank?"

Teigen looked at Dahl, unsure what to say.

"Actually, sir." Dahl cleared his throat. "Hansen doesn't know this, but he's being promoted to sergeant today."

"It's well deserved, sir," Selby interjected. "As his commanding officer I can attest to his capabilities."

Teigen watched Selby as she offered the completely unexpected compliment. She didn't look at him, but she had a slight smile on her face.

"Thank you, Lieutenant Hovland," he said as sincerely as he could. He wanted her to know he meant it.

She did glance at him then, but said nothing more.

"And Sergeant Wilhelmsen," Dahl indicated a beaming Bennett, "is being promoted to Lieutenant."

"Hearty congratulations to both of you. And keep up the excellent work." Hauge stood again, reminding Teigen of the children's toy that popped out of a box when the crank was turned. "I'm afraid I do have to go, but I wanted to grab this opportunity while I could."

He faced Colonel Berntsen and shook his hand. "Carry on."

Hauge exited the dressing room, donning his swirling coat as he did.

For a moment, the remaining group just stared at each other, expressions of awe now making their appearances.

"Wow. That was *him*." Gunter's words seem to express a commonly shared reaction.

"And he's too busy to visit just anyone," Berntsen stated. "He really *is* impressed with what you've all done."

"And our famous teacher," Bennett teased.

"Shut up," Teigen warned.

For the next several minutes, Dahl and Berntsen discussed a laundry list of logistical details, finances, and confirmed the promotions. Teigen watched Selby, who still wouldn't look at him. Even so, she appeared calm.

At least she's not upset with me at the moment.

Teigen would take what he could get from her, and if 'not upset' was the best she gave for now, then he was satisfied.

"And now to the matter of Elsa Borg," Berntsen said, jerking Teigen's attention from Selby.

"Yes, sir?"

"I understand that you and Miss Borg were engaged?"

Teigen nodded. "For three years. We were *supposed* to get married in early May of 1940."

"Ah, yes." Berntsen understood the significance of the date. "Are you still engaged?"

"No. She broke off our engagement the day I signed and mailed my refusal to join Quisling's Norwegian Teachers Union. February tenth of last year." His pulse surged as her parting words—*go to hell*—resounded in his memory.

"When were you arrested?"

"On March twenty-fourth. I was sent to Grini." A date he'd never forget.

"Did you have any contact with Elsa Borg between February tenth and March twenty-fourth?" Now Berntsen sounded like the lawyer.

"No, sir." Teigen hesitated only a moment before asking, "Did she really have a baby?"

Berntsen nodded. "She did. On December twenty-seventh."

Teigen spread his hands, painfully ignoring the jagged knife those words drove through his heart. "Then it couldn't be mine. Obviously."

"Actually..."

Teigen turned and stared at Selby. "What?"

"The baby was born exactly nine months after your arrest," she said. "It's your word against hers."

"But I'm telling the truth!" Teigen blurted. "Besides the fact that we hadn't been, uh..." His cheeks were on fire again. "...*together* like that since she moved in with her parents the year before."

"Well, we can't prosecute her without proof," Berntsen said.

Teigen glared at the colonel, his eyes narrowing. "Then I'll get your proof."

"How?" Selby asked.

Teigen's seething regard moved to hers. "From her own mouth."

ᚾ ᚾ ᚾ

Selby was frightened by the sudden fury in Teigen's expression and the anger in his quiet voice. She wrapped her arms across her chest as if to protect herself from his wrath and pressed her spine against her chair.

"You'll need witnesses," Dahl warned him. "Someone needs to hear her admit that she lied."

"So I'll meet her in a public place.'

"Will she agree to meet you?" Bennett asked.

Some of the rage seemed to seep from Teigen's frame. "I don't know."

"Maybe if she thinks she's meeting someone else," Bennett suggested.

Teigen nodded. "Yes. It'll have to be that."

"Do you know anyone?" Selby asked.

Teigen looked at her again. His gaze was already clearer, calmer. The storm seemed to be passing as quickly as it hit.

Was that possible?

He shook his head slowly. "She didn't have many friends back then. I don't think I could name one."

Berntsen leaned forward. "Does she like the theater?"

Gunter grinned. "We'll give her free tickets!"

"And ambush her in her seat?" Teigen made a face. "That won't work."

"No… but what if we offered her a backstage tour as part of the prize?" Selby sat forward again. "She won't see *you* until she's backstage."

"And we'll all hide out of sight," Bennett said. "But we'll hear everything."

Teigen looked around the area as if judging the viability of that plan. "That might work."

"You can meet her in my changing room so it's private," Selby offered. "She won't realize we're all listening."

Teigen tipped his head sideways. "She won't come alone…"

"Then give her two tickets." Berntsen shrugged. "She can bring anyone she wants to. That doesn't matter."

Teigen rubbed his chin, his expression skeptical. "One last detail—how did she win this prize if she never entered a contest?"

Selby hated to keep pressing his sore spot, but the only possibility that was believable was, "From the hospital."

Teigen frowned at her. "What?"

"We'll tell her that there was a drawing. For all the women who gave birth there in the month of December." Selby gave Teigen a tender look and said softly, "She won…"

No one spoke, but all eyes were on Teigen, waiting.

His features were drawn and somber as he stared at the floor, elbows on his knees and his hands clasped loosely in front of them.

"How soon can we do this?"

Dahl answered him quietly, "We can deliver the tickets today."

Teigen sniffed. Selby swore she saw a drop of moisture hit the floor. He drew a deep breath, straightened, and didn't bother to wipe his wet eyes.

Selby's heart constricted with unexpected compassion. She recognized the man's gentle and caring core which he strove so hard to protect.

"Good," he grunted. "Let's get it done."

ᚿ ᚿ ᚿ

Teigen walked quickly through the icy streets straight to Oslo Secondary School. He asked Dahl to give him an hour to himself and the actor surprised him by offering three.

"I know you've taken more hits than any of us," Dahl said with definite respect in his voice. "Take the time you need. No problem."

As Teigen pulled open the school's heavy steel front doors, the familiar aromas of chalk, floor wax, steam heat, and wet wool hit him like a solid wall. Memories flooded him and threatened to drown him.

So much had happened to him in the last year that he felt like he was returning to another lifetime.

It was *another lifetime.*

Teigen walked into the office, stopping to see who was still there that he knew before the arrests.

"Teigen Hansen!" Oskar Jung, his erstwhile *Overlærer* bolted out of his office. "Good God, man! What happened to you?"

"Mister Hansen?" Sophie, Oskar's secretary scurried around a corner and stopped dead when she saw him. Then she burst into tears. "Oh, Mister Hansen—we were so worried about you!"

"I'm serious, Teigen." Oskar's brow was so low it nearly obscured his concerned gaze. "Have you been in Grini all this time?"

Teigen blinked. Did they not know?

And who would have told them?

Certainly not the Nazis who snuck him and four hundred and ninety-nine other teachers out of Oslo in middle of the night.

"No, Oskar." Teigen paused. "I was in Kirkenes."

Sophie let out a wail that rivaled a siren.

Oskar paled. "Can you stay a while? Do you have time to talk?"

Teigen nodded. "Yes."

"All right, go wait in my office." Oskar turned to the hysterical secretary. "Please call Jorgen Lasse and Dierks Halle to my office right away. Have someone cover their classes if you need to, but get them in here. Now."

Teigen followed Oskar into his glass-walled office and sat next to a pile of sturdy boxes. He looked questioningly at his former principal. "Are these new books?"

"Yes, they just came." Oskar walked around his desk and sat, looking at Teigen like he had returned from the dead.

In a way I did.

"I thought the Nazis wouldn't allow us to print any new textbooks that weren't German-edited." Teigen frowned. "Have the schools capitulated?"

"Of course not." Oskar finally smiled. "We outsmarted them. We dated these nineteen thirty-nine."

Teigen's jaw fell slack, then he roared his delighted laughter.

Dierks, the physics teacher, reached the office first. He whooped when he saw Teigen and fell on him with a bear hug.

"Aren't you a sight!" He backed away. "How *are* you?"

"Better now, I guarantee." Teigen's eyes fell to the paperclip on Dierks' lapel. "Why are—"

"Teigen?" Jorgen, the head of the sciences department, stood in the doorway. "Oh my God, Teigen!"

Jorgen pumped his hand and slapped his back. "I never thought I'd see you again!"

"You almost didn't," Teigen admitted. He tapped the paperclip on Jorgen's lapel. "What's the deal with people wearing paperclips?"

"It means stay together," Jorgen said. "Everyone started wearing them last spring. It's a non-violent protest, I guess you could say."

"Non-violent for us, true, but not for the Germans." Dierks laughed. "The Nazis hate them and they tried to pull them off our clothes."

Jorgen grinned and flipped his lapel over exposing a razor blade under the paper clip. "This stopped them."

Teigen laughed again. "Serves the bastards right."

"Sit. Sit," Oskar urged. Dierks and Jorgen obeyed and all three men faced Teigen. Even Sophie calmed herself enough to stand in the doorway.

Oskar clasped his hands on the desk. "All right. Now—tell us everything."

CHAPTER TWENTY ONE

The plan was for Karolina to find Elsa during intermission, congratulate her on winning the tickets, and instruct her to remain in her seat when the play ended so she could be escorted backstage for her tour.

Teigen was going to wait behind the door inside Selby's changing room. Karolina would have Elsa walk inside first, then step back and pull the door shut revealing Teigen's presence. What happened next was up to him.

He moved through the production like an automaton, moving set pieces with Bennett and Jonas, and working the curtains like he had done dozens of times before. Of course he knew which seats were given to Elsa, and he peeked through the curtains before the play began, waiting for her to appear.

Teigen needed to see her before she saw him. He needed that tactical advantage.

"Sure, you need to see her first," Bennett said the fourth time Teigen went to look for her. "You can't be distracted by surprise if you want to control the interview."

"She's there now." Teigen pulled away from the split in the fabric. "She brought her mother."

Bennett looked for himself. "The blonde in the blue dress?"

"Yeah... she wears blue a lot to make her eyes look bluer."

Teigen hated that he remembered that.

Bennett stepped back. "I'm sorry to say it, but she's beautiful."

"On the outside," Teigen qualified. "Turns out what's inside isn't so attractive after all, is it."

The play, *A Midsummer Night's Dream*, was finished and the curtains closed. Teigen opened them for the first curtain call as the cast of seven bowed. If the applause demanded it, he was ready for a second curtain call.

Part of him wanted to delay what was about to transpire, but the rest of him wanted to get it over with as soon as possible.

He caught Jonas' eye across the stage. Jonas nodded. They opened the curtains one last time.

When the curtains were closed, Teigen crossed the stage and ducked back into the dressing area. Gunter patted his back, and Karolina stood on her tiptoes to kiss his cheek.

"Good luck," she whispered before heading to the front of the house to collect Elsa and her mother.

Teigen knocked on the slightly open door to Selby's little changing room.

"Come in."

Teigen pushed the door open. Selby was still in costume, but had changed her wig and shoes.

"I normally would have a date on opening night," she said casually as she watched herself in the mirror and adjusted the wig she wore in public. "But I sent him a message that some of Quisling's high-ranking staff were rumored to be attending tonight and I needed to postpone until tomorrow."

Teigen knew that Selby's role as Nazi consort was only a role, and a valuable one at times, but he still hated that she did it. When he didn't say anything she turned to look at him.

"You'll do fine."

Teigen drew a chestfull of air and let it out slowly. "I honestly don't know what can make it fine."

Selby closed the space between them and took his larger rough hands in her smaller softer ones. "Say what you *need* to say, Teig. We don't all get the chance to confront those who wronged us, so make the best of it."

Teigen knew she was talking about her own mysterious past, and he hoped that someday he would learn her story. For now, he just needed to follow her advice.

"Thanks."

Selby let go of his hands and looped her arms around his neck. The kiss she planted on his cheek was entirely different than the brief peck from Karolina.

As she pulled away, Teigen stared into her eyes, surprised. For a moment she didn't move.

"I need to get out of the way." Selby turned and quickly left the room.

Teigen blew another deep breath and hid himself behind the open door. His body was zinging with adrenaline.

God be with me.

※ ※ ※

"This is where we do our hair and make-up," Karolina trilled. "And, by the way, I absolutely love yours!"

"Thank you." That was Elsa.

"What do you use on your skin?" Karolina's voice wasn't moving closer.

"Whatever I can find, I'm afraid. I'm dying to get my hands on some cold cream."

"Maybe I can slip you a little before you go," Karolina said in a conspiratorial tone. "We all use it to remove stage makeup."

"I would love that—thank you!"

Teigen heard their footsteps approaching. "And here's the lead actress's changing room. It's kind of small, so I'll let you ladies go in first."

The door pressed briefly against his chest, and then swung away and clicked closed. Teigen moved to block the only exit as Elsa and Dina Borg whirled and stared at him in shock.

"Teigen?" Dina squeaked.

Elsa's eyes flashed with anger. "What the hell are you doing here?"

"I'm part of the troupe." Simple unemotional answers on his part seemed the best plan.

"Really? You're not teaching anymore? That's no surprise," Elsa scoffed. "When were you released from Grini?"

Teigen stared at her, trying to hold back his burgeoning anger. "Three weeks after I was arrested…"

Her eyes rounded. "Wha—"

"And I was taken to Kirkenes."

Dina clapped her hands against her cheeks. "Oh nooo..." she moaned.

"You were?" Elsa scrambled to hide the surprise she clearly didn't mean to show. "I didn't know. I mean, *no* one knew that would happen."

Teigen felt like the ground wobbled under his feet. "Did you report me? Are you the reason I was arrested?"

Elsa's mouth opened and closed.

Teigen's hands turned into fists. "How could you do that?" he shouted.

Unemotional answers be damned.

"I made plans... it was necessary." She glared at him. "You were so stubborn and wouldn't listen to reason. You were your own worst enemy and so you got what you deserved."

"Elsa!" Dina's jaw dropped and her cheeks drained of color. "How can you say such a thing?"

Teigen grabbed the doorknob to steady himself. His face felt numb. "What sort of plans, Elsa?"

She lifted her chin and stared down her nose. "I was in demand."

"Demand?" That didn't make sense. "For what?"

"The program is called *Lebensborn*," she said proudly. "Heinrich Himmler started it years ago to assure the continued births of superior children."

Superior?

"Are you out of your mind, Elsa?" Teigen couldn't believe what he was hearing. "What'd you do? Go fuck a German?"

"There's no reason to be vulgar about it. He was an officer. A major," Elsa snipped. She folded her arms and spoke as if he were the errant one. "Norwegian girls with blue eyes and blonde hair are being recruited because of our pure Aryan blood."

Teigen shifted his shocked regard to Dina. "Did you know about this?"

Tears were streaming down the older woman's cheeks. "Not until she was three months gone. But what could I do then?"

"And once I was, they treated me like a princess," Elsa bragged.

Unthinkable pieces were falling into their terrible place. "You had to turn me in to prove your loyalty. So they would accept you."

Elsa flipped an unconcerned hand. "You were *begging* to be

caught with all your self-important loyalist decisions. I just sped up the process is all."

"But after you conceived," Teigen growled, "you told the Resistance that the baby was mine and you collected my salary from them."

"Oh... Did you know about that?" Elsa was momentarily diverted.

"I didn't!" Dina grabbed her daughter's arm. "I thought all the money was from the Nazi officer. What *else* have you done?"

"Where is the baby now?" Teigen demanded before Elsa could answer.

"With his father's family." Elsa's haughty gaze faltered momentarily and Teigen saw the first glimmer of regret. "They live outside of Berlin."

Teigen slumped against the door and rubbed his eyes. This situation was far, far worse than he thought. The woman he would never again think of as the former love of his life had just shown her true and traitorous colors.

"Oh, Elsa," he said quietly without looking at her. "You are in trouble. Deep, deep trouble."

"No, I'm not," she objected. "Hitler is going to win. And when he does, I'm going to move to Germany and live with my son and his father."

Teigen would have laughed if the situation wasn't so horribly tragic.

He met her defiant gaze. "None of that's going to happen, Elsa. Hitler will be soundly defeated, and then you'll never see your son or his father again."

She scowled. "You don't know that."

"Yes. I do." Teigen spoke with calm authority. There was one more thing that needed to happen before this interview was concluded. "Now, tell your mother that there's no way the baby could have been mine, because we were never intimate once you moved into their home."

"Of course the baby's not yours," Elsa sneered. "I already made that clear."

Teigen stepped to the side and opened the door. "Have you heard enough?"

ᚾ ᚾ ᚾ

Elsa sat in a chair, visibly stunned by what was happening around her.

While the actors went about the business of taking off their costumes and hanging them carefully in place, donning their modern clothes, removing their makeup and wigs, and replacing prop in their spots for tomorrow night, she waited to find out what was going to happen to her.

Teigen stood behind Colonel Berntsen, reading and correcting the notes the Milorg officer made. Berntsen nodded and turned to Elsa.

"All right. Let's get started."

Selby was in her changing room, and Teigen wondered why she hadn't come out yet. Dina was sobbing in a corner periodically wailing anew when she heard what Berntsen was telling her daughter.

"Milorg is now part of the Norwegian Army," Berntsen said to Elsa. "That gives us the authority to arrest you now, and put you on trial for treason once the war is over."

"Not if Germany wins," she snapped.

"True. But they won't." Berntsen gave her a tight, confident smile. "And delayed justice is still justice."

"So where do you think you're going to lock me up now?"

He looked at the paper he was writing more notes on. "We can send you to Grini."

Elsa straightened in her chair. "No you can't. That's a Nazi prison."

"No, Elsa," he said patiently. "It's a Norwegian prison. And your theft of Teigen Hansen's salary was a Norwegian crime."

For the first time, Elsa Borg looked terrified. "No!"

"If she pays the money back will the charge be dropped?" Teigen asked.

Berntsen looked up at him, his expression pensive. "The theft, yes. The treason, no."

Teigen shifted his gaze to Elsa. "What do you say to that, Elsa? If you're so certain Germany will win, it sounds like a perfect solution."

"How am I supposed to pay back so much money?" she scoffed.

"One kroner at a time."

Elsa flopped back in her seat and folded her arms angrily.

"That's a ridiculous answer."

"Fine, then." Teigen turned his attention back to Berntsen. "I'd like to place a lien on the Borg home in the amount of twelve thousand kroner."

"*What?*" burst from Elsa's lips.

Her mother wailed anew.

"I do believe that's fair." Berntsen made more notes.

"No, it's not!" Elsa cried. "We could lose our home!"

Berntsen lifted his eyes to hers. "Yes, you could."

Teigen walked around her chair and stood over Elsa. He leaned forward so she was forced to tilt her head back to look up at him. He lifted one stiff finger in front of her face.

"Let me be extremely clear about this. You gave my name to the Nazis accusing me of who-knows-what. Didn't you?"

She shrugged.

"As a result of your actions, I spent a month in prison and seven months—SEVEN MONTHS!"

Elsa jumped when he shouted. There was no insolence in her expression anymore.

"Seven months deep in the Arctic Circle, crowded in a hut made out of cardboard—CARDBOARD!"

Elsa winced.

"I did hard physical labor twelve hours a day. Every. Single. DAY."

Elsa's lower lip began to quiver.

"I was freezing, and I was starving, Elsa. And why *was* that, exactly?"

She shook her head.

He leaned closer. "ANSWER ME!"

She was crying in gulping sobs. "Be-because I g-gave them your name."

"And *why* did you give them my name, exactly?"

She covered her face shook her head again.

"I'll tell you why—because you are nothing more than a spoiled and selfish girl who has no thought for anyone but herself."

Teigen straightened. "And then you *lied*, and you stole *my* salary from your countrymen."

Elsa's wracking sobs echoed from behind her palms.

Teigen spoke slowly and clearly. "If all that happens to you now is that I foreclose on your house, then you need to count yourself very, *very* lucky."

Teigen looked around the dressing room. Eight of his troupe members watched him silently, soberly. Selby opened the door to her changing room and stared at him, half-hidden by the door.

Teigen heaved a heavy sigh. He'd said almost everything he needed to say to Elsa. Only one thing remained. He waited until she lowered her hands to look at him.

"Your last words to me told me to go to hell." His voice was low and calm. "And I did. Now it's your turn."

Teigen turned around, grabbed his coat, and walked out the stage door in search of a tavern.

CHAPTER TWENTY TWO

Selby pulled on her coat and ran out the door after Teigen. He was already half a block away.

"Teigen!" she shouted. She ran as fast as she dared on the icy pavement. "Teigen!"

His voice floated back to her, frigid as the air that carried it. "Go away."

Selby struggled onward. "You shouldn't be alone right now."

He was gaining distance. "The taverns aren't empty, I'm pretty certain of it."

"I want to talk to you!"

"I don't want to talk to you."

She slipped badly and nearly fell; her arms wind-milled to keep her balance and she was glad he didn't see.

Teigen turned a corner. She was going to lose him.

"Sergeant! Halt!" she bellowed as loud as she could.

She found a bare spot and rushed forward.

Teigen reappeared around the corner looking back at her like he could spit fire. "Are you *joking?*"

Selby didn't say anything until she was standing in front of him. The streetlight at the corner encircled them both in an incongruently romantic light and gave Teigen an angelic halo of blond hair and frosted breath.

Neither idea could be farther from the truth.

"You don't want to talk to *me*," Selby panted. "Or you don't want to talk to anyone."

The man looked miserable; that was no surprise. "Anyone." That was the answer she hoped for. "Well, I just wanted to tell you that you were brilliant just now."

"Brilliant?" Teigen's face crumpled in confusion. "I was horrible."

Now Selby's expression imitated his. "Horrible? What are you talking about?"

"I just—I don't want to talk about it." He started to take a step, but stopped himself. "Am I free to go, Lieutenant?"

Selby pulled rank, glad at the moment that she could. "No. Not until we get this cleared up."

Teigen threw his hands in the air, growled, and turned in a frustrated circle. Then he planted both feet and leaned toward her.

"I'm not proud of what I said to Elsa. Is that clear enough?"

That surprised her. "But you only said what was true."

"I called her names!"

"No, you didn't." Selby had heard everything clearly. "You called her spoiled and selfish. And her actions obviously deserved that description."

Teigen straightened and dragged his fingers over his bare head. It made his hair stick up, enhancing the halo effect. "But I *yelled* at her."

Selby was stunned. In her experience with men, name calling and yelling were just the beginning. Yet Teigen seemed to believe he had severely transgressed.

"I would've yelled at her, too," Selby admitted. "She didn't have any idea what her actions cost you and she needed to know."

Teigen rested his hands on his hips pushing aside the open front of his coat. Selby responded by pulling her coat tighter.

Is the man never *cold?*

"She'll be arrested for treason when the war is over…" His low tone and pained expression displayed the sorrow that knowledge brought him.

"But not for theft," Selby reminded him sternly. "You couldn't save her from her terrible choice to consort with the enemy. But if she pays you back, the theft charges will be dropped."

"And if she doesn't, then I throw her and her parents out of their home," he reminded her.

"That'll be your choice to make at the time." Selby risked resting a hand on his arm. "You could rent it to them for a kroner a year if you wanted, and only claim it when they die."

Teigen stared at her, his chin jutting forward and his eyes wide. Then his gaze dropped to the ground. For a minute he didn't move or speak before he raised his head and considered her again, now with a furrowed brow.

"Why are you doing this?"

Selby hesitated. "Doing what?"

"Coming after me, telling me I was brilliant, talking to me like... I don't know."

Selby felt unexplained tears prick her eyelids. She knew the reason, but she was afraid tell him, to let her wall crack. She couldn't afford a breech.

"Selby?" Teigen looked concerned. "What's wrong?"

She wiped her cheeks. "Damn it."

Teigen looped his arm through hers and started walking toward the tavern with the *fårikål*. "I'm not disobeying your orders because I'm still in your presence, Lieutenant."

Selby couldn't respond. She was crying in earnest now.

When they reached the door, Teigen opened it and pushed her inside. Then he led her to a booth in the farthest corner and sat her on the side which put her back to the room.

"Are you hungry?"

She shook her head.

"Aquavit and beer," he told the barmaid. "Two."

Selby felt like a complete idiot, crying for no reason.

Teigen pushed his coat off his shoulders and leaned his elbows on the table. "Tell me what's wrong."

She shook her head and wiped her cheeks. "I don't want to talk about it."

"To me? Or to anyone?" he parroted her earlier challenge.

"I don't know..."

"Well, since I talked to you when I didn't want to, I believe it's your turn now." He waited for the barmaid to set down their drinks and leave before he continued. "That's only fair."

Not ready to down the aquavit, Selby took a sip of the beer. She hoped it would clear her throat enough that she could speak somewhat normally.

She raised blurry eyes to his. "It's not something I ever talk about."

Teigen looked surprised. "Even to your friends?"

Selby made a face. "I don't have friends."

Teigen leaned back and folded his arms. "What about Dahl? Or Bennett?"

"They're men." *Obviously.*

"Karolina?"

Selby laughed a little. "She's… an actress."

"So are you."

Selby shook her head. "No. Being an actress is a role I play. Just like the street urchin. Or Nazi girlfriend. It's not who I am."

Teigen's gaze pinned her. "Who are you, Selby?"

There was no chance in hell she was going to answer that. Instead, she lifted the shot glass of aquavit to her lips, threw her head back, and let the burning alcohol sear its way to her stomach.

ᚾ ᚾ ᚾ

Teigen watched Selby gulp her aquavit and follow it with a long swallow of beer. One thing was clear: she was not going to answer the question.

Time to change the course of the conversation.

"I'm still a teacher, I think," he said in a matter-of-fact tone, acting as if she hadn't definitively ignored his question. "It's sort of a personality type. Not something you can change about yourself."

Selby set her beer down and looked at him through narrowed eyes. "I know what you're doing."

He shrugged. "What?"

She tilted her head as she looked at him. "I won't answer your question, so you're pretending you didn't ask it."

Did she really think that?

Teigen leaned forward. "No, Selby. I'm not pretending anything." He smiled a little. "I'm just respecting your reluctance to answer."

Teigen straightened and downed his own shot. As he chased it with a sip of the cooled beer, he watched her over the rim of his glass.

His response seemed to bring her near to tears again. What had happened to her? Teigen wanted to pull her into his arms and protect her from whatever had hurt her.

She'd scratch my eyes out if I did.

He bit his lips and wiped his mouth to keep from laughing at the mental image of what that would look like.

"I'm... not used to... that kind of respect," she managed finally.

"Dahl respects you, Selby. I think he's in love with you." *Not that he knows what to do about it.* "Am I wrong?"

"No." Selby sighed. "But he walks on eggshells around me and I hate it. That's not respect. It's fear."

If what Teigen had observed could be trusted, he knew the answer; but he asked anyway.

"Are you in love with him?"

She gave him a resigned look. "No. I've never been in love with anyone."

Teigen gave a little chuckle. "Turns out, neither have I. At least not real, unconditional, I'd-die-for-you love."

"Don't hold your breath waiting, Teig. That doesn't exist." Selby closed her eyes and sipped her beer.

Teigen wondered if that was true. It seemed his parents had that sort of love, but he couldn't know what went on between them behind closed doors.

Now he sighed. "You could be right about love." He pointed a finger at her. "But do I know that friendship exists."

"I suppose..." She set down her empty beer glass. "I guess I've never taken the time to make friends."

"That's not true," Teigen stated. "You did tonight."

Selby looked surprised. "Tonight?"

Teigen laughed. "Yeah! You chased after me, Sel. You even ordered me to halt so you could catch up with me."

She waved her hand. "I only did that because you wouldn't stop."

"No—you did it so you could tell me that you thought I was brilliant, even after I said I didn't want to talk to you." Teigen gave her a satisfied smile. "That's what friends do."

She stared at him and twirled her empty beer glass on the table. "And you brought me in here and took care of me when I fell apart for absolutely no reason."

He let the *no reason* go for now. "I've had practice being a friend."

Selby's brow quirked. "I've never had a man talk to me the way you have tonight."

"And I've never had a woman pull rank on me so she could compliment me." He gulped the last of his beer and set the glass down. "We should go—it's almost curfew."

※ ※ ※

Selby didn't feel like talking as Teigen held her elbow and steadied her on the slippery walk back to the hotel. So much happened that surprised her tonight that she really needed to think about how those things made her feel.

Some of it was shaking her long-held convictions about men. Well, about *one* man. Teigen Hansen was definitely unique.

Inside the lobby, Teigen let go of her arm and walked beside her to the foot of the stairs. "Thanks for… you know."

Was he blushing? Or were his cheeks just red from the cold?

"Thank you, too." Selby stuck out her hand on impulse.

Bemused, Teigen took it.

Selby shook his hand. "Friends shake hands, right?"

Teigen grinned. "Yep."

Shelby dropped his hand, turned and climbed the stairs. She couldn't stop smiling.

February 19, 1943
Oslo, Norway

Dahl found Teigen touching up the paint on a worn scenery flat. "I need to talk to you."

"Okay." Teigen stuck his paintbrush into a jar of turpentine. His first unlikely thought was that this conversation was going to be about Selby.

Then he saw the letter in Dahl's hand. "What's going on?"

Dahl gave him a crooked grin. "You're going to love this. Let's go in the front of the house to talk."

Teigen followed Dahl halfway into the audience seats. The men sat one chair apart and faced each other.

Dahl handed Teigen the letter. "Read this."

A master carpenter in Ålesund has begun building desks with a small space in the back which is intended for a bomb. His plan is that the desks will be delivered to the Nazi SS offices when Milorg knows there are few Norwegians in the building.

When the SS officer opens the front drawer it will trigger a bomb which explodes when he closes it again.

I seem to recall that Sergeant Hansen was a chemistry teacher. Ask him to start working on a bomb that fits this plan immediately. I want to see something when you return.

Major Hans Helgesen
Bergen

Teigen looked up at Dahl, surprised that the common joke was becoming a reality. "I'm really going to build bombs?"

"Can you?" Dahl asked. "I mean, can you make bombs that fit that scenario?"

"I'll sure try, won't I!" Teigen's mind was already working. "There has to be a detonator, and the explosive material. But it has to be stable enough to be jostled around when the desk is moved…"

"Maybe when the drawer opens, it pulls the pin from a grenade," Dahl suggested.

Teigen looked at him, surprised. His mind went straight to the heavily guarded crates of ammunition that he unloaded at the docks in Kirkenes. "Can we get hold of grenades?"

Dahl's mouth twisted. "No, not easily."

Teigen nodded and handed the letter back to Dahl. "You'll destroy that, right?"

"Yep." Dahl stood. "I'll leave this to you, then. Let me know if you need anything."

Teigen stood as well. "When I finish the flat, I need to go out for an hour or so. To start working on this before we leave Oslo."

"Okay…" Dahl raised his brows in silent question.

"I have sources here. Trustworthy ones." Teigen winked. "I need to pick their brains while I can."

N N N

"Oh, this is going to be fun." Dierks Halle, Teigen's physics teacher friend rubbed his hands together. "Blowing up SS assholes is a dream come true."

"The first problem is I don't know how big the compartment is," Teigen said. "And the second is that the bomb needs to be powerful enough to kill the man and destroy at least ten feet around him."

Dierks nodded. "Yeah. Yeah. You don't want to leave clues. I got it."

Teigen sat on the edge of Dierks' desk, pencil and paper in hand. "So, ideas?"

"Does it have to blow up when he closes the drawer? Or can it blow when he opens it?"

Teigen thought about that. "Good question. I don't think it would matter."

Dierks stroked his chin. "So the detonator could be something like a regular cigarette lighter where the flint gets struck when the desk is opened..."

"Or a piston that mixes something when the drawer opens, and it explodes when it's compressed." Teigen wrote both ideas down. "The key is we have to use materials that don't rouse suspicion when we collect them."

"Gunpowder is easy to make. It's just sulfur, charcoal, and potassium nitrate—saltpeter," Dierks said.

"Yeah. I just hope I don't have to go digging around manure piles for it." Teigen tapped the pencil against his chin. "If you mix glycerin with potassium permanganate it'll catch fire after a few minutes."

"Engineer the bomb so they get mixed when the drawer opens, then they ignite the gunpowder when they flame up."

"That could work." Teigen wrote it down. "What else?"

"Dry aluminum powder and dry powdered iodine?" Dierks suggested.

Teigen shook his head. "There's too much smoke before they flame. It'd be a warning."

"True..."

"What about hydrogen peroxide and potassium iodide?" Teigen mused. "That produces heat, plus a huge amount of oxygen which is highly flammable."

Dierks shook his head. "The oxygen is too hard to contain."

"Yeah, you're right." Teigen looked at the clock. "I need to get back to the theater. At least I have a start."

He folded the paper and stuck it in his pocket. "Why don't you come to the play?"

Dierks wrinkled his nose. "Not one for Shakespeare. But thanks."

Teigen put his coat on. "Are you interested in helping me make some explosions?"

Dierks' eyes lit up like detonators. "You bet I am!"

CHAPTER TWENTY THREE

February 25, 1943
Oslo, Norway

Teigen watched the explosion from behind a rock. When the experimental bomb exploded, Dierks slapped him on the back.

"I think we've got it," he said. "Two viable options."

Teigen walked toward the scorched earth to measure the circumference of the snow circle, encouraged by their long day of trial and error. Today was the troupe's last day in Oslo so Teigen had hurried to collect the supplies they needed. He wanted to make use of Dierks' knowledge while he could.

Dierks had a car, so he drove them ten miles outside of Oslo into the surrounding mountains.

The men, both scientists, tried a few different combinations and machinations, along with meticulously measuring and logging the amount of the ingredients to control the size of the blast.

"So option one is immediate: rig up a cigarette lighter so the flint sparks when the drawer is opened," Teigen clarified. "And that ignites the pouch of gunpowder."

"Yep. You could also have the drawer depress it when it's closing instead." Dierks shrugged. "Depending on how the desk is actually constructed."

Teigen handed Dierks one end of the measuring tape. "Don't

look around, but we're being watched," he whispered.

Dierks' eyes widened. "Germans?"

Teigen shook his head and spoke in a normal tone as he turned and walked to the edge of the blackened ground. "I'm guessing twelve feet."

He squatted there and glanced around, searching for more of the movement that had caught his eye.

"Close! It's thirteen." Dierks walked back toward him, his face pale. "What do you want to do now?"

Teigen stood. A flash of dingy blue appeared beside their pile of equipment about thirty yards away and quickly disappeared.

"We need at least one more try with the glycerin and potassium permanganate." Teigen turned and took long strides toward their stash with Dierks hurrying to keep up. "I need to time the lag between the glycerin hitting the mixture and the actual flame."

"Are we safe?" Dierks murmured.

Teigen hoped his friend would understand his answer. "We're safe as two men can be when they play with explosives." In other words, there was no external threat.

"Got it."

Dierks filled a tiny flask with glycerin and topped it with a cork into which they had fastened a tiny eye screw attached to a thin wire. Then he clamped the flask to a block of wood at a forty-five degree angle.

Teigen held a pre-filled fabric pouch of gunpowder and a tin lid with the potassium permanganate. "We'll use the same spot."

So I can keep an eye on our intruder.

It was hard to determine where there were new tracks in the snow since Teigen and Dierks had stomped around the area all day and even made a couple trips into the woods to pee. But as the pair walked away from the jumble of supplies, Teigen whispered, "My lunch sack is gone."

Dierks shot him a side glance but said nothing.

The men set up the bomb in the center of the blackened circle. Then they backed away about twenty feet and crouched behind a tree.

"We can see our camp better from here," Teigen explained when Dierks looked surprised that they weren't going back behind the rock.

Dierks held up his watch. "I'm ready when you are."

Teigen called out, "Three. Two. One."

He pulled in the wire, uncorking the glycerin which poured over the potassium. Then he sprang to his feet and bolted after the flash of blue reappeared.

Teigen reached their supplies before he heard the explosion behind him. The intruder was about twenty-five yards ahead of him, scrambling through the woods.

At this point, Teigen only needed to follow the fresh tracks in the snow. And judging by the length of their strides, Teigen had a definite advantage over the thief.

"Hey!" he shouted. "I'm not going to hurt you!"

The fugitive apparently didn't believe him because he continued to flee.

"I'm going to catch you!" Teigen forced the words past his gulping breaths—they were running uphill. "Just stop!"

The figure stumbled then and fell flat out. Teigen reached the spot before the flailing escapee could regain footing and he tackled the blue-clad frame.

"Let me go!" cried an adolescent male voice.

Teigen was shocked at the thin, bony body in his grip and understanding flooded his mind. "You can have the food," he said. "I don't care! Just calm down."

The boy stopped struggling, but his body was as stiff as the towering trees surrounding them. Teigen loosened his hold a little.

"What are you doing out here?"

The boy sniffed, but didn't answer. Teigen had hold of him from behind so he couldn't see the young man's face.

"Hiding from the brown bastards?"

The boy hesitated, then nodded.

"Are you alone?" Teigen pressed.

He nodded again.

Teigen felt the boy's body relax in increments. "If I let go, will you stay and talk to me?"

When he didn't answer, Teigen offered, "I'm a sergeant with Milorg. I can help you."

At that the boy twisted to look at him. Scared brown eyes searched his from under a filthy mop of what looked like blond straw.

Even in the freezing air, Teigen could smell the dirt on the boy's body.

Teigen let go and rolled to the side, sitting in the snow. "What's your name?"

The boy sat up, warily brushing snow from the front of his clothes. "B-ben."

"My name's Teigen." He held out his hand. After a pause, Ben accepted it and gave it a firm shake. "Nice to meet you. Why are you hiding, Ben?"

Ben looked like he was going to cry. "My full name is Benjamin. Benjamin Isaksen."

Teigen's shoulders slumped. "You're Jewish."

"My father's Jewish." Ben shot Teigen a challenging look. "My mother's family has been in Norway since the Vikings."

"Doesn't matter to those Nazi assholes, though, does it?"

Ben shook his head.

"Have you been in the mountains for the last four months?"

"Some of them, yeah."

"So none of your family is still in Norway?"

Ben's composure crumbled like fresh snow. "They—they shot my mother the night they came to take us." He wiped his cheeks leaving streaks of dirt across his face. "They—they said she was a traitor for breeding with filth. They left her body lying in the yard."

"And your father?" Teigen asked gently.

"They said they were taking him to Germany for 'experimentation'—him and my older brother." Raw gasping sobs convulsed Ben's overly-thin frame.

Teigen fought his own empathetic tears. "How'd you get away?"

"I was hiding in a closet—the one with the coal chute. I climbed out and ran."

Ben's face fell into his hands as fresh spasms gripped him. Teigen wiped his eyes before pulling the boy into his arms. Ben's cold and starving existence was so close to his own recent imprisonment that fear and hopelessness exploded in his chest, leaving him shaking.

He held Ben while they both calmed, rocking him slowly in the snow, until the boy's sobs abated to gasping, hiccoughing breaths.

"How old are you?" he asked when he thought the boy could speak again.

The answer came from behind his arm. "Fifteen."

Teigen unwound his arms and grabbed Ben's shoulders. The

realization that his own arms probably felt this thin just a few months ago solidified his resolve.

He looked into the boy's eyes. "You're my cousin now, do you understand what I'm saying?"

Ben's brow furrowed. "No."

"I'm taking you with me," Teigen stated. "We'll get you new papers and a new name. As far as the brown bastards will know, you're my cousin and I'm tutoring you for your secondary school exams."

"Are you a teacher?" was apparently the first question that came to Ben's mind.

Teigen smiled crookedly. "I used to be. Now I work with a traveling group of Milorg actors."

Teigen climbed to his feet. "Come on. Follow me."

Ben clambered to his feet, awkward, long-legged and knobby as a newborn foal.

N N N

Dierks made no comment about Teigen's unexpected companion, his only response being to open the car windows a little when the heater intensified the boy's unwashed aroma.

"He's about my size. I'll bring over some clothes," Dierks offered as he and Teigen carefully unloaded the backpacks of explosive materials from the trunk of the car.

Teigen shouldered the packs while Ben stood nearby, hunch-shouldered and clearly frightened. "Thanks for everything, Dierks."

Dierks grinned. "It's been fun. And I'll follow the news to see if our efforts are successful."

Teigen grinned and shook his friend's hand. "I'll see you in six months."

As Dierks drove away, Teigen led Ben into the hotel's lobby. "Just keep your eyes forward and walk beside me."

Once safely in the elevator, Ben heaved a shaky breath.

"After we get you cleaned up and in new clothes, no one's going to give you a second look because you're with me," Teigen assured him. "Do you mind being called a Hansen?"

Ben said no, but his face resembled a woeful hound.

"It's not forever. You can be an Isaksen again when the Germans are defeated."

"Okay."

Teigen contemplated what to put on the boy's papers. "What was your mother's maiden name?"

"Thorkelsen."

The elevator doors opened and Teigen led Ben down the hall to the room he shared with Bennett.

"After we leave Oslo tomorrow, I'll make sure you have a bed." Teigen unlocked the door and opened it. "But for tonight, sleeping on the floor beats sleeping in the snow, at least."

Ben walked into the room. "Leave Oslo?"

"I told you—it's a traveling troupe." Teigen crossed to the bathroom and turned on the water. "Come on in here and take a shower. Dierks is bringing you some new clothes."

Ben stood in the white-tiled bathroom doorway looking like he'd entered heaven.

"You can use the soap and the shampoo there." Teigen pointed to his own toiletries. "And that comb, if you don't have lice." Teigen leaned closer, examining the boy's hair. "Do you have lice?"

"No. I stole gasoline and used it to keep the nits away."

Teigen nodded. "Good."

He stepped out of the small, white-tiled room. "Toss your clothes out after you take them off. If they're not too worn, I'll have the hotel laundress wash them tonight."

Ben gazed at him, looking stunned. "Thanks."

"Okay. Get to it. I'll see about supper." Teigen almost closed the door before he remembered to ask, "Are there things you don't eat?"

"No, we didn't observe the laws. I'll eat anything." He looked like he was going to cry again. "We even celebrated Christmas."

Teigen smiled reassuringly and pulled the bathroom door solidly shut. Well. That's that.

Now what?

※ ※ ※

Bennett, Teigen's unflappable roommate, accepted the story of Teigen's new charge without blinking.

"I'd have done the same thing," he said softly. "I mean, you couldn't just leave him out there by himself."

"I hope Dahl agrees." Teigen stretched out on his bed while he waited for the shower to turn off. "I'll take financial responsibility for him, of course."

"We could make him part of the troupe," Bennett suggested while he changed clothes for dinner. "We can always use another hand, and at his age he might be able to pass information without attracting unwanted attention."

Teigen's mouth twisted. "I don't want to put him in danger. He's had enough of that."

Bennett stood in front of the mirror, watching himself button his shirt. "Are you really going to tutor him?"

"Sure. Why not?"

"Just wondering." Bennett spun to face him. "How do I look?"

Teigen laughed. "Like the ladies better be careful. Where're you going?"

"Supper and a dance hall. You pay five kroner to dance with a girl."

While that sounded like hell for himself, it sounded like fun for his gregarious friend. "Who's going with you?"

"Gunter." Bennett frowned. "Do you think he'll get all the good-looking girls?"

"No, I think you'll do fine." Teigen laughed again. "He's not Dahl, after all."

Bennett rolled his eyes. "No kidding. When our glorious star is around, women don't notice anyone else."

The bathroom door opened and Ben exited in a cloud of rising steam. One white towel was wrapped around his head and a second around his waist. His gaze jumped to Bennett.

"Uh…"

"Hi, Ben. I'm Bennett." The props manager held out a hand. "Welcome to the Royal Shakespearean Acting Troupe."

Ben kept a tight grip on the towel at his waist with one hand but shook Bennett's hand with the other. "Shakespeare? Really?"

Bennett nodded. "You like Shakespeare?"

"I love Shakespeare."

"Really?" Teigen sat up. "You do?"

The adolescent blushed. "I've read *Romeo and Juliet* at least a dozen times."

"Well, we've focused on the comedies," Bennett explained. "Considering the condition of the world at the moment."

There was a knock at the door.

Ben leapt back into the bathroom and closed that door.

Bennett answered the knock and was handed a pile of clothes tied with a rope. "Uh, thank you?"

Teigen climbed off the bed to claim the clothing. "That's for Ben. From Dierks."

"I'll take this opportunity to leave you then." Bennett stepped into the hall. "Have a good evening."

"You, too," Teigen said as the door closed. He walked to the bathroom door and rapped a knuckle against it. "Hey, Ben—the clothes are here. I'll leave them on the bed and take yours down to the laundry."

"Okay."

"After that our supper should be about ready."

"Okay."

Teigen hefted the sack of filthy clothes over his shoulder and left the room, locking the door behind him.

CHAPTER TWENTY FOUR

February 26, 1943
Oslo, Norway

Teigen spent last night on the floor. After their supper he went to speak with Dahl about his changed situation, and brought the troupe's captain to meet Ben. He found the boy curled in a ball on his bed, dead to the world.

"Guess I'll meet him tomorrow," Dahl said when they retreated into the hallway. He gave Teigen a scrutinizing look. "Are you sure you want to take him on?"

No.

But sometimes in life doing the right thing was required, even if it was less than convenient. Or even downright hard.

"Bennett suggested we could use him as a runner," Teigen floated the idea. "He thinks that being so young, Ben won't attract suspicious attention."

"That'll be Ben's decision, I think." Dahl said as he turned to leave. "In the meantime we'll definitely put him to work."

Teigen stretched and knocked on the bathroom door. "Are you almost ready for breakfast? I think my navel is touching my backbone."

Ben opened the door, dressed in his new clothes. He looked embarrassed. "I wanted to shave…"

Teigen considered the adolescent's nearly invisible blond sprouts. "You shaved last night for the first time in months. Give your face a rest until tomorrow."

Ben nodded. "I just want to look respectable."

Teigen's gaze traveled over the clothes that were the right length, but hung on Ben's skinny frame. "You look fine. Now let's apply our efforts to fattening you up."

ᚾ ᚾ ᚾ

Selby heard all about Teigen's new acquisition from Dahl when they shared a breakfast table. When Dahl finished eating and went to settle the troupe's hotel bill, Selby decided to wait in the dining room to see for herself.

What was Teigen thinking, she wondered as the waiter cleared the dirty dishes. What unmarried man would drag a teen-aged stranger out of the woods and give him his own bed?

Selby stared out the window at the blustery morning and sipped her tea. Teigen was certainly interesting.

"Selby?"

She turned and looked up into Teigen's bright green eyes. Her heart lurched a little. "Good morning."

"May we join you for breakfast?"

"Um, yes. Of course." Selby set her cup down and waved at the empty chairs. "I've already eaten, but I'll stay and keep you company."

A tall, lanky teen stepped out from behind Teigen and claimed a chair. His blond hair was overlong, his brown eyes wary, and his clothes were loose.

"Thank you, ma'am," he said in a voice that sounded uncomfortable with its newly lower range.

Teigen pulled out the chair next to Selby. "Selby Sunde, meet Ben Thorkelsen Hansen. The newest member of our troupe."

Ben's gaze shot to Teigen. "That's my name?"

Teigen unfolded his napkin. "Do you object?"

"No. I like it." Ben blushed, his cheeks turning a blotchy red. "Thanks."

Selby watched Teigen encourage Ben to order as much food as he wanted. His attention to the boy was matter-of-fact, respectful. As if talking to a peer. Nothing like she expected.

"I'll be tutoring Ben while we travel," Teigen said after taking a bracing sip of coffee. "So when this mess is finally over, he can take his university exams."

"Mister Hansen says he taught upper secondary school," Ben ventured.

Of course he knows how to treat the boy. He'd taught that age in school for the last several years.

Teigen leaned toward Ben. "If we are to be believed as cousins and troupe mates, you'll need to call me Teigen."

Ben's face reddened again. "Yes, sir."

Teigen flashed a crooked grin. "Considering our age difference, I'll allow *sir* if that's what you're comfortable with."

Ben's eyes widened as his breakfast plate was place in front of him.

"Eat as much as you can," Teigen instructed. "But don't make yourself sick. Remember what I told you last night."

Selby's curiosity was awakened. "What did you tell him?"

Teigen waited until his own plate was set in front of him before he answered. "When you've been starving, it's hard on your body to eat too much too soon. And what you eat is important. Nothing too hard to digest."

He knows because… Once again his terrible ordeal rose up in front of her.

"Did you have trouble when you got back?" she asked.

Ben looked at her, surprised. With his mouth full he asked, "Back from where?"

Teigen's expression sobered and a haunted look dimmed his gaze. "I was one of the teachers taken to the work camp in Kirkenes. Do you know about that?"

Ben stopped chewing and stared at Teigen. "How long were you there?"

Teigen cleared his throat. "Start to finish."

Ben's gaze stayed fixed on Teigen. "So you know what it's like…"

He nodded. "I do."

At that moment, Selby understood everything. "No wonder you rescued Ben."

Teigen's brow twitched and he looked at her as if she was dense. "I've been freezing and starving and hopeless, it's all true—but I wasn't alone. Ben's situation was far worse than mine. There's no way that I would've left him out there."

Selby's throat thickened. "Some men would have."

Teigen shook his head and speared his potatoes with his fork. "A real man would not."

Ben looked suddenly uncomfortable. "I—I think I need to go upstairs…"

Teigen handed him the room key. "Come back down when you're done. I'll wait here."

Ben grabbed the key and bolted.

Selby was still a little hesitant about the wisdom of Teigen's unorthodox actions. "Aren't you afraid he'll steal from you again?"

Teigen coughed a laugh. "There's nothing to steal."

Selby frowned. "I thought you collected your things from the boarding house."

"I did." He smiled at her. "But I was a bachelor living alone in a single room. I didn't have much."

Selby pointed at the unfamiliar sweater he was wearing. "Is that sweater from before?"

"Yep." Teigen looked down at the traditionally Nordic pattern. The shade of green around his shoulders perfectly matched his eyes. "I'm glad it was still there. It's one of my favorites."

Selby blinked in surprise. "Wasn't everything still there?"

"Mostly. All my clothes, my shaving kit—thank goodness—and the wooden chest from my chemistry class which came in very handy this week, I have to say."

That was it? "You certainly led a Spartan existence."

Teigen shrugged. "I don't need much. But now I'm glad that my textbooks were in the box. I was going to give them back to the school, but instead I'll use them with Ben."

At the mention of his new 'cousin' Selby's composure began to slip again. This man's actions were so… *unexpected.*

"I need to go." Selby stood and dropped her napkin on the table. "I'll see you when we leave."

She turned and hurried out of the dining room before Teigen could see her tears.

ᚾ ᚾ ᚾ

Selby lay on her bed and sobbed. Teigen Hansen's character was shaking her to her core—and she hated him for it.

Every wall that she so carefully constructed—resting firmly on the foundation that all men were, at heart, brutish, selfish and cruel—was threatening to crumble in the face of the teacher.

Even when Teigen faced the scheming Elsa and her lies, the worst he did was shout. And then he unbelievably offered her a way out of at least part of the hole she'd dug for herself; the only part he held some control over.

He might even have done more if he could. That thought prompted a fresh wash of tears.

And now, when a fugitive half-Jewish boy stole his food out in the wooded mountains, Teigen responded by pulling the adolescent under his protection. Without hesitation he provided food, clothing, and shelter for now, and tutoring so Ben could resume his life when the Germans were defeated at last.

What kind of man does something like that?

The kind who tells you that you're better than you know.

Teigen's startling words to her about how she should lead the men under her authority had changed her life. Since then, she made an effort to loosen the reins and allow the troupe's soldiers to act on their own ideas. As a result the troupe was accomplishing more.

Selby sat up and wiped her cheeks. She needed to be at the ship in just over an hour for the journey to Kristiansand, and she needed to be clear-headed for their on-board rehearsals of *The Winter's Tale.*

Teigen mustn't know how her feelings toward him were changing; she couldn't give him that power over her. If he knew she might someday be willing to explore a relationship with him it would ruin the friendship they were building.

She washed her face, combed the blonde wig, and applied lipstick. The actress looked somberly back at her from the mirror.

When will you stop acting?

Selby heaved a ragged sigh. Teigen's reply to her dangerous question, when would he know if he'd found another woman who interested him, was stuck firmly in her head.

When she does, I suppose.

"Do you know yet, Selby Hovland?" she murmured to her reflection.

Then she resolutely shook her head, closed her travel case, and returned to the bedroom to finish packing her suitcases.

⚡ ⚡ ⚡

"Have you ever been on a ship?" Teigen asked Ben. The pair braved the fitful weather to stand on the stern deck as belching tugboats pushed the ship away from the Oslo dock.

"No, sir." Ben looked a little apprehensive. "It won't sink, will it?"

Teigen caught sight of a pair of brown-clad SS officers standing at the rear of the ship. "Well, we won't be attacked by the Germans because they're on board. And, of course, the allies won't attack because there are Norwegians on board."

Ben squinted at the sky. A gust of damp wind spit in their faces. "What about the weather?"

Teigen gave him a reassuring grin. "These captains sail the Norwegian coast day after day all year. They know how and when to seek shelter along the inner passages, if that becomes necessary."

Ben nodded. "If you say so."

The ship was being turned around to face toward the North Sea, about sixty miles to the south. Teigen pointed up at Akershus Festning, the medieval fortress standing on the bluff overlooking Oslo harbor.

"Did you know the Norwegian soldiers at Akershus blocked the German's entry into Oslo when they attacked us?"

Ben rolled his eyes. "Of course. That's how the royal family, the *Storting*, and the treasury got out." He looked up at Teigen, his expression skeptical. "Are you going to be teaching me all the time?"

Teigen laughed. "Probably."

"Great." Ben made a face, but for the first time since Teigen met him he saw a glimmer of humor in the boy's eyes. "Is it too late for me to go back to the woods?"

⚡ ⚡ ⚡

Selby knew she'd have to face Teigen again today. She couldn't hide from the man forever, no matter how off-balance she felt about him at the moment.

So after checking her face one last time, and not seeing any obvious reminder of her former tears, Selby exited her cabin and went to join the actors in the ship's dining room for their final read-

through of *The Winter's Tale* before their off-book rehearsal later.
At least Teigen's not an actor and won't be there.
Selby strode into the dinning room.
Damn it. Why is he here?
Teigen stood when he saw her. "I thought it'd be a good start for Ben to see how the troupe operates, from read-through to performance."
Selby's brow lowered. "Don't you have lessons to teach?"
Ben smiled and then covered his mouth
Teigen gave an apologetic shrug. "I'm accomplished in the sciences and mathematics, of course, and I have a strong grasp of vocabulary, grammar, spelling and punctuation," he said. "But I'm a little weak in literature."
"So now that's *our* job?"
Teigen's expression was sculpted by confusion. "Is everything all right?"
Selby glanced at Ben who was starting to squirm. Her unfounded irritation with Teigen had nothing to do with the poor teen, so she backed off.
"Everything's fine." She forced her face to relax and look pleasant. "A little rehearsal jitters is all."
"Since when—"
"It's *fine*, Teigen," she interrupted. To further make the point she gestured toward to a pair of empty chairs. "Come sit beside me, Ben. You can read the script while we go through it."
Ben hopped up, clearly relieved. "Thanks, Miss Sunde."
Selby looked back at Teigen once she and Ben were settled in their seats. "You're not staying, are you?"
"I, um…" He looked even more confused than before. "I've got some letters to write."
Selby watched him leave, half relieved that he was gone and half wishing she could run after him.
Damn it.

CHAPTER TWENTY FIVE

March 1, 1943
Kristiansand, Norway

"We have to lay out all the flats and select the ones we'll use for this play," Bennett told Ben once everything was unloaded from the ship and transported to the theater in Kristiansand.

"Then the four of us will repaint what we need to," Teigen said.

"And fix what needs fixing," Jonas added.

Ben nodded. "I'm pretty good with a paint brush."

Teigen smiled at Ben's enthusiasm. Though the youth struggled with the ship's constantly rocking movement the first day of their voyage, Ben adapted pretty well after that. And with their regular meals the boy's face was already showing signs of filling out; at least he'd lost the gaunt look he had when Teigen found him.

And some of the fear.

The first test of his new name and papers happened when they boarded the ship in Oslo—and thankfully he walked onto the ship unchallenged. Teigen would be lying if he claimed he wasn't worried, but the forger in Oslo was very, very good.

Even so, he advised Ben to avoid the Nazi soldiers on board the ship if he could do it without looking like he was running away from them.

"Now's a good time to start practicing the skill of avoiding attention," Teigen told him. "Can you do that?"

Turns out, he could.

So could Selby.

Teigen hardly saw her at all on the journey, but when he did, all she would say to him was that she was learning her lines in her cabin and practicing with Karolina.

Except that Karolina was visible most of the days. Something was clearly wrong with Selby, but in spite of his efforts Teigen hadn't succeeded in finding out what.

Bennett pointed at one of the larger flats. "That one needs to be changed from *Much Ado's* Italian pillars and landscape to *Winter's* English stone and countryside." He handed Ben a geographic picture book. "We use this for reference."

Ben flipped the book open, turned a few pages, and then nodded. "I can do that."

"Really?" Bennett looked pleased. "Come on, then. Let's get you some paint."

Jonas tapped Teigen on the arm and waved a hand-written list in the air. "Let's sort through the props and get these ready."

March 4, 1943
Kristiansand, Norway

Opening night of any of their plays still set Selby's nerves on edge. She wasn't nervous about performing—amazing in itself because she'd never acted before the troupe was formed—but because opening night was the night she always arranged her assignations with her SS officers.

Tonight's lucky man was Lieutenant Colonel August Bernhardt, a forty-year-old redhead with a slight stutter—but his Norse was excellent.

When she walked out of her dressing room in the slinky dark blue silk dress that she bought in Oslo for their trip north, with her wig in place, her luscious Arctic fox coat around her shoulders, and her new red shoes, she thought poor young Ben would have a heart attack.

"M-miss Sunde," he stammered. "You look *very* nice."

The expression on his face screamed the question: who was she dressed up for? There was no way she was going to answer that now.

Selby smiled politely. "Thank you, Ben."

She walked to the stage door and looped her arm through Dahl's before he pushed the heavy door open to the expected flashes of camera bulbs and the cries of adoring fans who waited months between the troupe's appearances.

Bennett had served the lieutenant colonel a glass of aquavit to prime his pump, so to speak, and when the officer saw Selby, his ruddy cheeks split in a gap-toothed grin.

Selby walked down the short flight of steps and held out her hands toward the officer as Bennett claimed the empty glass and moved quietly out of the way.

"August, you're looking well." She stood on her toes to kiss him on both cheeks.

"And you, my darling, are as s-stunning as always." He tucked her arm in his and turned away from the scowling crowd. "I have a very s-special surprise for you t-tonight. I hope you will love it."

Selby smiled charmingly, though a German Nazi's idea of a special surprise was unlikely to be the same as hers. "I do hope it involves food," she demurred. "Putting on these plays always leaves me starving."

The surprise turned out to be a private yacht in the Kristiansand harbor. "We c-confiscated this boat from a Jewish merchant back in O-october," August bragged as he helped Selby climb on board. "But don't worry, my d-dear. Every surface has been thoroughly d-disinfected."

Selby turned her face toward the cabin of the expensive boat to hide any trace of revulsion that might have leaked past her resolve. "It's beautiful, August."

"And preparing our supper this evening is my p-personal chef, Leo Herrmann."

As if waiting for a stage cue, Leo appeared through the cabin door, smiling in his white uniform. "Welcome."

August led her inside to a white-covered table gleaming with silver and china. "Here we can see the lights of K-kristiansand and still be p-protected from the chill."

Selby sat in the seat he held for her, wondering how she was going to get the officer drunk if he was controlling their alcohol. She resigned herself to a wasted evening rather than a frustrated one and tried to relax. Rather than help however, that mindset exacerbated her already dour mood.

Something had shifted inside Selby, and she blamed Teigen Hansen for every last bit of it. The teacher had shown her that maybe her categorization of his gender was too broad and, at least in his case, unfair.

How was she supposed to flirt and deceive her Nazi contacts if she started thinking differently about men in general?

Think about Germans specifically.

No, think about Nazis specifically. Nazi officers.

Damn it.

Selby downed her first shot of aquavit purely out of irritated rebellion.

"D-don't get ahead of me, *liebchen*." August swallowed his as well, and reached for the bottle to refill both of their glasses. "Are you p-pleased with my surprise?"

"Yes. It's truly lovely." *You thieving racist pig of a man.*

That helped.

Because the aquavit was clear and alcohol evaporated fairly quickly, Selby poured hers on the wooden floor of the cabin as often as she could. She pretended to be getting tipsy during her exquisite supper of smoked salmon, beef Wellington, and cauliflower topped with cheese and swimming in butter.

When their chocolate mousse was served, Selby abandoned hers and climbed onto August's lap. She giggled like a schoolgirl as she fed him the decadent dessert, barely suppressing the urge to jam the spoon down his brown-collared throat.

"How is the war going for you, August?" she cooed and held a glass of Aquavit to his lips.

He accepted the drink, swallowing and wiping his mouth with the back of his hand before he answered.

"For me?" He shrugged. "It's not so bad."

Selby knew he was inebriated because he stopped stuttering. She offered him the last bite of mousse but he pushed it away and fixed a bleary gaze on her.

"Adolf is not so happy with Norway right now," he stage-whispered loud enough to be heard outside on the boat's deck. "You need to be very careful, *mein liebchen*."

The troupe heard an encouraging report the day they docked in Kristiansand and her assignment tonight was to ferret out the details. "What happened?"

"Some men snuck into the Vemork Hydroelectric Plant a few days ago..."

Selby played dumb. "Where is that?"

August waved a limp wrist. "Someplace called Telemark."

Selby shook her head and refilled August's glass. "Never been there."

August snorted and accepted the drink. "Well, do not go now!"

"Why not?" Selby pretended to take another shot.

"The bastards stuck explosives on the heavy water electrolysis chambers and blew them up." August shook his head. "Adolf is furious."

Selby ran her hand through the lieutenant colonel's wavy red hair. "I don't know what any of that means," she whined. "Why would anyone want to blow up water?"

August gave her a condescending albeit unfocused look. "Heavy water is for bombs."

Selby screwed up her face. "Bombs made out of water?"

"No, *liebchen*. The water from the electrolysis is for atomic bombs."

Selby's heart thudded though she kept her expression disinterested. The confirmation that a man like Adolf Hitler was trying to make atomic bombs was truly terrifying.

"So just make more electroly-things," she said flippantly.

"He will. But they're expensive. And—" August drained the glass she poured for him. "Apparently it takes a long time to make *enough* heavy water."

Selby heaved a petulant sigh. "When will this stupid war be over?"

The lieutenant colonel's shoulders sagged. "Because of this sabotage, our Fuhrer's glorious victory will take longer now."

"That's too bad." Selby kissed the top of August's head, but she was smiling.

ᚾ ᚾ ᚾ

Ben glowered at Teigen. "She's dating German officers?"

"Not really," Teigen clarified. "She pretends to like them, gets them drunk, and steals information."

"I don't like it." Ben's strong reaction indicated how smitten the youth was with Selby.

Get in line, son.

"It doesn't seem safe."

Teigen agreed, but,

"She's been doing it since the troupe started."

"I'm staying up until she gets back." Ben slid off his bed and walked to their hotel room's door. "I'll wait in the lobby."

He opened the door and cast an angry look back at Teigen. "Are you coming?"

Hell, yes.

The pair descended the stairs from the fourth floor—this hotel didn't have an elevator—and settled into two of the four big and worn leather chairs tucked into the lobby's leaded glass bay window.

Teigen grabbed someone's discarded newspaper and shared it with Ben. The two read the Nazi-controlled news in silence until Selby finally appeared.

She stopped in surprise when she saw them. "What are you two doing down here?"

In the face of the beautiful actress, Ben seemed to have lost his bluster. His face reddened and he jammed his hands into his pockets.

"Waiting for you to get back," Teigen answered for him. The true reason wouldn't do, so Teigen added, "We're curious about what you found out."

Selby took off her fox coat as she walked over to one of the leather chairs. When she sat down she kicked off her shoes and rubbed her silk-stockinged feet, sighing as she did.

Glancing back at the empty clerk's counter before she spoke, Selby faced Teigen and Ben, her expression serious. "Well first of all, it's completely true that Hitler's trying to make atomic bombs," she said softly.

"What?" Ben blurted.

"Quiet," Teigen warned him. "We never want to attract attention."

His face flushed again and he glanced at Selby. "Sorry."

She gave the teen a tired smile before she continued. "It's also true that the heavy water electrolysis chambers were blown up."

"All of them?" Teigen asked.

"That's not clear," Selby admitted. "But enough of them to put Adolf's plans back at least a year."

Teigen exhaled a sigh of relief. "That's good news."

Ben stared at Selby like he was about to explode himself. "How do you stand being with them?"

Selby was obviously startled by the boy's thankfully hushed outburst. She hesitated a moment then said, "It's a role I play."

Ben's lips pressed together and he scowled at her.

"Think of it this way, Ben." Selby leaned forward. "I hate…"

Teigen saw her falter. What did that mean?

"I hate the Nazis as much as you do," she ran at it again. "They're vile racist pigs to a man."

Ben nodded but his expression didn't change.

She gave a one-shoulder shrug and a corner of her mouth lifted. "Which is why I don't have a problem with deceiving any of them. Does that make sense?"

"I suppose," he muttered. "But it's dangerous."

"It's only dangerous if I make a mistake, Ben." Selby gave him a reassuring look. "And I'm very careful to never let them see what I *really* think of them and their damned Reich."

"Selby is a professional, Ben," Teigen added. "She knows what she's doing."

The appreciative look Selby gave him when he spoke those words shot straight to his groin.

Then she yawned.

"Go on up to bed, Ben," Teigen told the youth. "I'll be up in a minute. I have something to ask Selby about first."

Ben's curious glance bounced between the adults. "Yes, sir."

He stood and lumbered toward the staircase, shooting one look back when he reached the first landing.

Selby frowned at Teigen. "What is it?"

There was no point in beating around the bush. "Are you upset that I brought Ben into the troupe without asking you first?"

She shook her head. "No. Of course not. It was a very unusual situation and you did what needed to be done."

Teigen lifted his hands in frustrated supplication. "Then why have you been avoiding me ever since?"

Selby recoiled. "I haven't."

"Yes, you have," Teigen pressed. "Have I done something else to hurt you, or offend you, or make you angry?"

"No…" She picked up her shoes and slid them back on her feet while Teigen watched and waited for her to continue. "Quite the opposite, actually."

Teigen's jaw slackened. "What does that mean?"

Selby was fighting a visible war within herself. "It means... You are different from any man I ever knew."

Teigen frowned. "Different how?"

"You're... kind."

"Dahl is kind." Teigen hated that he was saying this. "And he's in love with you."

She shook her head almost frantically. "But he's not like you... I don't know how to describe it."

"Try using words."

"Fine." Selby glared at him. "Rough. Strong. Strong-willed. Stubborn. Unpredictable. And dangerous."

Teigen was taken aback. "Am *I* all those things?"

"Yes! But you're kind. And you're compassionate. And level-headed." She looked like she was going to cry. "And those things don't go together."

Teigen hesitated, struggling to understand the point she was trying to make—but he was completely lost.

"Selby," he said softly. "That doesn't make sense."

"I know!" She stood and grabbed her fur coat from the back of the leather chair. "That's what I'm saying!"

She turned and headed for the stairs. Teigen was beside her in three strides.

She shot him a sideways look. "What are you doing?"

"Walking you to your room."

"You don't need to."

Teigen grunted. "Yes I do."

Selby opened her mouth then snapped it shut. They climbed the steps to the second floor in silence, turned left, and walked down the hall, the carpet runner muffling their matching footsteps.

Selby stopped in front of a door near the end and dug a key from the pocket of her coat. She rammed the key into the lock and turned it. She pushed the door open.

Before she disappeared into the dimly lit room, Teigen took hold of her arm and turned her to face him.

She looked up at him, her pale eyes wide and their color eaten by her dilated pupils. Her lips parted. That was the invitation Teigen hoped for.

He leaned down and kissed her.

CHAPTER TWENTY SIX

Selby broke away from the kiss and stared up at Teigen, horrified. "Why did you do that?"

"Because you needed to be kissed." He stepped away from her and she felt like she was being torn in half. "I'll see you in the morning."

When Teigen turned to leave she reached out and grabbed his arm. "You shouldn't have done that. I'm your commanding officer."

"I know."

He obviously didn't understand the impact of what he'd done. "But—what will we say to each other tomorrow?"

"Good morning?" Teigen stepped closer again. "It was a kiss, Sel. Not a marriage proposal."

Her temper flashed. "How dare—"

"Come here."

He pulled her into a hug and held her against his chest until she stopped resisting and relaxed. "I kissed you because you are a beautiful, talented, and intelligent woman who I'm understandably attracted to. Is that what you wanted to hear?"

"No."

Yes, damn it.

Teigen chuckled. "Then I won't kiss you the next time. It's

your turn to kiss me."

He let go of her and her knees buckled. She grabbed the doorjamb for support. "You'll be waiting a long time, soldier."

"That's Sergeant, Lieutenant Hovland." He sighed and looked at her sadly. "Just be my friend, Sel. I've really missed you."

This time she didn't stop him when he walked away.

ᚾ ᚾ ᚾ

What the hell were you thinking?

Teigen climbed the two stories to his own floor, arguing that question back and forth in his mind. In the end, there were as many reasons not to kiss Selby as there were reasons for doing it.

But one reason broke the tie: Teigen had to face the fact that he'd developed real feelings for her. Was he in love?

No. Not yet.

Would he fall in love with her?

It was possible, sure.

And the first step toward that possibility was to kiss her. Not with an overwhelming, urgent, tongue shoved into her mouth sort of kiss, but with a tender exploring sort of kiss. A kiss to see how she responded.

She kissed me back.

That right there was what he needed to discover—would she shove him away or pull him closer. She did shove him away but only with her words, and not immediately. There was something between them for her as well, though she was trying to deny it.

Teigen smiled and opened his unlocked hotel room door.

Ben was in bed, but the light on the nightstand was blazing. "Is she okay?"

"Yeah. She's fine." Teigen opened the closet door and began to undress. "I hate what she does, just like you do, Ben," he admitted while he hung his shirt. "But I only joined the troupe in November, and she outranks me, so I have no say."

"November?" Ben sat up. "When you got out of the labor camp?"

"Yep." Teigen removed his shoes and dropped his socks on his laundry pile. "When we get to Bergen you'll get to meet Falko Jensen, the man who recruited me."

Teigen hung up his trousers and walked barefoot to the

bathroom. When he opened the door again, Ben was lying down with his eyes at half mast. Teigen crossed to his bed and switched off the light before throwing back the covers and climbing under them.

"Teigen?"

"What?"

"Did you kiss her?"

Teigen grinned into the darkness. "Go to sleep."

"That means yes." Ben's bed creaked as he turned over to face the other way. "G'night."

Teigen tucked his hands under his head and relived his conversation with Selby in the lobby. There was no other word for it but *odd*.

Selby called him kind.

He said Dahl was kind.

She replied by saying that Dahl wasn't rough, strong, strong-willed, stubborn, unpredictable, and dangerous. Those weren't compliments, they were attributes of angry men. Mean men.

So was she saying he was mean?

No, she said he was kind, compassionate, and level-headed.

That doesn't make sense.

Unless…

Teigen would've sat up in shock if he wasn't afraid of disturbing Ben.

Unless Selby had been the victim of mean men in the past. Was that why she found it so easy to treat the German men with such deceit and disdain? Because they were mean men and deserved it?

That made sense.

And if all of that was true, when she saw characteristics in Teigen that she associated with mean men, she was confused when he displayed the opposite characteristics that those mean men never owned.

That made sense, too.

Of course, until she told him these things for herself he couldn't know for sure. And he certainly couldn't ask her about it. He'd just have to wait. Be patient. Be her friend. Wait for her to learn to trust him enough to tell him about her past.

He believed Selby would come to that point if he let her do it at her own pace.

After all, she kissed me back.

ᚾ ᚾ ᚾ

Selby leaned against the door and slid down its length until she was seated on the floor. She covered her face with her hands and moaned into them.

Why did I kiss him back?

This was an epic disaster. And the worst part was that once it started she honestly didn't want the kiss to end.

What was going to happen now? He said, *just be my friend.* But men and women couldn't be friends—could they? At least she didn't believe she could be friends with Teigen. He was too... much. Too handsome. Too kind. Too sincere.

Too perfect.

Too perfect for her, anyway.

I'm damaged goods.

Selby climbed to her feet and stripped off her clothes before heading toward her bathroom.

Teigen noticed she was avoiding him, so that had to stop. Really the only thing she could do now was act friendly toward the man and hope for peace.

And not kiss him, of course.

She removed her wig and turned on the shower. After one of her dates she couldn't sleep until she washed away every trace of the Nazi officer and her evening of lies.

She stepped under the hot spray and washed her short hair. Then she scrubbed away all the makeup and perfume she had applied until she was down to clean, bare skin.

Down to Selby Hovland.

The troupe had four more performances to put on before they moved on to Bergen, a key location in both the German occupation and Milorg activity. Once they were in Bergen they'd all be busy. And when they were on the ship heading there, she could claim female issues were keeping her uncomfortable and closeted if she needed to be away from him.

True or not, that excuse always cowed men.

She turned off the shower and reached for her towels, wrapping one around her head and drying her body with the other. Tomorrow she'd go exploring in Kristiansand, claiming she needed to shop. That also sounded true, and men never wanted to come along.

Selby grinned wickedly.

I'll even invite Teigen to join me.
That was perfect. It would prove she was being his friend, while avoiding his presence at the same time. The perfect solution.

March 5, 1943
Kristiansand, Norway

"I'd love to come shopping with you."

Selby stared up at Teigen, stunned. "You would?"

"Yeah—but could we drag Ben along?" Teigen flashed an imploring smile. "At least for part of the time?"

"I guess. Sure." Selby's gaze shifted to the adolescent eating breakfast with Bennett at the other side of the dining room. She didn't imagine he would be pleased with the plan. "But why?"

"Look at his clothes, Sel. Nothing fits him."

"Oh! Yes. You're right." She returned her regard to Teigen. "Does he have any money?"

"He has his salary for March. And I've got my raise, so I can chip in if he runs short."

Generous, too?

Selby sighed and tried to look unconcerned. "Maybe we could have lunch somewhere."

Shut up.

Teigen smiled and his green eyes brightened. "That'd be great."

Change the subject.

"Hey, I meant to ask you—did you paint that backdrop with the stone pillars and English countryside?"

Teigen shook his head. "No, Ben did. Why?"

"Ben did?" Selby looked at the table across the room with an entirely different attitude. "It's gorgeous!"

"I thought he did a great job myself." Teigen chuckled. "Who knew we rescued an artist?"

Selby looked at him over the rim of her teacup. "I'll be sure to say something to him about it."

"He'll be so happy he'll probably have palpitations." Teigen winked at her. "I'll bring some ammonia inhalants, just in case."

"What?"

"Smelling salts."

Selby rolled her eyes. "Spoken like a chemist. Again."

ᚿ ᚿ ᚿ

The day spent shopping was actually pleasant. Initially reluctant, Ben perked up when he tried on trousers and shirts that fit his still-growing frame. The trio had lunch in a small diner overlooking the water because the salesgirl in the shop told them that the proprietors caught their own fish off the dock and kept most of it for themselves.

"Stupid Nazis don't know how many fish can be in a net," she whispered. "It's easy to lie to them."

The freshly fried fish was delicious, as were the mashed turnips served with the fillets.

So when they returned to their hotel rooms to get ready for the performance Teigen was shocked when Ben broke down in tears.

"What's wrong?"

"Everything…" he wailed.

Teigen lowered himself to the floor and leaned against Ben's bed next to the distraught boy. "Tell me."

It took him a moment for Ben to find his voice, and when he did it was raw and choked. "How can I be happy? How can I smile? Or laugh?"

Teigen understood what the youth was talking about right away. *Grief.*

"You forget for a while, then you feel guilty when you remember."

Ben nodded. He pressed the heels of his hands against his eyes. "My mother is dead," he moaned. "I don't even know what happened to her body…"

Though he tried to put himself in the teen's place, Teigen honestly couldn't know what young Ben was going through.

"And you may never see your father or brother again," he said softly.

The boy nodded and his sobs intensified. "So how can I go on with my life?"

Teigen didn't have an answer for that. But he did ask, "What would your mother want you to do?"

Ben dropped his hands and stared at Teigen. His cheeks were awash with tears and his nose was running.

"My mother?" he snuffled.

"Yes. If she was standing in front of you right now, what would she tell you to do?"

He gulped. "I don't know."

"Sure you do," Teigen said kindly. "Would she tell you to never be sad about what happened?"

He frowned. "No."

"You'll always remember and be sad when you do. That's okay." Teigen was fishing his way through this awkward moment. "But would she tell you to stop living your own life?"

Ben's chin quivered. "No."

"What would she want you to do?"

He ran his sleeve under his streaming nose. "She wanted me to finish school."

"And you will," Teigen assured him. "What else?"

"Get married."

"All mothers want that for their sons." Teigen nudged him. "My mother's still waiting. What else?"

"She wanted grandchildren." His tears spilled again. "Now she'll never see them."

"What do Jews believe about life after death?"

"I-I'm not sure..." Ben heaved a jagged sigh. "My dad used to say that his ancestors could see him, though."

Teigen patted Ben's leg. "There you are."

His brow furrowed. "My mom's not Jewish."

"Doesn't God take up Christians, too?"

Ben looked like a klieg light had lit up in his head. "Yeah. He does."

"So talk to your mother like she can hear you. Not all the time, of course, or you'll sound like a lunatic," Teigen cautioned. "But when something important happens, tell her."

"You mean like..." Ben sniffed and wiped again. "Like when I was rescued in the woods by a teacher who gave me a new life?"

Teigen eyes filled suddenly. "Yeah. Like that."

Ben wasn't looking at him. "I was going to die."

Teigen nodded slowly. "Yeah. You were."

"You saved my life."

"Well God gave *me* a new life when I was released from the camp, so..." Teigen dried his eyes with the cuff of his shirt. "I figured I should do the same for you."

"Thank you." Ben waved his hand. "For all this stuff."

Teigen examined his own interwoven fingers, trying to say the right words in the right way. "Look, I know there will be times when the sadness overwhelms you. Don't be embarrassed about that, okay?"

"Okay."

"But on the other side of the coin, don't ever feel guilty for living your life and being happy about it." He looked at Ben then. "Does that make sense?"

"Yeah. It does."

Teigen climbed to his feet. "I need to get to the theater. You can come later, if you need some time."

"No, I'll go with you. Just give me a minute." Ben got to his feet as well and went into the bathroom to wash his face.

When he came out he said, "I want to make sure that the flat Miss Sunde was so impressed with is handled carefully tonight.

He gave Teigen a shy, embarrassed grin. "Apparently, it's a work of art."

CHAPTER TWENTY SEVEN

March 14, 1943
Sailing to Bergen

Selby threw back her covers and swung her legs over the side of her narrow bed, sliding her feet into the slippers she abandoned there hours earlier. Sleep was eluding her tonight and even the gentle rocking of the ship wasn't helping.

She pulled on a pair of trousers, tucking the hem of her nightgown into the waistband, and donned her fox-fur coat. She left her little cabin and walked down the hallway to the door opening onto the deck.

The air was cool and damp, but the chill of winter was gone. She walked along the railing toward the stern of the ship with the intention of sitting in a chair and watching the wake of the ship glow in the waning moonlight until it made her feel sleepy.

Apparently she wasn't the only wakeful soul on board. In the light of the nearly-full moon she could see Teigen's familiar form draped over one of the teakwood chairs, while another chair acted as his ottoman. He stiffened and turned to look at her when she dropped into the chair next to his.

His brows shot upward. "Hi."

"You couldn't sleep either?" she asked.

"No." His body relaxed and he huffed an irritated sigh. "I'm still figuring out the bomb I'm supposed to present to the honorable Major Hans Helgesen in less than forty-eight hours."

Selby tucked one foot under her and turned her body to face Teigen. "I thought you had it worked out already. Back in Oslo."

"I have the explosives worked out," he clarified. "But I'm still not sure of how to detonate them."

Selby considered the long and shifting trail of churning water that the ship was leaving in the otherwise calm sea. "Tell me what the problem is. We can work on it together."

And then you won't ask me why I'm out here.

Teigen folded his hands, his elbows on the arms of the chair. "Part of the problem is that I don't know the size or shape of the compartment that the bomb needs to fit into."

"But that can be changed if it needs to be—right?"

"I expect so. But that leaves me wondering what *would* be the best choice if I *do* redesign it."

Selby pulled her gaze from the mesmerizing water. "What are your unchangeable conditions?"

Teigen held up one hand and ticked off fingers as he spoke. "First, the parts of the explosive must be secured and stable so they aren't accidentally set off."

"Okay." Selby rested her chin on her hand. "What are the parts?"

Teigen's hand remained in the air when he turned to look at her. "Either a cigarette lighter and a pouch of gunpowder, or two chemicals which flame up when they're mixed—and the pouch of gunpowder."

Selby nodded. "Got it."

Teigen return to counting on his fingers. "Second, the detonator must be triggered by a specific movement—the opening or closing of a drawer."

"So the movement either lights the lighter, or mixes the chemicals." Selby drummed her fingertips against her cheek. "Could the drawer act like a thumb and flick the flint on the lighter?"

"That's what I was thinking initially, and it might still work." Teigen's hand lowered a little. "I'd have to make sure that the lighter is fastened so securely in place that moving the desk doesn't knock it out of alignment."

"Lighters don't always spark on the first try, either," Selby observed. "Would that be a problem?"

Teigen's expression changed. He looked hopefully surprised. "Actually, that might be an advantage. If the desk doesn't explode the first day, then the men delivering it can say the bomb was placed there later."

That was an interesting idea. "*Could* the bombs be placed there later?" she asked.

"No. They have to be securely attached… Ha!" Teigen clapped his hands together and whooped.

Selby sat up straight and giggled. "What?"

Teigen's whole body turned to face her. "But the packet of gunpowder could be put in later! At least if we use a lighter!"

"And it won't set the desk on fire because the flame goes out when the lighter closes." Selby pointed at him. "You'll have to be careful where you put it."

"But won't work with the chemicals, because they *will* set the desk on fire." Teigen was pensive again. "I'm thinking something spring-loaded for that. When the drawer opens, it drops one chemical into the other, and when it closes it mixes them somehow."

Selby sat back and snuggled into her fox coat. "It sounds like you do have it worked out."

"I have the concepts, true. I guess that'll have to suffice for now. I'll figure out the actual construction when I see the desk."

Teigen peered at her. "So why are you out here?"

И И И

Selby's mouth opened, but no words came out.

Because she doesn't want to tell me.

He waited.

She shrugged, the movement nearly smothered by the thick fur. "I just couldn't sleep."

Teigen lifted one accusing brow. "If a person can't sleep, it's because something unpleasant is weighing on them."

Selby frowned. "Not necessarily. They could be figuring out a problem, like you. Or just be wakeful."

"Are you just wakeful tonight, Selby Hovland?" he pressed. "Or is it something that you don't want to talk to me about?"

Selby turned away and looked toward the water churning

behind the ship. In the moonlight Teigen could see her delicate profile and her pale blue eyes appeared colorless.

"I don't think I ever told you how much I love your hair," he said.

One hand jumped to her short locks and she turned back to him, obviously surprised. "You do? Why?"

Teigen's gaze moved over her face. "Because the wigs overwhelm your features. When I see you like this I notice your cheekbones and the curve of your jaw."

She cringed. "I don't have any makeup on."

Teigen shrugged. "You don't need makeup. You're beautiful just as you are."

For some reason, that angered her. "Why do you say things like that?" she growled.

"Like what?" Teigen was knocked sideway by the question. "Do you mean compliments?"

"Yes. What do you hope to gain?"

Gain?

"Nothing!"

Her eyes narrowed. "I don't believe you. Men always want something."

"When have I ever... What do you think I..." Teigen sputtered his frustration at the unfounded suggestion. Then his recent suspicion about Selby's past ran to the front of his mind, jumped up and down, and waved its hands.

It's time to address this.

"Good God, Selby—what happened to you?"

When she jumped to her feet he thought she was going to bolt. Then when she clenched her fists, he was sure she was going to punch him.

Instead she froze.

Teigen slowly reached for her hand, which was shaking, and pulled her down into the chair he had been using to prop his feet.

"I'm sorry. You don't have to tell me," he said gently. "I shouldn't have asked."

The moon was behind her now, so her face was harder to see. When she didn't speak he continued, saying what he needed to say to her.

"It just seems like your general mistrust of men must have come from something that happened in your past."

She tried to pull her hand from his when he said that, but he wouldn't let her. Instead, he placed his other hand over the one he grasped.

"You don't have to tell me anything, Sel. It's none of my business."

Her arm relaxed at that, no longer tugging her hand toward escape.

"But I do have one thing to say that I feel very strongly about."

Her eyes, which had been staring to the side unfocused and blank, jumped to his.

"What?" she rasped.

Teigen squeezed her hand as he spoke. "I. Am. Not. That. Man."

Selby gasped, wide-eyed. Her free hand clamped over her mouth.

"Do you hear me?" Teigen probed.

She gave him the tiniest nod.

"I promise you, I will never harm you in any way. In fact…" Teigen decided at that moment to go all in. "If at all possible, I'll protect you from anyone *else* who tries to harm you."

Her hand dropped to her lap. "Why?" she whispered.

"I need to redeem my gender."

Her brow flickered. "What?"

Teigen's heart drummed in his chest. Was it too soon to be fully honest?

If I'm not, how can I expect her to be?

"Redeem my gender." He looked at her in a way that he hoped telegraphed his feelings. "I was afraid that if I said it was because I love you, you might get upset."

Selby was silent, her eyes intently fixed on his.

"Did you hear me?" he ventured.

She nodded. "Do you? Love me?"

"I might." *Don't be a coward.* "Yes."

She bowed her head then. He couldn't see even a shadowed version of her face.

"Please believe me, Sel, I don't expect you to fall in love with me. No one can control who they fall for. I think my own sad experience proves that."

Nothing. No reaction.

He squeezed her hand again. "But I really want you to stop

thinking the worst about me at every turn, just because I happen to be a man."

She sighed and gave another tiny nod.

Good. Move on.

"So was there something else that wouldn't let you sleep tonight?"

"I don't know."

Encouraged that she spoke, Teigen asked. "Do you want to stay out here a while? I'll go in if you want to be alone."

She didn't seem to know what she wanted to do.

"I guess I'll head back to my cabin then." Teigen let go of her hand and stood. "Try to get some sleep."

He turned to leave.

"Wait."

He looked down at the petite woman engulfed in expensive fur. She looked up at him so that the moon illuminated her face again.

"Thank you."

Don't ask for what.

He smiled a little. "You're welcome."

"I'm sorry but I—I can't tell you."

"Don't apologize. I shouldn't have asked."

Selby rose to her feet so that she stood in front of him. "You're a good man, Teigen Hansen. I'm going to try and remember that."

He chuckled. "I'd appreciate it."

When she made no move to leave, he asked, "Is there something else?"

She chewed her bottom lip and nodded.

"What?"

"I want to give you something, but I don't want you to misunderstand the gesture."

Teigen put his hands up in surrender and kept his tone light. "Okay. So it's just a what, a peace offering? A simple sign of friendship?"

Selby looked very relieved. "Yes. Exactly that."

Teigen waited.

Selby looked at the chair he had just vacated and stepped on its seat, eliminating their twelve-inch difference in height. She now faced him eye-to-eye.

Which a resolute sigh she placed her hands on his cheeks, leaned forward, and kissed him.

CHAPTER TWENTY EIGHT

March 16, 1943
Bergen, Norway

Major Hans Helgesen had a hidden office in the back of a barn on a plot of land that overlooked Bergen's bustling harbor, and that's where today's meeting was taking place.

The troupe's ranking officers, Dahl, Selby, and Bennett, along with a grinning Falko Jensen, stood in a semi-circle around a beautifully crafted office desk while Teigen explained his ideas to the major.

"I like it, Hansen." Helgesen rubbed his chin and his eyes narrowed. "You're right about the lighter not striking right away, and that delay offering an alibi... But once you test both methods we'll know for sure."

"Yes, sir," Teigen agreed, relieved that Helgesen was pleased. One obstacle was cleared. "When can I start working on them?"

"I see no reason to delay." The major looked at Dahl. "Can you spare him until he figures it out?"

Dahl nodded. "We've picked up a stray, so we'll be fine."

Helgesen's gaze hit each of the troupe's three officers. "What do you mean by a stray?"

"Hansen was testing explosives in the woods one day and he came back with a fifteen-year-old Jewish fugitive." Dahl looked

amused. "He's a good worker. So we kept him."
Selby's elbow hit Dahl with enough force to make Teigen wince. "Don't talk about Ben like he's a dog."
"Ow!" Dahl rubbed his side. "I'm just giving Teig a hard time."
Helgesen's gaze pinned Teigen. "You gave him papers, of course."
Teigen nodded. "Before we left Oslo. Benjamin Isaksen is now Ben Thorkelsen Hansen."
The major's brow quirked. "Hansen?"
"I'm claiming him as a cousin," Teigen explained. "And he's traveling with me because I'm tutoring him for his university exams."
"Which he actually is," Selby interjected without looking at him. "Tutoring, I mean."
"Because you're a teacher, obviously." Helgesen nodded. "That's a believable story." He returned his regard to Dahl. "So can this boy take up the slack while Hansen works on the desk?"
Dahl was still rubbing his side. "Yes, sir."
"And if you don't object, sir," Falko spoke up. "I'd like to work with Hansen on this project. That way when the kinks are worked out, there'll be two of us who know how to assemble the bombs."
The major nodded. "Good thinking, Jensen."
Falko grinned at Teigen, who smiled back. He was looking forward to working with his friend again.
"All right, then." Helgesen grinned. "Let's get to work."

N N N

After everyone left, Teigen lined up his chemical supply on a plank. "So how have you been? Has your leg healed?"
"Oh, yeah. I'm fine. See?" Falko hopped on the shot leg. "What about you?"
Teigen smacked his belly with both hands. "Back to fighting weight. You, too, I see."
Falko chuckled. "I may have added a few extra pounds in reserve. Just in case."
"Well, you look good."
"Thanks. You too." Falko leaned against the desk, crossed his arms, and pointed toward the door with his head. "What's up with you and her?"

Teigen looked at his friend in surprise. "Selby?"

"Yeah. Are you two…" Falko unfolded his arms and clasped his hands together."

Teigen laughed. "What? Dating?"

He refolded his arms. "I was thinking something a little more intimate than that."

"I haven't bedded her, no." Teigen set the wooden case on the end of the plank. "And why would you even ask me that?"

"Because she's obviously interested in you."

Teigen rested his hands on his hips, incredulous. "What did you see here that I didn't?"

"Dahl made a joke out of you sheltering that kid, and she let him have it." Falko grinned. "You saw that, didn't you?"

He did, but, "That didn't mean anything."

"Sure it did. She was standing up for you." Falko pointed a finger at him. "And then she said the nice thing about you tutoring—what's his name, Ben?—to get him ready for his exams."

Could Falko be right? Was Selby sending messages that he'd been missing?

Wouldn't surprise him; he wasn't exactly experienced in the romance arena.

Falko's lips curved as he added, "And I would bet money that it's mutual."

Teigen walked over and leaned against the desk next to his friend. "It is," he admitted. "But it's a slow burn."

"Have you kissed her?"

"Once." Teigen smiled. "And she kissed *me* once."

Falko laughed. "Four months and that's it? That *is* a slow burn."

Teigen spread his hands in a gesture of helplessness. "We're at war. It's not like we could get married and start a family anytime soon, even if we wanted to. There isn't a future for any one of us until somebody beats the other guy."

Falko looked resigned. "And gets the hell out of Norway."

"To that end, we need to arm some desks so they explode." Teigen pointed at the line-up of glass containers. "We'll need to make more gunpowder, for sure. And we'll need to go buy a couple cigarette lighters."

"What if I could get you some gunpowder?"

Teigen looked at Falko. "Can you?"

He winked. "I have connections."

"Great!" Teigen straightened. "Then let's go buy some lighters—and maybe a beer or two."

March 17, 1943

Selby sat at her backstage dressing table wondering if she could send Captain Rolf Schmidt a note begging off for the night. Today was her twenty-ninth birthday and she really just wanted to hole up in her room with a bottle of wine.

If only she had one.

The European war had thrown her life into some weird universe where capricious and sullen men in brown uniforms controlled everything around her. And the idea of her controlling them in any way was far less probable than she wanted to admit.

"Sel?"

Selby turned toward Teigen's softly spoken greeting. "Hi."

"You have a minute?"

"Sure."

Teigen walked toward her and sat on the chair next to hers. "Is Ben doing okay? Working, I mean?"

"Yep. Doing great. He seems happier than ever." She waved a hand toward backstage. "He's even started repainting some of the other flats."

Teigen's shoulders relaxed. "Good. I didn't want to leave the troupe shorthanded."

Selby dipped her chin. "And we appreciate that. So—how's it going?"

Teigen's expression lit up. "Well, we tried figuring out how to install the bombs by turning the desk upside down, but that didn't work. So then we had to remove the top so we could reach the space in the back the man left for us to use."

That sounded like more work than was intended, and she said so.

Teigen waved an unconcerned hand. "It'll be fine. I asked Major Helgesen to let the craftsman know not to attach the desks' tops when he has them delivered to our outposts."

"So you'll attach the tops after the bombs are installed." That made sense.

"Plus we don't have to worry about *how* the desks are handled before we get them because they won't be armed." Teigen gave her a relieved look. "I have to admit, that was one of my biggest concerns."

Selby couldn't stop herself smiling at the man's enthusiasm for his task. "When do you think you'll be finished?"

His expression turned impish. "In plenty of time to deliver it here in Bergen and see how it goes."

Selby's mood soured. "Can you deliver it to Captain Rolf Schmidt?"

Teigen stiffened. "Is he giving you trouble?"

"No." Selby glanced at the third scribbled attempt to call off her date with the Nazi which waited on her dressing table. "I just don't feel like spending tonight with a Nazi German."

"Tonight?" *Ugh.* Of course he picked up her unfortunate designation. "Is tonight special for some reason?"

Selby heaved a resigned sigh. She might as well tell him.

"Today's my birthday."

"Are you joking?" Teigen's head fell back and he laughed. "Really? Today?"

Selby looked at him like he was as crazy as he was acting. "Why is that funny?"

Teigen grinned at her. "Because my birthday's tomorrow!"

Her jaw dropped. "How old are you?"

"I'll be twenty-eight at one minute past midnight." He raised his brows. "How about you?"

Selby cringed, inwardly and outwardly. Why did he have to younger than her?

Okay, only a year, but still...

"I'm twenty-nine."

"Ooh, an older woman," he teased. "I better watch myself."

"Yeah," Selby groused. "Or I might seduce you and have my way with you."

"Promises, promises." Teigen's features shifted and his eyes looked like green flames.

He leaned forward and spoke before her outrage reached her tongue. "But seriously, Sel. Push him off tonight. Let's celebrate our both surviving another year."

The offer was tempting. Too tempting to ignore.

"How long before the desk is ready?"

Teigen didn't seem put-off by her change of subject. Instead he pulled a cigarette lighter from his pocket. "If I can get this to light when the drawer closes, we can deliver the desk the next day."

Selby looked at her watch. It was only two o'clock. "Are you going back to work on it?"

"Yeah. Falko and I just finished lunch and he's picking up the gunpowder he somehow managed to round up." Teigen stood. "So after the show tonight, we'll have a late supper at the hotel. Deal?"

She looked up at him. "I'm serious about Schmidt."

"I know." Teigen's expression was grim. "He shot my friend in the middle of a crowd so I can't think of a better candidate."

"I've just sentenced a man to die."

"The world's at war, Selby. And Schmidt is the enemy." Teigen leaned over and kissed the top of her head. "I'll see you later."

Selby watched his back as he left and something swelled in her chest.

He'll protect me.

ᚾ ᚾ ᚾ

"Okay, try it now."

Falko pushed the desk's center drawer closed. The lever on the lighter depressed, but not quite far enough.

"That's closer, at least."

Teigen bent over the back of the desk and shoved another tiny shim between the desk's outer wall and the lighter's brace. The idea was for the back of the drawer to hit the lever and light the lighter.

After an hour and a half of trial and error, he and Falko had reached the point where they were ready to give up and start designing the more complicated two-chemical-reaction method.

Teigen straightened. "Try it again."

Falko closed the drawer.

A tiny flame sprung to life.

"Ha HA!" Teigen whooped. "Do it again."

Falko obliged. Eight more tries produced five more flames. "Ten tries and seven flames." Falko grinned at Teigen. "Is seventy percent good enough?"

"Maybe." Teigen was smiling as he bent over to watch the mechanics one more time. "Do it slowly…"

Falko did.

"Stop!" Teigen grabbed a shim and made a final adjustment. "Try it now."

Six closings of the drawer produced six flames. Falko spun in an elated circle. "We did it!"

"Now we need to replicate it." Teigen grabbed his tape measure and logged the placement and size of every component in his notepad. Then he drew an overall sketch, one view from above, and the other from the side.

He looked at Falko. "Where's the gunpowder?"

Falko handed him the little linen pouch. It was filled with the precise amount of the explosive material which Teigen and Dierks determined would get the job done. Teigen tacked it to the back of the closed drawer exactly one inch from the lighter.

"Won't do any good if the powder snuffs the flame…" he said.

He straightened and looked at Falko, his heart pounding and his hands shaking. "It's done."

Falko wrapped a tight strap around the desk to keep the top drawers—specifically the center one—from accidentally opening. To avoid rousing any suspicions, the lower drawers were strapped as well.

The two men carefully replaced the top on the desk, then stepped back to stare at it. Teigen wasn't sure what Falko was thinking, but he was terrified. The idea that he had designed and built a bomb for the purpose of killing a man had suddenly become very real.

I'm a science teacher, not a subversive murderer.

Images of the freezing labor camp and the death of Jans exploded in his mind, and he realized that everything about the man he had been was changed by that horrific experience.

I'm a soldier at war.

"Who's our lucky recipient?" Falko asked. "Did Helgesen tell you?"

"No. But I know who'll get this." Teigen turned to look at Falko. "The asshole who shot you."

Falko's smile looked more like a sneer. "I like the way you think."

Teigen moved to clean up the space and pack his chemicals away. "Let's see that this gets delivered tomorrow."

CHAPTER TWENTY NINE

March 18, 1943

Selby couldn't stop pacing.

First in her hotel room before she went down for breakfast. But that was mostly because her birthday supper with Teigen had been so intimate.

Not physically, of course. They were in a public setting. It was their conversation that was so startling.

Teigen had been fidgeting throughout the meal and he didn't finish it—a certain sign that something weighed on him. But when Selby pressed the point, he spoke to her in unrestrained honesty.

"I was angry at my brother for joining the Norwegian army the day we were attacked," he said. "Because I felt like I was forced to take a lesser path as a result."

Selby had heard him say this before. "Stay back and make sure your parents were all right."

Teigen nodded slowly. "So joining Milorg has given me the opportunity to do something here."

Selby lifted her wine goblet. "I believe you are about to say *but...*" She sipped the single glass of wine the hotel would serve her, nursing it the way the hotel nursed their meager supply.

"Yes. But." Teigen didn't smile. "It wasn't until I attached the pouch of gunpowder next to the lighter that I realized I was actually going to kill someone."

Selby was an excellent shot, and practiced whenever the rare opportunity arose. Trees, cans, and bottles weren't threats and she had never aimed her gun at a human. Except the night she broke into Teigen's hotel room, of course.

But I wasn't really going to shoot him.

And when she set her mother's house on fire, no one was inside it—she and her husband were already dead.

The reality of Teigen's words sank into her chest. "And I selected a man to die."

"We are at war with a terrible enemy, Sel. One who judges the value of a man by the color of his eyes and hair." Teigen was clearly speaking to himself as much as he was talking to her. "I was arrested and imprisoned, forced to work and live under inhuman conditions for seven months, because I disagreed with that philosophy."

Selby shuddered. "And look at what's happened to the Jews in Norway. Over two thousand have been sent to Auschwitz and Birkenau."

Teigen's face was drawn and his cheeks sunken. "We have to do what we can to stop—or at least hamper—Hitler's efforts. It's our moral duty, I think."

Selby reached over and laid her hand on his. "I agree with you, Teig. But I don't feel any better about it than you do."

His eyes narrowed. "Am I weak?"

Selby's breath caught. "No. Not at all. I think a man who kills or hurts without pause is weak. You're the strongest man I ever met."

His cheeks lifted in a regretful smile. "Tor is in the army, and he has to fight man-to-man. He shoots men whose eyes he can see. Before today I never understood that burden."

Selby intertwined her fingers with Teigen's, but didn't say anything. What was there to say?

Now she was pacing inside the theater. She came early, too nervous about the desk delivery to stay at the hotel. She knew Teigen was seeing to the final details and hoped he would come to the theater when he was finished.

"Helgesen's sending a couple men with a truck to meet us at the barn," he told her as he finished his hurried breakfast. "They're going to say they're stevedores from the dock, and that the desk was shipped by someone in Quisling's office as a reward for the captain's efforts here in Bergen."

Selby sighed. "At least he'll die happy."

And I'll be free of him.

The back door to the theater opened sending a bright and brief streak of sunlight across the stage. Selby ran to see who it was.

"Oh." She tried to hide her nervous disappointment. "Hi, Bennett."

"He's not back yet?"

"No."

Bennett looked around the backstage area as if trying to find a task to occupy his time, while at the same time appearing completely distracted.

Of course he was. They all were.

"Is Ben painting again?"

"Yeah." Selby chuckled. "He's redoing the Italian backdrops now."

Bennett grinned. "I sure can't complain about that. The kid's darn good."

"Are you talking about me?" Ben walked toward the work sink, dirty brushes in hand.

"Why, your ears burning?" Bennett teased.

"Nope. Just being modest." He smiled puckishly. "I knew it was me."

The door opened again and all three turned to see if Teigen would make his appearance.

"Hey, Dahl." Bennett's tone shouted his unfulfilled hopes.

"He's not back yet?"

Three voices chorused, "No."

The door opened again. Teigen stopped, surprised by the four troupe members clustered just inside. "Is everything all right?"

"You tell us!" Dahl pushed the door shut behind him. "We've been waiting for you."

Selby watched Teigen's face, looking for signs of his mood. He looked resigned. Nervous. And satisfied.

"We loaded the desk, told the guys to be *very* careful, and they drove off." He looked at his watch. "I expect they might have reached Nazi headquarters by now." Five pair of eyes moved around the little circle.

"What now?" Ben asked, the bouquet of dirty paint brushes still clutched in his fist.

Teigen looked at his charge. "We wait. See if it works."

Selby walked to the coat rack and grabbed her jacket. "I'm going out." She stopped and looked up at Teigen. "You coming?"

ᚿ ᚿ ᚿ

Teigen didn't need to be asked twice. He followed Selby out the door and back into the bright spring day. "Where're we going?"

"We're going out for lunch, somewhere within a block of the place."

"It's a little early for lunch, don't you think?"

She stopped her march and turned to face him. "Then we'll have coffee. Or shop. Or all three."

Teigen put up his hands to stop her tirade. "I know what you want to do, Sel, and I'm in complete agreement. I just don't want to draw any attention by doing something unusual."

She seemed to accept his logic. "Then what do we do?"

"If you don't mind acting a little," he began. "We could hold hands and take a leisurely stroll around the area. Like a loving couple enjoying the day."

The look she gave him would have wilted a weaker man. "Are you serious?"

He shrugged. "It's just an idea. Do you have a better one?"

Selby's lips squished together as if trying to hold back a string of inappropriate words.

Then she grabbed his hand. "Fine."

Teigen flexed his fingers under her viselike grip. "I'll probably need my hand to be in working order later."

She loosened her fingers.

They walked down the alley beside the theater, heading toward the street. "I actually would like a cup of coffee," he ventured.

When they reached the street, Selby turned him away from the front of the theater. "I know a little place about a block-and-a-half from the offices."

"Teigen?"

He stopped, and then slowly turned toward the voice.

The tall man in a Norwegian army uniform grinned crazily and ran down the theater's front steps. "It *is* you, brother!"

"Tor?" Teigen was stunned. "What are you doing here?"

"I came to find you, you idiot!" Tor launched himself at Teigen and wrapped him in a back-pounding hug that Teigen returned.

Tor came to find me.

Teigen's chest warmed with affection for his older brother.

"How?" he blurted.

"I was just in Arendal. Mamma told me where you were." Tor loosened his hold and fell back. "I wanted to see you before I left."

"Left?" Teigen frowned. "Where're you going now?"

Tor's blue eyes shone above his wide grin. "England first, then America. Camp Hale in Colorado."

"Why?" was the only response that came to Teigen's mind.

"Seems the American soldiers need to learn how to ski."

"And you're going to teach them?"

Tor looked a little taken aback by the question. "I did qualify for the Olympics, remember?"

"Yeah." Teigen spent his entire life trying to live up to Tor's legacy. "Too bad the war got in the way."

Tor turned to Selby. "We haven't met. I'm Captain Tor Hansen. Teigen's big brother."

"So I gathered." Teigen appreciated Selby's cool demeanor. Much like Dahl, Tor always seemed to attract female attention. "I'm—"

"The beautiful and talented Selby Sunde. Yes, I know." Tor smiled and gave a little bow. "I am very pleased to meet you."

Selby smiled sweetly. "We were just about to go get a cup of coffee. Would you care to join us?"

ᚾ ᚾ ᚾ

Teigen was so shocked by his brother's appearance that he didn't seem to know where to start their conversation.

Thankfully, Selby did. She looped her arms through both brothers' elbows and resumed walking away from the theater.

"The first thing you need to know, Tor, is that the acting troupe is a device which covers our true purpose. I'm a lieutenant in Milorg and your brother is a sergeant." She kept her voice low, watching surreptitiously for unwanted ears. "He joined after he was released from Kirkenes."

Tor turned to look at Teigen over Selby's head. "Mamma didn't tell me that."

"Mamma doesn't know," Teigen murmured. "She thinks I'm just helping the troupe. She doesn't know I'm active duty."

"He thought she'd worry too much if she knew," Selby added. "You understand—having both of her sons in danger."

Teigen squeezed her elbow.

She looked up at him. He smiled his thanks.

"So the whole troupe is Milorg?" Tor whispered.

Selby turned back to Tor. "Yes. And now that you know that, you'll understand if certain topics of conversation might have to wait until you two are alone."

"Absolutely."

"How long will you be in Bergen?" Teigen asked.

Tor's expression sobered. "I'm taking the Shetland Bus out of Telavåg tomorrow. I wish I could stay longer, but, well you know how it is."

The trio reached the café and claimed three metal chairs around a small rusting table.

"I'll go in and see about our coffee," Selby offered. "You two start catching up."

ᚿ ᚿ ᚿ

Teigen stared at Tor. The two brothers had often been mistaken for twins; the only significant difference in their looks was the color of their eyes. Tor's were blue.

"Mamma said you were in Kirkenes." Tor's voice held a surprising trace of awe. "What was that like?"

Teigen drew a deep breath and told Tor his story as Selby returned and took her seat by his side.

Having her there steadied him as he relived the nightmare: from the midnight beating and arrest, through Grini and the train ride north, down to every detail of the exhausting work schedule, substandard living conditions, hellish weather, and his eventual release.

Tor's expression grew more horrified with each sentence of the narrative. "God, Teig. I had no idea you were caught up in that."

"He has Elsa to thank. She turned him in." For some reason, Selby wanted Tor to know about Teigen's fiancée's betrayal.

"No!" Tor stared at Teigen. "You cut her loose, of course."

"More than that. I had her arrested."

Teigen explained about Elsa's fraudulent salary claim and her choice to become involved with the Nazis through the *Lebensborn* project.

"I can't believe it, Teig. "Tor wagged his head sadly. "What a selfish bitch she turned out to be."

Selby looked at her watch for the third time since they finished their weak coffee.

"Lighters don't spark every time."

Her gaze jumped to Teigen's. "I know. It's just... the waiting. And the wondering."

"Is something going on?" Tor asked.

"No. We just need to get back to the theater in time to get ready for tonight's performance," Teigen lied.

Teigen could see the front of the Nazi headquarters down the street. So far, there was no unusual activity as brown-clad bastards entered and left the peaceful building.

Maybe Schmidt was coming in late today.

Or not at all.

Teigen turned back to Tor. "Where are you staying?"

"At your hotel." Tor shrugged. "Figured I'd find you one way or another."

"Will you come to the show tonight?" Selby flashed that adorable smile she'd perfected.

Tor smiled back. "I wouldn't miss it for the worl—"

BOOM!

Tor leapt to his feet. "What's that?"

Smoke spewed from the front of the Nazi's headquarters as Teigen and Selby also stood to watch. German soldiers scrambled around the front of the building like frantic ants.

Tor looked like he was about to bolt down the street toward the chaos but Teigen grabbed his arm to stop him. "No! That's the Nazi headquarters."

Tor relaxed his stance and shaded his eyes as he watched. "Someone put a bomb in there?"

"Looks like it." Teigen leaned closer to his brother and shaded his eyes as well, pretending to get a better view.

He spoke so quietly he hoped Tor heard him. "Actually, I did."

Chapter Thirty

Teigen cleared his throat. "We better get back to the theater, Miss Sunde," he said loudly. "Back to safety until they figure out what happened."

The owner of the café appeared in the doorway in time to hear Teigen call the actress by name.

Perfect.

"Thank you," Selby said to the woman with a trembling smile. "But I believe he's right. I'm rather frightened at the moment."

The trio hurried away in the opposite direction from the offices. None of them spoke while they made their way to the theater and headed down the side alley to the backstage door.

When they opened it, cheers erupted from the troupe.

"You did it!" Dahl grabbed Teigen's hand and pumped his arm. "Bennett saw it with his own eyes!"

"It was a thing of beauty," Bennett declared. "Noise and smoke and Nazis scrambling over each other to get away."

As the moment passed, the group's curious gazes shifted to the uniformed soldier standing behind Teigen.

"As you can probably guess," he said. "This is my brother, Tor."

Introductions were made, all routine, until Ben stepped forward. "Hello, cousin."

Tor startled. "Are we related?"

"Well done, Ben." Teigen clapped the youth on the shoulder. "You couldn't know if he could be trusted, even with the uniform." Teigen grinned. "But he can."

Tor frowned. "What's going on?"

"Young Ben here is hiding from the Nazis in plain sight."

"I'm half Jewish, sir," Ben offered the explanation. "Your brother saved my life."

Tor looked impressed yet again. Teigen was thoroughly loving this brotherly reunion. "We gave him papers as Ben Thorkelsen Hansen. We say he's my cousin and I'm tutoring him for his university exams."

"But he really is tutoring me," Ben said with clear exasperation. "He's a slave driver."

Teigen laughed and gave Ben an affectionate shake. "And Ben is an accomplished artist. You'll see that later."

"Teigen, why don't you go back to the hotel with Tor," Selby suggested. "You only have a short time together. Make the most of it."

"Thank you, Lieutenant." Teigen smiled. "We'll be back for the play."

***

Selby was touching up her makeup during intermission when Bennett appeared, ashen faced, with two SS officers behind him. Selby set her brush down and turned slowly to face the men.

"Can I help you?" she asked gently.

"Miss Sunde?" The officer who spoke was worrying his hat in his hands and looked extremely uncomfortable. "We need to talk to you about an explosion at Headquarters today."

Selby's heart climbed up her gullet and threatened to choke her. She looked intentionally confused. "Headquarters?"

"Yes, ma'am. The German headquarters."

Selby widened her eyes and put her hand to her throat. She focused on her role as Nazi sympathizer in case these men had come here thinking she was something else. "An explosion? Was anyone hurt?"

He looked like he wanted to drop through the floor. "Yes, I'm afraid so."

Selby suddenly realized why these men were here. Relief made her feel weak, thankfully enhancing her performance. "Not—tell me it wasn't—"

She covered her mouth with a legitimately shaking hand.

"I'm afraid so, ma'am. Captain Rolf Schmidt perished from his wounds within an hour of the explosion. He was rushed to the hospital, but there was nothing they could do."

Selby let loose a wail that brought the stage crew running. The other actors in the dressing room fell into various impromptu supporting roles when they saw the uniformed Nazis,

Dahl fanned her while she pretended to swoon and barked for water—which Karolina brought. Gunter shoved a stool under her feet and removed her shoes. Bennett told the stage crew to go back to their positions but wait to start the second act until they knew if Selby—or her understudy—could go on.

Teigen actually brought the smelling salts and waved them under her nose, which made her eyes water convincingly.

Bennett faced the Germans.

"If that's all you came for, can you please go?" Bennett's tone was respectful and pleading. "We have a sold-out theater expecting the second half of *The Winter's Tale* and the troupe needs to figure out how to make that still happen. I'm sure you understand."

"Yes. Of course." The man looked relieved to be done with the distasteful job.

"Wait…" Selby appeared to struggle to sit up. "Did he say anything? Before he died?"

The misery was back. "No ma'am. I'm sorry. Apparently, he didn't have a face…"

Selby gagged. She slumped in her chair and blinked rapidly, struggling to remain conscious. Teigen applied the smelling salts with more intent and her mind cleared—but the nauseating image of the captain with nothing left but a bloody mass on the front of his head remained.

She barely noticed the Germans hurrying out the back door.

Dahl turned her face to his and examined her with concern. "Can you finish the play, Sel? Or should Karolina do it?" Tor's face rose to the front of her thoughts, and replaced the captain's imagined lack of one. She wanted—no, *needed*—to perform well tonight for Teigen's sake.

The older brother excelled at so much, at least as far as Teigen was concerned, that Selby couldn't let the troupe present a less than stellar performance when Tor was in the house.

She drew a steadying breath and straightened in her seat. "We did good work today. I can't let that stop now."

Teigen squatted beside her. "There's no shame in asking for help, Selby."

"No, there's not. But I won't let the Nazi bastards steal my glory. *Our* glory." She looked at the bank of concerned faces surrounding her and pushed herself to her feet. "Now let's get back out there and perform the hell out of Shakespeare."

ᚾ ᚾ ᚾ

Teigen watched Selby from backstage, utterly amazed. He knew she was faking her sorrow over the announcement that Schmidt was dead, but her reaction to the damage the bomb caused the captain obviously undid her.

I'll add more gunpowder next time, he decided. *So death is immediate.*

There was a difference between a clean kill and torture, after all.

The troupe was cheered back onstage for three curtain calls that night. Selby's determination clearly inspired the rest of the cast to give one of the best performances he had ever seen from them.

Tor was impressed as well. Teigen knew because his brother said so over and over again.

"Are you hungry?" Teigen asked when they finished cleaning up. "The hotel has a decent cook."

"That sounds good." Tor's blue eyes twinkled with mischief. "Are you going to invite your girlfriend to join us?"

"My—Selby?"

"She *is* your girlfriend, isn't she? You were holding hands when I found you."

"That was—we're just—not exactly," Teigen sputtered.

"Fine." Tor shrugged and twisted his neck to search the troupe milling in the backstage area. "Then I'll ask her."

"*I'll* ask her," Teigen grumbled. "I see you haven't changed. Still meddling in my life."

Tor's expression shifted. "No. You're wrong there, Teig. I have changed."

"Then why—"

"Because I like her," Tor cut him off. "And if you aren't out for her, I might as well give it a shot."

Teigen scoffed. "But you're leaving for America tomorrow."

"Which is why I'm glad I pressed the point." Tor's smile returned, but all trace of teasing was gone. "With you, brother, she's in the best possible hands."

N N N

Selby sat at dinner with the Hansen brothers believing herself to be dining with the two handsomest men in all of Norway. Both stood a lean and muscular half-a-foot over six feet with blond hair—Teigen's in a longer style that was popular, Tor's in a military cut—and both had the most expressive and beautiful eyes.

When Tor excused himself to wash his hands, Teigen turned to her. "What are you thinking so hard about?"

Selby felt her face warming. "That you two are the most handsome men in Norway."

Teigen laughed and wagged his head. "Then God help Norway."

Curiosity pushed her to ask, "Did Tor say anything about me?"

Teigen paused. "He asked if I was going to invite my girlfriend to join us for supper."

Selby pulled back in surprise. "Me? Your girlfriend?"

"We were, as he pointed out, holding hands when he found us."

"Oh. Of course."

"But we weren't when we met with Falko." Teigen gave her a significant look. "And *he* asked if we were dating. Or more."

Selby waited for her usual fear and revulsion to surface at the thought. It didn't. Instead, she wondered if being Teigen Hansen's girlfriend would be such a bad thing.

It's not an engagement, she reminded herself. Just a public acknowledgement of a mutual attraction. Nothing more.

Teigen glanced around to see who could hear them before saying in a sotto voice, "Even Ben asked me if I kissed you."

Selby bristled. "What have you been saying to everyone?"

Teigen laid a hand over his heart. "I swear, Selby, not one single word."

"So they all came up with the idea that we're an item all by themselves?"

Teigen lifted his beer to his lips. "Yep."

While he sipped it, Selby pulled up her mental bootstraps and made a decision, but she waited for him to set his glass down before she told him, to avoid his making a mess.

"All right then." It was all her nerves would allow her to say.

Teigen frowned. "All right then what?"

"I'll be your—if you *want* me to, of course. But if not, well that's fine, too. You know."

Teigen's jaw fell slack and he stared at her. "Are you having some sort of episode?"

Good Lord, I'm an actress. I can do better than that.

"No. I'm fine." Selby took another run at it. "Do you want to be my boyfriend?"

Tor reappeared at that exact moment and dropped into his seat. "I'll pick up the check for supper."

"Yes!" Teigen practically shouted. "No!"

"Are you having a fit, brother?" Tor chuckled. "Which is it?"

"Yes to you." Teigen pointed at Selby.

"And no to you." He pointed at Tor.

Selby burst out laughing.

"I can't speak for Selby, but I insist on buying your dinner." Tor's face was a mask of confusion. "It's your birthday, Teig. Who knows when I'll be able to celebrate with you again."

"Yes, Teigen." Selby couldn't stop giggling. "Let him buy your supper, for heaven's sake."

"And yours, too, Miss Sunde," Tor continued. "In gratitude for your excellent performance tonight."

"Let him, Selby. Tor always wins anyway." Teigen's smile couldn't be wider.

Tor sighed and rolled his eyes. "That's settled then."

"Yes it is. Finally." Teigen reached for Selby. "Come here."

Selby slid happily into his arms.

※ ※ ※

The kiss was quick, intense, and left him tingling like he'd stuck a screwdriver into an electrical outlet. Mindful that they were still in the hotel dining room, Teigen set Selby back in her chair as quickly as he'd pulled her from it.

Tor sat across the table, blinking like an owl. Selby's face was as red as a winter's sunset and she was still giggling. Teigen felt like he could conquer Germany single handedly.

Tor leaned one elbow on the table. "What exactly happened when I went to wash my hands?"

Teigen grinned at his brother. "Selby asked me to be her boyfriend."

"Oh. That's great." He blinked again. "So you weren't talking about the supper bill then, were you?"

"Part of the time I was, yeah." Teigen looked at his girlfriend. "Sel?"

She was radiant. "I tell you what, I'm going up to my room and relax before bed. It's been an eventful day, to say the least, and I'm done in."

Teigen started to object but she stopped him. "Why don't you and Tor stay down here and have a drink. I'll talk to you tomorrow."

Teigen looked at his brother and realized the wisdom of that suggestion. "I think that's a fine idea."

Tor gave Teigen's shoulder an affectionate pat. "Me, too."

Selby turned and left the dining room, and Teigen watched her go. "I hope she doesn't change her mind."

Tor laughed. "Do they have aquavit here?"

The Hansen brothers stayed up talking until after midnight. Even so, when Tor came down to the lobby early the next morning to catch his ride to Telavåg, Teigen was waiting for him.

"I wanted to say a proper goodbye," he said and stuck out his right hand.

Tor shook it with both of his. "It was really good to see you, Teig. I've missed you."

"I've missed you, too. But after this visit, I'll probably miss you more," Teigen admitted.

"I feel the same." Tor's brows pulled together. "I joined the army, but I think you've been through far more than I have."

"It's been tough, I won't lie." Teigen combed his fingers through his hair. "But I'm making up for lost time now."

Tor smiled. "In both love *and* war, it seems."

Teigen felt his cheeks tighten with the blush. "Yeah. I hope so."

"Well, good luck then." Tor shouldered his knapsack and turned to leave, but turned back to face Teigen. "I'm really proud to be your brother. I want you to know that."

Unexpected emotion thickened Teigen's throat. "Thank you for saying that. Your shoes are hard to fill."

Tor shook his head. "Don't follow me, Teig. Walk your own path."

"I will." Teigen wiped his wet eyes. "And you keep walking yours, Tor. Show the Americans what the Hansen men of Arendal are capable of."

The brothers hugged then; a tight, solid hug. The kind of hug that, if they never saw each other again, they would not find this moment lacking in any way.

"I love you, Tor."

"I love you too, brother."

And then he was gone.

CHAPTER THIRTY ONE

March 24, 1943

"What news is there?" Teigen asked Selby as they walked from the hotel to the theater.

"Jorgensen says there hasn't been any mention of it on the German transmissions." Selby glanced over her shoulder to make sure no one was within earshot. "It's as if the explosion never happened."

Interesting.

"And this Jorgensen is trustworthy?" he asked.

"So far the information he's given us has all been accurate." Selby looked up at Teigen. The sun made the pale blue in her eyes look like glacier ice. "He has a closet behind a closet that he hides his radio in. I know he's been suspected of spying, but the Nazis haven't found his hidey-hole yet."

Teigen dragged his fingers through his lengthening hair. "I'm always amazed at the risks people take. What about his family? He could easily end up in the prison camp right here in Bergen—or worse."

"It's a simpler choice for people like me," Selby admitted. "I don't have anyone else in the world I need to worry about."

Though that wasn't at all true, Teigen replied with, "And I

don't have a wife or children."
Yet.
"You have your parents."
Teigen shrugged. "And besides me, they have Tor."
"Don't forget Ben," Selby chided. "He adores you."
"I suppose he does." Teigen smiled softly. "And I do care about him."
The pair walked on in silence, passing uniformed soldiers without looking them in the eye. The sun shone weakly through gauzy clouds and a damp and lazy sea breeze brushed Teigen's cheeks.

When they reached the theater he opened the stage door and held it for Selby. Ben was already there. He left the hotel early saying that he wanted to make sure the paint was dry enough on his latest creation before anyone packed it.

The young man showed so much promise as an artist, that Teigen was rethinking how best to teach him. Once the war ended, it might turn out better for the youth to enter a fine arts program rather than a strictly academic university.

We'll talk about it when the time comes.

In the meantime, he would continue their regular lessons.

Today's task was packing the flats, costumes, and props in preparation for the start their journey to Ålesund the next day. After so many repetitions the job had fallen into an easy routine with each member of the small troupe responsible for particular items.

Teigen and Bennett were loading flats onto a trolley when Falko opened the door and strode into the backstage area.

"I came to say goodbye," he said as he shook Teigen's hand. "And to say that you did a fine job here."

"Thanks." Teigen chuckled and considered his friend. "Is it bad that I wish the explosion had more impact?"

Falko grinned. "You might be surprised. Helgesen was very pleased. He's talking about ordering more desks."

"He is?" That was good news.

Falko nodded. "Yep. So who knows?"

Teigen made a gesture of hopeful helplessness. "Then I guess I'll have to wait and see."

"In the meantime, I think you should make a few copies of the schematic for the desk." Falko winked. "Just in case."

October 26, 1943
Trondheim, Norway

It was a good thing that Teigen decided to act on Falko's parting suggestion. Over the last seven months, five of the special desks had been built and shipped to Milorg groups in Oslo, Kristiansand, Stavanger, Trondheim, and Narvik—all Norwegian ports where the Germans originally attacked and still maintained strongholds.

And, except for the far northern city of Narvik, all were regular stops for the Royal Shakespearean Acting Troupe.

Teigen's arming of the new desks had begun in Oslo three months ago. He worked with Milorg and showed his designated partner how to install the cigarette lighter and gunpowder.

"Don't add the powder until you're sure that the lighter will light," he cautioned. "And then immediately strap the drawer closed. Tightly closed."

The man nodded nervously. "Got it."

The newly built desks were made with hinged tops; Helgesen had obviously passed Teigen's comments on to the craftsman. The polished tops could be latched in place once the desk was armed, so that was very helpful. And Teigen realized right away that he needed to buy several of the same style of cigarette lighter—ones with push levers—so that his design would work consistently.

"I thought of something else," he told Colonel Berntsen once the Oslo desk was armed and ready to be delivered to the Germans. "The desks need to be delivered to the Nazis at different times in every city so that they don't explode either while the troupe is in town or right after the troupe leaves."

Berntsen nodded. "Good thinking, Hansen. Though I'm not sure the Germans are smart enough to connect your presence with the sabotage, it pays to be cautious. I'll notify the various outposts."

The next concern Teigen had needed to be discussed with Selby. "I know you asked for Schmidt to be the target in Bergen, but we can't designate a target in every city."

Selby rolled her eyes and looked at him like he was simple.

"Obviously. The explosions happen in cities where we perform, so if all the victims are known consorts of mine that would shine a klieg light on us as the culprit."

He should have known she'd be a step ahead of him. "Right. So we're in agreement."

Selby nodded. "In Oslo, Kristiansand, and Stavanger I don't care who gets targeted. Or even if it's someone specific or just whoever's unlucky enough to open the drawer..."

Teigen noted her omission. "But in Trondheim..."

Selby's expression turned to hardened steel. "Fritz Walder needs to die."

Teigen knew about Walder's attack on Selby. The officer had been transferred from Ålesund to Trondheim as a result of being found lacking. Apparently winding up in a gutter passed out drunk and being discovered there by local Norwegians didn't present the image the Nazis strove for.

Plus, waking up in a gutter with a nasty bump on the head and clutching an empty bottle of aquavit left some doubt as to exactly what had occurred. Walder couldn't retaliate for Selby's dumping him because he couldn't prove what happened.

But Selby was keenly aware. "I mean it, Teigen. Fritz needs to receive that desk."

"That's fair," he agreed. "I'll do what I can."

And that's exactly what he was working on now.

"Major Berntsen says we're supposed to deliver this desk while you're still here," Teigen's contact Karl told him. "He says that the troupe was in town for Bergen, but gone for Oslo, Kristiansand, and Stavanger. He wants to change the pattern."

"Understood." *Selby will be happy to hear that.* "What have you heard about the other explosions?"

"Reports of the exploding desks are always circulated on the Milorg underground radio," Karl said. "But the Germans are keeping quiet officially, as I'm sure you've noticed—I think they're afraid of giving ideas to other resisters."

Teigen chuckled as he opened the hinged top on the desk. "I don't think Milorg is lacking ideas."

Karl leaned over the opened desk. He pointed to the gap behind the front drawer. "So the bomb goes here?"

И И И

Selby sat in her hotel room that whole afternoon trying to memorize her lines for *Taming of the Shrew* but she couldn't concentrate. She looked at the clock on the nightstand, wondering

when Teigen would return and tell her when Fritz was going to receive the armed desk.
I hope it's while we're still here.
The troupe had already vacated the previous three cities for various lengths of time for the last explosions. In each city, however, there were arrests and imprisonments afterwards.
"But breaking the pattern is important," she muttered. "And we don't even perform in Narvik."
Falko Jensen had drawn the assignment of traveling north to arm that desk. In fact, he should be there now. Having two explosions in close proximity time-wise, but several hundred miles apart geographically, would keep suspicion away from the troupe.
Selby looked at the clock again. If the second hand wasn't moving, she would have sworn the cursed thing had stopped.
A knock on her door made her jump.
Selby tossed the script onto her bed and ran to the door. When she yanked it open and saw Dahl standing in the hall she had to struggle not to look disappointed.
"Hi." She stepped back so the actor could enter. "Come on in."
"I'm glad you're here." Dahl held up his script as he walked past her. "Would you mind running lines with me?"
"No, not at all." At least it would be a useful distraction. "Sit wherever you want."
Dahl looked at the bed and then sat in the only chair in the room. His tall, masculine frame was at odds with the worn floral fabric covering the decidedly feminine chair.
Selby walked to the bed, retrieved her own script, and sat leaning against the traditionally painted wooden headboard.
"Where do you want to begin?"
He flipped a few pages. "Act Two. When Katherine and Petruchio are alone for the first time."
Selby turned to the page. She read over the scene quickly then looked at Dahl. "Okay. I'm ready."
As the pair spoke William Shakespeare's centuries-old dialog to each other, Selby realized how similar her relationship with Dahl was with Kate's relationship with Petruchio.
The strong-willed and determined Katherine had never met a man like Petruchio before. When she insults him, he replies sweetly. When she goads him, he offers clever responses. She belittles him, and he still treats her with patience and offers kind words.

True, Selby had never been mean to Dahl; but she did continually refuse his gentle advances—and yet he persisted. No matter how thoughtful and consistent the man had been, Selby always held him at arm's length.

So how was Teigen Hansen able to bash through her concrete wall without even trying?

"Selby?"

She blinked and stared at Dahl. "I'm sorry. Could you say that line again?"

Dahl's brows pulled together. "What on your mind? Is it the desk?"

"No. Well yes, but..." Selby's pulse surged as she considered how honest to be. "I was just struck by Kate and Petruchio's conversation."

Dahl set his script aside. "Struck how?"

Time to jump in. "How similar she is to me, and Petruchio to you."

Dahl looked like someone had just punched him in the chest. "I have to disagree, Sel. You've never treated me like Kate treats Petruchio."

"No, I haven't been mean or rude to you," she began. "But I have refused your romantic advances. Every time."

Dahl's eyes rounded. "And now?"

Oh, no.

This was going in the wrong direction.

Selby shook her head and leaned forward. "You are an amazing man, Dahl. You're brave, talented, smart. And way too handsome for your own good."

"But..." His shoulders slumped. "You aren't interested."

He looked so crestfallen that Selby wanted to cry. "We're not a good match." Tears stung her eyelids. "I'm not good enough for you."

"Good enough!" Dahl looked incredulous. "Selby, how can you say something like that?"

"There are things you don't know about my past. I'm... damaged." A single tear dripped down one cheek. "I don't think I'll be good for anyone."

Dahl looked desperate. "I don't care if you're not a virgin."

Selby huffed a laugh in spite of the severity of their conversation and wiped the lone tear away. "Actually, I *am* still a virgin. Barely."

Dahl abandoned the girly chair and crossed to the bed. He sat by her feet. "Then what is it?"

Selby's composure took another hit. Dahl's expression was so compassionate and loving that she wondered for the first time if she was completely wrong about absolutely everything.

"I can't tell you," she deferred. Her palms began to sweat.

"Don't you trust me?"

Selby gasped. "Of course I trust you. But I care very deeply about what you think of me."

He leaned back a little. "And you're afraid that if you tell me your deep, dark secret that my opinion of you will change?"

She gave an apologetic shrug. "It will."

Dahl's gaze fell to his hands. His fingers twisted together like he was fervently trying to hold on to something but it was slipping from his grasp.

"You're wrong, Selby."

Her voice was very small. "I don't think I am."

Dahl lifted his devastated regard to hers. "Does Hansen know?"

Selby gasped again, this inhalation ragged with shock.

"What? No!" Her heart tried to break out of her chest and she held it inside with a fist pressed to her sternum. "Why would you ask me that?"

Dahl wagged his head. "I'm hopeful, not blind."

"Blind?" Was their relationship that obvious?

Dahl snorted. "It's clear to all of us that Hansen is smitten with you, if not downright in love. And you two spend so much time together."

Selby knew it was true, even of she hadn't allowed herself to fully believe it. "That doesn't mean anything. We're really just good friends."

Dahl was clearly skeptical. "You're not in love with him?"

Am I?

No. I can't be.

"I am not." Selby willed it to be true.

Dahl's eyes narrowed. "I don't think you know yourself, Selby Hovland."

Selby glared at him. "Don't insult me, Petruchio. It's not your role."

Dahl startled. "Sorry, Kate. It was only an observation, not an insult." He reached for her. "Forgive me?"

Selby pulled a deep breath and let it out slowly. Dahl was right—she was overreacting. She accepted his proffered hand.

"Yes, of course. I'm sorry, too."

Dahl smiled weakly. "Friends at least?"

"Friends forever, I hope. Dear ones," Selby said truthfully. "I do love you in that way."

The actor looked resigned. "Well, that's something."

Another knock on her door launched Selby from the bed. She stopped and tried to calm her skyrocketing anticipation before she opened the door.

Teigen stood in the hall grinning. "The desk is delivered."

Relief washed over her nerves. "That's fantastic!"

Teigen's gaze moved past her and into the room. Selby turned to see what Teigen saw: Dahl sitting on her bed and the crumpled bedspread.

She whirled back to look at him. "We were rehearsing."

Teigen's smile disappeared. "Sorry I interrupted."

He turned away and strode down the hall.

Selby followed, quickly pulling the door closed behind her so Dahl couldn't hear any conversation she and Teigen might be about to have.

"Wait!"

Teigen took two more steps before he halted.

Selby ran around him and planted herself in front of him. "We were working on Scene Two," she said quietly. "Nothing more."

He looked down his nose at her. "It's none of my business what you do with him."

She punched his arm. "I wasn't doing anything with him!"

Teigen lifted his hands. "If you say so."

Selby glared up at him demanding, "Why don't you believe me?"

He leaned down and met her eyes. "Why do you care so much what I believe?"

"You're impossible!" Selby punched his arm again before rushing back to her room.

CHAPTER THIRTY TWO

October 27, 1943

Selby kept to herself the rest of the night and had dinner sent up to her room. In the morning she skipped breakfast, too nervous to eat. Instead, she dressed in the boy clothes—shirt, trousers, jacket, shoes, and cap—and slipped out of the hotel through the kitchen's back door.

Her brief argument with Teigen left her unsettled. She did care what he thought she was doing alone in a hotel room on a rumpled bed with Dahl. Teigen was technically her boyfriend, though not much between them had changed. She still held him at arm's length.

She knew that if she told Teigen about her stepfather and the rough things he had done to her before he murdered her mother and killed himself that Teigen would know she was soiled.

Not to mention she was a thief and an arsonist.

No man, even in this enlightened age, would see her as wifeworthy, even if she *could* bring herself to let a man whom she cared about touch her intimately.

The fumbled caresses of drunken Nazi fools were disgusting, not arousing, and she never let them go too far. Those groping and unemotional attempts at sex didn't bother her.

On the other hand, kissing Teigen lit her up inside in ways that were dangerously treacherous to her resolve.

"What if I let him get closer and was revolted by our physical contact?" she wondered softly as she walked through the early morning streets of Trondheim. "That would ruin everything."

Selby reached the long block where the Nazis' Trondheim headquarters were housed. She walked down the length of the block, looking for an obscure place to settle while she waited for the explosion that was sure to happen this morning.

Teigen said he would see what he could do about ensuring that Fritz Walder was the officer who received the desk. Asking God's forgiveness even as she prayed, Selby asked Him to make sure things would turn out that way.

She did wonder how her conscience could stand condemning two men to death, but told herself once again that she was at war and these men were her sworn enemies.

Selby tucked herself into the doorway of an abandoned shop and watched the German officers enter the building to start their workday. As time passed with no sign of Walder she began to wonder with disappointment if Fritz was taking the day off.

Damn.

Today of all days.

Eventually her patience was dubiously rewarded when she saw the lieutenant swaggering down the street. His familiar face burned her stomach as the memory of his angry assault on her flamed anew in her mind.

Go to your death, you bastard.

As soon as the man disappeared into the building, Selby moved to find a closer place to wait in. She wanted—no *needed*—to be certain that Fritz was dead after the explosion happened.

Her pulse surged as she waited, making her chest feel tight and her head feel as if it might roll off her shoulders. She tried to breathe deeply but it was hard when she expected the *boom* of the desk at any moment.

Come on, Fritz... Open your—

BOOM!

Smoke streamed from the front door which was blown open by the blast. Norwegians rushed toward the building as Germans scrambled over each other to get out of it. Selby stood and walked forward to stand with her countrymen.

"Careful, boy," an older man warned her. "There could be

another explosion or a fire."

Selby nodded and took half a step back without meeting the man's eyes.

It's done.

Satisfaction soothed her core. Fritz Walder would never attack another woman again.

And then the unthinkable happened.

His face still recognizable under a layer of smoky soot, the very lieutenant whom Selby hoped would die stumbled through the smoke and into the street.

No. No no no.

Frozen in disbelief, Selby stared wide-eyed at the Nazi officer. With a shock, she realized that was a mistake. Spinning around, she began to push her way through the crowd.

"Boy!" Fritz shouted. "Stop!"

Selby ignored the order and the crowd of Norwegians made no effort to impede her progress. Some went so far as to step in her wake. She was nearly free when a hand clamped down on her shoulder with the strength of a crane's claw.

"I've got him, sir!" the brown bastard shouted.

Selby struggled to break free. The soldier grunted as bystanders' blows were surreptitiously added to hers.

An ear-rupturing gunshot brought all movement to a halt.

"Make way!" a voice demanded, angry and hoarse from smoke. "Now!"

An expanding opening in the crowd put Selby face to face with Fritz. At least it would have if she was looking anywhere but her feet.

"Did you have something to do with this?" Fritz barked.

Selby shook her head violently and grunted, "Uh uh."

"Look at me when I speak to you, boy." Fritz grabbed Selby's jaw and jerked her face upwards. "Show due respect to your— *you?*"

The lieutenant stared at Selby's face in disbelief. His free hand yanked the cap from her head. "What the hell!"

Selby shot visual daggers at Fritz but said nothing.

"You little bitch!" he bellowed as the once-protective crowd faded from her range of vision. "Did you set that bomb?"

"No," Selby ground out with her jaw still painfully held in Walder's tightening grip. "But I wish I had."

The lieutenant's fist dove into her midsection taking every last bit of her breath with it.

᛫ ᛫ ᛫

Teigen edged closer to Walder and Selby, trying to figure out how to rescue her before the Nazi killed her.

The enraged officer pummeled the petite actress over and over, until Teigen coiled to jump in and intervene.

"No." Hands attached to the sotto voice gripped him from behind. "You'll make it worse."

Selby lay senseless on the ground while Walder shouted his spitting vitriol at the actress, Selby Sunde, and landed a few extra kicks.

God help her.

Now.

Another officer stepped to Walder's side and grabbed his arm, pulling the man's attention from his victim. The officer said something that Teigen couldn't hear into Walder's ear.

Walder nodded.

He looked down and spat at the unconscious Selby before following the other man back into the smoking building.

᛫ ᛫ ᛫

Teigen leapt forward and quickly gathered the actress in his arms. He asked the crowd, "Where can I take her?"

"There's a Norwegian doctor two blocks that way on the left, next to the grocer," said a man about Teigen's age. "He's a *good* doctor."

A young boy of ten or eleven bolted in that direction, leading the way.

"Thanks." Teigen followed, running as fast as he could without jarring his precious cargo too roughly. He understood the man's designation of *good* meant that the Norwegian doctor held no loyalty to their brutal occupiers.

Teigen pushed through the door to the medical office. "Help!"

A nurse motioned to him from an interior door while the boy panted in a corner, his eyes wide. "This way."

"Thank you," Teigen said to both the nurse and the boy.

When he laid Selby on the examination table he was gratified that she squirmed a little and moaned. He leaned down and spoke soothingly in her ear.

"You're with a doctor. He's going to help you."

"Hurts…"

"Shhh." Teigen pushed her cropped hair off her swollen and bruising face. "You're going to be fine."

Please God. Please please please.

"The boy says she was beaten." The doctor's clipped words as he entered the exam room were spoken without wasting time on pleasantries. He jammed the earpieces of his stethoscope into place and pushed the chestpiece under Selby's shirt.

Teigen nodded, his regard fixed on the doctor's face. "A Nazi officer recognized her."

The doctor frowned and moved the chestpiece, still listening. "Recognized?"

"This is Selby Sunde. The lead actress with the Royal Shakespearean Acting Troupe."

The doctor's gaze jumped to Teigen's. "Is that why he hit her face so often?"

Teigen looked at Selby. Her nose was definitely broken. Both eyes were swelling shut and turning a vivid shade of reddish purple as was her jaw.

"Is her jaw broken?"

The doctor moved it slowly. "I don't think so, but I'll need x-rays to be sure."

Selby moaned again. Tears leaked from her swollen eyes.

"Can you hear me, Miss Sunde?" the doctor asked.

"Uh huh."

"Good." He shot Teigen a reassuring glance. "I'm going to have you transported to a safe hospital. Do you understand me?"

Pause. "Uh huh."

This time the doctor hesitated. "You're going to be fine."

Teigen's chest constricted when the doctor straightened and met his gaze with a severe one of his own. "I'll get the car."

◢ ◢ ◢

That evening Teigen sat beside Selby's hospital bed and watched the chest of the woman he loved more than anyone else on this planet rise and fall in shallow but thankfully regular breaths.

X-rays proved three cracked ribs on her left side—thankfully still in place and not puncturing her lung. But there was fluid in both of her lungs and she was put on penicillin to keep it from turning into pneumonia.

Her jaw was cracked as well, but only a painful hairline fracture which could be treated with rest and soft foods.

The doctor saw internal bleeding in the x-ray of her abdomen so nurses came in and examined her every hour to see if it had worsened. So far, it had not.

Teigen passed the time by mentally flaying Lieutenant Fritz Walder in the slowest and most painful way he could imagine.

I will retaliate, Teigen resolved. The vile man would pay for hurting this woman, no matter how long it took.

A movement in his peripheral vision drew Teigen's attention to the door. "Dahl. Come on in."

The actor was good, but not good enough to hide the horror that claimed him when he saw Selby. "Oh, God."

"She's going to be fine, Dahl," Teigen reassured. "As long as the internal bleeding stops."

Dahl sank into the other chair by the bed. "Internal bleeding?"

"Yeah. Walder didn't hold back." *Fuck the bastard.* "She's got three cracked ribs and a cracked jaw."

"Shit."

"Exactly."

The men sat in silence until the nurse came in to examine Selby's abdomen and left again.

"Her face…" Dahl began. "Looks like her nose is broken."

"It is."

"I hate to mention this, but—"

"What's she going to look like now?" Teigen guessed.

Dahl looked appalled at his own words. "She's our lead actress."

"No. Not anymore," Teigen stated.

Dahl's jaw dropped. "She's not going to be *that* much changed!"

"Not for that reason!" Teigen felt his face heating with embarrassment at what Dahl thought he meant. "I meant because she has been exposed."

Dahl's face paled. "How badly?"

"That asshole Walder shouted her name to the crowd—and she was in her urchin disguise at the time."

"But that's not too—"

Teigen lifted one hand to stop him. "And he asked her if she set the bomb."

Dahl's shoulders fell. He closed his eyes and tipped his head back. "Oh, Lord. What'd she say?"

"No, but I wish I had," Teigen quoted.

"Damn."

"She's done, Dahl. And if she comes back even to visit the troupe you'll all be done." He didn't say *we'll* for a reason, and wondered if Dahl caught it. Teigen was not going to leave Selby's side ever again for any reason.

Dahl looked like the light had gone out of his life. "We'll have to issue a public statement of some sort."

"Agreed."

The men were quiet again until Dahl spoke. "I'll say she had nothing to do with the bomb, and was working on a disguise for a future role when she was recognized."

"Dahl—"

Now Dahl lifted a silencing hand. "Hear me out, Hansen. We'll say that this is the second time that Lieutenant Walder has attacked her for absolutely no reason, and because of that she has left the troupe *temporarily* for rest and recuperation."

Teigen frowned. "Temporarily?"

"If we say it's permanent, she looks guilty."

Teigen heaved a sigh. "Damn it. You're right."

"And that way," Dahl seemed to be thinking out loud, "if she wants to come back in a different capacity, or even the same one, she can."

"After everything blows over?"

Or Walder is dead.

Dahl shrugged. "Yep. That's what I'm thinking."

It was a workable plan, Teigen had to admit. "I can agree to that."

Dahl looked at the sleeping woman. His surprising expression reflected deep loss and Teigen wondered what had really happened yesterday between Dahl and Selby.

"The Shetland Bus leaves from Ålesund," Dahl broke into Teigen's musings with the stunning suggestion. "That's the closest boat."

"Leave Norway?" he clarified.

Dahl nodded. "For now."

"I'll take her," Teigen declared. "How do we get there? Should we take the Hurtigruten?"

"It's just under two hundred miles by land. That might be safer. Milorg can get you a car."

"Alright."

Dahl stood. "Are you coming back to the hotel?"

"Not yet." Teigen looked at the woman who seemed so small and fragile in the stark hospital bed. "I'll be there later to pack."

"I'll have Karolina pack Selby's things and put them in your room under Ben's guard." Dahl shot him a rueful smile. "And I'll tell her to practice Selby's lines."

Teigen stood and held out his hand. "Thank you, Dahl. For everything."

Dahl swallowed visibly. "You love her. Don't you."

Teigen's first impulse was to deny it, but the haunted look on the actor's face cut through any façade he might have hidden behind.

"More than I care to admit," he conceded.

"Good. She deserves it." Dahl bounced a determined nod and swallowed again. "She has no interest in me, by the way. In case you thought she did."

Teigen didn't know what to say to that, so he said nothing; but now he knew how totally wrong his assumption was yesterday. No wonder Selby was so angry at him.

She had a right to be.

"Anyway, I wish you luck." Dahl walked to the door of the ward. "She's a tough nut."

Teigen allowed a relieved smile, careful not to gloat visibly over this unexpected turn. "So am I. We might be doomed."

CHAPTER THIRTY THREE

November 1, 1943
Ålesund, Norway

Pain.

Sometimes it dragged her from sleep and wild dreams with the intensity of a sledgehammer. And then, after a while, it would fade to the background, still throbbing, but at least she could breathe.

She couldn't think clearly. Something had happened to her... the bomb. The bomb exploded. That was good.

But afterwards something bad had happened.

If only her brain wasn't so fuzzy she might be able to put the pieces together.

Sometimes she awoke lying in the back seat of a car, jostling over rough roads. Other times she was lying on a cot, rocking with the movement of waves. Then she was in a car again.

Where am I?

What happened to me?

She was being lifted from the car's bench. Lifted gently in strong arms. She tried to open her eyes but she couldn't manage more than a slit.

Teigen? Teigen was carrying her?

What happened?

"You can put her in here." A woman's voice. Soft and kind.

"Thank you." *Teigen.*

"The boat's due the day after tomorrow." The woman again. "In the meantime, what can I get you?"

She felt herself being lowered onto a bed. The softness of it soothed the pains which seemed to claim every inch of her frame. She hummed a moan of relief.

"Selby? Are you awake?" Teigen's unshaven face moved into her slice of vision. "Do you need more pain medicine?"

Pain medicine. Opiates.

That explained the dreams and fuzzy-headed fog.

She pried her tongue from the roof of her mouth and grunted, "No."

"Water?" Teigen offered. "Maybe some broth?"

"Uh huh."

His arms slid behind her shoulders and sat her up, causing her head to pound and sending daggers through her left side. A straw prodded her lips.

Selby latched onto the straw and sucked the cold liquid, relishing the feel of it sliding down her parched throat. With each swallow she felt more alert.

When she pulled her mouth away from the straw, Teigen leaned her back, now against a stack of pillows that elevated her from the waist up.

The woman must have done that.

"I'll go make some broth," she said. "And something a bit more substantial for you."

Teigen said, "Thank you."

"Wha…"

"Don't try to talk, Selby. Just rest. I'll be right back."

When Teigen reappeared at her side, he laid cold cloths over her eyes and nose as he spoke to her.

"Do you remember what happened?"

"No. Some." Her voice sounded like an old lady.

"Do you want me to tell you now? Or later?"

Selby didn't need to think about that. "Now."

Teigen began to comb her short hair. "All right. I'll start at the beginning of that day." He set the comb aside and slipped his hand under hers. "If you have a question, or want me to stop, squeeze my hand."

She squeezed it to show him she understood.

Teigen drew a deep breath. "We had delivered the desk with the bomb to Lieutenant Walder's office the day before. That morning, I went to your hotel room to see if you wanted to have breakfast with me, but you weren't there. And when I went down to the dining room, you weren't there either. That's when I knew you had gone to Nazi headquarters."

Yes. I did. I remember.

She left the hotel at dawn. Dressed like a boy.

"By the time I reached the building, the bomb had just exploded. I couldn't see you in the crowd at first. But I did see Walder come out the door through the smoke, still alive."

Yes.

That was the bad thing. Fritz Walder wasn't dead.

"I saw you then, trying to make your escape through the crowd." Teigen paused and cleared his throat. "Do you remember that?"

Vague images spurred by panic flooded her mind. "Uh huh."

"Do you remember what happened next?"

She remembered looking into the lieutenant's eyes and telling him she wished she *had* planted the bomb.

After that, nothing.

"No."

Teigen removed the cold cloths from her eyes, rinsed them, and replaced them. He did the same with the cloth across her nose. The fresh chill was soothing.

His hesitation was not.

Selby squeezed his hand.

Teigen's voice was low and calm. "He beat you, Selby. Badly. Right there in the street."

Stinging hot tears filled her eyes and rewet the underside of the damp cloths. She felt the tears leaking out the sides of her eyes and rolling down her temples.

Teigen lifted the cloths and refreshed them. "I shouldn't have told you."

"Yes," she managed. "More."

"More?" He sounded puzzled. "More cold cloths?"

"No." Why did it hurt to talk? "How... bad?"

"Your injuries?" His tone screamed his reluctance to answer.

She squeezed his hand as hard as she could. "Every... one."

As Teigen listed the damage—concussion, broken nose,

cracked ribs, fractured jaw, internal bleeding, and deep bruising over her whole body—Selby's tears flowed continuously. She didn't remember the pummeling, and was thankful for that mercy.

Someday, however she would claim her revenge.

"You were in the hospital for three days, waiting for the internal bleeding to stop, which it did on the second day," Teigen continued. "Milorg found me a car and sent word here, in Ålesund, that we would need passage on the Shetland Bus. It took two days of driving and ferries to get us here. And the boat sails the day after tomorrow."

She frowned, though doubted Teigen could see that. "Why?"

"Why are we leaving Norway?"

She squeezed his hand again.

"Because he called you out by name—Selby Sunde. Everyone there saw you with your short hair and boy clothes." Teigen cleared his throat again. "Dahl will make a formal statement that you had nothing to do with the bomb and were testing a disguise for a future role."

Dahl. Always looking out for her.

Fresh tears.

"He's going to tell everyone that this is the second time that Walder's attacked you for absolutely no reason."

Fucking bastard.

"That's why you've left the troupe *temporarily*—to rest and recuperate."

Selby squeezed his hand. "Go back?"

"If you want to go back to the troupe you can. But no more dating Nazis."

She was fine with that. "When?"

Teigen chuckled a little. "You've got at least two months of healing before we even start to talk about it."

Footsteps and the quiet rattle of a tray being set down nearby halted their conversation. "Here's the broth. I hope it's not too hot."

"Name?" Selby croaked.

"Call me Anna."

A common woman's name, probably a pseudonym, and no surname. Always striving to be safe.

"Thanks, Anna."

When Anna's footsteps faded away, Teigen asked Selby if she wanted the straw for the broth, or would she rather he feed her with a spoon.

Selby chose the less humiliating path. "Straw."

The broth was delicious. The rich flavor of the bone marrow was salted just enough and the warmth of the soup relaxed her.

The conversation, however, seemed to have drained all of her strength.

When she pushed the bowl away, Teigen said, "You sleep now. I'll get settled and check in on you later."

Selby had one more question first. "Why you?"

"Why me?" Through the slit in her swollen eyes, Selby saw his surprise as well as heard it. "Do you mean why am I the one taking you to safety?"

"Yes."

Teigen smiled and set the bowl on the tray. "Don't you remember my promise? I told you I would always protect you."

She remembered, but she thought his words were rhetorical, not literal.

"I'm not a man who goes back on his word." Teigen lifted her hand to his lips as kissed it. "Get some rest."

He stood and carried the tray from the room, pulling the door closed behind him.

November 3, 1943
Ålesund, Norway

Because the Shetland Bus network recruited Norwegian fishermen to sail between the British Shetland Islands and the west coast of Norway right under the Germans' noses, anything appearing too military or showy would be suspect, leading to stop-and-search maneuvers.

The two-masted sixty-foot fishing boat waiting for them—a Møre Cutter from Ålesund—was as unremarkable as was to be expected. But Møre Cutters were supposed to be the strongest and best-fitted vessels for the rough weather common in the North Sea.

"Nobody would notice this bucket," Teigen muttered. He hoped the thing was more seaworthy that she looked.

"What?" Selby hobbled next to him at about fifty percent under her own power.

"Nothing. Can you manage the gangway or should I carry

you?" When she looked up the incline and didn't answer right away, Teigen swooped her up in his arms. "Here we go."

Thankfully the inside of the boat was in considerably better shape than the outside.

"Keeps them from looking at us too sharply." The Norse captain winked and worked very hard not to look at Selby. "Let's get the lady settled in. There's a hidden cabin we get through in the galley."

Teigen shifted Selby in his arms. "The galley?"

"It's labeled *Cold Storage*. In case we get stopped." The captain beckoned. "Follow me."

When Teigen set her on her feet inside her little cabin, Selby looked around the space. "Mirror?"

Up to now, Teigen had refused her repeated request. "You'll look worse before you look better," he told her yet again, thankful the tiny cabin lacked that bit of vanity. "There's no reason to upset yourself needlessly."

Selby shuffled to the bed and sat. "He wouldn't look."

"The captain?" Teigen was getting pretty good at intuiting what Selby's clipped sentences meant. "Don't worry about that. Just keep healing."

She might have glared at him. Hard to tell with her eyes still swollen. "I'm going to find my cabin, then find out about bringing your meals down here."

Selby flipped an irritated hand in his direction before she curled on the bunk.

Teigen's same-sized cabin was next door. He was sharing it with a man his same age who was escaping Norway to go to America and live with relatives. That man had already claimed the bottom bunk, so Teigen tossed his satchel on the top bunk and went in search of the captain and the galley.

"Three hundred and sixty miles," the captain answered Teigen's query. "I'll crank up her seventy-horsepower engine, and if we get good winds we should land in Lerwick late tomorrow afternoon."

The *tonk-tonk-tonk* of the semi-diesel engine had already begun. Teigen excused himself and went below to tell Selby what he discovered, but she was sleeping.

As the boat began to move away from the dock and sway with the coastal swells, Teigen went to his own cabin and climbed to the upper bunk to rest. This past week of worrying about and taking care of Selby had drained him and he was looking forward to doing very little for the next thirty hours.

What strange turns his life had taken over the last eighteen months: the dissolution of his engagement, his arrest, surviving the Arctic labor camp, joining a traveling acting troupe, becoming a Milorg officer, taking charge of a half-Jewish teenaged refugee, making Nazi desks explode, and now escorting the woman he loved to a British island to recover from a severe public beating.

He would never have predicted any of that even in his most incredible imaginings.

Teigen didn't know what to expect from their coming months in Shetland exile, but he was pretty sure that both Selby's appearance and his relationship with her were not going to be the same when they returned to Norway.

Whether that was good or bad he could only wait and see.

CHAPTER THIRTY FOUR

November 4, 1943
Lerwick, Shetland Islands

Selby was a bit more steady on her feet the next afternoon when Teigen came to collect her and escort her off the ship. She was glad he grabbed her Arctic fox coat when they made their escape. Even though the coat was far too showy for their humble surroundings, above all else it was warm. She appreciated that quality most of all when she climbed to the deck and sleet hit her battered face.

She looped her arm through Teigen's and held up the coat's thick fur collar to protect herself.

People stared at her. She was used to getting attention, but for a much different reason than today. She tried to tuck herself out of sight behind Teigen's arm. Besides avoiding notice, it kept the icy rain from stinging her eyes.

At least she could see out of them now. During the last two days the swelling had dramatically decreased even if the tenderness had not.

Teigen led her slowly, allowing the other passengers to disembark first, before leading her carefully down the gangway.

"Do you know where we go?" she asked. Her jaw still ached, but she decided to stop sounding like a simpleton and form more complete sentences.

"We're all being met by a Scotsman named James Adie," Teigen spoke over her head as he looked around. They walked forward, following the straggling group of refugees down the pier as Teigen continued, "He and his Norwegian wife built a refugee center here in a herring factory."

A man of middle height with bushy auburn hair approached the group. He was accompanied by a blonde woman of the same stature, and she was the one who addressed the Norwegians in their own language.

"I am Helga Adie. Welcome to Lerwick and to freedom," she said in a voice that carried surprisingly well. "My husband James and I will see to your needs and get you on your continued way as soon as possible."

Her roaming gaze landed on Selby, then quickly moved away. Selby thought she was blushing, judging by the tightening of her skin.

"Please follow us."

The walk to the herring factory was only two blocks but it left Selby panting and sweating. Teigen hadn't offered to carry her and she wondered if he was unconcerned, or if he knew she would have refused.

It was bad enough to look like she did. She didn't need *helpless invalid* added to her list of odd qualities.

"You're a proud woman, Selby Hovland," Teigen murmured in her ear. "But don't push yourself too hard."

Selby tightened her grip on his arm but said nothing.

Once inside the repurposed building, each person was assigned to a curtained area in either the men's dorm or the women's. But when Selby and Teigen reached the front of the line, she was given different instructions.

Helga Adie smiled at her kindly. "Miss Sunde, your room is on the second floor, in our medical wing."

That was a relief. She'd be with others who also weren't in their best form. "Thank you."

"She'll need help," Teigen said quietly.

Helga motioned to a stout woman in a white nurse's uniform. "Erin will help you. She knows a little Norse, but will call me if you run into trouble."

Selby did her best to smile, but was afraid all she did was grimace. "Thank you."

As she walked away from Teigen, Selby felt an unexpected surge of panic. This was the first moment since the beating that he wasn't going to be near her, and the thought of being alone terrified her.

She grabbed Erin's sturdy arm. "Can he come?"

"He?" The nurse turned around to look at Teigen who was intently watching them. Then she turned back to Selby and shook her head. "I'm sorry. Women's ward, yes?"

Selby tried to slow her breathing and told herself she was being ridiculous. "Yes. Of course."

You are going to be fine.

"I—I can't climb the stairs."

Erin smiled and pointed to an elevator. "All sick people use."

A quarter of an hour later, Selby was settled into her own curtained space in the medical ward. Erin said that a doctor would come examine her, and she should rest.

Selby lay down on the firm cot and then curled on her right side—she couldn't put pressure on her cracked left ribs. She stared blankly at the white linen curtain, wondering why she panicked.

Because Teigen makes me feel safe.

He promised to protect her and he was doing a fine and uncomplaining job of it. Maybe if she had trusted him enough and asked him to go wait for the explosion with her, she wouldn't be in this situation now.

Or maybe he would have been beaten and *arrested.*

She must have dozed because the doctor's greeting startled her. Selby sat up slowly, glad to see Helga Adie at the man's side.

"I'm Doctor McKean and my Norse is getting better," he began with a grin. "But I always have Lady Adie with me in case I get confused. You are Selby Sunde?"

"That's my stage name. My real name is Selby Hovland."

"Stage name?"

"I'm—well I *was*,"—she would think about that later—"lead actress in the Royal Shakespearean Acting Troupe. All of the troupe members are Milorg."

"I see." Dr. McKean swept a pointed finger from her head to her feet. "And how did this happen?"

"I was publicly beaten by a vengeful Nazi lieutenant."

With Helga's help, Selby told her story with enough detail that the doctor understood. With his stethoscope and gentle hands, he examined every injury she sustained until he was familiar with the extent of her damages.

"You are a lucky woman," he said. "All we can do for you now is make you rest, take fluids, and eat as much as you're able with your jaw so painful."

Selby wanted to check Teigen's claim. "How long will I be here?"

"Eight weeks." Dr. McKean looked at her over the rim of his glasses. "Not a day less, and maybe several more."

"Where will you go then?" Helga asked.

That was an odd question. "Back to Norway, of course. Why do you ask?"

"Most of the people who make it this far are headed toward safety," Helga replied. "Yet you plan to return to the occupation?"

Selby lifted her chin. "I'm a soldier. A Milorg lieutenant. I'm at war, and I don't have a choice."

December 24, 1943

During the last seven weeks of Selby's convalescence, Teigen spent all available hours with her. He went to the second floor and either sat with her in the hall, or escorted her down to the first floor for a short walk.

On the few days that the weather on this small northern island cooperated he walked outside with her. With Selby bundled warmly in the fox fur and draped in a scarf, they explored shops together along the narrow streets or watched the activity on the pier from a distance.

Over time her bruises faded and her eyes looked like her eyes again; thick brown lashes surrounding the purest pale blue Teigen had ever seen. Her hair had grown an inch since the incident—which is how they both agreed to refer to the vicious beating—and now brushed her cheekbones in a way the shorter cut hadn't.

Karolina didn't think to pack any of Selby's cosmetics in the rush to get her out of harm's way, and even through Selby groused about that on a regular basis, Teigen told her repeatedly that she had never been more beautiful.

Three weeks ago Selby had stared intently at her reflection in the mirror Teigen eventually provided. "My nose isn't straight."

"It's still swollen," he countered.

Her gaze bounced from the mirror to him and back. "I don't look the same."

Teigen leaned over and looked closely. "I can see what you're talking about."

Selby looked stricken. "So I'm *not* imagining it?"

"I'm afraid not." She stared at the mirror again and tried pushing on her nose. When she winced, Teigen told her to stop.

"Leave it alone, Sel. If it heals with a little angle to it that only adds character to your face."

"So I'm a character actress now?" She let the mirror fall to her lap.

"We should talk about that." Teigen reached over and took the mirror from her grip. He set it on the table beside her bed, as far from her as he could.

Selby's brows gathered above the offending feature. "About what?"

"Acting. And the troupe." Teigen leaned back in his seat. "What are your thoughts?"

"I'm going back, of course," she declared. "There's no doubt about that."

"As whom?" he prodded. "As Selby Sunde the blonde bombshell—even though everyone now knows that's not what you look like?"

Selby stared at him, her expression sober. "You think I should return as mousey Selby Hovland with the crooked nose?"

Teigen laughed at that. "Good God, woman. You are the furthest thing from mousey!"

Selby made a *pffft* sound. "Don't try to swell my ego."

"I'm not!" Teigen continued to chuckle. "I'm serious, Sel. You possess a true and *natural* beauty."

Selby crossed her arms and glared at him. "So what do you suggest?"

Teigen had actually given this matter quite a bit of thought.

"First of all, I suggest you return as Selby Sunde, because that name is known. You don't want to lose that draw. Besides, you're probably even more famous since the incident."

Her expression didn't change. "And?"

"And secondly, ditch the wigs and appear in public the way you look now."

Selby's hand moved to her hair. "And let my hair grow?"

Teigen shook his head. "No. Keep it short. It suits you."

She looked skeptical. "Really?"

"Really." Teigen leaned forward again. "Frame your eyes with some liner and mascara, and get a lipstick in a softer color than that red you always wore."

He smiled. "You'll look stunning."

Selby started to giggle. "Is the big manly high school teacher giving the actress make-up tips?"

Still grinning, Teigen winked at her. "After spending a full year watching you all transform your looks with greasepaint, I might have picked up a thing or two."

After that conversation, Selby seemed to relax—at least where her next move was concerned. The mirror was still at her bedside, but Teigen noticed it wasn't moved nearly as often.

N N N

It's Christmas Eve.

Selby combed her hair with her fingers and considered Teigen's words—as she did every time she looked at her reflection. Her critical examination of her features grew less condemning, and she decided he was right. The short haircut was flattering. And once she could buy make-up again, she'd try his suggestions.

Her nose was, well, her nose. She was stuck with it.

Throughout the whole ordeal Teigen had been her rock. Her honest and kind rock. Her uncomplaining rock. The rock that saved her life.

I wish I had a Christmas gift for him.

Maybe when they returned to Norway. Hopefully she'd get the doctor's blessing and they could sail on New Year's Day; but even if she didn't, she decided it was time to go back.

Her ribs still ached when it was cold and damp, which was every winter's day on this island, but they didn't hurt when she breathed normally anymore. And her jaw only pained her if she tried to chew something hard.

Selby wondered how the troupe was faring. Dahl had sent a couple letters to assure her that she wasn't implicated in the explosion and there was no backlash against them. Karolina was doing fine as lead actress, but she wasn't as beloved by the audiences.

That made Selby feel good in an unflattering sort of way.

Mostly she felt like life was passing her by and she needed to re-board that train.

"That means you're completely healed, in my book," Teigen said when she told him.

He held her chair while she sat at a festively adorned table in the warehouse section of the erstwhile herring factory. James and Helga Adie had clearly put a lot of effort into making their temporary Norwegian refugees feel celebratory during their first Christmas in exile.

"I hope Doctor McKean agrees," Selby muttered. "Even if he doesn't, I'm leaving as soon as I can."

"Don't you mean *we* are leaving?"

Selby looked up at him, startled by his words. "Yes. *We* are leaving. Right?"

"Right." Teigen gave her an odd look. "But you always talk as though it's only you."

Do I?

"I don't mean it that way."

Teigen flashed a crooked smile. "I'm glad to hear it. Because *I'm* going back with you."

Selby stared at the candles in the center of the table. Though she wasn't aware that she spoke in singular terms, the reason she did was obvious.

"I've been alone since I was fifteen," she murmured. "And I'll be thirty in March." She lifted her eyes to Teigen's. "That's a long time to only have yourself to think about."

"That's true."

It looked like Teigen was about to say something else but he was interrupted by other Norwegians joining their table.

After brief introductions, the conversation shifted to an exchange of war and occupation stories while their traditional Norwegian Christmas Eve dinner of salted and smoked lamb ribs was served. Every man and woman in this building had a reason to leave their beloved homeland behind, and some of them were truly horrific.

Many refugees had relatives in other countries, but just as many others did not. Those souls, forced into bravery, were headed toward America where they were determined to forge new lives.

Minnesota. Wisconsin. Iowa. They said the names as if trying to make them feel familiar, welcoming, comfortable.

"But you're going back?" The woman stared at Selby while their supper dishes were cleared. "Why?"

"I'm a lieutenant in Milorg," she explained to her shocked tablemates. "I was brought here to recuperate after I was—I was severely beaten in the streets of Trondheim. By a Nazi officer."

"Are you an actress?" the man beside her asked. "I heard something like that on the resistance radio."

"Yes." The fact that she looked so different now made her suddenly self-conscious. "With the Royal Shakespearean Acting Troupe."

Another man across the table stared at her. "I've seen them perform. *A Midsummer Night's Dream*. Which part was yours?"

Selby wanted to sink through the floor. She felt her cheeks burning. "Titania."

"The lead?" He frowned. "What'd you say your name is?"

Under the table Teigen's hand moved to rest on her thigh. The heat of his palm seemed to ground her. She glanced at him and flashed a tiny smile of acknowledgement.

"Selby Sunde." Out of long-standing habit she never introduced herself as Selby Hovland. "You're used to seeing me in a blonde wig."

The man snapped his fingers. "That's right! Now I recognize you!"

The first woman looked confused. "Are you an actress or Milorg?"

"Both," Teigen answered before Selby could. "The entire troupe is Milorg, and we pass information and supplies as we travel up and down the west coast."

"And what about you?" the woman asked Teigen.

"I was a high school chemistry teacher in Oslo before I was arrested. After I was released from the Kirkenes labor camp a little over a year ago I joined Milorg and the troupe. I work backstage, and I arm Nazi desks to explode."

As the attention focused on Teigen's startling succession of statements Selby sat back and helped herself to the Christmas biscuits and cookies that were set on the table. She knew him well enough to know that he had no love for the spotlight.

What he had just done was take a figurative bullet and pulled the uncomfortable scrutiny away from her.
Now her palm moved to his thigh.
His glance slid to hers and he smiled.
"Well, at least you have each other," the woman said to Teigen after the initial hubbub calmed somewhat. "And your beautiful wife is a very lucky woman."

CHAPTER THIRTY FIVE

Selby stiffened. "He's—"

"Thank you," Teigen cut her off and his hand clamped over hers under the table. "I happen to agree with you."

What the hell was he doing?

She dug her nails into his thigh, gripping the muscle like a claw. He pulled her hand away and stood.

"While we have enjoyed the time, I don't want Selby to tire herself. She needs to be completely recovered before we sail."

Selby glared up at him as he pulled her chair back. "Ready?"

Realizing that her reputation still mattered, Selby stood and smiled sweetly at their tablemates. "Happy Christmas."

Teigen took her arm and guided her from the room.

Selby rounded on him in the factory hallway. "Explain yourself!"

Teigen's jaw was set. "Let's go somewhere private."

Selby turned and headed for the elevator. "There are unused offices on the second floor."

Tense silence filled the elevator car as it rumbled creakily to the second level. When the doors opened Selby turned away from the medical ward and headed down a dim hallway until she reached the first door.

Inside the office she flipped on the light. Fluorescent lights blinked to harsh life above them. Selby planted her feet and crossed her arms.

"Okay. Talk."

Teigen crossed to the dusty desk and sat on it. His eyes were now level with hers. "There is something that I wanted to speak with you about before we leave the island."

"What?"

Teigen squinted at the lights on the ceiling. "This isn't the setting I imagined."

Selby huffed. "Just say it."

Teigen's green eyes rested on hers. He looked as if he was steeling himself against her coming response.

"Will you marry me, Selby?"

She was struck momentarily speechless. She should have guessed this was coming, but...

"I am deeply in love with you," Teigen said, filling the deserted office with his words. "And I almost lost you. This life is too precarious for me to believe we can safely wait for another chance."

Selby found her voice, though it was nearly strangled by the lump in her throat. "You don't want me."

"But I do."

"No..." Selby couldn't look him in the eye. "I'm... broken."

She heard Teigen breathing. She waited.

"I know you don't trust men in general," he said finally. "But I think you'll agree that I've proven *myself* to be extremely trustworthy."

"You have," she said to the floor.

"So what's broken?"

"Me," she whispered.

Teigen's knuckle slid under her chin and tipped her head up toward his. "How are you broken, Selby?"

Tears blurred his handsome face. "If I tell you, then nothing between us will ever be the same."

"If that means you'll be my wife, then I'll be satisfied." His eyes pinned hers. "Tell me."

"You won't want to marry me anymore."

"Try me."

Selby desperately wanted to tell Teigen about her past. And just

as desperately she wanted to believe he would still want to marry her after he heard her story.
Because I love him, too.
But what if it ruined everything?

ᚾ ᚾ ᚾ

Teigen watched Selby carefully. Whatever had happened to her, or whatever she had done, didn't matter to him. For over a year he had lived and worked by her side, and he knew what sort of woman she was.

And he knew that he didn't want to live the rest of his life without her.

She seemed to come to a decision. "I need to sit down."

Teigen got off the desk and walked around behind it. He pulled the wooden desk chair forward and placed it in the center of the office. Then he flipped the little metal trash can upside down and sat on it in front of her.

He took one of her hands and gently massaged it. "When you're ready," he said softly.

Selby watched his ministrations as if in a daze. "This is terrifying."

"I'm here with you, remember? I'll protect you," he assured her.

She did look at him then. "You can't change the past."

"No," he admitted. "But I can change the future."

After pulling a ragged sigh of resolution, Selby started her tale. "My father died in the Great War and the man my mother married afterwards was as cruel and perverted as any Nazi. I always hid in my closet when he raged at her."

Teigen turned her hand over and rubbed her wrist. "What was that like?"

"He always accused her of sleeping with Russians, for some reason. And he threatened to kill her."

"As a child, I'm sure you thought he might actually do it."

Selby nodded, watching the movement of his fingers over her skin. "So I prayed that God would strike him dead."

"How long did this last?"

"When I was twelve or thirteen I started stepping between him and my mother."

Teigen wagged his head. "I can't imagine he was happy about that."

"No."

"Did he turn on you?"

A full minute passed before Selby uttered the tiny word, "Yes."

Teigen set her hand down and lifted the other. "Did he rape you?"

※ ※ ※

His tone was no more intense than if he had asked if she wanted coffee or tea with supper. But somehow that matter-of-fact tone unlocked a deep-seated and violent fury inside her.

"No. But I think what he did was worse." Her voice hardened along with her determination. If Teigen really wanted to hear about her past, then she wasn't going to hold back.

You'll see.

And then you'll know I'm right.

"Whenever I stopped him from beating my mother his rage turned into lust. He dragged me to my bedroom and threw me on the floor. He stripped me from the waist down. Then he opened his pants."

The words were gushing out of her like a dam had broken. "He used his hands on me while he pleasured himself. He was rough and mean, but he slapped me if I made any sound. He said I was trying to make him to have sex with me."

Teigen watched her silently, all the while rubbing her wrist and then moving up her arm.

"He always said exactly the same thing: I know what you want, bitch, but I won't let you give me the clap, you filthy whore." She still could hear the rasp of his sneering taunt. "I think sometimes he started up with my mother *hoping* I would interfere."

The muscle in Teigen's jaw rippled, but his expression remained calm. "And your mother?"

"She tried to stop me from getting into it with him, and then she tried to stop him from hurting me. All that got her were multiple broken noses and teeth." Selby reflexively touched her own damaged nose. "I finally couldn't take it anymore. I ran away when I was fifteen."

"I don't blame you." Teigen switched hands again. "From what you've said before, I assume your mother is no longer alive."

Selby shook her head. "A month after I left, that man shot her and then himself."

He hummed a sympathetic sigh. "I'm so sorry, Sel."

"I went back to the house and cried for a week." Fresh grief rolled down her cheeks. "I kept thinking that if I had stayed then he wouldn't have killed her."

Teigen stopped the massage but he still held her hand. He looked at her sadly. "You know that's not true, don't you. He probably would have killed both of you."

That thought had occurred to her. Selby wiped her cheeks. "You might be right."

"Is that everything?"

"Except that I stole everything I could use or pawn from the house before I left the second time."

"It wasn't stealing," Teigen countered. "You were collecting your inheritance."

"And then…" She drew a steadying breath. "I burned the house down."

↗ ↗ ↗

Teigen was actually relieved. His worst-case expectation was that Selby had been raped multiple times.

He let go of her hands and looked her in the eye. "Let me see if I understand your situation: you were beaten and attacked by a madman multiple times, you ran away to save your own life, and using what you could scavenge from your own home, you started a new life?"

Selby looked confused. "Y—yes. And I burned the house down."

"It was your house."

"But—"

"There wasn't anyone inside?" Teigen clarified.

She frowned. "Of course not."

Teigen shrugged. "Then you had every right to do whatever you wanted with it."

Selby stared at him. "Are you insane?"

"Nooo," he said slowly. "I don't think so."

"Did you listen to what I said?" she snapped. "I burned a house down!"

Teigen watched her carefully. "It all could have been so much worse for you than it was. You could have been raped or killed. Or did I get part of this wrong?"

Her mouth opened, then closed. Finally, "No—I guess not."

"Good." He gave her an encouraging look. "Now explain the broken part."

"What?" she snapped.

"You said you're damaged but—unless there's more that you haven't told me—you're still a virgin?"

"Physically. Yes." She looked angry. "But he ruined me."

Teigen was honestly confused by that. "I don't understand."

"People who get married have sex."

He nodded. "That's usually the case."

Selby smacked her palm against her chest. "I can't let a man touch me in that way without being revolted."

"Have you tried?" The question was sincere. "Have you had a boyfriend before?"

"No!" Selby stood suddenly and circled behind her chair. Her white-knuckled fingers gripped its back. "There's no point, is there? Because I already know what will happen."

Teigen remained perched on his wastebasket-cum-stool and looked up at her. "You're a grown woman now, Selby. Not a frightened little girl."

"No, Teigen—I *am* a frightened little girl!" she cried. "Don't you understand that? I'll always be!"

"I understand your words, but they don't make sense to me." He hesitated a moment before bringing up the dangerous subject. "What about when you were with the German officers?"

N N N

Selby straightened. "How *dare* you!"

Teigen jumped to his feet. "Don't misunderstand me—I'm not suggesting you did *anything* wrong!"

"Then what?"

"When you were plying them for information. Didn't they touch you?" Teigen's face grew violently red. Obviously he was embarrassed by his own question.

She jammed her hands on her hips. "Of course they did. It was part of the ruse. But I *never* let it go far."

"Were you revolted?" he pressed.

"Every single minute!"

Who wouldn't be?

"That makes sense…" Teigen stood. He dragged his fingers through his hair and walked a jerky circle around the desk while Selby watched him.

Frustrated by his silence she demanded, "Do you have something else to say?"

"I do." He looked at her, his expression pensive. "I'm putting it together."

"Well hurry up. I'm getting tired." Selby walked the rest of the way around her chair and dropped back into the seat. She crossed her arms and her legs tightly.

"Okay. Hear me out. Promise?" Teigen looked so hopeful that she couldn't deny him.

"Fine."

He perched back on top of the little metal wastebasket. He looked so ridiculous that if their discussion wasn't so intense she might have laughed.

"You have only had sexual contact with two kinds of men: your violent stepfather and your worst enemy." Teigen paused. When she didn't answer him, he prompted, "Isn't that right?"

Unsettled by the question, she tried to explain. "I was able to lead the German bastards on because at that point I believed that all men were like the man my mother married."

I'll never call him my stepfather.

Teigen pounced like a bird on a worm. "At that point?"

"Ugh!" she grunted angrily. "Yes. You've shown me differently. Satisfied?"

"Very." Thankfully Teigen didn't grin. If he had, she might have slapped it right off his face.

He readjusted his weight on the creaking wastebasket in preparation before launching his next volley. "Has it ever occurred to you that the element of attraction was absent from every single one of those encounters?"

Damn it.

She unfolded her arms to plead with him. "I see where you're going, but—"

He stuck a stiff finger in her face. "No buts! You promised to hear me out."

"I know, but—"

"Selby." His stern tone silenced her.

She pressed fisted hands into her lap. "Keep your finger out of my face."

Teigen retracted the offending digit then leaned toward her. "Have you ever in your life been physical with a man you were attracted to?"

Her pulse surged. She felt her cheeks tighten.

"Selby?" he said softly. "Tell me the truth."

"You know the answer."

He shrugged. "Even if I do, you need to say it out loud."

She narrowed her eyes. "Why?"

"Because then you and I will be starting from the same place."

Starting?

"Starting what?"

His brow twitched and she saw his heart displayed across his features as clearly as if the words *I love you* were tattooed on his forehead. "Starting our life together."

He still…

Don't get your hopes up.

Selby swallowed thickly. "No. I have never in my life been physical with a man I was attracted to."

A slow and sultry smile spread over Teigen's face. "Then it's time."

CHAPTER THIRTY SIX

Selby blinked. "What?"

Teigen rose from his awkward seat, moved it aside, and sat on the desktop again. He stretched a hand toward Selby.

"Come here."

She couldn't move. Whatever was about to happen here, in this dingy deserted factory office on a foreign island in the middle of the North Sea during a world-wide war, was going to define the rest of her life.

"I'm scared," she admitted.

Teigen looked at her so kindly it hurt. "There's nothing to be scared of."

"Yes there is."

His hand didn't move. "What?"

"That nothing changes." Selby bit her lower lip and watched him.

He gave her a small, reassuring smile. "But it will."

"You don't know that."

"But I do."

Still planted in the wooden chair, Selby shook her head. "You can't."

"I can." Teigen motioned with the extended hand. "Let me show you."

Selby realized that to remain in the chair, unmoving, was stupid. Nothing in her fraught life had kept her from making brave choices until now and this was yet another one.

"We'll still be friends, no matter what?"

Teigen's brow smoothed. "I expect to be by your side for the rest of our lives."

Selby gripped the arms of the chair and pushed herself to her feet. She took three small steps toward him thinking this must be how a convicted criminal felt walking into his lifetime of imprisonment.

She laid her hand in Teigen's and let him pull her the rest of the way until she stood between his knees.

"I'm just going to kiss you," he assured her. "Nothing else."

"Oh." Surprised relief calmed her nerves. "Okay."

Teigen let go of her hand and placed one palm on either side of her head.

Selby closed her eyes.

When Teigen's lips touched hers she immediately knew that this kiss wasn't going to be like the first one. Nor was it going to be like the time she kissed him.

And it certainly wasn't going to resemble the nightly affectionate pecks he began giving her once her jaw felt better.

This kiss was going to rock her to her very center.

His lips invited her in. Again. And again.

When she didn't resist the kiss deepened until his tongue played with hers. She felt his breath on her cheek and the roughness of his days-old beard.

It felt surprisingly good. Teigen was a big man with a strong and hardened frame—one that could harm her or protect her. To understand that he chose to protect her with his body sent a hot tendril of hope through her veins.

Selby hummed a surprised sigh and leaned into Teigen.

His hands moved down her neck and around her back. He slid forward a little and held her tightly against him, chest to chest and hips to hips. Selby clearly felt his arousal.

She waited fearfully for revulsion to douse her with glacier water and end this precarious experiment once and for all.

It didn't.

Selby decided to push the issue. She looped her arms around his neck and pressed her hips against his groin. Then she moved just a little from side to side.

Teigen groaned. His hands dropped to her hips and held them still. He broke away from the kiss, panting, and rested his forehead against hers.

"Good God, woman. What are you doing?" he croaked.

"I have to know," she whispered. "I have to know when I'll break."

"*Are* you going to break?"

She swallowed. "Not yet."

Teigen pulled back and looked at her. His pupils were so wide that there was only the faintest ring of green around them. The intensity in his gaze screamed his desire for her.

But it didn't scare her.

When he leaned in to kiss her again she met him full force. They held on to each other, one deep and passionate kiss following another, until her lips were swollen and her cheek sore from the scratch of his whiskers.

Selby pulled away at last. "That's enough."

Teigen ran one finger gently along her jaw line. "How do you feel?"

Hopeful. "I—I liked it," she admitted.

"Me, too." Teigen smiled crookedly. "Obviously."

Even his reference to his arousal didn't shake her. What was happening to her?

"We should go…" Her suggestion to call it a night, though logical, felt wrong somehow, and that made her uncomfortable in a way she didn't expect. "Tomorrow's Christmas."

What does that have to do with anything?

She needed time alone right now. She had a lot to think about.

"You're right." Teigen pushed her back and got off the desk. He adjusted his trousers. "I'll walk you to your door as usual."

"Nothing's changed," she murmured, knowing it was a lie.

"Same as before." Teigen's grin proved he knew it was a lie as well. "Happy Christmas, my love."

December 25, 1943

Teigen sat at breakfast waiting for Selby and reading the letter he had just been handed when she dropped into the seat beside him.

"Good morning." Her voice was soft and held the hint of their secret. "Did you sleep well?"

"Not very, to be honest." He examined her expression looking for hints of her thoughts. "You?"

"Better than I expected." She reached for the platter of eggs in the middle of the table. "But not for the first three hours."

Deciding to move away from the personal topic for now, Teigen held up the letter. "This came from Dahl."

Selby's brow shot upward. "He wrote to you? But I'm the ranking officer."

Teigen pressed back every trace of a smile that the petulant tone in her voice prompted. "To be fair, I wrote him first. I sent him a note saying we arrived safely and that you were going to be all right."

"Oh." Her expression eased and she looked contrite. "That was good of you."

"And I wrote him again a couple weeks ago saying that we'd be returning soon." Teigen handed her the letter which he had already read.

Greetings.

I'm glad to hear that both of you are well and anxious to return to the Troupe. That will be good news to the rest.

As for us, Karolina sufficed as Kate. We completed our performances in Trondheim and Ålesund, but the terrible and unprovoked treatment Selby received at the hand of the Nazi officer has weighed heavily on all of us.

I decided to postpone our Bergen performances until after the New Year, and all the members of the Troupe were given time off for Christmas. Those who wish to continue to be part of our group will meet in Bergen the first week of January.

Ben sends his greeting especially, but says while he misses you, he doesn't miss his lessons. He and Bennett are staying with me in Bergen for the holiday. Watch out ladies: three bachelors on the prowl. Ha!

I hope you and Selby will be able to join us here soon.
Happy Christmas to you both.
Dahl

Selby raised her eyes to his. "That settles it. We'll leave on the next Shetland Bus."

Teigen reclaimed his letter. "I still want Doctor McKean to check you over one last time."

Selby rolled her eyes. "I'm fine. Or I will be. When *is* the next Shetland Bus?"

ᚅ ᚅ ᚅ

"January first. New Year's Day," James Adie told Teigen later. "We figure that even Germans celebrate the incoming year with plenty of drink, so it's a safe time to sail from that perspective."

"The boat lands here on the thirty-first and sails back the next day?" Teigen clarified. "Selby and I would like to be on it."

"You're sure about going back?"

Teigen nodded. "We're both Milorg officers and we want to rejoin our troupe."

James looked uncertain. "Is it safe?"

Teigen huffed a laugh. "Nowhere in Norway is safe. But that doesn't change anything, does it?"

After finishing his conversation with James, Teigen went in search of Selby. Since last night his resolve was firmly set and time was running out.

"Where does the boat land?" she asked when he told her he'd secured their passage.

"Telavåg. Do you know it?" That's where Tor had sailed from.

Selby frowned in thought. "It's a village on the outer coast. About twenty-five miles from Bergen, I think."

"Good. That's not too far." Teigen nodded his satisfaction. "We can hire a driver to take us into Bergen from there."

Selby sighed. "This is going to be a very long week."

"That depends on what we have to accomplish before we go," Teigen offered.

Selby shot him a skeptical look. "What do we have to accomplish? Neither one of us has much to pack."

"Well…" Teigen looked directly into Selby's eyes, willing her to agree with his plan. "There's our wedding."

Her shoulders fell. "Oh, Teig."

He stepped closer and pulled her into his arms. He kissed her as deeply as he had the night before, and he didn't stop until he felt her stiffened frame relax.

"It only makes sense, Sel," he whispered into her hair as he clasped her against his chest. "If we go back as husband and wife then we can share a hotel room. We can continue working on what we started last night."

"But what if it *doesn't* work?" she mumbled against his shirt.

"We won't know until we try." He rubbed her back. "And there's no way for us to have any privacy here."

Selby tilted her head back and looked up at him. "Why don't we just share a hotel room anyway? The world already believes I'm a Nazi whore."

Teigen shook his head. "But you're not. And I won't let the world think you are for one minute longer."

"Does it matter?" she pressed.

"It does to me," he declared. "I won't have the mother of my children be thought of like that."

That seemed to startle her. "You're really serious about this."

"Of course I am."

"You want to marry me here before we leave, and take the risk of a sexless marriage?"

"Not exactly," he said quietly. "I expect you to let me put a couple of children in you before you shut me out of your bed forever."

Her jaw dropped in shock, but he continued, "That won't happen until after the war, of course. Assuming we're both still alive."

That last statement definitely startled her. "We can't wait for another chance…"

He pushed her head against his heart and rested his chin in her hair. "Do *you* think we can?"

For a long time she held him without answering, her arms wrapped around his waist and her ear to his heart. Teigen literally bit his tongue to keep from saying anything else. This was Selby's moment of truth and she needed to come to her decision by herself.

He felt her take a breath and she cleared her throat with it.

"Ask me again."

Teigen loosened his grip and looked down at her. "Selby Hovland, will you do me the honor of becoming my wife?"

Though she looked as frightened as the scared little girl she claimed to be, her jaw was set. "Yes, Teigen. I will."

December 29, 1944

Selby stood in the narthex of the fifty-year-old Garthspool Evangelical Church in the center of Lerwick and wondered if she'd completely lost her mind.

Helga Adie was so excited about the impromptu wedding that she managed to find Selby a cream-colored wedding dress that reached her ankles, a short veil, and a few hot-house flowers.

"We'll have your reception lunch here, of course." Helga adjusted the shoulders of the dress. "Let me take in the back a little."

"You don't have to go to all that trouble," Selby objected.

"Oh yes I do!" Helga said between the pins now held in her teeth. "I needed something happy to end another terrible year with, and the love story between you and Teigen is just the thing."

"We don't have rings," Selby pointed out to her fiancé after the fitting. "This is too rushed."

"I'll take care of it," Teigen promised. "Trust me."

The chapel was filled with current residents from the refugee center, mostly new arrivals and total strangers to her. Apparently Helga wasn't the only person grasping at straws of normalcy and hope.

When the organist began to play, Selby stepped into the opening from the narthex and looked down the aisle. Teigen, wearing a dark blue suit that almost fit, waited for her by the altar with a ridiculously happy grin on his face.

Since she had no one to give her away, Selby walked the length of the chapel by herself. Her heartbeat thumped in her chest and the hot-house flowers trembled visibly in her hands.

When she reached Teigen she stood beside him and faced the pastor. The ceremony passed her in a blur, and it wasn't until Teigen slipped a ring on her finger that her thoughts cleared.

She looked down at the gold band encircling her third finger, then up at her new husband. "Where—"

He winked and tapped his forefinger against his lips.

"...man and wife. You may kiss your bride."

When he did, Selby forgot her question. All she could think was: *Faenmeg! I'm married.*

CHAPTER THIRTY SEVEN

January 3, 1944
Bergen, Norway

Teigen watched his wife sleep. Today they were meeting up with The Royal Shakespearean Acting Troupe to resume their positions. He wondered if any of their former colleagues had jumped ship during the hiatus or if all had remained committed to their mission.

He and Selby also needed to collect their last two months' salaries. He planned to use his to buy wedding rings to replace the one he borrowed for their ceremony and returned afterward.

And today they would tell the rest of the troupe that he and Selby were married.

Teigen stretched under the covers and yawned while Selby slept peacefully beside him. That was step one.

He had been careful to respect her pace. He didn't sleep in the same room as she until they left the center in Lerwick. They slept in the same cabin on the fishing boat—in bunks. Now settled in at their regular hotel, he finally spent the night in the same bed as his wife.

Full intimacy was still a long way off. But Teigen had learned patience in the labor camp. Take each day as it comes and don't look too far ahead. One foot in front of the other.

That was how you remained sane.
Selby stirred and stretched.
"Good morning," he greeted her.
Selby's eyes fluttered open and she smiled. "Looks like I'll never be cold again. Lying next to you is like lying next to a radiator."
Teigen chuckled. "You're welcome."
"What time is it?"
Teigen looked over his shoulder at the clock on his night table. "Seven forty-five. We better get going."
Half an hour later they descended the stairs to the lobby.
"It doesn't take me as long in the morning without messing with the wigs," Selby told him as she exited the bathroom. "But I do need to find out where my make-up case is."
Teigen shaved the night before after checking into the hotel and borrowing a razor from Ben. Apparently the teen had spent the last three days in the lobby waiting for him to arrive.
He greeted Teigen with a bear hug and followed him and Selby up to their shared room. When Teigen let Selby go in first and prepared to follow her, Ben looked alarmed.
"Don't worry, Ben," Teigen told him. "Nothing is going on that won't be explained tomorrow."
"Okay…" Ben considered him suspiciously from under lowered brows. "I'll bring the razor."
When they walked into the dining room Dahl, Ben, Bennett, and Karolina were already there. While Karolina jumped up and hugged Selby, the waiter hurried over and pulled a second table alongside the first to make room for the new arrivals to join the group.
"You made it!" Dahl stood and shook Teigen's hand. "It's good to see you both again!"
Teigen observed all the curious glances at Selby. Not only were the others wondering about her recovery, but she appeared this morning in her natural hair and without make-up.
He saw her cheeks brighten as she took a seat at the expanded table. Clearly she noticed the scrutiny, too.
Dahl was the first to speak. "You look wonderful, Sel."
The color in her cheeks deepened. "Thanks."
"How do you feel?" Bennett asked.
"My ribs and jaw still hurt a little," she said. "And of course my

nose will never be the same."

Ben frowned. "I think it looks fine."

Selby smiled at the teen. "Thank you, Ben. That's sweet."

The boy's blush outstripped Selby's.

Teigen sat next to Selby as he asked Dahl. "Is everyone coming back?"

"As far as I know, yes." He threw up flat palms. "That's a relief. We can go forward without scrambling."

"Except for the role of Kate," Karolina said softly. She looked at Dahl, not Selby.

"No, the role is yours," Selby stated. "You started it, so you might as well finish it."

Karolina turned to Selby. Her eyes rounded hopefully. "Are you sure?"

"I am. I'll start working on what's next." Selby glanced at Dahl. "If that's okay with you, of course."

Teigen noticed the brief disappointment that dampened Dahl's expression but it disappeared quickly. "If you still need time to heal, I have no objection."

After stubbornly insisting to Teigen that she was fine, he wondered if Selby would rise to the bait. He was surprised when she didn't.

"I've been thinking about switching roles anyway." His wife's declaration surprised everyone at the table, including Teigen. "I'm not going to play Nazi consort any more, so it makes sense to let someone else have the spotlight."

Dahl leaned forward, concern sculpting his face. "Are you afraid of something like that happening again?"

Selby blanched and glanced at Teigen. "I might be."

"Because you can still be lead actress and *not* date Nazis," the director and leading man pointed out.

Karolina looked pouty. "Maybe we could take turns?"

Selby faced her. "Turns at what? Dating Nazis or taking the lead role?"

Now Karolina blanched. "I don't want to date Nazis."

"Maybe taking turns as the lead actress would be a good idea." Dahl was obviously trying not to lose Selby. "Or deciding depending on the play…"

Selby turned back to Dahl. "What's the next play?"

He looked like a man in the crosshairs. "I haven't decided. Do you have a suggestion?"

"*The Comedy of Errors* has two lead female parts." The occupants of the table turned surprised faces to Ben.

"What?" He looked at the other five people at the table. "I told you I love Shakespeare."

"That's actually a very good suggestion, Ben." Selby returned her regard to Dahl. "What do you think?"

Teigen would bet his coming two months' salary that Dahl would do anything to keep Selby prominently onstage—especially since her beating was national news—so the actor's answer was no surprise.

"I love it!"

Plates of food were set in front of everyone in the group, halting conversation for the moment. But as soon as the waiter moved away, Teigen asked about the money owed to himself and Selby.

"Yes, of course. Gunter should be here by noon. He can pay you both then." Dahl gave Teigen a sly look. "That's a lot of money. Don't spend it all in one place."

Teigen turned to look at his wife. The time had come.

"I'm afraid I'll have to—or at least a good chunk of it."

"Don't go overboard Teigen," Selby cautioned him sternly. "I told you simple, and I mean it."

Bennett frowned. "What's going on?"

Ben, however, began to laugh.

Karolina looked at Dahl, clearly confused.

Dahl paled. "What's—what *is* going on?"

Teigen intertwined his fingers with Selby's and their joined hands rested on the white tablecloth. He couldn't hold back his joy and he grinned at the group.

"Selby and I were married in Lerwick. I need to buy rings."

ᚾ ᚾ ᚾ

"That's why you slept in her room last night!" Ben clapped his hands while Selby wanted to slide under the table.

"You did?" Dahl looked like his dog just died.

Teigen spoke to Ben. "I told you everything was fine."

Karolina squealed and Bennett shook Teigen's hand across Ben's chest.

Selby sat silently.

They think we had sex.

She managed a look at Dahl. Her counterpart was also silent. Stunned by the news. Why wouldn't he be?

The very last time they were together, the night before the explosion in Trondheim and her beating, she told him *I'm damaged. I don't think I'll be good for anyone.*

And now, just over two months later, she was married to another man. He'd asked her *does Hansen know.* Dahl knew her heart better than she did.

"Yes," she blurted as if Dahl had asked the question just a moment ago. "And we're working on it."

Conversation around the table died.

Selby ignored everyone except Dahl while her face burst into painful flames. "Do you understand?"

Dahl shook his head slowly. "I understand your words, Sel. But I don't understand you."

Selby turned to Teigen. "I'm not hungry."

He looked down at her, his face a mask of confusion. "What do you want to do?"

"Buy our rings." She stood and dropped her napkin over her untouched breakfast. "Let's go."

И И И

After her outburst at breakfast, Teigen took Selby to two jewelry stores and convinced her to accept a pair of rings, one with a small diamond flanked by two emeralds.

"I want to give this to you," he insisted. "Please let me."

Though her acceptance seemed reluctant, Teigen noticed during their lunch that she played with her empty finger. After they met with Gunter and collected their back pay, he and Selby returned to the store where the rings were on hold and he paid for them.

He slid the plain gold band onto her finger first, and the little diamond and emerald one next.

"With these rings, I thee wed," he said before kissing her right there in the shop.

Selby then slid the thicker plain gold band onto his finger.

"I didn't even have a prop when we spoke our vows," she said before she looked up into his eyes. "But with this ring, I wed you right back."

By suppertime everyone in the troupe knew that Teigen and Selby had married while in the Shetland Islands. When they walked into the hotel dining room for supper they were greeted with a standing ovation. There was even a bottle of champagne chilling on the table set for twelve.

"Where did this come from?" Teigen asked, lifting the dripping bottle.

"From me!" Falko Jensen pounded him on the back. "You sly dog!"

Teigen realized that some sort of explanation was in order. He encouraged everyone to sit while the waiter doled out a dozen tiny servings of the scarce wine. He took his place next to his wife, who kept surreptitiously staring at her hand and smiling.

"A toast," he said finally, lifting his glass. "I know that my marriage to Selby seems sudden. The truth is I've loved her for months."

Several of his troupe mates looked surprised, but a few smiled smugly. He guessed some wagers would be paid off later.

"I was willing to wait for her to realize that she loved me in return—which of course she did." He smiled as chuckles rose around the table. "But because we're at war, hurrying to settle down and start a family wasn't the best idea."

Heads wagged as the actors and actresses glanced sadly at each other.

"However..." Teigen paused to gather his composure. "On October twenty-seventh my opinion was changed in an instant."

Every face at the table sobered, and every pair of eyes shifted to Selby. Her cheeks reddened but her gaze remained fixed on his.

"I realized at that moment that I couldn't wait to make Selby my wife. Our future wasn't a guarantee."

Teigen looked directly at Dahl now. "Whatever obstacles were keeping us apart, are obstacles that we'll now face together."

Then he moved his gaze around the table so as not to obviously target Dahl with his words. "Whatever future we are blessed to have, starts now."

He grinned at Selby then and lifted her to her feet. Her smiling eyes glittered up at him with happy tears.

"*Skål!*" He clinked his champagne glass against hers.

"*Skål!*" she replied.

He emptied his glass in one gulp.

ᚾ ᚾ ᚾ

"I need to talk to Falko," Teigen said to Selby after their celebratory dinner was finally finished. "Do you mind?"

She shook her head. "I'll shower and get ready for bed before you come up."

Teigen gave her a tender but brief kiss on the lips. "I won't be too long."

He watched her leave and then turned his attention to his friend. "Thanks for the champagne."

"It's the least I could do." Falko walked away from the big table where their waiter and a busboy were cleaning up the dishes. "Will this do?" he asked pointing to a table for two in the corner.

"Sure." Teigen sat with his back to the room knowing that Falko preferred to keep an eye on who came and left. "Can I buy you a drink?"

"I won't say no."

Teigen caught the waiter's attention. "Two aquavits when you're finished, please."

The waiter nodded.

"So," Teigen turned back to his friend. "Tell me about the desks."

"Six explosions, five targets dead."

"Walder was the one that escaped?"

Falko sighed. "Yeah. Some dumb private opened the drawer apparently."

Too bad. "Are more desks coming?"

"No. Colonel Berntsen in Oslo put a halt to it. He said the Nazis were retaliating too strongly." Falko shrugged. "I can't argue with him on that."

The two shots of aquavit arrived. Teigen paid the waiter. Then he lifted his glass. "It was good while it lasted."

Falko touched Teigen's glass with his. "Yes it was."

The men downed the drinks.

"Anything else we can work on?" Teigen asked.

"I'll let you know—after I tell Dahl, of course." *Right. Chain of command.* "So is there a secret story about Selby?"

Teigen stared at his empty glass while he decided what to say. Falko, after all, was his best friend. The only one who understood

Kirkenes.

"She had it rough at home. Stepfather who wasn't nice. She hasn't trusted men since." Teigen lifted one shoulder in an offhanded shrug. "Until she met me, of course."

"That's right. You two had that mystical connection on the pier." Falko chuckled and signaled for another drink. "This one's on me."

Teigen went upstairs after the second drink. He took off his shoes and socks then padded barefoot into the bathroom to wash and undress. He switched off the light, paused a moment to let his eyes adjust, then made his way to the bed.

Once under the covers, he curled around Selby who was lying on her side facing away from him. He looped his arm over her and cupped the breast closest to the mattress.

"Good night," she whispered sleepily.

She didn't remove his hand.

CHAPTER THIRTY EIGHT

March 12, 1944
Oslo, Norway

"This is going to be disastrous." Dahl handed Teigen the newspaper at breakfast. "Quisling has come up with the brilliant idea to draft Norwegian men into the German army."

"*What?* When?" Teigen scanned the article. "It says the draft notices will go out starting next week."

"We need to have a troupe meeting as soon as we all get to the theater." Dahl gave Selby a tight-lipped smile as she slid into her chair. "I'll let everyone know."

"Sorry I'm late," she said. "What did I miss?"

Teigen handed Selby the newspaper as Dahl walked away.

Her eyes followed the actor from the dining room. "I'm not sure he knows how to talk to me anymore."

"He has a lot on his mind." Teigen pointed at the article. "This is the latest."

Selby read, brow lowering and eyes widening. Teigen watched his wife. Though their marriage wasn't consummated yet, she was making consistent progress in her comfortable level of intimacy.

After they were in bed at night and the light was off, she let him touch her body over her nightgown—her *entire* body. What was even more encouraging, she was now touching his.

After a couple weeks of marriage Teigen began changing clothes in front of Selby and walking out of the bathroom naked after his shower. She stopped blushing after a week or so.

Selby hadn't been naked in front of him yet, but last night she stripped to her bra and panties before disappearing behind the bathroom door to put her nightgown on.

Teigen smiled. Progress was progress.

Selby lifted her eyes from the paper. "Teigen, this is really frightening. What are we going to do?"

Teigen reached for her hand. The sight of her wedding rings always lifted his mood. "We'll figure that out today. But no matter what, I'm not leaving you behind."

*****

I'm not leaving you behind.

Selby loved her husband so much more than she imagined was possible. She just wished she wasn't still afraid to *love* her husband.

Give it time, she chided herself. It will come.

It has to.

Dahl stood in front of the other nine members of the acting troupe plus Ben. He read the Oslo newspaper article aloud so that everyone had the same information before they started making a plan.

"What's the worst that can happen?" Gunter started the conversation. "That all seven of the men here are drafted and the troupe is finished."

"That's a very real possibility," Bennett said. "We're all the right age—not too old, and not boys."

"Ben's a boy," Jonas stated.

"My papers say I'm almost eighteen," Ben countered. "And even though I'm still sixteen, that's old enough to be drafted."

"Do you think that because we officially exist to entertain the Germans that we might be exempt?" Selby asked hopefully.

Dahl's mouth twisted in disgust. "The thing is, Quisling is the one who decided to force his countrymen to join the Germans. Terboven's not making the call, Quisling is."

"Maybe we appeal to Terboven anyway," Gunter suggested. "I don't see a way that could make things any worse."

Teigen grunted. "Trust me. Quisling always finds a way to

make everything worse. I know that from experience."

"Retaliation for going over his head." Bennett looked at the others. "That could get ugly."

Selby felt panic tighten her chest. "So what are our options?"

Dahl held up one hand and grabbed his index finger. "We men get drafted and the troupe shuts down."

"None of us will join the Germans, so I guess we'll go into hiding, then. Resist from the woods." Gunter looked at Teigen. "Right?"

Teigen shrugged. "Or leave the country."

Selby shot him a disapproving look.

He gave his head a tiny shake and mouthed, *we'll stay.*

"Moving on." Dahl grabbed the next finger. "We go to Terboven and ask for special dispensation, and he agrees."

"Then we continue as we have been, knowing Quisling has a target on our backs?" Jonas looked uncertain. "How long will we last?"

"There's no way to know," Dahl admitted. "But it would buy us time to make other arrangements."

Bennett nodded his agreement. "That's not a bad thing."

Dahl's hand moved to the third finger. "Or, we go to Terboven and he disagrees. Assuming we're drafted, that puts us back at number one."

"We'll be drafted, there's no doubt. I mean, look around this room." Gunter's arm moved in a sweeping semi-circle. "The Royal Shakespearean Acting Troupe has a certain amount of fame. If its members joined the German army, Quisling would have his very own role models of Norwegian support."

"Except we *won't*," Bennett growled.

Gunter leaned toward his troupe mate. "Quisling's too stupid to know that. He'll try it."

"It seems like approaching Terboven is our best next move, then," Selby ventured. "And if he agrees, then we have time to discuss what's next."

"And if he says no…" Dahl sighed and rested his hands on his hips. "Then I think we need to leave Oslo immediately. Get out of Quisling's reach before he can draft us"

Everyone in the room was silent.

Selby reached for her husband's hand. It was big and strong and warm and it pulled her back from the panic that threatened to drown her. Teigen closed his fingers around hers.

"Where would we go?" Ben asked when no one else did.

"Not to Kristiansand." Teigen looked to Dahl for confirmation. "Because that's our next stop. It's where they'd expect us to go."

Gunter cleared his throat loudly, drawing all eyes to him. "If Terboven says no, then the troupe is finished."

Dahl nodded, his expression grim. "Yep. And even if he says yes, our time is limited."

Selby looked around at the men and women with whom she'd spent the last three years of her life. She was going to miss them. Even the frivolous Karolina.

"We'll still be members of Milorg and active resistance," she reminded them. "Even if we aren't working together we'll still be fighting the same war."

"And we might be working together, at least for a while." Bennett looked optimistic. "We won't know until we ask."

Dahl looked directly at Selby then. "Are you ready for your most important role?"

She nodded and squeezed her husband's hand. "I'll go dress the part. Selby Sunde will be stunning."

ᚾ ᚾ ᚾ

Selby and Dahl waited in the room outside *Reichskommissar* Josef Terboven's office. As the two lead actors in the troupe, it made sense for them to be the ones to lay the request at Terboven's feet.

Selby counted to one hundred in her head over and over to keep her thoughts from running amok. Her emerald green dress, blonde wig, shiny black spike-heeled pumps, and red lipstick were all designed to attract a man's attention and hold it.

She already knew her smile looked sincere. Men fell for it every time.

The intercom on the SS-uniformed secretary's desk buzzed. He picked up the receiver and nodded. "Yes, sir."

He set the handset in its cradle before looking at Selby and Dahl. "You may go in."

Terboven's private office was a huge wood-paneled affair whose purpose was clearly to intimidate. Maps, flags, and an enormous desk with an equally enormous leather chair faced the door. Gleaming silver tea, coffee, and liquor services graced the sideboard to Selby's right, opposite a bank of paned-glass windows that she estimated must stretch eight feet above the pierced-metal enclosed registers.

The man himself was unremarkable. Still handsome in his mid-forties, he was tall and slim—though not as tall as her husband. His hair was short, parted on one side, and he wore glasses with round metal frames. The blue eyes they framed showed no emotion.

"Good afternoon," he said in Norse. "What can I do for you?"

Dahl and Selby stood in front of the desk—they had not been asked to sit. "My name is Dahl Holter and this lovely woman is Selby Sunde."

Selby gave Terboven her shy smile. He didn't return it.

"We are lead actor and actress in the Royal Shakespearean Acting Troupe and we are currently performing in Oslo."

The Nazi's gaze flicked from Dahl to Selby and back. "Currently?"

"We're a traveling troupe, *Reichskommissar*," Selby said. "We travel from Oslo to Trondheim and back, twice a year, entertaining German officers."

"Hm." He seemed unimpressed.

"What we've brought you today are tickets for tonight's performance." Dahl reached inside his jacket and pulled out an envelope which he set on Terboven's desk. "Twenty-four to be exact."

Selby's smile brightened. "We thought that you and your officers, along with wives or lady friends, would enjoy our production of *A Comedy of Errors*."

Terboven picked up the envelope and looked inside. "This is very generous of you." He dropped the envelope back on the polished desktop. "Why today? Why not the times you have performed in Oslo before?"

Selby spoke before Dahl could, intending to send him a message. "May we be honest?"

Terboven's regard was intense. "I expect nothing *but* honesty, Miss Sunde."

Dahl shifted his stance and gave the *Reichskommissar* his best casual look.

"Of course you're aware that Minister-President Quisling will begin drafting Norwegians for service in the German army," Dahl began. "We're hoping that you'll see the value in how we currently serve the Reich and exempt our actors from that draft."

"Hm." Terboven stroked his lower lip. "Do you feel the two forms of service are equal?"

"All forms of service vary," Selby risked. "Don't their values vary as well, based on the recipient?"

One side of Terboven's mouth lifted. "That's a pretty sentiment, Miss Sunde. But it's no more than a sentiment, I'm afraid."

Damn.

"In any case, we hope to see you tonight. We do believe you'll enjoy the play." Dahl dipped his chin. "Thank you for your time, *Reichskommissar.*"

As Selby and Dahl turned to leave, Terboven stood up. He clicked his heels together and stuck out a rigid arm. "*Heil* Hitler!"

Dahl met Selby's eye. She nodded so slightly she wasn't sure he'd notice. But he did.

Dahl faced Terboven and lifted a hand. "*Heil.* Hitler."

ᚾ ᚾ ᚾ

"That was horrible," he grumbled once they were clear of the office.

"You had to do it," Selby assured him. "Otherwise there was no chance at all."

Dahl shook his head. "There still isn't. Not with that bastard."

"We still have Quisling himself. Don't give up hope."

Selby and Dahl didn't speak again until they reached the Minister-President's offices. Dahl was waiting outside for this meeting, just in case the traitor decided to start his draft immediately once the well-known actor was standing in front of him.

"Good luck, Sel," Dahl murmured.

Selby was quickly ushered into Vidkun Quisling's smarmy presence, the envelope of six tickets for tonight in her hand. The hope was that if the Germans came in force, Quisling might be cowed by the Nazi's apparent interest in the traveling troupe and exempt the actors from his draft.

There was no reason *not* to appeal to both sides on this one.

"My dear Selby Sunde," Quisling cooed. "What a lovely gift."

Selby gave him the sincere-looking smile. "We realized that we haven't seen you at any of our performances Minister-President, and we wanted to make that right."

He tipped his head. "Well, your unexpected generosity is greatly appreciated."

"Of course, we're also hoping that you'll see the value in how we currently serve the Reich," Selby said sweetly. "And that you'll consider exempting our actors from additional service to the Germans."

Quisling's smile dimmed. "I see. You mean the draft."

"Until tonight, then." Selby held out a gloved hand and flashed a conspiratorial grin, hoping to distract the man from thinking too hard about her last statement. "I'm *really* looking forward to hearing how you and your wife like the play."

Vidkun took her hand and kissed her glove, but his expression had hardened. "Until tonight."

Chapter Thirty Eight

The Royal Shakespearean Acting Troupe closed the curtain for the last time on the final performance of their career at half past nine.

When Dahl heard how Quisling reacted to Selby's request earlier, he went straight to the Oslo harbor and found a fishing boat that would sail the troupe away from the city that same night. Though curfew in the city was ten o'clock, the troupe was always given an extra hour to remove the accoutrements of the stage before walking back to their hotel.

That dispensation was crucial tonight.

In order to keep their exit a secret, a car driven by a Milorg member from Oslo was hired to meet them at the hotel at six. Once there, a bellman loaded the troupe's luggage into the vehicle—a normal activity for any hotel. The Milorg officer then drove the loaded car to the pier and waited for the troupe's arrival after the play.

Troupe members had to leave everything related to the stage productions behind and could only pack their personal possessions—much to Ben's disappointment.

"Can't I cut the canvas out of *one* of the painted flats?" he begged Teigen. "I can fold it and fit it in my suitcase. I promise."

Teigen relented because he knew how much the paintings

meant to the youth. Besides, he might actually be able to use it later when he applied to art school."

"*Only* one," Teigen said sternly. "And it can't be one that we're using tonight because we need to leave right after Selby gets changed."

"Thank you!" Ben spun around and headed for the flats.

"Make sure you hide the empty frame in the middle of the stack," Teigen called after him. "It can't look like we're not coming back."

The plan of intimidating Quisling might have worked if more than a handful of Nazis showed up that night. The empty chairs surrounding the few brown-clad SS officers clearly showed that the troupe members were not getting Terboven's protection.

The Minister-President did bring his wife backstage after the play, however. While she gushed over each actor's performance, Quisling handed every one of the men—including Ben—his card.

"Come see me tomorrow, would you?" His grin did not even begin to look sincere. "I have a proposal for you."

Like hell I will.

"Yes, sir." Teigen stuffed the card in his back pocket.

Once Quisling left, troupe members vacated the building in four pairs plus the trio of Teigen, Selby, and Ben. The exits were staggered so that they didn't all walk to the pier en masse. And each pair took a different route.

Teigen, his wife, and foster son were the next to last to leave the theater. Dahl and Gunter would follow in ten minutes.

"It's a beautiful night," Teigen observed aloud in case any brown bastards were nearby. "We have a little time. Let's take the long way back and enjoy the weather."

As the three of them strolled in a zig-zagged path to the pier, Teigen kept watch for any hint that they were being followed.

"So far, so good," he whispered to Selby.

She answered by tucking her arm into his and keeping her eyes focused forward.

The car waited at the pier as planned.

"How has it gone?" Teigen asked the driver while the three of them collected their luggage.

"Fine. I had a couple curious dogs come sniffing around, but I told them I was delivering Terboven's mistress's bags and was told to wait here until she showed up." The man chuckled deeply. "You should've seen their faces when I suggested they check the story with him."

"Brilliant." Teigen clasped the man's shoulder and shook his hand. "Thanks for your help."

Dahl and Gunter boarded the boat at half past eleven, having been stopped by a drunken SS officer.

"We showed him our curfew passes but he wasn't having anything to do with them," Gunter said as he hefted his trunk onto the deck of the fishing boat.

"Nope. In fact..." Dahl grunted as his suitcase also made it onto the deck. "He set them on fire."

Teigen frowned. "Didn't that draw some attention?"

"It would have, I guess." Gunter held up a swelling hand with split knuckles. "If I hadn't cold-cocked him and he smothered the flames with his chest."

Teigen coughed a laugh. "Your farewell to Oslo. I approve."

Dahl looked at the deck, empty but for the three of them and the captain. "Everyone here?"

"Yes, sir." Teigen motioned a faint salute. "All below deck and accounted for."

"Then let's go."

※ ※ ※

Fredrikstad was about sixty-five miles southeast of Oslo on land, and would take just over four hours to reach sailing through Oslo Fjord. Even though the boat would dock before four o'clock in the morning, disembarking in what was essentially the middle of the night during curfew wouldn't be wise. The troupe would need to wait until sunrise or later.

"At least our absence isn't going to be noticed as yet," Teigen said as he helped Selby climb down a rope ladder to the Fredrikstad pier. "And there's no reason for anyone to think we've come here."

Dahl's escape plan included not checking out of the hotel and not informing the theater owner or any of the employees that the troupe was leaving. That meant that they wouldn't be missed for another ten or twelve hours.

No one in the group had managed to sleep during the night. Instead, they huddled together and talked about what they would do next. Dahl gave each member their salaries, plus a letter of introduction and recommendation which stated their rank in Milorg. "In case you want to relocate and continue," he explained. "Which I hope you all do. It's been my honor to work with you."

※ ※ ※

As the night and their collective exhaustion wore on, tears were shed and promises made to stay in touch. Final goodbyes were said before they all left the little fishing ship and the group split up to find separate lodging on their own.

Dahl and Bennett, however, remained with Teigen and his little family.

"Bergen makes the most sense for me because Falko's there," Teigen said at some point during the night. He turned to Selby. "What's your preference?"

She honestly didn't have one, as long as they were far away from Oslo, Terboven, and Quisling. Selby rubbed her eyes, dry from lack of sleep. "I like Bergen. It's not so cold there."

She dropped her hands and looked at her husband. "And Rolf Schmidt is dead so no one there will harass me."

"I like Bergen, too," Ben chimed in. "In case anybody cares."

Teigen ruffled the teen's hair, leaving it sticking out at odd angles. "Of course we care, Ben. We're family, remember?"

Ben's expression shifted as though he heard—and believed—those words for the first time.

"You're like a son to me," Teigen admitted. "And I mean to treat you like one."

Ben's eyes brightened mischievously. "Does that mean you're not going to teach me anymore?"

Teigen laughed. "No. It means I'll take a fatherly interest in your marks."

Selby watched the pair with warm affection suffusing her chest. Teigen's care for Ben was obvious, and the youth practically worshipped her husband. The only flaw in their family was her reluctance to open herself fully to Teigen.

Patience.

Soon she would be able to risk it. Just not quite yet. Her happiness was still too new to risk.

"I was thinking of Bergen, too." Dahl's gaze moved between Teigen and Selby. "If you two don't object, that is."

"I don't," Selby answered a little too quickly. She turned and asked Teigen, "Do you?"

Teigen gave her an odd look. "Of course not. I'd be happy to continue working together. We make a great team."

"Would you mind if I joined that team?" Bennett offered.

"That would be great!" Ben blurted. He and Bennett—the youngest member of the troupe at twenty-two—had become great friends working backstage together.

Dahl looked at Teigen, grinning. "The four Musketeers plus an impudent mascot?"

"Hey!" Ben barked.

"Totally impudent." Teigen winked at Selby. "But I think we can work with him."

"I do have one suggestion," Selby said to Teigen. "Dahl and Bennett should head to Bergen as soon as possible and let Major Helgesen know we're joining them. Maybe start looking for a place for us to live."

Teigen looked confused. "What are we going to do in Fredrikstad in the meantime?"

Selby shook her head. "Not Fredrikstad."

"Then where?"

She smiled. "Arendal. It's time your parents met your wife, and your foster son. Don't you agree?"

March 21, 1944
Arendal, Norway

Teigen did agree. The minute Selby suggested it he was embarrassed that he hadn't thought of it himself.

In his defense, however, this was the first time in two full years that his time was truly his own. Grini prison, the Kirkenes labor camp, and the troupe's unyielding schedule all held him captive during those many months without any respite.

As their ship navigated past the lighthouse and into Arendal's inlet, Teigen caught his first glimpse of his ancestral hometown. Though a mile still distant, his emotions were pitching a battle with each other.

On the one hand, he couldn't wait to see his mother and father again, and tell them that he had seen Tor in Bergen this time last year as his brother was headed to America to teach their soldiers to ski.

He wasn't sure his parents were aware of the tension between their two sons—and he certainly wouldn't mention it. But in case they were, he would be sure to tell them how happy the unexpected reunion was for both brothers, and how he and Tor parted with expressed affection for each other.

On the other hand, Teigen hadn't seen his parents for three years. Because of his relationship with his spoiled fiancée Elsa, he hadn't gone home for Christmas in December of nineteen forty-one. Once his world blew apart two months later he had deeply regretted that omission.

What would his parents look like now? Had the strictures of occupation aged them? Were they well, or had they succumbed to deprivation-induced illnesses?

If only I could have sent them money.

But he received no income for a year—and what *was* owed him during that time Elsa had stolen. His salary with the troupe had barely covered his own needs, especially after he took Ben under his protection.

Still. I could have managed some if I'd really tried.

"Guilt is a useless emotion," Selby told him when he mentioned some of his thoughts. "It eats you up and accomplishes nothing."

He wagged his head. "But—"

"Tell them how you feel, because you have the opportunity to. And then do what you can going forward," she advised.

Teigen pulled her into his arms. "You're a wise woman, Selby Hovland."

"Selby Hovland Hansen," she mumbled into his chest. "I need to make that official one of these days."

"We will," he assured her. "Once this mess is finished."

When the bluff west of town came into sight around one of the many rock outcroppings in the inlet, Teigen nudged Selby. "The house is up there."

Part Viking tower, part medieval fortress, and part eighteenth century addition, Hansen Hall had been inhabited by one of Teigen's direct ancestors for over a thousand years. Only a mile from the center of Arendal, the town had grown up to meet the once-solitary structure.

"Do you see the church spire in the middle?" he asked Ben.

"That used to be a stave church at one time. It burned down at some point, and in eighteen eighty-eight it was replaced with this. It's the second tallest church in all of Norway."

Ben, oblivious to the fact that Teigen expected him to be impressed, asked, "Where's the tallest?"

"Trondheim," Selby answered for him. "You've seen it. *Nidaros Domkirke.*"

Ben wrinkled his nose. "That big ugly mess of gray stone?" He shook his head and squinted toward the town. "I think I'll like this one better."

Teigen smiled at Selby, his pride in his home placated. "The boy really *is* an artist, isn't he?"

ᚾ ᚾ ᚾ

Teigen hailed a taxi and the trio took the short but steep ride up the hill to Hansen Hall. The front door banged open before he unloaded their suitcases from the trunk of the running car.

"Go," Selby said. "I'll pay him."

Teigen turned to face his father. *"Pappa!"*

Nikolai Hansen was still tall and straight at fifty-eight. His full head of brown hair was gray at the edges and trimmed short to minimize the effect. "Teigen!"

Father and son embraced until they were pushed apart by Matilda. "Give his mother a turn, you selfish old man!"

Teigen laughed and lifted his mother in a bear hug and spun in a circle. She was a tall woman—half a foot taller than Selby—but was much thinner than when he last saw her. The feel of her bones in his arms worried him.

He set her down and she gripped his arm for balance. "Is this my daughter?"

Selby tucked her remaining money into a small pouch as she approached. "Hello, Matilda. I'm Selby."

"And I'm *Mamma* Matilda to you." She let go of Teigen and held out her arms. "Or just *Mamma* if you prefer."

Selby slipped into his mother's embrace and remained for a long moment. "I'm glad to meet you, *Mamma.*"

"Who's this young man?" Nikolai asked, his tone jovial. He walked toward Ben and the pile of luggage. "Let me help you with that."

Teigen stepped forward. "*Mamma, Pappa*, this is Ben Thorkelsen Hansen."

"Hansen?" his father asked, picking up two of the suitcases. "Are we related?"

Teigen decided the minute he saw his parents to tell them the same story he was telling the world. It was safer for Nikolai and Matilda that way. He just hoped Ben didn't contradict what he was about to say.

"He's some sort of cousin. Ben was orphaned when his parents were shipped to a German camp last year." Teigen glanced at Ben. The boy's expression remained thankfully impassive. "I found him alone in Oslo and took him in."

If his parents doubted the story, they didn't let on.

"Welcome to our side of the family, Ben," his mother said sweetly.

His cheeks flushed and he looked like he might cry. "Thank you, ma'am."

"We're *Bestefar* and *Bestemor* to you now. Don't forget it." She looked up at Teigen. "Are you hungry?"

CHAPTER THIRTY NINE

March 31, 1944
Arendal, Norway

Teigen told Selby that they would stay in Arendal four or five days. They stayed ten.

Matilda's health worried her son, who petted over her incessantly. He made trips to the market every day and brought back any food he could find that might put weight on her frame.

After several days Selby pulled Nikolai aside. "Would you like to take a walk? It's a beautiful day."

"On the arm of such a beauty, how can I say no?" he teased.

Stepping out the front door, Selby suggested Nikolai take the lead. "I have no idea where I am," she laughed. "Show me Arendal."

Wife and father-in-law strolled away from town and around the back of the estate. Nikolai started the conversation with, "Why did you want to talk to me alone?"

Selby chuckled. "I can see where Teigen gets his astute observation skills."

"It's about Matilda," he ventured. "Isn't it."

"Yes." Selby sighed. "Teigen is really worried. Has he said anything to you?"

Nikolai shook his head. "No. Not directly."

"Can you tell me?" Selby asked gently, adding, "I won't tell him if you don't want me to."

"There's no secret, really. The doctor says it's a combination of worry over the boys and inadequate foods."

Selby smiled inwardly at the reference to Tor and Teigen as *the boys*. She'd never seen a pair of such manly men.

"Tor is safe in America, isn't he?"

"For now." Nikolai rubbed his brow. "But if the American soldiers learn to ski well enough, they will come back and fight the Germans."

Selby's heart sank. "And Tor will fight with them."

"Everyday she prays that the war will end before that happens." Nikolai cleared his throat. "I—I do, too."

"As will I," Selby offered. "But Teigen is relatively safe here in Norway."

Nikolai scoffed. "So we thought. Until he was arrested and sent to die in that labor camp so far north that no one even knew where it was!"

True. "But he didn't die."

"We couldn't know he would survive and be released," Nikolai reminded her. "We thought it would kill him."

Selby and Nikolai walked in silence for a few minutes.

"What can we do?" she finally asked.

"She needs meat. Beef, pork, chicken." Nikolai lifted his hands in the same helpless gesture that Teigen often made. "But the Nazis take it all. They come to the farms and make notes of how many piglets are born, and then come back later when they're grown to take them away."

He heaved a frustrated sigh. "Sure, we try to hide some, but it's hard to make a pig or a cow invisible. They must have shelter, they can't be left out in the cold."

"It's that way everywhere…" The realization that she and Teigen would no longer enjoy the perks of living in well-stocked hotels punched her in the gut. "Our lives are certainly going to change now that the troupe has disbanded."

The pair had circled the Hansen estate. Nikolai stopped and gazed up at the circular Viking tower. "This very spot has been our home for a thousand years."

"Tor will come back." It was as much a prayer as a statement.

Nikolai rubbed his forehead again. "I don't know…"

Selby laid her hand on his arm. "Have faith, *Pappa*."

"It's not that..." Nikolai winced a little. "I'm not sure he wants to."

Selby frowned. "What do you mean?"

"I love my son. And I couldn't be prouder of him." Nikolai's face brightened. "Did you know that before the war he made the Olympic ski team?"

Selby smiled. "I do."

Nikolai's expression dimmed again. "He's the type of man who gets restless, though. Always the first to act. Never foolishly, don't misunderstand me. He's a smart man. But he doesn't have that same steady determination that Teigen does."

"You want Teigen to inherit Hansen Hall." The startling realization shocked her. "Am I right?"

Nikolai looked pained. "I can't do that to Tor."

Selby pressed her lips together and considered the situation. "Maybe after the war and Tor comes home, you could ask him what he thinks."

Nikolai nodded slowly. "Yes. I should do that." He turned his attention back to Selby. "Would Teigen take it?"

Selby's heart lurched with sudden hope. To live here and truly become part of an ancient and honorable family would turn a dream, one which she never thought to dream, into reality.

"I'd make him," she declared. "What better place to start a family—s-someday?"

Selby felt the blush her own words prompted. *Someday*. She promised Teigen that at the least.

Nikolai chuckled. "I'm glad we had this talk, Selby."

She took her father-in-law's arm and they walked toward the front door of the big house. "So am I, *Pappa*."

ᚿ ᚿ ᚿ

Teigen followed a rumor and was eventually able to talk a farmer into giving up one of his newly weaned piglets. If his father could manage to hide the animal until it was fully grown then his mother would have the meat her body needed.

He and Ben spent three days building a pen deep in the woods under an outcropping of rock. They even transplanted several pine saplings to further hide the pen's presence.

"That's the best we can do." Teigen clapped dirt from his hands. "I hope it works."

Until then, the chicken he bought his parents would provide them with eggs. And live in the wooden coop Teigen and Ben built and tucked inside the ancient chapel in the medieval section of the house.

"Sorry, Rydar. Sorry, Grier. It's just temporary," Teigen said to the oldest graves in the stone room as he carried straw inside and spread it over the centuries-old floor. "I'm sure you would do the same under the circumstances."

Selby found him there. "We need to leave soon or we'll miss the boat."

"I know." He looked at his wife. "But I hate to leave them."

"We'll be back," she assured him. "Maybe someday to stay."

Teigen found that surprising. "Would you want to live here?"

Selby shrugged. "We'll have to wait and see what happens. Right now, we need to win a war. We can't make any real plans until that's accomplished."

Teigen walked to the doorway and wrapped his wife in his arms, resting his chin on her head as he usually did. "Do you know how much I love you?"

"Not as much as I love you."

"We're going to get through this," he whispered. "All of this."

April 9, 1944
Bergen, Norway

"Bergen is starting to feel like home to me," Teigen said as their ship sailed into the harbor. "So much has happened here."

"It's going to be odd not to be at the hotel." Selby looked up at him. "Is Falko taking us to the flat?"

"He said so." Teigen's gaze combed the crowd waiting for the boat. "I think I see him."

"There are more German ships than last time." Selby shuddered visibly.

Teigen glanced at the trio of SS officers standing about twenty feet away. "Careful."

Selby followed his gaze. She grunted her disdain but didn't say anything else.

Falko met the trio at the bottom of the gangway. He hugged Selby and shook Ben and Teigen's hands. "On to new adventures, eh?"

Selby looked sad. "We are, I'm afraid."

Falko stepped back and considered Ben. "Have you grown, boy?"

Ben blushed. "Yep."

He had. He was six feet tall at least.

"Keeping him fed is our biggest challenge," Teigen teased. "I'm going to have to get a second job."

"Speaking of that." Falko motioned for them to follow him. They hefted their suitcases—Teigen carrying his own and his wife's—and trailed along behind Falko. He didn't continue speaking until there weren't any Nazis in earshot. "We're raising your salary."

"Really?" Teigen glanced at Selby. "That's good news, but why?"

"Because now that the troupe isn't buying your room and board, you'll have to be able to afford that on your own." He gave Teigen a pensive glance. "But you getting a job of some sort *is* a good cover."

"What about me?" Selby asked.

"You're the wife." Falko shrugged. "That's your cover."

"Will I get a raise?"

Falko looked like she was pointing a gun at him. "Um…"

"I'm a lieutenant! He's just a sergeant!"

Falko cringed. "He's been promoted."

Selby stopped still. "*What?*"

Falko threw up his hands in surrender. "It was Helgesen's decision. Please don't kill the messenger."

"That's not fair!" she stormed. "I want to have a word with him."

Teigen understood Selby's anger, but honestly her situation *had* changed—she was a married woman with a husband who was responsible for taking care of her. And now that the troupe was disbanded they were on their own and waiting for new assignments.

"Let's all calm down for the moment," he said gently. "We'll get everything sorted out in time. But first, we do need to know where we're sleeping tonight."

Selby made a face at him but didn't reply.

Falko looked like a man who dodged a bullet. "It's not much farther."

He started walking again. Selby stomped behind him with her arms crossed. Teigen glanced at Ben who looked as startled as Falko.

"There's a boarding house that only houses resistance members so conversation there is safe. Bennett and Dahl already have rooms there." Falko glanced over his shoulder. "Bennett is expecting Ben to stay with him, if that's all right with you."

Ben grinned. "That's great!"

"Good. Saves you some money, Hansen." Falko ran up the wooden steps in front of the narrow four-story row house. "Here we are."

The house was clean and sparingly furnished. A sturdy middle-aged woman with ruddy cheeks rushed out of the kitchen, drying her hands on an embroidered towel.

Falko smiled. "This is Gunnhild. She's the owner of the house."

Introductions were quickly made and Gunnhild led them up to the second floor. "This room is for Mister and Missus Hansen. The boy is on the third floor with the single men. The attic is for storage."

Teigen stepped inside and set their suitcases down. He looked at Selby, who seemed to have calmed down some. "What do you think?"

⁂

Selby walked to the middle of the room and turned in a slow circle, trying to focus on the room and not the recent news.

Everything was neat and looked clean. Instead of a closet, there was a large old-fashioned pine wardrobe, painted with traditional Norwegian designs. A six-drawer dresser—also painted—stood on one side of the big iron bed, and a three-drawer nightstand was on the other. Two upholstered chairs completed the furnishings.

Selby looked back at Gunnhild. "The bathroom?"

"You have a toilet and sink through that door. The tub and shower are down the hall."

I have been spoiled.

Selby forced a smile past that realization. "Thank you. This will do nicely."

"I'm going to go get Ben settled," Teigen said. "Do you want to come up?"

Gunnhild put up an imperious hand. "Sorry. No women are allowed on the third floor."

"That answers that." Selby was actually glad to hear the rule. "I'll start unpacking."

Once she was alone, Selby grumbled about the unfairness of Major Helgesen's decisions. She jammed hangers into her blouses and shoved them onto the wardrobe's rail. She yanked drawers open and stuffed her sweaters into them.

She slowed her pace when she started placing her lingerie into the drawers. The silk was too delicate and rare to risk damaging it.

She carried her train case into the small bathroom and started placing her toiletries on one of the shelves. The idea of sharing a tub and shower with strangers wasn't a pleasant one after three years of rarified hotel living, but it was one she needed to get used to.

Besides, after I meet the other occupants of this floor, they won't be strangers anymore.

"Selby?"

"In here." She set the last jar of face cream on the shelf and closed the lid on her case. Teigen's face appeared in the doorway. "Did you get Ben settled?"

"I did." He peered at her. "Are you all right?"

Selby blew through her lips. "No. But I will be."

Teigen stepped aside and let her pass. "Are you unpacked?"

"I am." She set her empty train case beside her empty suitcase and faced her tall husband. "Can you please put these on top of the wardrobe?"

He obliged easily. "Did you leave me any room?"

That made her laugh. "Of course. You don't have a lot of clothes, but the clothes you do have are huge."

"True." Teigen smiled at her. "By the way, we're having supper with Dahl, Bennett, and Falko tonight. Helgesen's treat."

Selby wrinkled her nose. "Well the man's done one thing right." She opened the door of the wardrobe. "Welcome home, husband. Do you want help unpacking?"

CHAPTER FORTY

During supper in the private dining room of a nearby hotel Falko filled them in on the latest Milorg news. "Estimates claim seventy thousand men have gone into hiding to avoid Quisling's draft."

Teigen wagged his head at the number. "I knew some men would bolt, but had no idea it would be so many. I assume Milorg's seeing that they're fed and housed?"

"Yep." Falko flashed a wry grin. "It's a good thing King Harald made it out with the treasury when Hitler invaded. Not all the governments-in-exile were so quick to act."

"Exactly," Dahl concurred. "We don't have to worry about funds. Just about getting them back into the country."

Teigen lifted his glass—water with a drop or two of aquavit. "A toast to the Shetland Bus."

"We have more new resistance volunteers than we know what to do with, at the moment," Dahl said after they drank. "But we're coming up with ideas."

"What kind of ideas?" Selby asked.

"The Linge men working with Gunnar Sønsteby are doing sabotage raids around Oslo. We could do things like that around Bergen." Dahl looked at Selby and frowned. "Did we meet him?"

She shook her head. "No, we met Jens Hauge."

"Oh. Right."

"There's another option that a lot of men are choosing. Harald's created a new Norwegian police force and they're training in England. For cleaning up the country after the war." Falko finished off his glass of watered aquavit.

"He hopes Hitler will be defeated?" Bennett asked. "Or he knows?"

"The evil bastard's been fighting for five years and he's losing ground," Teigen answered. "I think we can all see how this ends. We just can't see when."

"As long as he doesn't get the atomic bomb," Selby murmured. "God help us if he does."

"And—" Dahl pointed his fork at the supper group. "Hopefully he doesn't do even more damage once he realizes he's going down."

Falko pressed his lips into a grim line. "We just need to keep fighting. In any way we can."

"Can I go to England and join the police?" Ben asked.

Teigen looked at the youth, surprised. "I thought you wanted to be an artist."

"I can do both."

Falko shrugged. "Sorry, kid, but you have to be eighteen."

"My papers say I am. Almost."

Teigen put down a metaphorical foot. "No. You're going back to your real identity when this is over, remember?"

Ben's brow twitched uncertainly. "Do I have to?"

Selby's jaw dropped. "Why wouldn't you?"

"Because…" Ben looked like a trapped rat. "I—I don't want to leave you."

Teigen grabbed Ben's hand. "You're not going anywhere, do you understand? You're stuck with us."

Ben's wide eyes were fixed on Teigen's but he said nothing.

"Your name may change from Hansen back to Isaksen, but you'll always be part of our family." Teigen squeezed Ben's hand. "Unless *you* decide otherwise."

Ben voice was very small. "I won't. Ever."

"Good." Teigen let go of Ben's hand and smacked him on the shoulder. "Now eat up. This might be your last free meal for a while."

April 17, 1944
Bergen, Norway

Someone was pounding on their door.

Teigen came out of the washroom. "I'll see who it is."

Selby held her robe closed and folded her newspaper on her lap.

Falko stood in the hall looking like he was about to burst. "Did I catch you shaving? Sorry. But this couldn't wait."

Teigen stood soap-faced with a towel in one hand and the razor in the other. Falko had an amazing grasp of the obvious.

"What couldn't wait?"

"We have an opportunity," he answered esoterically. "So go finish up. Helgesen wants to see you."

Teigen looked at Selby.

"You heard him," she said in a resigned tone. "*Your* presence is needed."

Teigen faced Falko. "I'll be down in five minutes."

With his shave finished and his shirt donned, Teigen hurried down the stairs.

"Let's go." Falko practically ran from the boarding house.

"Hey—slow down," Teigen barked.

They rounded the row of tall houses and Falko tipped his head toward the harbor. "See what's arrived?"

A huge gray warship rested in the center. *Voorbode* was painted on her prow.

"Foreboding?" Teigen translated. "That's an odd name."

"Could be appropriate if things turn out right."

Teigen turned his startled regard to Falko. "What are you talking about?"

"You'll see."

※ ※ ※

"We received intelligence today concerning the ship that dropped anchor in Bergen harbor yesterday evening." Helgesen slid the paper across his desk toward Teigen. "Read this."

He did. "The cargo is dynamite, fuses and blasting caps?"

"It's a munitions ship." Helgesen gave Teigen a significant look. "And we're going to blow it up."

Teigen stared at the major, stunned. "How big of an explosion will that be?"

"According to regulations, only ships with less than fifty tons of explosives are allowed into the harbor." Helgesen gave an acknowledging shrug. "It'll still make an impressive point."

His presence at this meeting became obvious. "You want me to make the bomb."

"You did an excellent job with the desks, Hansen." The major smiled. "I know you'll do the same here."

Teigen's mind was whirling. "How do we get the bomb on the ship?"

"That's my part to play," Helgesen stated. "You make the bomb." He smiled coldly. "You have three days."

※ ※ ※

"Three days?" Selby stared at Teigen. "Can you do it?"

"I don't have a choice." He rummaged through his things and retrieved the one chemistry book which had survived his travels. "I'm meeting Falko for lunch and we're going to look for supplies after that."

Selby looked skeptical. "It took you *how* long to figure out the desks?"

Teigen straightened. "That was different. There were mechanics involved."

"And this?"

"This will be one single bomb with a fuse long enough to allow the man who places it to escape before it explodes." Teigen steeled himself for her response.

Her pale eyes shot icy daggers at him. "And *you're* that man?"

"Not necessarily," he deflected. "Helgesen said that how the bomb is put in place is his responsibility to figure out."

"This is terrifying, Teigen." Selby struggled not to let her emotions show. "I don't want you to do it."

"I'll make the bomb," he said. "I don't have to agree to take it to the ship."

But could I trust anyone else not to kill themselves doing it?

Selby closed her eyes. "Go. Just go."

Teigen stepped forward and planted a robust kiss on her mouth. "I'll be back for supper."

₦ ₦ ₦

Selby spent the afternoon wandering through the scantily stocked shops in central Bergen. All the while, she could see the hulking gray munitions ship dominating the harbor.

Blow your own damn self up. Don't make my husband do it.

Great.

Now she was talking to ships in her head.

With nothing else to do, she sat on a bench. She didn't dare spend money on a cup of tea or coffee yet. Until they had a couple of months' experience in paying their own bills behind them, she and Teigen agreed to no purchases that weren't necessities.

She ran her fingers through her hair, wondering if she should cut it short again. It had grown three inches since she cut it last and the sides brushed against her neck in a very annoying tickle. It was also hard to style with its undecided length.

Teigen said he liked it short. He hadn't said anything else about her hair since it had grown.

That's it. I'll cut it tonight.

The physical intimacy between the two of them had stalled out once they were in Arendal. And it hadn't picked up again since arriving back in Bergen. The most surprising thing about that was that Selby was truthfully missing Teigen's touch.

Maybe after she cut and washed her hair tonight, she would initiate something. Maybe let him touch her more intimately than she had before. It was time to take another step.

And that called for a bottle of wine.

This is a necessity. I'm sure he'll agree.

Selby rose from the bench, threw another mental curse at the ship, and walked to the only liquor store she knew of. She greeted the proprietor and wandered down the half-empty aisles looking for a bottle she could afford.

A voice from the front of the store sent ice through her veins.

It can't be.

He's hundreds of miles away.

In Trondheim.

Selby peeked around the shelves. What she saw stole her ability to breathe. She backed up and grabbed the nearest wooden shelf to steady herself.

Lieutenant Fritz Walder was here. In Bergen.

Why didn't I bring my gun?

Because, she chided herself, you don't want to die because you killed him in public. You want to do it cleverly.

She heard footsteps coming down the other aisle. Selby turned around and tip-toed to the front of the store. She pretended to examine a bottle of something until she saw movement at the spot she just vacated.

When she did, she crossed to the door, smiled at the man behind the counter, and walked out.

ᛝ ᛝ ᛝ

Selby stood in front of the mirror in their boarding house washroom, scissors in hand, and cut the first lock of her hair. There was no going back now.

After every few snips she took a tiny sip of the wine she went back to buy after Walder left the liquor store. Her hands stopped shaking after the first cut and she moved forward, remembering how she'd done this countless times before.

She used her hand mirror to check the back and make necessary corrections. When she finished, she examined her reflection critically.

Teigen was right. Her eyes were more noticeable with the wispy fringe above them. She tucked the sides behind her ears, and then pulled out a strand on either side. She used the edge of the scissor's blade to turn them into wisps that curled under her cheekbones.

Satisfied with the result, she replaced her clothes with her robe, grabbed her towel, and headed to the shower.

ᛝ ᛝ ᛝ

Teigen couldn't stop staring at his wife. With the black eyeliner, burgundy lips, and short hair she was stunning. And he told her so. Several times.

Her resultant smile made his nether regions sit up and take notice.

Down boy. Not yet.

During supper she told him about seeing Fritz Walder in town. That doused his arousal with a rage so visceral that he struggled to hold himself in his seat and not charge out into the evening to strangle the man.

"Can Falko find out why he's here?" Selby asked.

"I'm sure he can. Why?"

"The lieutenant might be summoned to a ship right before it blows up."

Her voice was so calm and sweet it took Teigen a moment to realize what she suggested. It was brilliant.

"Yes. Yes, he might."

Once back in their room Selby poured him a glass of the wine. "This was a necessary purchase," she forestalled his question. "I was so disturbed by running into you-know-who that I almost lost my train of thought."

Teigen looked at her curiously. "Are you trying to seduce me?"

"Sort of." She poured her own glass. "I want to start moving forward again."

She set the bottle on the dresser and turned her back to him. "Unzip me?"

N N N

Selby laid on the bed in Teigen's arms. The only light in the room came through the cracked-open washroom door and the full moon outside. She answered his kisses and his caresses until he slid his hand between her thighs.

Nothing stood in the way but her flimsy silk panties.

She gasped a little.

"Relax, sweetheart," he whispered between intoxicating kisses which she accepted with increasing curiosity.

As his fingers gently stroked her through the silk, she opened her legs a little to give his large hand room to move.

"Oh, no," she murmured in dismay. "Did I wet myself?"

To his credit, Teigen didn't laugh at her. "No, that's how your body prepares for my eventual entry. It's normal. It's good."

Relieved, Selby relaxed. Teigen's touches sent chills over her skin while a ball of heat was growing low in her belly. She pressed her hips against his hand. It felt so good she wanted more.

"Don't stop," she whispered against his lips. She sensed she was building to something but she had no idea what it was. She just needed him to keep doing what he was doing.

Without warning a spasm of intense pleasure shot through her, zinging outward from her core to the tips of her fingers and toes. Selby stiffened, shook and whimpered. Her breaths came in huffs.

When it passed, she was limp as wet grass. For a moment she couldn't find her voice. Or open her eyes.

Teigen kissed her softly on the lips.

"What... what happened?" she rasped.

He ran his lips along her jaw. "I believe you just experienced your first orgasm, my love."

CHAPTER FORTY ONE

April 18, 1944

"The resistance paper said that 'public outrage against Lieutenant Fritz Walder for the unprovoked beating of beloved actress Selby Sunde resulted in the officer being relocated to Bergen.' It also claimed that his pending promotion was withdrawn." Falko nudged Teigen. "Are you listening?"

"What? Yes. Of course." Teigen tried to push last night's play with Selby from his mind. He didn't succeed. "That's good."

"So what are you thinking of?"

Selby's pleasure releasing in my hand. "Selby, uh, suggested that the lieutenant might be summoned to the ship right before it explodes."

"Oh! That's brilliant!" Falko whooped. "We need to make sure that happens."

Teigen blinked himself stoically back into the conversation. "Do you know where he lives?"

"I know where he works, isn't that good enough?"

Of course. "The same office where we blew up Schmidt."

Falko nodded. "Right."

"Okay. Back to work." Teigen stared at the scattered items on the table in the back of the same barn where he armed the first desk to explode. "The main thing we need to assure is that the bomb doesn't explode too soon. We need a slow-burning fuse."

Falko lifted a coil of treated flax cord. "This is slow burning, I think."

"Let's test it."

Teigen lit the end of the fuse and timed its burn for sixty seconds before cutting the little piece from the coil and watching it sputter out. "How far was that?"

"Not even an inch."

"Perfect. Let's try it again." They did.

"This was actually half an inch," Falko said.

"And the tip only glows," Teigen approved. "No flame to draw attention or risk setting anything else on fire." He looked at Falko. "Where did you get this?"

"I found it."

"Where?"

Falko tossed a thumb over his shoulder. "Back there. Under a bunch of stuff."

Teigen huffed a laugh. "Did you know it was a fuse?"

Falko's eyes twinkled. "Nope."

N N N

The plan was set: insert a fifteen-inch length of the slow burning flax cord into a pouch of gunpowder, light it, and tuck it out of sight as close to the cargo hold as possible. That would give the operative thirty minutes to get to safety.

"Are you certain of the timing?" Helgesen asked.

Teigen nodded. "We tested it five times. Every test had the same burn rate."

"And how much gunpowder will you use?"

"Three times as much as we did for the desks."

Helgesen looked impressed. "So could we expect a thirty-foot radius in the explosion?"

"Yes, sir," Falko answered. "If for some reason it doesn't ignite the dynamite, it will start one heck of a fire."

"And that fire will detonate anything it touches" Teigen stated the obvious.

"Simple and effective. Good work Hansen."

"Thank you sir."

Falko shifted his stance and looked unconcerned. "Do you know who will be placing the bomb?"

Helgesen looked a little less confident. "We're talking to a pair of mechanics who've worked on German ships before. They can actually board the ship without being questioned."

Teigen sighed his relief. *Selby will be happy to hear that.* "That's good."

The major looked at Teigen for an uncomfortably silent moment before saying, "Come back tomorrow at four. I'll have the rest of the details for you then."

Selby was, indeed, happy—in spite of the fact she was in bed with a hot water bottle and cramps. Any hope of repeating last night's experience, and maybe taking their intimacy a step further, was now delayed for a few days.

"I'm sorry," she croaked.

"Sorry? For what?" Teigen tried to act as if nothing of importance had happened. "This happens every month. It's normal."

"I know. But, well... I don't know." Selby's lips twisted and pressed together.

Teigen kissed her until her lips untwisted and softened. "It's only a few days."

April 19, 1944

Teigen and Falko stood in front of Major Hans Helgesen's desk for the third day in a row.

"Here's the plan," the major began as he handed Teigen a small map of Bergen Harbor. "You'll meet two men, Lauritz Sletten and Lars Hamre, at seven-thirty tomorrow morning at this point here." He pointed to a dock in the area marked *Nordnes*. "Show them how to set and light the bomb and make sure they understand exactly what to do."

"Yes, sir."

"They're going to row a boat across this way," the major's finger traced a path over the water, "to the ship. They'll board, set the bomb, and leave."

Helgesen met Teigen's gaze. "It's a simple business. Any questions?"

"No, sir."

Helgesen looked relieved. "One last thing, gentlemen."

Teigen waited, apprehensive about what might come next. He glanced at Falko who looked as uncertain as he felt.

"Tomorrow is Adolf Hitler's fifty-fifth birthday." Helgesen smiled crookedly. "Let's give him something to remember the day by."

Teigen grinned. "Yes, sir!"

As they left the office, Teigen turned to Falko. "It's time to send a note to Walder."

"Agreed."

Teigen wrote the note, since he spoke German fluently:

> Lieutenant Walder,
> Would you please join me for breakfast on the bridge of the Voorbode on Thursday, April 20th at 08:00? I would like to learn more about our offices in Trondheim and I understand you spent some time there.
> I look forward to meeting with you.
> Captain R. M. Forsen
> ST Voorbode

Falko saw that it was delivered directly into Walder's hands that same afternoon.

April 20, 1944

The weather the next morning was cloudy and cold with a substantial breeze. Falko came along with Teigen as moral support, though he seemed as giddy as a schoolgirl. Teigen suspected Falko wanted to be there just to be part of the objective.

They arrived at the rendezvous spot a few minutes early but the engineers were already waiting there. After completing their introductions, Teigen pulled out the length of fuse and the linen pouch of gunpowder.

"Tie the end of this cord—it's the fuse—into the pouch of powder before you light the fuse," he instructed.

Lauritz Sletten looked alarmed. "Why is the fuse so short?"

"It burns very slowly," Teigen answered. "Half an inch a minute."

Falko pointed at the cord. "That's fifteen inches, so you'll have half an hour to get out of the way."

Lauritz shifted his gaze to his partner. "Lars, do you trust this?"

Lars Hamre shrugged. "Helgesen said this man knows what he's doing."

"It's really very simple. Look." Teigen held the pouch and the fuse together. "We can even tie it now if you want."

"Let me." Falko took the parts and used a thin piece of wire to secure them together. "There."

He handed the bomb back to Lauritz but the mechanic put up his hands. "I'm sorry. I can't do this."

"Come on, Lauritz," Lars cajoled. "In and out. And then we run away while the shitheads blow up."

Lauritz shook his head. "They'll know we did it. They'll come after us."

"You don't have to set the bomb right away," Teigen suggested. "You could stay and pretend to work for a while."

"Then say you have to go get a part and you'll be back," Falko added.

Teigen nodded his agreement. "Exactly. And light the fuse right before you leave."

Lauritz shook his head and backed away. "No. I can't. I can't do this."

Teigen grunted his frustration. "Fine. Give me your jacket."

Now Falko looked alarmed. "Selby will kill you, man."

Teigen wiggled his fingers to hurry the mechanic up. "In and out. She'll never need to know." He looked at Lars. "You lead the way."

Lars nodded uncertainly. "And you'll light the fuse?"

"Yes."

Five minutes later Teigen was wearing Lauritz Sletten's jacket and hat and sitting in the prow of the boat as Lars rowed them toward the ship.

"The lower deck door is on the other side," he said to Teigen. "It's usually open when the ship's at anchor."

"Have you worked on this ship before?"

"Not this one, no." He squinted into the glare of the cloud-covered sun. "But they're all the same."

"You do the talking."

Lars nodded. "I will."

They reached the side of the ship with the lower deck door and it was open. Lars edged the rowboat between the ship and the dock while Teigen tossed the rope to a waiting sailor.

"We're here to take a look at your engines," Lars shouted. "Captain Forsen said they're running rough."

The sailor nodded and handed the men aboard. "Do you know where to go?"

"We'll find it. Ships are all the same." Lars lifted his toolbox and walked inside the vessel with a silent Teigen following.

"Engines are in the back," he told Teigen. "Cargo is in front."

The men turned toward the front. After walking a several yards, Teigen stopped. "Do you smell that?"

Lars turned startled eyes to his. "Smoke."

Both men looked up.

A layer of hazy yellowish gray was creeping along the ceiling and heading toward them.

"The open door is pulling the smoke," Lars started to back away.

Teigen spun around. "And where there's smoke—RUN!"

Lars dropped his tool box. Both men ran back the way they came as fast as they were able.

"FIRE!" Teigen shouted at the startled sailors guarding the open door.

He leapt from the ship to the rowboat and fell to his knees. His weight and the direction he was headed pushed the little boat closer to the dock. Teigen regained his balance and scrambled out the other side onto the pier.

He heard the sailors behind him start to shout. And he heard a splash. Apparently Lars Hamre had panicked and chose to swim for safety.

Teigen's focus was on reaching the boarding house and getting Selby and the others to safety before the *Voorbode* blew upon its own. He ran to the end of the pier and turned to his left to circle the edge of the bay. When he turned left again, he looked across the water at the ship.

The crew was pouring from the open doorway, leaping for the pier the same way Teigen had. A loud BANG sent a hatch cover fifty feet in the air.

"Oh, God." Teigen resumed his frantic pace. People on the edge of the water were stopping and staring at the *Voorbode*.

"Look! The ship's on fire!"

"There's so much smoke!"

"That flame's got to be ten stories tall!"

Teigen shouted at them as he passed. "Get to safety now! It's a *munitions* ship!"

He didn't wait to see whether they heeded his advice. Rounding a corner he pushed his burning legs to keep going until he reached the boarding house. He jumped to the porch and threw the door open.

"Everyone! Go to the cellar! NOW!" he bellowed as he climbed the stairs two at a time. "GET IN THE CELLAR!"

Selby opened the door to their room, her eyes wide with alarm. "What's wrong?"

"The ship's on fire!" He grabbed her arm and pulled her into the hall. "Go down to the cellar right now! HURRY!"

He pushed her in that direction and ran past her to the stairs. "I'll get Ben. GO!"

Selby seemed to grasp his panic-stricken message and she ran down the stairs while he ran up.

"Go to the cellar!" he shouted, pounding on doors he ran past toward Ben and Bennett's room. He opened their door without knocking.

"The ship's on fire," he managing past heaving breaths. "Get to the cellar—NOW."

※ ※ ※

The occupants of the boarding house who believed Teigen's warning huddled in the damp and dim stone-walled cellar below their four-story clapboard row house. Ben sat on the floor next to Bennett facing Teigen and their legs straddled his. Dahl wasn't in his room.

Selby sat on the floor next to her husband, her shoulder tucked under his arm.

She hadn't asked him why he was wearing a jacket and hat he didn't own, but she had an angry suspicion that he had boarded the ship and started the fire himself.

After he told me he wouldn't.

She clenched her jaw to keep from asking him now, in front of witnesses, resistance or not.

"Tell me why we're here," a man demanded. "I'm supposed to be at work by nine and it's already eight-thirty."

Teigen was catching his breath. "The ship—*Voorbode*—is on fire. And—she's a munitions ship—meaning her cargo is mainly explosives."

A murmur of concern rumbled through the enclosure.

"How long do we need to stay down here, do you think?" Bennett asked.

"I don't know," Teigen admitted, still breathing hard. "Until we're sure—the fire's put out."

Gunnhild had her ever-present kitchen towel twisted around her work-reddened hands. "I hope it's soon. I have a cake in the oven."

Teigen looked at Selby. "I suppose if nothing happens in another fifteen minutes I could go up and look."

"What if it blows up when you're up there?" she demanded.

He didn't seem to have an answer.

She glared at him. "Give it thirty."

"But I'll be late for work!" the man protested.

Teigen faced him. "So then pray you'll still have a workplace to be late to."

The group fell uncomfortably quiet; the only sounds in the stuffy cellar were sniffing and throat clearing. Selby decided to be a good wife and show some her support for her husband; she'd deal with his dishonesty later.

She slipped her hand into the pocket of the unfamiliar jacket.

Something was there. A pouch tied to a cord.

Selby drew a sharp breath through her nose.

Could it be?

She turned and looked up at Teigen in shock. "Is that…"

She left the question dangling, knowing he'd understand if she meant was it the bomb.

"Yes." He heaved a jagged sigh. "The ship was already on fire."

CHAPTER FORTY TWO

The explosive *BOOM* seemed to come up from below the ground as the cellar floor shivered.

"Oh, God!" Gunnhild wailed. "My house!"

No one in the enclosure moved. Selby wondered if they were even breathing.

Nine minutes had passed since the man berated Teigen, saying they shouldn't have to wait below the house for so long.

Nine minutes.

The man's face paled. "I could be dead."

"You're welcome," Teigen growled.

No one in the cellar looked irritated anymore. In fact, they looked at Teigen like he was some kind of deity.

"You saved our lives," Ben said, looking at his foster father in awe. "If you hadn't run back and warned us…"

A woman started to cry.

"Is it safe to go see the damage?" Bennett asked.

Teigen shrugged. "I don't believe it can explode twice."

People reclaimed their feet and helped others to theirs. Teigen opened the cellar door for Gunnhild because she couldn't get through the crowded cellar and open it herself.

Acrid smoke and ashes wafted down to them. Something was definitely on fire. Selby hoped it wasn't the city itself.

Teigen helped people up the steep wooden steps to the kitchen until only he, Ben, Bennett, and Selby remained.

"Ladies first." Teigen practically pushed her through the opening.

The smoke-filled air stung Selby's eyes.

Gunnhild was picking up dishes from the floor. A few platters survived, but the majority of her plates were broken.

"Watch your step, dear," she said to Selby. "The windows blew out of their frames."

Selby looked down at the floor covered in tiny glittering glass shards. "I'll help you clean up."

Gunnhild didn't meet Selby's eyes. "Thank you, dear."

Teigen appeared and looked around at the mess. "I'm going outside to see the extent of the damage."

Bennett stepped out from behind him. "I'm coming with you."

"Me, too." Ben looked terrified but determined.

Selby grabbed the front of Teigen's unfamiliar jacket in a tight fist, her expression stern. "Be careful. I mean it."

"I will."

She shook the jacket before she let go of it. "Promise me. And keep it this time."

Teigen's eyes widened briefly; he knew he was found out. "I will."

She turned her back so he wouldn't see the tears that threatened and went to find the broom and dustpan.

ᚾ ᚾ ᚾ

The scene that Teigen met was surreal. In one moment the city of Bergen had been damaged beyond anything he would have believed. Everything near the water's edge was reduced to rubble. And wet.

"You wouldn't believe it," a man kept saying to anyone walking close to him—he was obviously in shock. "Water shot hundreds of feet in the air. Hundreds. You wouldn't believe it."

The thing Teigen didn't expect to see were so many bodies lying sprawled on the pier.

"What happened to them?" Ben asked quietly.

Teigen turned him around. "Don't look."

Ben's somber gaze met Teigen's. "But what happened?"

"Either they were too late running away, or they were watching the first flames and didn't believe they were in danger." Teigen recognized one couple he had shouted warnings at.

Damn it.

"The force of a close explosion causes internal injuries. If it knocks you down, you die."

Ben's eye rounded. "How do you know that?"

"First, I'm a scientist. And second..." Teigen heaved a steadying sigh. "My father fought in the last war and he told me."

"This looks like war," Bennett murmured. "Like a bomb was dropped here."

"That's actually what happened. That cargo was one big bomb." Teigen's gut turned over and he felt like he might vomit.

I almost caused this.

He started walking, leaving Ben and Bennett to follow. He was shaking with shock and knew he couldn't trust his voice.

If I set the bomb, all these deaths would be on my shoulders.

It wouldn't have mattered that Major Helgesen ordered him to make the bomb. And it wouldn't have mattered if Lars or Lauritz had been the one to place the bomb and light the fuse. Teigen gave them the weapon.

What about Dahl and Falko?

Teigen squinted against the smoke and tried without success to see the spot where he and Falko met the mechanics. All he could tell was that the majority of the damage from the blast seemed to be on this side of the inlet, not that side.

Fire trucks screeched past the trio toward the burning rubble. The sky above them was a thick gray mix of smoke and cloud. The roof of the medieval Bergenhus Fortress was in flames.

All around them people were shouting, Germans and Norwegians alike. Buckets of water were being thrown against the wooden buildings still standing. Bodies were being covered with blankets.

Teigen pulled himself together enough to ask, "Where was Dahl this morning?"

Bennett's stunned expression didn't change when he answered. "I don't know."

"Did he go out early?" Teigen pressed. "Or was he out all night?"

When Ben tugged on the sleeve of Sletten's jacket, Teigen

realized he still wore the mechanic's clothes. And that the bomb was still in the pocket.

I need to get rid of it.

He looked at his foster son. "What?"

"He had a date." Ben looked awkwardly embarrassed. "I think... he said something about..."

"Sex." Bennett rescued the youth. "This is one time I hope he was right."

"Do you know where she lives?" Teigen asked even though he doubted they did.

Bennett swept his arm toward the destruction and flames. "Hopefully not here."

Teigen's eyes followed the sweep of Bennett's arm.

I could have done this.

Teigen's knees gave way. He dropped to the ground and covered his eyes.

"Teigen?" Ben's trembling voice was right in his ear. "Are you okay?"

Pull yourself together.

You did not *do this.*

No one in Norway did. If anyone had set the ship on fire it was a German. So it had to be an accident, because no one who knew what her cargo was would do something so foolish.

Teigen sucked a deep smoky breath and coughed it out. He nodded and lifted watering eyes to the pair.

"I'm okay. I just got light-headed. From the smoke, I think."

"Yeah. It's bad." Bennett pointed away from the burning pier. "Let's see how far the damage goes."

Teigen climbed carefully to his feet. "I have to do something first."

He stumbled to the water's closest edge. Reaching into the pocket of Sletten's coat, he palmed the heavy linen pouch of gun powder.

God forgive me for what I almost caused.

And thank You that I didn't.

He pulled the bomb from his pocket and in one seamless motion pitched it as far as he could into the sea.

ᚾ ᚾ ᚾ

Dahl showed up at supper.

Selby leapt from the table and launched herself toward him. She threw her arms around him.

"Where were you? I was so worried!" she sobbed.

The erstwhile actor didn't seem to be able to hide his shattered emotions. "I was with a lady friend," he managed. "We stayed out late and had a lot to drink. I—I slept on her couch."

Selby didn't believe that for a minute but she wasn't about to call him out now. She let go of him and stepped back.

"So you were safe?"

His face was pale. "Mostly. We were both awakened when the windows in her house shattered."

"Did you hear the explosion?" Teigen asked.

Dahl nodded. "I was afraid you were killed."

Selby cut her eyes toward Teigen, silently thanking God that her beloved husband had escaped unscathed.

In spite of his foolishness.

"What have you been doing all day?" he asked Dahl.

Dahl stepped to the closest chair at the boarding house's communal table, set with the mismatched pieces of china and pottery that had somehow survived the blast, and dropped heavily onto it. Selby reclaimed her seat next to Teigen.

"I reported to Helgesen immediately." Dahl accepted the cracked platter of sausages Bennett handed him. "We spent the day gathering information."

"What did you find out?" Bennett asked.

Dahl scooped potatoes onto his chipped plate. "The papers the *Voorbode's* captain filed with the harbormaster weren't accurate. The ship was carrying more explosives than were allowed."

Teigen dropped his fork. "How *much* more?"

"One hundred tons of dynamite, fifty tons of fuses and one hundred and eighty thousand blasting caps."

"*Two times* what's allowed?" Teigen shouted. "No *wonder* the blast was so big!"

Bennett jabbed his fork at Dahl, his expression volatile. "And the damage was so severe! What in *hell* were they thinking?"

"One of our men intercepted a letter from the captain. He copied it down and sent it to Helgesen today." Dahl heaved a sad sigh. "Forsen knew exactly what he was carrying."

Selby shuddered. "Of course he did. He had to have!"

Ben, their still-growing charge, paused the continuous shoveling of food into his mouth long enough to ask, "What did the letter say?"

"As best I can quote it," Dahl began, "It was something like, *We're sitting ducks with a hold full of dynamite. One bullet through the hull, and there won't be anything left of the crew or the ship.*"

"Damn." Teigen's expression was thunderous. "And he sailed it right into Bergen's harbor anyway."

"The ship was having mechanical trouble," Selby reminded him. "Isn't that why the two engineers were boarding?"

Teigen shot her a guilty look. "Yes."

He knows I know.

Teigen leaned forward. "Have you seen Falko?"

Dahl nodded. "About an hour ago. He looked a mess, but he's not mortally wounded."

"Thank God!" Teigen seemed to melt into his chair.

"He gave me a message for you and Selby," Dahl said with his mouth full. "He said to tell you both that Fritz Walder was definitely on the ship when it exploded."

Selby gasped and turned to Teigen. "Did you know?"

"I only hoped." Teigen looked at her like he was extending her a peace offering. "We sent him an invitation from the captain to join him for breakfast this morning."

Selby's anger softened a little with the knowledge of her husband's endeavor on her behalf. "Thank you."

"The good news is that the Nazis have lost a massive amount of explosives—twice what we thought. Plus a warship." Dahl lifted his jar of watery beer with a wry smile. "Happy fifty-fifth birthday, Adolf. May it be your last."

ᚾ ᚾ ᚾ

"You know I'm still angry with you, don't you." Selby's statement was clearly not a question. "Even though I do have to thank you for making sure Walder got his just reward."

Teigen sat in one of the chairs in their room and removed his shoes before he faced his wife.

"I swear to you, Sel. I didn't lie to you. I never intended to board that ship."

She crossed her arms and glared at him from her stiff perch on the edge of their bed. "So why did you?"

"Sletten got cold feet at the last minute." Teigen's pulse sped up with the recollection. "He refused to set the bomb."

"And so you decided to go in his place."

Teigen spread his hands in a gesture of helplessness. "The Germans were expecting two men. And Lars Hamre would never have done it on his own. If I didn't pretend to be Sletten and go with him then the plan was over."

Selby's crossed arms dropped a little. "What happened when you boarded the ship?"

"We headed toward the cargo hold." Teigen wondered if his heart was actually going to beat itself to death inside his chest. He drew a steadying breath hoping to slow it down. "But there was smoke. The ship was on fire. We turned and ran. We even warned the Germans to jump ship."

At least we did that.

Her shoulders relaxed. "And then you came home."

"All the way here I was running and shouting at people to take cover." Teigen dragged his hands through his hair. "I *told* them the ship was a munitions ship! But so many of them just *stood* there, watching the flames shoot through a hatch cover."

The horror of what happened to those people began to drown him. "They wouldn't listen. They just stood there."

Teigen slid off the chair and knelt on the carpet. "It was like a bad dream. One where no matter how hard you try, you can't do the thing you need to do."

His shoulders began to shake. "I saw so many of them afterwards. Lying on the ground. Dead."

Somehow Selby was on the floor in front of him. "You did everything you could, Teig. It wasn't your fault."

He covered his face with his hands. "But don't you see? It could have been! If I *had* put the bomb on that ship, *all* of this would be my doing. All the dead people. All the destroyed buildings…"

He knew he was crying. Sobbing. Loudly.

He rocked back and forth, shaking with terror at the horrific destiny he so narrowly missed.

"Oh God, Sel!" he cried from behind his hands. "Can you even imagine such a terrible thing?"

Selby's arms were around him.

"God saved you from it," she said over and over again. "You aren't guilty of anything."

Teigen had no idea how long he knelt on the floor, panicking over the fate that he so narrowly missed, but Selby never left his side. All he knew was that he needed to thank God every single day for the rest of his life for not turning him into a mass murderer, a man no better than Hitler himself.

"Come to bed," his wife whispered.

Teigen realized he had been holding her quietly for some time. His heart had settled into its normal pace. His tears were dry.

He let go of her and unfolded himself from the floor. His stiff legs were numb and Selby had to steady him as he moved to the bed. She helped him undress until he only wore his boxer shorts.

"Get under the covers," she said softly as she put his clothes in the laundry hamper. "Do you want some tea?"

He shook his head, unable to make coherent sounds come out of his mouth.

Selby undressed and donned her nightgown. Then she turned off the light and got into bed.

When she snuggled next to him he held her close.

"I need you, Sel," he finally whispered, daring to hope his wife understood the depths of his request.

Selby didn't hesitate. She pushed the covers away and rolled on top of him, straddling his hips with her knees. Her nightgown was somehow around her waist. She leaned forward and kissed him softly.

"Take me then," she whispered back.

He did.

Selby lifted herself so Teigen could push his boxers out of the way. When she settled back against him they were skin to skin.

She whispered again, "Show me what to do."

Teigen kissed her deeply, running his hands over her skin. He waited, his hardness pressed to her softness, until he was sure she was ready.

He gripped her hips, lifted her and aimed himself. When she lowered herself and took him in, she moaned; the primal sound rose from deep in her throat.

Loving Selby was nothing like his experiences with Elsa. Teigen realized at that moment that he never really loved Elsa—he only lusted after her. Joining with Selby truly made them one flesh in every sense of that word.

His release carried his anguish with it, draining him physically and emotionally. Selby cried out with her own climax before collapsing over him. Her panting breaths matched his. He felt her heart beating against his.

"I love you," he rasped. "More than you know."

Selby didn't answer him with words, but she held on to him as if her life depended on it.

Exhausted by everything that occurred that fateful day, he fell into a peaceful sleep with his beloved wife still resting on top of him.

May 20, 1944
Bergen, Norway

During the past month, the Bergen Milorg group had found out in bits and pieces what happened after the explosion.

Fifty-six German sailors and soldiers died when the ship blew up.

Ninety-eight Norwegians died, some from proximity to the blast and others when their homes were suddenly knocked to the ground on top of them. One-hundred-and-thirty-one homes were destroyed in all, leaving nearly five thousand Bergen residents wounded and homeless.

After the explosion Lauritz Sletten and Lars Hamre were arrested and imprisoned for three weeks—Lauritz choosing to keep Teigen's secret while the Germans investigated the blast. When the Nazis didn't find proof that the mechanics had done anything wrong, the men were thankfully released.

"Maybe the Nazis know it was German sabotage and they're trying to blame us," Helgesen told Teigen the same day he also told him about the promotion. "And that's why they've targeted two of our known Milorg members, Rolf Olsen and Trygve Havnes, for arrest on sight."

"But they didn't have anything to do with the explosion," Teigen replied. "They aren't even *in* Bergen anymore."

Helgesen shrugged. "My guess is that after they had to let Sletten and Hamre go, and the German Navy Court threw their own harbormaster into prison, they needed to find some way to blame

Norway for their losses."

The most interesting tidbit they discovered was the location where a portion of the *Voorbode's* anchor was found: almost two miles from the harbor and high in the mountains above Bergen.

"Thirteen hundred feet above sea level," Falko said as the Milorg group stared, astounded, at the recovered chunk of debris. "That's how strong the blast was."

The rubble from the explosion was slowly being cleared, but it would take years—probably decades—before everything that was leveled could be rebuilt.

Gunnhild's boarding house and the other houses in her row only sustained superficial damage. Her male boarders were working together to replace her windows, fallen clapboards, and roofing tiles in exchange for a little deduction in their rent.

Since the night of the explosion, Teigen and Selby experienced a full marriage. She came eagerly and often into his arms at night, her childhood demons finally conquered and forever banished.

And though during the last month Teigen still experienced occasional twinges of shaky relief that he wasn't responsible for the devastation in Bergen, he never had any of the nightmares he feared he would suffer from after that horrible day.

He believed he had his wife to thank for that. And so he thanked her often—and vigorously, much to her expressed delight.

CHAPTER FORTY THREE

February 21, 1945
Bergen, Norway

"Teigen, look at this headline." Selby handed her husband the Norwegian Resistance's newspaper. "Isn't this what Tor went to America for?"

Teigen grabbed the paper and read the headline out loud. "Ski Patrol Defeats Germans in the Alps."

> *On February 18th, under the cover of darkness, nine hundred men from the 86th Mountain Infantry Regiment attacked Riva Ridge in the Italian Alps, climbing the ice-coved ridge with ropes in complete silence. They were able to surprise and subdue the German lookouts and subsequently captured the Ridge.*
>
> *American casualties numbered seventeen dead, thirty-eight wounded, and three missing.*
>
> *These soldiers were taught to ski at Camp Hale in Colorado, USA by a group of experienced skiers led by Norway's own Tor Hansen, who qualified in downhill skiing for the cancelled 1940 Winter Olympics.*

Teigen looked up from the newspaper. "Of course the report

mentions him by name. He's very famous."

Selby lifted one brow. "Are you jealous?"

"No. I'm famous, too, remember?" Teigen chuckled. "Though my status as *arrested teacher returned from Kirkenes* has faded a bit."

"Don't worry. History will always remember." Selby reached for the newspaper and he handed it back to her. "Any idea what's our next project?"

"Nope. I guess we'll find out from Helgesen this afternoon."

The Milorg meeting was held in the familiar secret room behind the barn where Teigen and Falko armed the exploding desk. The people who gathered in the unheated room huddled together in their heavy coats and snow boots, their breath creating little clouds of fog in front of their faces.

Selby, of course, wore her Arctic fox coat.

Major Helgesen stood at one end of the room. "I'll keep this short so you can all get back home. We're going to be part of a plan called Operation Cement Mixer. It's a coordinated effort between Milorg and the Linge men, and it's scheduled to take place three weeks from today—March fourteenth."

Selby leaned over to Teigen and whispered, "Whatever that is, it's going to be big."

"The goal is to blow up railroad lines all throughout Norway on the same day in a hundred or more key locations," Helgesen explained. "Germany is losing the war, and they have thousands of troops just sitting here in the occupation. We intend to hobble the train system so they can't transfer those troops back to Germany and keep fighting."

Approving murmurs rumbled around the room. Teigen looked across at Falko. Falko grinned and winked at him. His friend knew Teigen would be on the ground with this initiative because of his experience with blowing things up.

And Falko would be by his side.

Helgesen waved his hand to quiet the room. "Our points of disruption are outside of Bergen, Dale, and Vossevangen if we can get there through the snow. We'll need a team for each location."

Dahl raised his hand. "How far is it from Bergen to Dale and Vossevangen?"

"Dale is about forty miles and Vossevangen is about sixty-five."

"How many men per team?" another man asked.

"At least four."

Teigen raised his hand. It was better to volunteer first and take the assignment he preferred. "I'll take Dale."

I've had enough with explosions in Bergen.

Dahl, Bennett—and of course Falko—all threw their hands in the air.

"I'll go."

"Me, too."

"I'm in."

Major Helgesen shook his head, smiling. "I don't know what it is, Hansen. But you do seem to inspire loyalty. Okay, Dale is covered. Who wants Bergen?"

March 14, 1945
Dale, Norway

The road to Dale was piled so high with snow on either side that all Teigen could see was the path in front of him. The quartet left Bergen when the sun rose at seven in order to make the most of their day.

"I'll try to be home by noon," he promised Selby when he kissed her goodbye. "One at the latest."

"Be careful," she warned. "And don't rush anything. You need to come home safely."

Teigen crossed his heart. "I promise. No heroics."

"Thank you." Selby kissed him again. "I'll be right here when you get back."

"There it is." Falko pointed forward. "I see the church spire."

"Do they know we're coming?" Bennett asked.

"I don't think so," Dahl replied. "The element of surprise is important for this to work."

Teigen rolled the car into the village. "Do you see the train station?"

Falko pointed again. "To the right."

Teigen parked the car in front of the wooden shed that protected waiting passengers. "Let's go."

The four men climbed out of the car and wrapped their faces with woolen scarves. The wind was biting even though the sun shone.

Dahl opened the trunk of the car and each man grabbed a sack. Inside each sack was a packet of gunpowder, a length of fuse, and a cigarette lighter.

"Four explosions, twenty-five yards apart," Teigen reminded them. "I'll lead out. When we're far enough from here, you three double back and space yourselves."

The men began walking the track. Teigen counted his strides and stopped when he hit one hundred and fifty.

"This is it." He turned around. "Go twenty-five paces and set your bomb. Shout out when you're ready. We'll all light our fuses at the same time."

"Yes, sir." Falko saluted, smiling.

The men turned and retraced their steps.

Teigen tucked his packet of gunpowder under a rail and stuck the fifteen inch fuse into it. There was enough gunpowder to cause an explosion with a thirty to forty foot radius and he wanted the thirty minutes for them all to escape safely.

Dahl called out. Then Bennett. And Falko.

"Okay!" Teigen shouted. "Light 'em!"

Once his fuse was burning he jogged back toward the village. Dahl, Bennett, and Falko joined him in turn, each keeping up with his pace.

Back at the car, the men climbed inside to get away from the wind. The sun shining through the glass warmed the interior a little.

Falko settled in the front seat and closed his eyes. "Now we wait."

No one talked as the minutes ticked by. Teigen opened the driver's side window a few inches to listen for the explosions.

Instead, he heard a train whistle in the distance.

He looked back at Dahl in alarm. "There isn't supposed to be a train."

Dahl wagged his head. "No. There isn't."

"Did you all put your bombs under the rail?" Teigen asked.

They nodded.

"So the train can go over them without displacing them?"

"Yes," they chorused.

Teigen slumped in his seat. "How much time do we have left?"

Falko looked at his watch. "Ten minutes."

It was a matter of time whether the tracks blew up before the train crossed, after the train crossed, or just as the train rolled over the bombs. Clearly the train that was approaching wasn't a scheduled run. That probably meant it was carrying German soldiers toward the port at Bergen.

Teigen heaved a sigh. "There's nothing we can do now but wait and see what happens."

Time seemed to have stopped. The train whistled again, definitely closer. It didn't seem to be in a hurry or it might have reached Dale by now.

Teigen looked at Falko. "How much time is left now?"

"Four minutes."

"If the tracks are destroyed before the train gets there it'll derail," Bennett observed. "And if the bombs go off while it's riding over them the cars will be thrown off the track."

"But..." Dahl leaned forward. "If they explode after the train arrives at this station, we are sitting ducks for the Germans to pick off."

"Good point." Teigen started the engine. "We'll have to trust our work and—"

BOOM! BOOM! BOOM! BOOM!

The screech of metal tore the air and pierced Teigen's ears. The crashing of train cars and the screams of men clearly carried toward the car on the wind.

Teigen put the car in reverse and backed up.

As he shifted into drive, the engine of the train skidded into view. There were no cars attached, and only the fluttering of swastika-festooned flags confirmed what the men thought.

Teigen hit the gas.

ᚾ ᚾ ᚾ

When Teigen opened the door to their room at the boarding house, one look at Selby's distraught expression and flowing tears erased the satisfaction of their job well done.

"What's happened?" The worst possibility rushed to the front of his thoughts and demanded to be spoken. "Has someone died?"

She nodded while her lips disappeared, pinned between her teeth.

"My father? My mother?"

Selby shook her head slowly.

"Not—oh God!" Teigen sank to his knees. "Tor?"

Selby handed him the letter, which he accepted with trembling hands.

> *Dearest Son,*
> *We received the worst possible news today. Your brother was killed in battle in Italy. The telegram didn't say how it happened, but it did say he will receive a Silver Star. It's the third highest military award that the Americans bestow, awarded for gallantry in action against an enemy of the United States.*
> *His body is being sent back to America...*

Teigen looked up at Selby. "America? Why not Norway?"

Selby wiped her streaming eyes. "Keep reading."

> *...back to America and his wife.*

"Wife?" Teigen smacked his head. "He got married? To an American?"

Selby gave him an empathetic half-smile. "So it seems."

> *She will receive his Silver Star posthumously during his military burial there.*
> *Your father and I are going to try and find out more about her and will tell you when we do. In the meantime, please try to keep yourself safe. You're all we have.*
> *All our love,*
> *Mamma*

Teigen was so stunned he couldn't cry. He couldn't move. He felt numb.

Tor had always gone ahead of him, blazing a trail that he could never match—or so it felt. Now his impulsive brother was dead. There would be no more shoes to fill. No more shadows to step out from. No more stories of his glorious exploits.

Teigen was his parents' only son.

"The future of the family rests on my shoulders now." His voice sounded strange. Distant. Flat. "I'll—*we'll*—need to move back to Arendal as soon as possible."

"Leave Milorg." Selby said it before he had to.

"Yes." Teigen stared at his wife, still dry-eyed. "We won't miss much. If every location was as successful as we were today, the Germans will be crippled."

She looked hopeful. "So it went well?"

Teigen nodded, the letter still clutched in his hand. "There was an unscheduled train. It came through just when the bombs went off."

Selby's eyes widened. "Oh no!"

Teigen held up his empty hand. "It's okay. It was filled with Germans. Probably on the way to the port here."

"So Operation Cement Mixer happened just in time." She heaved a sigh. "The war should end soon."

"Milorg won't miss us."

Selby slid off her chair and knelt in front of Teigen. "I am so, *so* sorry about Tor. I know there's nothing that will ever replace him in your life."

Teigen gave her a resigned look. "I had a feeling. Ever since we parted last. Somehow I knew he wasn't going to survive this war. He was too... big. I knew he'd be in the thick of it."

"I do have something else to tell you." Selby's voice and expression were hesitant. "But maybe it should wait."

He felt punched in the belly. "Is it good news or bad?"

Her face softened. "It's good. But I don't know if I want you to always remember this letter every time you think of it."

"Tell me something good, Sel. Please. Tell me something that makes all of this struggle and fighting and dying worth it." He reached for her hand. "What's the good news?"

Her smile was shaky at first. "Are you ready?"

He drew a deep breath and squeezed her hand. "Yes."

"All right then." Her pale blue eyes, full of love, met his. "I'm going to have a baby."

Teigen fell sideways off his knees. "Swear it's true, Sel. Don't tease."

Her smile grew radiant then. "It's true. I saw the doctor today."

Teigen was gobsmacked. "Wh—when?"

"He'll be born in September. At Hansen Hall." Now Selby squeezed his hand. "And we'll name him Tor."

EPILOGUE

Less than a month after Operation Cement Mixer—which destroyed train tracks in over a hundred locations around Norway—the Norwegian resistance ended its sabotage operations so as not to provoke the Germans into making a last stand in Norway.

On April 30, 1945 Adolf Hitler shot himself in his *Führerbunker* in Berlin. His wife Eva committed suicide with him by taking cyanide.

On May 7, 1945 the Germans unconditionally surrendered all of their forces to the Allies in a meeting at US General Eisenhower's headquarters in France.

Terboven was despised by both the Norwegians and his own men. The *Reichskommissar* killed himself by detonating a hundred pounds of dynamite in a bunker after Germany's surrender.

May 8, 1945 brought a new day in Norway. Church bells rang while people filled the streets to celebrate and sing. Milorg and the new Norwegian Police force appeared in uniform and began mass arrests of Nazi Party members.

At seven o'clock in the morning on May 9, 1945 and knowing they were defeated, Vidkun Quisling along with six other German ministers arrived at the Oslo Police Headquarters to be arrested. Two hours later, Norwegians listened to the first free Norwegian radio broadcast in five years.

On May 13, 1945 Norway's Crown Prince Philip, along with some of the government-in-exile ministers, returned from England to reclaim his throne in Oslo. The Norwegian people greeted him with a parade of welcome.

King Haakon received the same welcome when he arrived in Oslo on June 7, 1945—5 years to the day after he left Norway for exile in Britain. This was also the 40th Anniversary of Norway's Independence, won in 1905.

And on September 10, 1945 at Hansen Hall in Arendal, Selby presented Teigen with a healthy eight-pound baby girl, named Torhild after her heroic uncle.

Read Chapter One of:

Battles Abroad

THE NORSEMEN'S WAR

Book 2:
Tor & Kyle

Kris Tualla

CHAPTER ONE

November 18, 1943
Denver, Colorado

Captain Tor Hansen of the Norwegian Army had been delayed in getting to America and he was as tense and fidgety as a man standing on the edge of a cracking glacier. After eight months of red tape and passports and military negotiations he was finally about to land in Denver, Colorado and take up his commission as an adjunct to the United States Army.

Seems that the American soldiers needed to learn how to ski.

And after being denied the chance to compete in the cancelled nineteen forty Winter Olympic Games—thanks that bastard Adolf Hitler starting this war—Tor was itching to get back on the slopes and show off his skills.

But as he stared out the window of the airplane from the cramped, far-too-small-for-his-frame seat, the prospect of finding those slopes seemed unlikely. Since leaving Chicago on this third and final leg of his long and exhausting journey from London, Tor saw nothing below him except miles and miles of flat ground.

Sure, a hill rose up now and then. And the farmland was occasionally relieved by clusters of denuded trees or small gray-green lakes. But the further west they flew the farms gave way to vast expanses of yellow-grassed prairie land. Not a mountain in sight.

Where in hell are we supposed to ski?

His travel-weary body must have succumbed to a light sleep because he was jerked awake by the sudden and plane-jolting rise and drop of the aircraft. He grabbed the arms of his seat and looked around to see if anyone else seemed concerned as their path grew increasingly turbulent.

His head became dizzy from the constant motion. His belly, so disrupted by the last twenty-four hours' time-of-day shifts, sporadic sleep, and unfamiliar food, threatened to empty whatever it still held onto Tor's lap. He reached into the seat pocket in front of him and fumbled for the little waxed sack.

"It's always like this, coming into Denver," his seatmate assured him. "It's because the airport is so close to the mountains."

Mountains?

Tor turned back to the window. All he could see was the unending roll of the prairie.

He faced the man beside him again. "What mountains?"

"The Rocky Mountains." The man smiled knowingly. "Wait until we turn around to land. You'll see them then."

In Tor's experience, a landscape never just shifted from vast plains to tall mountains without many miles of gradually increasing foothills. He saw no sign of the sort of foothills that would lead to mountains high enough to require his expertise.

His view disappeared as the two-propeller wing lifted and the plane dipped to its left. Looking across to the windows on the other side, all he could see was brown, snow-dusted ground.

And then, the aircraft leveled out.

Tor's jaw dropped. Rising suddenly from the plains as if all the land had been scraped from the east to form them, the majestic Rockies stretched north, south, and west as far as he could see.

Jagged peaks were crowned in glorious white—the kind that never melts completely away. They both dwarfed and protected the city that knelt at their feet. As the plane continued its bone-shaking bounces and violent swerves on its downward path, Tor smiled in spite of his discomfort.

This was what he expected to see. This was the sort of landscape he was familiar with.

I'm home.

He hurriedly opened the wax sack and completely emptied his stomach into it.

⋈ ⋈ ⋈

Tor straightened his drab-green Norwegian Army captain's uniform with its three-starred collars and King Harald's crest on his arm, and checked once more for any stray flecks of vomit that might have missed the sack. It wouldn't do to give his hosts a bad impression at first glance.

Satisfied that he looked presentable, he settled his cap on his head and stepped into the aisle to gratefully exit the airplane. A bitterly cold wind slapped his bare face as he carefully descended the steps to the frosted tarmac and followed the other passengers into the terminal. His scarf was in his duffle bag. He didn't care; it was a short walk.

Thank God my feet are on the ground.

Once inside he swept a gaze over the crowd waiting for the deplaning passengers. He was supposed to be met by an American soldier from his destination, Camp Hale—a Lieutenant Kyle Solberg. Tor had no idea what the man looked like but figured that, as the only Norwegian soldier on the flight, he stood out enough for the man to find him.

When he saw no one who fit the bill, he turned to follow the baggage collection signs, assuming the lieutenant was waiting there for him.

"*Unnskyld meg, sir,*" The feminine voice at his shoulder addressed him in Norsk. "*Er du Kaptein Hansen?*"

Tor stopped and looked down at the blonde woman in what he thought was a lieutenant's uniform based on the information he was given during his cross-cultural training.

"Yes, I am," he answered in the same language. "And you are?"

She flashed a relieved smile and saluted him before continuing their conversation in Norsk. "I'm Lieutenant Kyle Solberg. I'll be your translator while you're stationed at Camp Hale."

Translator?

And Kyle Solberg is a woman?

Under different circumstances, Tor might have admitted that he spoke English fairly well after training in England for a cumulative fourteen months over the last three years. But at the moment he was far from his best.

His head pounded and was still woozy from motion sickness. His empty stomach simultaneously begged for food while promising to reject anything that might appear. He was so tired from lack of sleep he was ready to topple over. And every muscle in his tall frame was cramped and aching.

So instead, all he said was, "I'm glad to meet you, Lieutenant."

She extended one hand in the direction of the baggage claim. "Shall we collect your bags?"

※ ※ ※

Once his heavily stuffed duffle bag was retrieved and crammed into the trunk of the lieutenant's little black sedan, Tor folded himself into the passenger seat.

Lieutenant Solberg noticed. "There's some room to put the seat back," she offered. "How tall are you, exactly?"

"Six feet and six inches. Just like my brother."

Now why did I mention him?

That was only going to lead to small talk. Tor pressed his lips together and pulled the door closed to shut off the windy blast that swept over the parking lot. Clouds scudded across the sky as if undecided whether to gather or move on.

Solberg started the engine. Cold air blew from the car's vents; he found it refreshing.

"It should warm up soon."

Relieved that she was going to ignore the comment about his brother, Tor said truthfully, "It's fine. I like it cold."

She reached down and turned a knob. "It's a three hour drive to the camp. Are you hungry?"

"Not at the moment."

"Okay. Then I guess we're on our way." She backed out of the parking space and turned the car toward the exit. "We should get there before supper is served at six, but if you want to stop along the road just let me know."

"Thank you." Tor shifted his weight, trying to straighten his legs without success.

"So is your brother in the Norwegian Army, too?"

Damn.

He looked at the lieutenant. Her profile was classically Norse: high brow, high cheekbones, straight nose. She was actually very attractive. In another setting…

Stop.

"No. But he's a sergeant in Milorg. That's short for Military

Organization."

"The Resistance?" she clarified.

"Yes."

"Does he look like you, too?"

Tor blinked heavily. The motion of the car was already making him sleepy. "The truth is we've often been mistaken for twins. The most obvious difference in our appearance is that he has green eyes and mine are blue."

Solberg briefly glanced at him. "I always wanted blue eyes."

He couldn't see the color of her eyes when she faced the road, but he thought he saw they were gray. Maybe greenish gray. He yawned.

She noticed that, too. "It's okay if you want to grab a nap. The seat leans pretty far back."

"If you don't mind..." Tor felt for the lever. "I've been traveling since sometime yesterday."

"Not at all, sir."

He found the level and pulled it. The back of his seat fell backwards to a forty-five-degree angle. He resettled and closed his eyes.

What should he do about Lieutenant Kyle Solberg?

The idea that he would be provided a translator surprised him initially, but as he thought about it the accommodation made sense. He didn't mean to puff himself up, but he held a significant military rank and he was an exceptional skier. For him to come to America and teach others to ski as well as he did was sort of a big deal.

And of course no one would assume he knew English; he hailed from a proud but small and internationally unimportant kingdom.

Hell, Hitler walked in and claimed the entire country in just a five hour siege.

There was resistance now, sure, but no battles. No actual war. Most of the world probably had no idea what was going on in Norway for that matter.

So—here he was with a translator. A woman. An attractive woman. He'd be a fool to put a stop to this before he got a chance to know her.

She spoke Norsk like a native. He'd have to ask her about that. In the meantime, a lot could be gained by not admitting he understood the conversations that took place around him.

Tor smiled inwardly.

This could be fun.

Thus resolved to continue the ruse and speak nothing but Norsk for as long as it suited him, he shifted his position in the car once again before allowing the steady hum of the engine and the gentle motion of the vehicle to lull him into a much-needed nap.

※ ※ ※

Kyle listened to the captain's soft snores as she drove into the shadows of the Rocky Mountains. Night came swiftly here, the sun hidden long before it fell level with the valleys. The fact that he slept, trusting her with his life, warmed her heart in a stupid, silly way.

He's just exhausted, she told herself. *Who wouldn't be?*

She looked over at him again, before the interior of the car grew too dark for her to see his face.

Damn, he's handsome.

Kyle never swore out loud—it wasn't acceptable for women in her mind, even in the military. But since joining the Women's Army Corps as a translator and being stationed at Camp Hale she'd certainly heard an abundance of colorful language.

The fact that Captain Tor Hansen was an exceptionally good-looking individual wasn't going to be helpful in her situation. She couldn't allow herself to become infatuated with the Norseman because she was engaged to be married.

When the war ended Kyle would return home to Viking, the tiny town in northern Minnesota where she was born, and marry Erik Olsen. She'd live on his farm, and together they'd eke out a decent living. They'd grow a variety of grains during the fleeting summer months, and tend cows and pigs indoors when the arctic winds froze everything solid.

That was what was expected from her.

And then the call came on the radio, asking for a translator for a Norwegian officer. Kyle answered on a whim, not expecting anything to come from the interview. And then the notice arrived, instructing her to go to Minneapolis and accept her commission.

Basic training was easy for a farm girl.

And the weather in Colorado wasn't any worse than Minnesota.

She slid into the role with intriguing ease.

Captain Hansen sat up, halting her musings. "Where are we?"

"We have about half an hour to go." She looked at him in the dusk. He was frowning a little and seemed uneasy. "Do you need something?"

"I need to piss."

Kyle blushed, glad that he couldn't see it in the car's dim interior. "I'll pull over."

She stopped the car well on the shoulder. Tor opened the passenger door and exited in a blast of frigid air sprinkled with tiny dancing snow pellets. She watched in the car's mirrors as he moved to the back of the sedan, fidgeted with his clothes, and then stood still.

He didn't move for at least half a minute.

When he did, he put himself back together before squatting and scooping up a double handful of snow which he scrubbed against his face and rubbed between his hands.

Then he dragged his fingers through his cropped military haircut before he turned around and came back inside the car to reclaim his seat.

His cheeks were damp and reddened and he looked more awake than he had in the airport. "Thank you."

"Yes, sir." Kyle shifted and pressed on the gas. "Did the nap help?"

"Yes." He smiled at her. "At least my face won't fall in my soup."

"After you taste Cooky's soup, you might regret that," Kyle teased, surprised at her sudden temerity. "Let's hope for the best."

Captain Tor Hansen's head fell back and he loosed a deep, delighted laugh.

Damn, he's handsome.

NOTES for ENEMIES & TRAITORS:

Teigen, Selby, and the other characters in this story are fictional. The things they experienced, however, are not. At times I was forced to make up names for real people when I couldn't find the actual names documented, as in the captain of the *Voorbode*.

Other details proved elusive as well. For example, the number of imprisoned teachers who were sent back from Kirkenes and when they sailed varied from source to source. I used the numbers and dates that made sense to the story and timeline.

Some of my best information, however, was gleaned from relatives of brave Norwegians who lived through the occupation:

Linda Jorgensen Guilbert: "My uncle in Bergen had a closet behind a closet from which he sent and received information on whereabouts of the Nazis. The house was bombed at least once and there's still a German bunker within easy sight of the house."

Kori Breivik Emerson: "Harald Breivik, my Bestefar (grandfather), built desks that later blew up SS officers. He was one of the best master carpenters at the time. He built the desks with a small space in the back for the underground to put a bomb in. They would deliver the desk when they knew there would be fewer Norwegians in the building. The SS officer would sit down to the desk. What is the first thing you do when you get a new desk? Sit down and open the front. When it was closed BOOM!"

The following is documented historical fact:

The Special Operations Executive (SOE) trained men and women, and gathered supplies and weapons to fight alongside the Allies in any future invasion of Norway. By 1944 there were about 35,000 Norwegian men and women in Milorg.

There were 2173 Jews in Norway in 1942 and most of them lived in Oslo and Trondheim. At first the Nazi regime collected their names, registered their property, and stamped **J** on their identification cards. Later they arrested Jews and seized their property.

On October 24, 1942 (while Teigen was in Kirkenes) an order was issued to arrest all Jewish males over the age of fifteen and to confiscate their property. The Norwegian resistance alerted the Jews and about 850 escaped to Sweden and Britain, while others went into hiding in Norway.

On October 26, 1942 the remaining Jewish men were rounded up and sent to jails and concentration camps. A month later all Jewish women and children in Norway were arrested and transported to the death camps Auschwitz and Birkenau. Any remaining Jews in Norway were sent to Auschwitz on February 24, 1943.

Telavåg is a fishing village south west of Bergen and one of the many landing places for the Shetland Bus.

The explosion in Bergen remains one of the most tragic events of the occupation:

Against all regulations, the Dutch boat *Voorbode*, which does mean forewarning or omen, carried 100 tons of dynamite, 50 tons of fuses and 180,000 blasting caps. According to regulations, only ships with less than 50 tons of explosives were allowed into the Bergen harbor.

The ship arrived at 5:00pm on Sunday, April 16, 1944. The papers filed with the harbor captain did not tell exactly what was onboard, and the crew kept silent. The captain on the *Voorbode* did write a letter on the evening before the explosion stating: *"We are of course sitting ducks, a cargo hold full of dynamite, one bullet through the hull, and you won't find anything left of the crew or the ship."*

Two Norwegian mechanics, Lauritz Sletten and Lars Hamre, arrived in a row boat at 8:05am. Shortly after they came onboard, they saw smoke coming from the cargo hold. Sletten jumped onto the dock. Hamre dived into the sea. At 8:39am the ship exploded.

Hitler eventually lost patience with Quisling as the civilians throughout Norway were literally in revolt. Hitler gave Terboven control of the Norwegian government and any communications from Quisling to Hitler had to be directed through him.

On March 14, 1945 over a thousand Milorg and Linge men carried out Operation Cement Mixer and blew up railroad lines in over 100 places throughout Norway.

The Norwegian death toll in World War II exceeded 10,000 including approximately 4000 sailors, 2000 members of the armed forces, and 2000 resistance fighters. 3940 Norwegians were killed in concentration camps; more than half were Norwegian Jews.

THE HANSEN FAMILY TREE

Sveyn Hansen* (b. 1035 ~ Arendal, Norway)

***

Rydar Hansen (b. 1324 ~ Arendal, Norway)
Grier MacInnes (b. 1328 ~ Durness, Scotland)

Eryndal Bell Hansen (b. 1327 ~ Bedford, England)
Andrew Drummond (b. 1325 ~ Falkirk, Scotland)

***

Jakob Petter Hansen (b. 1485 ~ Arendal, Norway)
Avery Galaviz de Mendoza (b. 1483 ~ Madrid, Spain)

***

Brander Hansen (b. 1689 ~ Arendal, Norway)
Regin Kildahl (b. 1693 ~ Hamar, Norway)

***

Martin Hansen (b. 1721 ~ Arendal, Norway)
Dagne Sivertsen (b. 1725 ~ Ljan, Norway)

Reidar Hansen (b. 1750 ~ Boston, Massachusetts)
Kristen Sven (b. 1754 ~ Philadelphia, Pennsylvania)

Nicolas Hansen (b. 1787 ~ Cheltenham, Missouri Territory)
Siobhan Sydney Bell (b. 1789 ~ Shelbyville, Kentucky)

Stefan Hansen (b. 1813 ~ Cheltenham, Missouri)
Kirsten Hansen (b. 1820 ~ Cheltenham, Missouri)
Leif Fredericksen Hansen (b. 1809 ~ Christiania, Norway)

***

Tor Hansen (b. 1913 ~ Arendal, Norway)
Kyle Solberg (b. 1919 ~ Viking, Minnesota)

Teigen Hansen (b. 1915 ~ Arendal, Norway)
Selby Hovland (b. 1914 ~ Trondheim, Norway)

***

*Hollis McKenna Hansen (b. Sparta, Wisconsin)

Kris Tualla is a dynamic, award-winning, and internationally published author of historical romance and suspense. She started in 2006 with nothing but a nugget of a character in mind, and has created a dynasty with The Hansen Series, and its spin-off, The Discreet Gentleman Series. Find out more at: www.KrisTualla.com

Kris is an active PAN member of Romance Writers of America, the Historical Novel Society, and Sisters in Crime, and was invited to be a guest instructor at the Piper Writing Center at Arizona State University.

"In the Historical Romance genre, there have been countless kilted warrior stories told. I say it's time for a new breed of heroes. Come along with me and find out why: **Norway IS the new Scotland!***"*

Made in the USA
Columbia, SC
04 November 2017